A Sea Cold and Deep

David Niemitz

Annie

Descending

June 13th, 2128

"How can anyone live here," Lieutenant Commander Annie Winters muttered under her breath, looking down at the surface of Europa as she descended from the docked carrier, *Scipio.* She stood inside one of three orbital elevators which allowed orbiting ships to transfer passengers and cargo to the surface settlements. 'Surface settlements', in this case, was a somewhat inaccurate label. Everyone who did live on Europa, one of Jupiter's sixty-seven moons, lived beneath the ocean.

Laid out beneath her, through the triple paned glass observation window, was Europa. She had thought an ice planet would be white, or blue, or gray - and Europa was all of those colors. But it also was pink and orange and green, with strange lines of varying thicknesses cutting across it irregularly. Some were straight slashes, some wandering like rivers or streams, but all of them, she knew, were cracks or ridges in the ice. Her smart lenses tracked the movement of her eyes, and digitally generated labels popped up across her field of vision. She could use her fingers to expand one into an article on a feature of geography, or whatever the label corresponded to; instead, she raised her hand before her face and swiped with two fingers extended to dismiss the app. The motion nearly sent her spinning, and she had to reach out a hand to grab onto one of the handles attached to the bulkhead.

"At least there will be gravity here," she grumbled.

"You alright, Commander," Serafina asked her, and Annie nodded. The beginning and end of the sixteen month journey aboard the *Scipio* had taught her that she was not the kind of person who ever adapted to living in zero-g. At either end of her hibernation cycle, the trip from the Martian moon of Deimos to Jupiter's orbit had been full of missteps just like this, and she still ended every 'day' feeling clumsier than the last.

The elevator lurched, then began to descend. Above and below her stretched a cable of woven carbon nanotubes, hanging down from the orbital satellite which they had just disconnected from to Icebreaker 2, the spaceport below. At first, the motors of the elevator acted to put it into motion: the satellite, and thus, the elevator, were positioned in a stable orbit around the moon, where the force of Europa's gravity was just enough to keep them from flying off into space. After moving a short distance, the motors began to serve their secondary function: as brakes.

The closer to the moon's icy surface they came, the greater the force that Europa's gravity exerted. They no longer needed to propel the elevator downward - they needed to slow its descent to a safe speed. If this had been Mars, they would also have had to deal with heat generated by the friction of falling into the atmosphere. Here, that would be less of a problem: Europa's thin atmosphere was much less dense than that of Mars. As a result, she was able to watch their descent from the window for much longer than she was used to, but eventually ceramic heat shields were deployed to cover the glass. A moment later, the 'fasten restraints' sign lit up, and Sera sat to her left.

Once the view was gone, Annie used a light push off the wall to reorient herself facing into the passenger compartment, and slid into her seat. The five pilots under her command were scattered around the compartment, along with perhaps a dozen civilians taking the same ride, and Captain Varga of the *Scipio*. They all may have shared the physical space here, but not much else: the civilians were careful to maintain distance from the military officers. Intangible things separated the two groups, as well: bearing, for one. Even in zero-g, her pilots held themselves erect, conditioned by long hours of training, and now they buckled themselves into their descent restraints quickly and efficiently. Captain Varga, a dark haired man who probably hadn't spent half his lifetime in a gravity well, looked less like a ramrod and more like a predatory cat, coiled to push off from the nearest surface at any moment.

The officers of the 101st Wing - her included - wore black fatigues and boots, with a minimum of rank insignia, to discourage snipers. With a simple hand motion, tracked by her smart lenses, a signal would be transmitted to the micro-computer inside the clothing, and electricity passed through the nanotubes woven into the fabric, sending heat out into the area around her body and bending light waves to produce a mirage effect. To the casual observer, her clothing, and the body behind it, would disappear from view, leaving a floating head, a pair of slender hands, and probably a lot of confusion. These were not the sort of clothes civilians could get away with wearing.

Her hair would single her out as well. It wasn't the longer style Annie had worn before she was a commissioned officer, but she'd done her best within the regulations. Pale blonde and, for the most part, straight, it had curled slightly at the ends before she'd chopped it all off. In the back, it was clipped close to her neck and then faded and angled into a pixie cut, not longer than an inch or two anywhere. She had to keep it short, not only by regulations, but for practicality: not only way long hair a mess in zero-g, but this made it easier to clean the Neural Shunt Port installed between her 6th and 7th vertebrae, just above where her neck met her shoulders. Again, civilians didn't generally have access to that kind of tech, unless they were recording pornography for one of the shadier sites on the local dark web, or were the sort to partake of those recordings. People like that would never show the Shunt in public, but hers was just peeking out from her back collar, open as you please.

Rafe sat down to her right, wedged in against her on the narrow bench, and buckled himself in. Annie resisted the urge to draw her body away from his - she should be use to tight conditions by now, and if anyone had the right to casual physical contact such as this, it was her subordinates, with whom she had made such a long journey, and had trained for so long. He didn't mean anything by it, and a man in her position would hardly even have noticed. The important thing was that every pilot of her wing was strapped in safely. She swept her eyes over them. They were 'European Stew,' as many of the third-generation settlers of Mars liked to joke: the planet had been heavily colonized by residents of the old European Union. Back when that was a thing that had existed.

Lieutenant Junior Grade Rafe Traugott was built something like a greyhound: lean and thin as a strand of tall grass. His dark hair was cut close to his skull like all of the men in her team, and as soon as his safety harness was secure, he was already leaning away from her, toward Laura, each of them with a secret smile on their lips.

Annie knew they were sleeping together, Rafe and Lieutenant Junior Grade Laura Ross. Laura's hair was even shorter than Annie's: a scattering of straight black spikes instead of bangs, shooting down toward her face but not even reaching her eyebrows. Somehow, it worked for her. Maybe it was the big blue eyes, or the sharp chin, or the long elegant neck - whatever it was, it had certainly snagged Rafe. Not that Annie was jealous, or anything - she could hardly have a relationship with a subordinate. And since she was in command of the wing, that meant she had spent a long, lonely voyage here. *It could have been worse*, she reminded herself. *I could have been awake for two and a half months.*

To her left was Lieutenant Junior Grade Serafine Moreau. Serafine, she thought, was something of an odd duck, but they'd gotten used to each other at Officer Training School, where they'd shared a room. At the moment, the brunette seemed to be completely lost in whatever her smart lenses were currently displaying. Her eyes didn't even flick downward as she secured the harness: she did it all by feel, with a fair bit of fumbling around before everything was clicked in correctly. This sort of behavior was what passed for normal with Serafine. Her head was generally somewhere in the web, and she seemed far more comfortable dealing with computers and machines than with people, which had resulted in Annie having to rescue her, more than once, from an awkward situation on Mars. When men hit on Serafine - which they did, often - she didn't seem capable of just ignoring them and continuing on her way. Instead, she felt obligated to stop and respond, and found herself trapped in uncomfortable conversations with overly aggressive men. Annie had finally resorted to a habit of just taking her by the hand, pulling her along, and shouting, "No thanks!"

On the other side of Serafine slouched Gavriil Ilyavich Semenov, blonde, broad, and loud of mouth. Annie had a suspicion - though she'd never been able to wrangle up an old image of him to prove it - that he'd been overweight before joining the service, and that boot camp had converted that fat into muscle. His face still had the softness of someone who'd carried a little too much fat, and she guessed that it was only a dedicated fitness regimen on the *Scipio*'s gigantic rotating gravity decks that had kept his current build from melting away after a long voyage in hibernation. In fact, Semenov was the reason she hadn't spent more time on those decks herself - it was inevitable that he would attempt to draw her into a conversation on black market neural recordings. If Serafine had a talent for the software side of things, Semenov was a prodigy with hardware. That wasn't to say that they didn't both often team up to take care of a problem, but Semenov was more comfortable up to his elbows in circuit boards with a soldering iron. No one in their right mind would bet money that his cockpit equipment remained standard issue, regardless of the regulations. As long as everything worked, she'd long since decided she didn't care to hassle him over it.

Finally, she looked over to her second in command, Lieutenant Richard Nolan. No one ever called him anything but Nolan, or by his rank. He was at least ten years older than the rest of them, a career officer who had never made the political connections to keep moving up, but managed to keep renewing his commission. Or maybe, Annie mused, he had the connections, but couldn't stomach kissing the requisite amount of ass. That seemed more like him. He reminded her a lot of a drill sergeant, and he'd scared the hell out of her at first, especially with his spiel about mixing genders in the same unit.

"Stupid as shit," he'd told her over their first dinner in the officer's mess aboard the *Scipio*, the night before they all went into hibernation. "Leads to a whole lot of fucking, VD, and pregnant soldiers. It's even worse in combat. But," he said with a shake of his head, "I get why they're doing it. We don't have the population to be picky anymore."

Most of the table had fallen silent for an uncomfortable moment as they all thought about Old Earth. Nineteen years before - twenty, now that they'd completed their voyage, Annie reminded herself - the war that humanity had spent a century and a half trying to avoid had finally come. In the space of only a few months, ninety percent of humanity - over eleven billion people - had died in a nuclear holocaust. Some had survived, was the conventional wisdom, in shelters, but the planet was so red-hot with radiation that no one was going to be crazy enough to try to land a ship there to rescue any of them. Humanity's homeworld even looked different from above - she'd seen pictures taken from Luna, or the O'Neill cylinders parked at the closer Lagrange points, and instead of the blue-green marble depicted in history files, the planet was now a muddy gray, still covered in thick clouds of dust and fallout thrown up by the explosions.

And that, of course, she reminded herself as gravity began to pull at her stomach, was the reason they were all here, descending to one of the outer colonies, instead of comfortably at home on Mars, or being tourists to Luna, or some other place civilized.

Non-proliferation treaties, clearly, had failed. In the

wake of the war on Old Earth That Was, the populations of Luna and Mars had voted to join under a single governmental body, and the Lagrange colonies had followed quickly. The Unified Colonies, or UC, had been the product of a political and popular movement which blamed the existence of nation-states for the catastrophe on earth. If all nuclear arms were under the control of a single government, the argument went, another war could be avoided. The Unified Colonies could continue to grow. And someday, perhaps, humanity could return to Earth.

It was necessary for every colony - even the outer colonies off of Jupiter, or Saturn - to be brought under central control. As soon as an organized military force could be mustered, the UCAF, or Unified Colonies Armed Forces, had blockaded each of the outer colonies. Unlike Luna, which had been first colonized three quarters of a century before, or Mars, which was nearly as well established, most of the outer colonies were nowhere near self sufficient. Even if they could scrape by on food grown in algae vats in their limited hydroponic facilities, they couldn't produce the manufactured goods needed to maintain their computer systems, nevermind any kind of luxury items. The greatest delay had been in simply moving soldiers and material from the inner colonies to the outer - within five years from the day the first bomb had dropped on earth, the Colony War was complete.

The end result of all of this was that Annie and Rafe and Laura and the others were here as part of an occupying force. It seemed ridiculous to her that anyone could have a problem with the UC after what had happened to Earth, but she supposed there were always people who just liked to be difficult. Or wrong-headed. Or selfish. So they were rotating in to replace the wing that had spent the last two years here as part of the occupation force, and of course every civilian on the elevator with them would know that. There wouldn't be any insurgents here: security was too tight for that. To go off-world or get access to the orbital elevators required background checks, letters of reference, and security clearances. Most Europans hadn't been off-world in twenty years, if ever.

So she wasn't worried about her safety yet, or the safety of the soldiers in her wing. Even once they got planetside, she couldn't imagine insurgents getting within a kilometer of the elevator. But she'd heard stories, and seen pictures on the web. Just a week ago, the Provost Marshal in charge of UCAF military police on Europa had been killed by a sniper.

Soldiers maimed in suicide bombings, coming back to Mars or Luna without an arm or a leg. Soldiers shot, coming back only as an electronic notice to their next of kin, their bodies too expensive to ship home. Soldiers coming back physically whole, but psychologically damaged, some committing suicide later. The danger had seemed distant during the journey over, but now that she was descending the elevator into a place where people would hate her and want to kill her because of the uniform she wore, it was hard not to think about it. Annie licked her lips, and tasted sweat. Breakfast - a ration of oatmeal, brown sugar, cinnamon, and raisins - knotted and coiled in her stomach, like a trapped animal desperate to get out of its cage. She wondered how it would affect unit morale and discipline if the commanding officer got sick, and decided it would be better to close her eyes and count slowly until the nausea passed.

The elevator shook and rattled as it fell through Europa's thin atmosphere. Annie didn't know exactly how long it was before the rattling stopped, but she had counted to five hundred and sixty seven. When the ride finally smoothed out, her jaw was sore from how hard she'd been grinding her teeth together. She opened her eyes. The 'fasten restraints' sign was dark, and the ceramic heat shields had retracted from their positions over the triple paned windows. Her hand shook as she unclipped her harness, and she hoped that none of her subordinates noticed. Her butt stayed where it was: they were out of zero-g now, and comfortably into Europa's gravity well.

That meant they were now falling out the the sky at a suicidal speed, depending on the braking systems to slow them before impact. She tried not to picture what would happen if those braking systems failed.

Annie stood up, knees a bit wobbly, and tried to get used to the gravity here. It was much less than that of Mars, but after spending so much time in zero-g, it was still like standing up straight with someone sitting on your shoulders. She tried to do math in her head. On Mars, she weighed about 24 kilograms. Here, she weighed just over eight - only a third of what she was used to, and a fraction of what she would have weighed on Old Earth, if she'd ever gone there. She knew what Earth gravity felt like, because that was what the spinning gravity decks on the *Scipio* were torturously set to mimic.

Gently, Annie pushed off of the floor with one boot, aiming toward a window about three meters away. A single long, bounding step was enough to take her there, and she threw up both her hands against the glass to catch herself. The elevator was much lower now, in the atmosphere - closer in height to the airplanes used for long distance transport on Mars than to orbit. She could see plumes of water shooting up into the air from where some of the surface ice had cracked.

A soft *thump* from her right signalled the arrival of Nolan. "Nervous," he asked her in a hushed tone clearly meant to be private.

She shot him a stern look intended as a warning: don't ask your superior officer personal questions. "No." *Did I look nervous?*

"I don't think anyone else noticed," he assured her. "Look, it's natural. You've never been in hostile territory before, and this place is about as hostile as they come." He waved a hand out over the view of the frozen moon. "Enough radiation to fry all your eggs. A layer of ice nearly a hundred kilometers thick that shifts and moves, and we have to go down through it. After that, another hundred and seventy kilometers of ocean, deeper than anything on Mars or Earth.

That's a lot of death waiting to rush in if anything goes wrong with the structure of one of the so-called cities built into the rock. And, oh yeah, on top of all that, a bunch of whacko terrorists that would like nothing better than to blow you up for being here. I get it. And honestly, you're keeping your shit together pretty well, all things considered."

Annie felt like scowling, but instead she did her best to keep a neutral expression. "Thank you, Lieutenant, but I don't really think this conversation is appropriate."

Nolan shrugged. "Nah, it isn't. But it's necessary. I asked around about you, and I've been watching you the whole trip out. You must have some real connections to pull the rank you've got, at your age. What are you, twenty-five?"

"Twenty-four," she admitted.

"Right. If you'd said twenty-nine, you'd still be young for a Lieutenant Commander. Anyway, below my limit by a couple of years. Look, I've been around. This is not my first rodeo." *What the hell did that mean,* she wondered. "And I can help you," Nolan continued. "You have something you want to talk about, and you're not sure you want to go to the base commander? I'll bring over a bottle of scotch. It stays between us. And I notice something, something about the other pilots? I'll bring it to you. Quiet like."

Annie hesitated. *I have to spend the next two years with this man,* she reminded herself. *And he's offering to help me. If I say no, I might make an enemy - but if I say yes, I might make an ally.* "I'm not sure what to say," she began slowly.

"Thank you' would be a good start," Nolan said with a smirk.

"Thank you," she repeated. "Yes. Perhaps after we've all settled in tonight then, we could could talk over your impressions of the other pilots."

Nolan nodded. "Yes, sir," he said loudly enough for everyone in the elevator to hear him clearly. That was something, at least. Out the window, there was a glint down below - something, a flash had caught her eye. She leaned down...

"I thought the surface of Europa was ice," she ventured cautiously.

"It is," Nolan confirmed.

"Then why does it look like we're coming down over a lake?"

Nolan leaned close to the glass, trying to look straight downward, or as close as he could get from inside the elevator. "Chemical reaction," he explained. "The salt water bubbles up through the cracks in the ice. Sometimes, enough of it reacts with sulfur from the volcanoes on Io that you get these semi-stable lakes or pockets of liquid. That's where they put all the Ice Breaker stations."

Annie nodded. "This elevator is connected to Icebreaker Two."

"Yeah," Nolan agreed. "There were supplemental notes about the chemistry attached to the briefing. Basically, the ice is constantly moving, cracking, and refreezing. You can't put a permanent installation on the ice, because sooner or later it would be caught between two continent sized chunks and crushed."

"So they put a floating installation in these surface lakes," she continued, remembering something about this from her mission briefing documents. She'd skipped over the science and spent most of her time reading about the politics.

"And they keep the reaction going artificially on a more or less constant basis," Nolan finished explaining. "So that ice moving in towards the pocket melts. And that's where they anchor the elevators - Icebreakers One, Two, and Three."

"I see." Annie thought back to the history of Europa. "And it was those installations we took over during the war."

"Without the Icebreaker installations and the Orbital Elevators," Nolan said, "There's no way off the planet. Hell, there's no way in or out of the ice."

The lake didn't stay in view for long, however, as the elevator was now rapidly approaching the surface. The cracks in the ice, which had seemed so thin at the beginning of their descent, now resolved into massive canyons and ridges in the frozen landscape, rising up to form a jagged horizon beyond which she could no longer make out the curvature of the moon.

Suddenly, the gravity of the moon seemed to increase drastically, and she knew the braking process had begun. For a moment, she thought her knees would buckle, and she used her hands to steady herself against the bulkhead. Finally, the pressure forcing her body down eased up, and she felt light again. Annie took a deep breath, then turned to face her soldiers, making eye contact with each and motioning them to stay as the civilians began to cluster around the automated door out of the passenger compartment.

"You all know the next step," Annie told them in what she hoped was an even, moderate tone. "We proceed to cargo compartment B-11 and start up the reactors. Once all the civilians are clear of the elevator and inside Icebreaker Station Two, we will transfer all combat vehicles into the station cargo shaft and proceed in an orderly fashion to the lowest level of the station. There, we will board our SubTee." All of the men and women under her command nodded. "Lieutenant Nolan will lead the way, and I will bring up the rear. Remember, we are now boots on the ground in a potentially hostile OZ. There's no particular reason to expect any kind of trouble, but keep your eyes open, pay attention to your sensor systems, and don't take any chances. You'd feel like a pretty big idiot if you never even made it beneath the ice before needing to be shipped home without a leg," she said in a lighter tone, giving them a smile to signal that it was alright to laugh.

Captain Varga stepped over to her, and she snapped him a salute. "Good luck down here, Lieutenant Commander," he said, extending a hand. "Once you're settled, look me up. I know one or two decent places to eat in Green Zone, and our turnaround time is usually about a week."

"Yes sir," Annie responded with a smile. "Thank you,

sir."

With a nod, Varga turned and, as the passenger compartment doors hissed open, strode out through the crowd of civilians, who parted before him like waves washing around rock. A moment later, the last of the civilians had exited the compartment, which was what she had been waiting for, and she clapped her hands together. "Let's move, people!"

Nolan led the way, walking at a careful but brisk pace that made her think he'd been exposed to low gravity at some point in the past. Rafe and Laura followed him, side by side, then Serafine, and finally Semenov. Annie took a second to sweep the compartment visually, more to see if anyone had left something behind accidentally than because she was worried about sabotage here, then stepped after them.

The elevator was clamped in place in its dock, suspended in the middle of a vast shaft that penetrated the entirety of Icebreaker Two. An extendable catwalk of metal had been secured to the open door of the passenger compartment, and it rattled underneath their boots as they walked across it. From there, the six soldiers moved quickly down a cramped metal staircase to bring themselves level with the elevator's cargo compartments. Here, Annie had to push to the front again - her biometrics were necessary, as commanding officer of the squad, to open the cargo bay in which the UCAF had stowed half a dozen highly classified combat vehicles.

Annie gingerly swung a ceramic-cased metal cover down to reveal a security panel with three step verification - the cover was still warm from re-entry, but not dangerously so. She placed her thumb onto a sensor pad, which read her print, then matched the grooves in her skin with the file on record. Then, she leaned her eye into a laser scanner, which nearly blinded her with green light as it mapped the interior of her right eye, again checking what it found. Finally, she whispered the passcode she had chosen at the time the vehicles were unloaded from the *Scipio*: "Whiskey, Tango, Foxtrot." Her lips curved in a smile at the old joke, and the cargo doors unlocked. A gust of wind blew past them as air rushed into the bay, and Nolan, waiting, led them inside.

Automated LED lighting panels on the ceiling flickered to life as the motion sensors tripped, and the pitch darkness of the cargo bay changed into a landscape of alternating harsh light and dim shadow. The six pilots split up, each making their way to a different vehicle, where rope ladders hung down from cockpits located nearly two stories off the ground. Annie, left hand on the lowest rung of her ladder, paused for just a moment to consider the machine towering above her.

"It's good to see you again," Annie whispered, though she knew it was silly to have an emotional connection to a piece of machinery - no matter how well engineered. But this was, aside from a few pieces of clothing and personal technology, all she had brought with her from Mars.

It was a thing of flat planes and angles, of a necessity. The fourth generation Chobham Armor - layered ceramic and metal components under pressure, descended from the combat vehicles of the 20th and 21st centuries - functioned best when enemy fire impacted it at a perpendicular angle, the exact opposite of the primitive steel armor worn by medieval knights, which had functioned by directing the force of a blow away on angles and grooves.

The engineers and the operational manuals referred to this particular combat vehicle as a NSIS: Neural Shunt Interface Shell. For a time, there had been an attempt to verbalize that as 'Ensis,' she'd heard from one of her instructors, but it was too awkward: in the end, everyone just referred to them as Shells.

They were shaped roughly like humans, in that they were bipedal, with two articulated and armored arms emerging from shoulder armor and a tightly packed array of dozens of sensors in the position of a head, but there was also a set of wings sprouting from the back, and fusion torches emanating from strategic points scattered around the body and limbs. It was a strange way to build a vehicle, she knew, and it drove the engineers crazy: if you wanted to build a combat vehicle efficiently for space, you wanted something much better at maneuvering in any given direction, and if you wanted to build something to operate in atmosphere you wanted it to be aerodynamic, which this was not, and if you wanted a land-based vehicle you wanted something more like a 21st century wheeled or treaded combat vehicle. If her Shell somehow ever made it to full Old Earth gravity, it wouldn't even be able to stand up without breaking its own legs.

But none of those other shapes worked particularly well with the Neural Shunt Interface, and that was what had changed everything.

Shaking the cobwebs out of her head, Annie reached up for a rung above her, carefully set her foot on the bottom rung of the ladder, and began to pull herself up. The low gravity made it easy to lift her own weight, but she had to be careful, because it also meant she could pull too hard, throw herself up into the air, and really foul up the ladder. As a result, it took her a little longer than usual to get to the torso of the shell.

There, she spoke again. "Open cockpit."

With a series of soft whirs and clicks, the Chobham Armor plates along the side of the upper torso opened, first revealing a seam, and then a doorway into the largest open physical space contained beneath the surface of the shell. It had to be, to fit a pilot inside, computer and life support systems, layers of aluminum and polyethylene radiation shielding, under external armor.

Annie pulled herself in, pressed a button to automatically reel up the rope ladder, and then scrambled into the padded chair which took up most of the interior space. She kicked off her boots and slid her feet into tight, padded plastic shells which reached up her calves, similar to the hard skiing boots that she'd worn as a girl when vacationing on the slopes of Olympus Mons. Levered buckles tightened the restraints around her feet and lower legs, and then she began strapping herself into the padded five point harness that reached over her shoulders, around her waist, and up between her legs. She pulled a moulded plastic wrapped metal bar in the shape of a 'u' down from above, settling it over her shoulders and chest, then pulling it tight until it clicked into place around her; it was padded, and fit close enough to keep her head from being knocked around.

With her hands, she reached back to the base of her neck, made sure her hair was well away from the neural shunt port, and by touch found the small button that opened it. With the fingers of one hand, she found the small cable and plug that came out below the chair's headrest and firmly inserted it into the back of her neck through the port. A small, green colored blinking icon appeared in her vision, but she ignored it until she'd shoved her lower arms and hands into the restraints along the chair's sides. Then, she focused on the icon and blinked three times.

Annie lost all awareness of her own body. The feeling of the chair against her was gone. The tightness of the restraints around her legs or arms, even the never-quite-comfortable sensation of the plug *in* the back of her neck, they all turned off instantly. Instead, she saw the cargo bay through the optical sensors mounted in the head of the shell. With as little effort as it took to move her pinky finger, she banished the human-style imaging in favor of a complex feed that blended low light optics and infrared sensors to paint her a much more clear picture. She'd fiddled with that blend herself for weeks to get it right.

Another thought cut loose the steel webbed restraints that held the Shell in place against the wall of the cargo hold, and then the fusion reactor was starting up like her own heartbeat so that she didn't need to draw power from the lithium-ion batteries. Around her in the hold, five other shells were stirring to mechanical life, and the bloom of their fusion reactors appeared, one by one, in her sensor feed.

Adjusting for local gravity, the Shell's OS told her in a

pleasant monotone. She gave it a second, and then began to walk.

This was the reason for the difficult to engineer, in all other ways impractical, humanoid shape of the Shells. The Neural Shunt bypassed the lower spinal cord and connected the human brain directly to the computer-aided control systems of the Shell. She lifted the right leg exactly as if it was her own, made of flesh and blood. No control system of pedals, sticks, wheels or buttons could compete with her movements, her reaction time, her balance. But try to put a neural shunt interface into something that *wasn't* roughly human shaped, and there were all sorts of problems. The brain expected the body to move a certain way, and if you messed with that too much, it didn't react well. Nausea. Headaches. Vertigo.

Annie moved quickly to the doorway of the cargo hold, taking the lead now. With a thought, she sent out a communication to the rest of her wing: "I'll take lead. Civilians should all have been moved out of the shaft by now. Wings and torches, straight down to our transport at the lowest level of the shaft." *Here's hoping Sera recalibrated our torch output correctly for the low gravity,* Annie thought, *or I'm going to collide with the top of the elevator shaft as soon as I light them off.*

As nimbly as she had jumped off the rocks of a martian waterfall at age ten, she dropped the Shell over the edge of the elevator and began to fall down the shaft. Her wings spread out behind and above her, the control surfaces shifting and moving to keep her oriented feet down. Fusion torches, connected directly to the reactor burning under her seat, began to fire from her feet, knees, and waist, using computer-calculated thrust guided by her own instincts to slow her fall. In less than ten seconds, she was flexing her knees to land with a deafening 'clang' at the bottom of the shaft, and then moving out of the way to make room for her subordinates to follow.

An incoming communication, manifesting as a single flashing gold star, pulsed for her attention, and Annie grabbed the icon with a thought. The star split into five, then these formed into a circle, rotated a few times, and after a second expanded into an audio/video feed in the bottom right corner of her vision. The AV feed showed a middle aged man in the black UCAF uniform of a Commander, hair cropped close to the skull, eyes protruding from sunken socket, nose reminding her of some sort of bird of prey - a hawk, or an eagle, perhaps.

"It's good to see that you've arrived safely, Lieutenant Commander," the as yet unnamed Commander nearly shouted. Annie turned down the volume on the AV feed with a thought. "I'm Commander Michael Clavinger, your superior for the duration of your stay here."

"Sir," she vocalized energetically, the NSI turning her thoughts into a reasonable approximation of her natural voice. "A pleasure to meet you, sir. We're glad to be here, Commander!"

The balding bird of prey nodded. "Move your people down the north hallway," he instructed her. "Your transport is a civilian ship named *The Nautilus*."

"As in Verne, sir?"

Clavinger scowled, and Annie realized he didn't know the reference. "Verne? No," her superior officer continued. "Pilot's name is Katakura. Local civilian, but you're in good hands. Security clearance green, last updated six months ago. Not an insurgent. In any event, who your pilot is doesn't matter. You secure your machines along the hull and hitch a ride down."

"Sir...." Annie hesitated, then went ahead and asked the question. "We're not putting the machines in a cargo bay?"

"Magnetic clamps," Clavinger confirmed. "You ride in your cockpits. Trip takes about two hours - a half hour or so down through the ice, the rest through the ocean. Your machines are rated for more than enough pressure to make it to the bottom. You dock at a secure UCAF facility in the Green Zone of Toshimayr City, unload the machines, walk through the city to your hanger in Blue Zone, then bring your people to my office. I'll send an ensign to bring you up, show you the way. All that clear, Lieutenant?"

"Yes, sir!" Annie had to stop herself from nodding the head of her Shell.

Clavinger, unencumbered by several tons of metal, did nod, curtly. "Good. Clavinger out."

The AV feed cut, and Annie reopened a channel to the rest of the wing. "You're going to love this, people. We're riding down the whole way on the outside of the SubTee, like one of those barnacles on the boats back on Mars."

"Seriously," Serafine half asked, half complained. "We're not even going to be behind any radiation shielding?" Sera sounded quite put out, and Annie didn't blame her.

"It is short trip," Semerov rebutted. "Less radiation than on *Scipio*. Drink your wine, take your iodide pills, trust to shielding in Shell, and let your T-proteins do their work."

"That's enough chatter," Nolan cut in. "You have your orders. Get a move on, people." He put action to words, turning his Shell to lumber slowly down the hallway marked out by their positioning systems. *I think I'm going to like Nolan,* Annie decided. *He can be the hard-ass so I don't have to be.*

The entire facility - Ice Breaker Two - felt like, Annie thought, a cross between an airport and a warehouse. This passage was big - sized for Shells like theirs, or cargo lifters, not passengers. A human would be dwarfed by it. But along the side, she noticed, to her left, ran two parallel moving walkways, one going the same direction as them, toward where their transport was docked, and the other inward toward the central shaft of the station.

As long as it might have taken a traveler on foot to hurry down those moving walkways, the Shells covered the ground quickly. In perhaps five minutes time, they emerged from the end of the passage into a vast, rectangular chamber half filled with dark water. The metal floor across which they moved continued out over the water as a walkway, secured to the SubTee moored there.

The cigar-shaped SubTee took up most of the room in

the chamber - there wasn't a great deal of space above it before the chamber's ceiling was reached, or to any side of it. She couldn't see the bottom of the chamber through her Shell's sensors, though she knew that if she wanted to she could send out a sonar ping to map it, after getting the Shell into the water. A new AV feed icon appeared on her screen, this one the blue circle of a civilian, and she accepted the contact.

The image of a young man appeared in the lower right of her field of vision. His skin wasn't tanned in the way hers might get after a few days in the sun, but a darker color, even though he'd likely never seen natural sunlight. His hair was long, black and unkempt, falling across his forehead and eyes, and those eyes - it was like she'd seen in briefings, news videos, and footage from the war. Not at all like anyone on Mars.

Europa had been settled primarily by citizens of the old Earth nation of Japan, from the islands east of the continent of Asia. Annie stared at the pilot, fascinated, for a long moment, before she realized that he was speaking to her.

"Repeat, this is *Nautilus* contacting Commanding Officer of incoming Shell wing. Anyone in there," the young man wondered, pushing back the mop of unruly hair and peering forward. Annie had not sent him a visual feed in return, only audio - that was the default setting she'd set up for her communications systems.

"This is Lieutenant Commander Winters," Annie confirmed.

The young man squinted out at her from the display as if waiting for a video feed to pop up. "Right. Well, grab yourself a nice spot on the hull, but stay away from anything that looks important, like the engines. And make sure your people hook on good - I don't want to lose anyone along the way."

For an instant, Annie imagined drifting in Europa's cold, dark ocean, with nothing solid for fifty klicks or more in every direction. "Acknowledged, *Nautilus*," was all she said before switching feeds to address her people. Her sensors had already identified the row of clamps laid out along the walkway. "This is how things are going to work. You take a clamp in each hand. Find yourself a good spot along the hull and turn the magnets on. I want everyone within sight of at least one other Shell. Maintain an open channel during the descent. Our torches aren't meant for long distances underwater, so this ship is our ride down. Get going!"

She waited for her subordinates to take clamps, and then lifted two herself. These were fairly standard items, used by all manner of construction or salvage oriented Shells to hitch a ride on transport ships when working in orbit. The articulated fingers of her shell grasped the handles easily, and she strode over to the edge of the walkway. Rafe and Laura had each stepped to either side of the walkway, affixed a single clamp, and swung out to the right and left to secure their second clamp. Serafine's Shell hesitated, but Semenov just dropped into the water to the right of the walkway. The infrared feed to her sensors tracked the heat bloom of his reactor, which sunk quickly under the water before stopping as he clamped onto the hull of the SubTee beneath the surface. Serafine watched what he was doing, then followed suit.

As Annie walked her Shell over, Nolan sent her a private AV feed. "Looks like everyone is secured."

"Good." She lit her fusion torches for half a second, thrusting her Shell up over the *Nautilus* in an arc. She bent the Shell's knees to absorb the impact as she came down on the top of the transport, hitting the hull with a loud ringing sound. A few meters away, Nolan's Shell clanked down next to hers. In the AV feed from the Nautilus, the pilot - Katakura, she remembered - swore. Ignoring him, Annie knelt the Shell and held the magnetic clamps against the hull, then twisted the handles, activating the magnetic bases.

"If you scratch my hull," Katakura warned her, "I'm going to submit a bill to the UCAF."

Annie looked down at the scratched, dented and dirty hull beneath her Shell, and let out a laugh. "Good luck with that. But it doesn't come out of my paycheck, either way."

"Is everyone secured," he asked her.

"Affirmative."

Her smart lenses informed her Katakura had switched to an open channel. "Here we go, ladies and gentlemen. Keep your hands and feet inside the ride at all times. Flooding the docking bay."

She assumed that he had sent some sort of signal to whatever person or computer system was in control of this dock, for gates in the outer walls of the docking bay opened and water began to pour in. Annie felt a rising panic as white foam and dark waves crashed and swirled about the Shell. She knew, in her head, that it was the Shell being submerged, and that it didn't breath, and that it wouldn't be swept away because the magnetic clamps were holding it in place. But with the Neural Shunt cutting her off from her own body, and feeding the sensor data of the Shell directly to her, she couldn't help a rising sense of panic, the feeling that she was about to drown in this dark water of an alien moon. If she'd been able to close her eyes, she would have; instead, she did the next best thing, accessing her internal memory core, pulling up image and sound files and throwing all of her sensor data off to one side, ready to be called back when she needed it.

The beach at Elysia Island sprang up around her, complete with the sound of breaking waves. Annie had recorded this with her Neural Shunt three days before she left Mars, and stored it on her internal memory core: a glass-encased chip, less than an inch in length, that could hold up to eight terabytes of data, inserted where her appendix used to be. As the saved sensory file ran, butterscotch-colored sand spread out beneath her, leading down to gently lapping waves of blue and green. The foam and the breakers and the crests of the waves sparkled under the light from the sun, and palm fronds danced overhead in the breeze. Once, she knew, the skies on Mars had looked red, primarily due to the scattering of dust, but that hadn't been the case since the earliest stages

DAVID NIEMITZ

of the terraforming process. All of her life, they had been a beautiful blue, like the pictures she had seen of Earth, and a few, stray, puffy white clouds made their way leisurely across the sky.

Her father had told her that on earth, the sand was different - more gritty, less soft. There, he'd explained to her when she was a young girl just learning to swim, the ocean sand was mostly made up of tiny pieces of crushed shells. On Mars, it was still mostly dust, and so when you waded into the water your feet squished into wet mud, kicking up swirls of it all around you. Someday, he'd told her, maybe in another hundred years, there would have been shellfish living in the terraformed oceans long enough to change the consistency. But she had giggled and told him that would feel strange and weird between her toes, and she preferred the mud.

She stayed there, on the beach at Elysia Island, for ten or fifteen minutes. Long enough, she hoped, that they'd be out of the dock and into the ocean. Then, she reopened her sensor feed.

A jagged slope of pale, greenish blue ice sped by, not five meters from the sensor inputs located in the head of her Shell. She gasped, then began to call up data, overlaying feeds from different types of sensors. The IR feeds did a splendid job of mapping out the crevice through which they moved: the water was significantly warmer than the ice to all sides, and she was even able to paint a zoomed out view of their descent in one corner of her vision. Her equipment told her they were moving fast - over eighty kilometers an hour, which was nothing in space or in the air, but quite a bit when frozen escarpments reared suddenly about her in all directions.

She re-opened an AV feed to the pilot. "Is this a safe speed," she asked him in a somewhat accusatory tone. "If you hit a Shell against one of those ice walls, the magnetic clamps aren't going to keep us on." *Nevermind prevent them from ripping through our armor*, she didn't say out loud.

"Oh yeah, it's fine," Katakura drawled lazily, without

24

looking at the camera. She hoped he was focused on piloting. "I could do this run in my sleep. You're riding with the best, sweetie."

"Excuse me?" If her Neural Shunt hadn't prevented it, she would have scowled. "I am not your 'sweetie.' You may address me as 'Lieutenant Commander Winters,' and that's it."

"I don't know," the Europan said slowly as they executed a turn that brought them perilously close to sharp-toothed ledges of ice that reminded her of the crest of a mountain range seen in profile - "You sound pretty sweet to me. I mean, don't get me wrong, you're not my type - those are some thick thighs you've got, the biggest feet I've ever seen, and the giant rocket launcher permanently attached to your shoulder is kind of a turn off - I'm not into that type of body modification, really, but hey, your voice sounds cute."

In spite of herself, she laughed. "That's not me, you idiot. That's my Shell."

"Sure," he said. "I know that. But now you're laughing and you forgot how scared you were."

"I was not-" she broke off as the *Nautilus* shot out of the crevice into open water - a vast, dark expanse, black as deep space on all sides of them. There were no stars, no moons or ringed planets to break up the emptiness.

"It's ok," Katakura commented after a moment. "I won't tell anyone. Anyway, dangerous part's over now. The SubTee could take us the rest of the way by herself. There's nothing between us and Toshimayr now but a hundred and sixty klicks of open ocean."

Somewhere far away, secured tightly in a cockpit deep under layers of armor, wires, frame, and computer systems, she was sure that her body was breathing out deeply in relief. "Wonderful," she said out loud over the AV feed. "Then there's no need for any further communication over this channel."

"Not unless you get bored," Katakura began, but she didn't hear the rest because she'd already shut off the feed. She went back to Elysia Beach for a while, but then, restless, closed that recorded video and looked out into the darkness, searching for something. A spot of light, color, or motion. She could track their progress by satellite, and even *see* the currents they were riding down by differences in temperature through her sensors, but something about the limitless abyss was both fascinating and terrifying, and she couldn't look away. Finally, she reopened her AV feed to the *Nautilus*.

"It's not a rocket launcher," she began quickly. "It's a Thales-Demios Type II Plasma Cannon."

Katakura, who looked to have been napping, opened one eye. "Yeah, still not sexy."

"Standard issue for UCAF occupation forces. It can be calibrated for crowd control. Projectiles, not so much."

"So you're coming down here with the intention of shooting people," he commented, opening both eyes to the camera and sitting up from his former slouch.

"No," she said. "But if it had to happen, this would be non-lethal."

"You're not coming off any better," Katakura laughed. She couldn't tell how serious he was.

"Look," she said. "I don't know this planet."

"Moon."

"Whatever. But we're not here to hurt anyone. We're only here to keep order. If you're not an insurgent, you've got nothing to worry about from us."

"Tell that to some of the kids who've lost legs to those 'non-lethal' guns," Katakura told her sharply, brushing back his mop of dark hair. "The UCAF-"

Annie never got to hear what he was about to say, because she shrieked as something thumped against her Shell. In her visual sensor feed, *something* with half a dozen semi-luminescent tentacles had latched onto her Shell. Set against the vast darkness of the Europan sea, it seemed at first horribly bright: its skin a kind of smoky, pale blue, broken by glowing orange-red spots or nodules. "What is that," she exclaimed, as her sensors began feeding her data. Fifteen meters in length, the computers were telling her as a giant eye blinked once, filling up the view from one of her optical sensors. 'Abraliopsis Morisii Europus,' her computer identified it.

"Light squid," Katakura answered her with a chuckle. "It'll let go when it realizes it can't eat you."

"Light squid," she repeated hesitantly.

"They taste great cooked up in a nice ginger and tomato sauce," he offered.

It was hard to stay frightened when you couldn't feel your heartbeat pounding in your chest. That was one of the reasons soldiers performed so well while operating with a Neural Shunt: complete lack of biofeedback. No adrenaline, no pounding pulse, no deep gulps of oxygen. Annie looked at the squid. She zoomed in and out, switching views between different cameras as the glow faded from red to purple to blue, pulsing through the spectrum. After a moment, she concluded, "It's beautiful."

Katakura said nothing, and she gazed at the light squid, watching the glow of its body, until it released her Shell and fell away into the ocean. She was sad to see it go, and focused her sensors on it, watching as it became smaller and less distinct. It wasn't like watching a person or a vehicle get farther away in atmosphere; there was too much in this water, microscopic forms of life and silt and who knew what else, and her visual sensors lost it long before it dropped off her IR feed.

Long moments later, Katakura closed their private channel and then addressed her entire unit over an open feed. "We're almost to Toshimayr," he told them. "Your sensors should be able to pick up the ocean floor by now. Same thing as when you got on, but in reverse: we'll maneuver into a bay, the doors will close, and pumps will lower the water level. At that point the airlocks to the loading areas will open, and you can walk your tin men out of the bay."

"Thank you, Mr. Katakura," she said in a crisp, professional tone. "We're grateful for your skilled piloting."

"Make sure to say that to my boss," Katakura said, and

she could picture a crooked smile on his face and the flip of his hair even though they didn't have a private feed open at the moment. "*Nautilus* out."

Annie switched to the wing's secure channel. "Again, loading and unloading is when we're most vulnerable. We made the move from the elevator through Icebreaker Two with no incident, but that's no reason to get sloppy now. Unload quickly and efficiently, and then I want Nolan to take point on moving us out of the bay. I'll bring up the rear. Pay attention to your sensor feeds."

"Roger that," Nolan confirmed, and the rest of her subordinates followed suit.

Compared to the hair-raising journey down through the ice, or the long plunge into the darkness of Europa's world-sea, it took very little time for the *Nautilus* to dock at Toshimayr City. As the pumps slowly did their work, water poured down off of her Shell's planes and angles in miniature cascades, streaming down along the sloped surfaces of the SubTee. Releasing the magnetic clamps, Annie stood her shell up on top of the hull to watch her subordinates offload, and experimentally cleared her fusion torches and thruster intakes. Once there was room, she lit the torches and spread the Shell's wings for a quick jump down to the walkways below.

As they passed out of the docking facilities into the Green Zone of Europa's largest city, Annie did her best to focus on the sensor data that would be immediately relevant in the event of an insurgent strike - or that might warn her of a strike with enough time to react. *I refuse to gape at everything around me like a clueless tourist,* she told herself as they stepped out into a massive excavated cavern. The architecture of the city was nothing like what one might see on Luna or Mars - instead of skyscrapers, the tallest structures stretched from the floor of the cavern to the ceiling, megalithic pillars anchored at either end.

She activated automated facial recognition software that scanned every person within view of her optical sensors and matched them against a database of convicted criminals and suspected terrorists. While that was running, she set her IR sensors to look for the heat bloom of rocket propelled grenades or anti-vehicle missiles, and still other sensors to scan for radioactive isotopes. Then, she tried to ignore the chanting crowd.

The UCAF had blocked off the streets in the immediate area, and no one without security clearances was allowed into the Green Zone to begin with, but there was still quite a mob. People were on rooftops, hanging out of windows, and down on the streets, where the soldiers kept them back, crowded up against the cordons but still in view, and hopefully too far away to pose a threat. *This is chaos,* she thought, and then made the mistake of turning on her audio. The roar of the protestors suddenly washed over her.

They had signs. "UCAF go home," read one. "Murderers," read another. "Baby-killers," read a third. They must have snuck the signs in. And they were chanting - she couldn't make it out clearly, and she cut the external audio again rather than try. It was too distracting.

Up ahead, Sera's Shell, passing under a bridge, flinched back as a rock hit it in the thigh. There was no way something like that could damage the Shell, but Annie could tell from the way she was moving that her friend was uncertain how to proceed. Even as Sera swung her torso around to locate the source, Annie spoke up on their secure channel. "Don't react," she ordered. "Keep walking. A rock isn't going to hurt you."

"I never thought it would be like this," Laura muttered over the comms.

"Cut the chatter," Nolan told her. "Keep this line clear."

And then time dilated.

She was familiar with the concept. Objectively, time dilated in relation to the speed you were travelling. The time that had passed for them on board the *Scipio* was less, by a small amount, than what had passed for their families and friends back home on Mars. But this wasn't about relative velocity. This was entirely subjective, and even with the Neural Shunt to cut out biofeedback, the human brain still moved into a different gear of processing speed in a life or death moment.

The bomb must have been dropped off the bridge - or been thrown - because it hit Laura's Shell from above. It was right on target, too: it exploded at a point where many of the sensors were located, on the left side of the head. The blast threw Laura's Shell sideways, and she must have instinctively thrown out a hand to try to steady herself, because then she was toppling into the building on her right side, arm outstretched, all the weight of the Shell concentrated into the outstretched hand that punched through the building's outer walls, sinking in up to the shoulder.

Laura recovered her balance quickly enough, considering, and spun out into the center of the street again, ripping out the mechanical arm, and a rain of debris in the process. On the street below, the crowd began to panic, with people fleeing in every direction. At least one protester was down, a chunk of cement next to her head and a pool of blood spreading around her. Laura must have been afraid of more bombs, especially since she was saying something over comms about losing sensor signals. Rafe was moving his shell to support her, but what caught Annie's attention was the swaying of the building.

There were people on the roof, people hanging out of windows, people below. Who knew how many people inside. Her facial recognition software began rapidly isolating and zooming in to individual faces: a dark haired girl, eyes wide in terror. An old man, hands raised to shelter his head.

In an instant, Annie had checked her rear optics to make sure her torches were only going to burn pavement, not people, and then she was flying through the air - or rather, her Shell was, faster than she'd meant, rocketing up over Nolan and Semenov and Sera. She had to use forward torches to brake herself so that she didn't overshoot the building, and then she was beneath it, arms and wings outstretched, holding the facade up as pieces of stone and metal and plaster fell about her shoulders.

She cut in her external speakers, so that her voice rang across the area, drowning out the chants of the crowds: "Evacuate this building!" She didn't know how long she could hold it back from collapse, but it wouldn't be long enough.

And then, the second bomb hit Laura's shell.

Kaito

Tako To Ama

June 13th, 2128

While Katakura Kaito waited for the UCAF Shells to scrape themselves, barnacle-like, off of his ship, he set three fingers together inside the field of vision his smart lenses recognized. The lenses weren't so hot picking up or displaying things in his peripheral vision, but they were the best he could afford. With familiar ease, he flicked his fingers open, signalling the software loaded into the lenses to respond.

A scrolling, semi-opaque menu appeared slightly to the left of his center of vision, and with the pointer finger of his left hand he began to swipe down through it. As a civilian contractor, he wouldn't be given official clearance to depart the *Nautilus* until the military Shells had left the bay. That meant he had a little time to kill.

He found an icon in the list that pulsed and changed, beginning as a black triangle outlined in silver, point down, with a horizontal silver line dividing it roughly in half. In the moment before he selected the icon, it winked to blue and lost the dividing line. He knew that if he gave it time, it would rotate through two more symbols before repeating itself, but with a tap against thin air he opened *Elyon*.

Here, in the Subtee, not much changed, but he knew if he'd been on just about any street in Toshimayr the world would have lit up with component icons, the auras of other players, and the occasional monster. His original menu faded away, and a number of small, unobtrusive icons scattered about the edges of his vision - not so far as to be in that troublesome peripheral region, but far enough not to interfere with whatever else he was doing. In the upper left a gold experience bar was displayed next to his current level in the game. It was perhaps three quarters filled, and when that gold bar was solid he would reach level eleven. In the lower left of his screen was a red heart, completely full, representing his health.

To the right side of his screen were a number of smaller icons, each of which represented a spell that he had pre-selected as Favorites. Most of these looked like dancing flames or shimmering balls of light, but a few were crystals of various colors. One, at the very top, was a yellow hand. None of this, however, was what he was looking for: he wanted the miniature HUD, or Heads-Up-Display, in the upper right. It was a sort of map, and with two fingers, he grabbed and expanded it to fill his vision as a translucent overlay.

Not many players had access to the docking bays in the Green Zone, and not many civilian contractors were players of *Elyon*. Kaito knew for a fact his boss would disapprove of anyone playing such a game on the clock, even if there was nothing better to do. However, the Augmented Reality game populated components and monsters automatically, using algorithms which matched elements of the game to GPS maps of the Europa Colony. Prior to the occupation, this bay - and the entire Green Zone - had been accessible by the public, routinely used, and clearly mapped. As a result, game elements spawned here just like they would anywhere else - and went uncollected for large stretches of time. In fact, as far as Kaito could tell since the game had launched just under a week ago, he was the only one grabbing resources in this area. It had been the same way with other games of the type, but with *Elyon* Kaito had managed to get in on the Beta Test, giving him something of a jump start and allowing him to really take advantage of these 'captive resources.'

During the ten minute wait, he made sure he knew where the nearest components were, then spent a while organizing his inventory and selling off low rarity components that he couldn't trade to other players. Then, after the Shells were out of sight and he'd been cleared to disembark, Kaito grabbed his thermos of tea with the *Date Shipping Inc* logo stamped on the side, bundled a worn and ragged knit sweater in a messy ball under his arm - it could sometimes get quite cold on the Subtee - and strolled out into the bay to collect the components which had spawned since he'd come through here on the way up. On his way down the ramp, he nodded to the maintenance crew heading into the *Nautilus* to shutdown the reactor while it was in port. He was off now, but they still had hours of work ahead of them before the Subtee was secure and the transport job was truly over.

His eyes scanned over the text boxes floating above the Components within line of sight. He ignored the metal catwalks and railings of the immense bay, which stretched off into ill-lit shadows. The glowing Component Icons were scattered between the heavy machinery lurking all about the bay: forklifts, pallet jacks and exoskeletons all waiting for the dockworkers to arrive and begin unloading the cargo from offworld. *Still mostly Water Aspected Components,* he grumbled internally. *But I can always trade them in Guild.* He selected the yellow hand icon from the spell menu on the right of his field of vision; this was an Air Aspected Spell named, quite aptly, *Far Hand.* Using it, he reached out in a sweeping gesture designed to encompass as many of the Components as he could at once. His smart lenses animated an arc of glittering yellow energy which passed through the various component icons overlaying the physical reality of the bay: a half dozen seashells, a piece of coral, and oyster shells with pearls inside. Each icon disappeared from his view as they entered his inventory, not to reappear in this bay until he'd left and given them time to respawn.

He'd picked up the *Far Hand* spell as soon as he could, because without it, he would have needed to actually wander around the bay and get right up to the GPS coordinates where the components were logged with the server as being located. If someone happened to glance at the security feeds, it would look pretty suspicious to be running back and forth across the hangar bay every time he went out on a job, but the Air Aspected spell solved that problem easily.

Just as he was walking up to the open airlock which led out of the bay, a final component spawned off to his left. He was about to keep walking - plenty of time to get it later, after all - but then he saw what it was and paused. The animation was of a boiling vent erupting from the water in the bay. Kaito had never seen that before. He fixed it in his field of vision, then tapped at it with a finger, and a textbox with a label and explanation popped up.

Gold, the textbox began. *Ultra-Rare Fire Aspect Component. Spawn Time: 6 Days. Epithermal Mineral Deposit formed in association with hot waters. Requires Heat Resistance Spell to collect (No Far Hand).*

Kaito's finger twitched, and he lingered at the edge of the bay. He looked out the airlock, down the hall where he knew the UCAF checkpoint was located, then at the animated icon, which continued to bubble and steam, then finally at the security cameras which monitored the room. After a moment's indecision, he called up the *Heat Resistance* spell, drew a triangle over his heart to activate it, and walked briskly to the edge of the dock. There, next to the metal rail, he crouched down and touched the icon where it hung above the surface of the water.

He didn't actually touch it, of course: Augmented Reality games were primarily visual, functioning through smart lenses. You could wear earbuds if you wanted to get sound, but there was often little point to doing that. But when his fingers were tracked as touching the component, it blinked out of existence, entering his inventory, not to reappear above the dark water for another six days. He jumped up, rushed back to the airlock and stepped out into the tunnel, feeling giddy as he called up his inventory. There it was. A lump of gold, sparkling in his inventory - the single most valuable component he'd collected since game launch. And no one knew where its spawn point was but him.

He picked up his pace a bit as he stepped onto the moving walkway heading out, almost stumbling as he called up his Guild Chat. As the walkway took him by a group of Date Shipping, Inc dockworkers engaged in a conversation with their mutual boss, he fixed his eyes at his feet. Right now, he did not want to deal with Mr. Date. Date Kunari, the owner of the shipping company generally referred to as 'DSI,' for which Kaito was a subcontractor, was in many ways cool for an old man, but he was, after all, *old*. He did not approve of employees playing AR games - or any type of games, for that matter - on the clock. But the walkway carried Kaito on without Date-sama's head, easily recognizable by his long, gray beard, turning in his direction.

"Found a UR Fire component," Kaito typed with one hand against the empty air as a translucent keyboard sprang up before him. By the time he'd made it to the end of the moving walkway, there were already three responses from the other members of *Ōchō*.

Cal: Nice
Rocky: *Are!* Where? *Saiko*, man. Fucking awesome.
P: Congrats, man. Is it someplace we can claim?

That was P, Kaito thought as he smiled. *Always thinking ahead.* P was the Guild leader, and he handled all the things no one else wanted to think about: recruitment, trimming the dead weight from the ranks, mathing out battle strategies, and that sort of thing. He was part of the core Dynasty group which had stuck together across three or four AR games over the past couple of years. Rocky was a more recent addition, from Atarashī kibō no machi, one of the other cities in the colony, and everyone was quietly convinced that he couldn't be a day over fourteen by how much he swore. Kaito quickly typed a response.

Kaito: Nope. Secret stash. *Mata ne!*

Mata ne was the guild's standard sign off in Japanese - it meant something like 'see you later' in English. As for 'secret stash,' they would all understand that phrase. Kaito had dropped enough hints that he had the security clearances to get into restricted areas in Green Zone during his time with the Guild that all the old-timers would get it, and not ask any more questions.

As he stepped off the moving walkway, Kaito swiped away the Guild Chat and headed over to the security checkpoint staffed by UCAF military police. "Hey guys," he said with a wave. "How's it going?"

At the security desk, situated next to a full body scanner, the two uniformed soldiers paused in their conversation - something about good places to eat in the Yellow Zone, but Kaito had only caught the end of it with half an ear. The shift had changed since his departure: he only recognized one of the men - the other must be new, or must have traded shifts with someone.

"Hey Kaito," Sergeant Van den Berg greeted him, with a familiar smile. He was a tall, dark skinned man with close cropped black hair and an artificial eye that didn't look quite right. "Easy trip?"

"Yeah," Kaito confirmed as he pressed his thumb to the scanner and waited for it to read his print. "A light squid latched onto one of the Shells for a minute or two, but that was it."

Van den Berg laughed. "Must have scared the shit out of the pilot."

Kaito shrugged. "I dunno. She seemed to keep it together ok." *Why did I just lie*, he wondered. That Lieutenant Commander - Winters, he remembered - had just about screamed his ear off, through the speakers.

"She, huh?" The other soldier commented with a smirk. He was smaller than Van den Berg, and younger. Kaito immediately disliked him. "She cute? *Bijin*?" Kaito held back a groan: the offworlder had mispronounced the Japanese slang word for someone beautiful. He'd probably gotten it off of some website giving advice trying to pick up Europan girls.

"Didn't see her," Kaito said as the sensor identified him and accepted his clearance. The display turned green and he walked into the body scanner. He held his arms over his head. "She was in the Shell the whole time."

"Anyway, he's talking about a Shell pilot," Van den Berg reminded his younger partner. "Whether she's cute or not, she's an officer and she outranks you, Moretti." With barely a glance at his monitor, he waved the Subtee pilot through. "See you later, Kaito."

"Later."

As he hurried away, he heard the younger officer, Moretti, continue: "I don't know why you're so friendly with them. You never know which of those guys is carrying a bomb or something..."

Kaito hunched his shoulders inward and picked up his pace before he could hear the rest of that, making his way out of the dock area and into the immense, excavated cavern which had been designated Green Zone by the UCAF. Here, artificial sunlight fell from enormous xenon arc lamps mounted at the cavern's apex, filtering its way between pillar-towers that supported the cavern's ceiling, and smaller buildings clustered around their bases. The buildings reminded him of mushrooms growing at the base of mature trees, back on Old Earth. He'd never seen such a thing in person, but there were plenty of images - both VR and flat - on the net.

The streets were clean, lined by shops and restaurants which catered to the occupational troops, civilians visiting from Mars, Luna, or one of the other colonies, and the upper class businessmen and bureaucrats of Toshimayr. As far as the UCAF went, this area was patronized mainly by the officers, he knew: the enlisted troops tended to prefer Yellow Zone. The tourist attractions here, such as tea shops, restaurants, clubs, bars, and clothing stores dealing in expensive imports from Luna, were too expensive for most of Europa's actual residents. The establishments all had English names designed to cater to the UCAF idea of Europa: *Jade Garden*, *Floating World*, and the like.

Above the shops and restaurants, the buildings were purposed as apartments, and so from the second or third floor on up there were windows and balconies looking out on the street. These apartments cost more than he could afford, and most of them were home to off worlders whose business or political interests brought them here for an extended stay. Just like in Yellow or Red Zone, however, their balconies teemed with potted plants: peas, beans, peppers, and the ubiquitous tomatoes, which were easy to grow and could be used for both salads and sauces. Fresh fruits and vegetables were expensive on Europa, because hydroponics space was at a premium: but for the price of a single fresh tomato, you could extract the seeds and grow your own. It usually didn't take long for off worlders to catch on to the trick.

Normally, Maple Street would be bustling, but he knew that it would have been cleared by the UCAF military police in advance of the *Nautilus'* arrival so that the Shells could be moved through safely. Kaito wasn't going that way, however. He was headed for Red Zone, so instead of following the path the Shells would have taken, he turned left toward the exit tunnel to Yellow. *I wonder if I can pick up any decent components on the way*, he thought, looking around for icons.

He paused under the awning of a tea shop, the kind that sold expensive sets of pots and cups and loose leaf tea to tourists, and pulled up a HUD view of the city. There weren't any particularly valuable components nearby, but there was something interesting: about two blocks toward Yellow Zone, an Epic Monster had spawned, and dozens of players either engaged with it, or raced toward it. Kaito smiled and began to pull up his spell list. *This will be a nice way to end my shift.*

That was when he heard the explosion.

It took a moment before he realized what he was hearing. It didn't sound like it did when you were watching an action scene in a VR movie. This was a low sound, somehow less loud than he had expected, but he could feel it vibrating through his bones and his body, even his teeth.

The sound had come from the route the Shells had taken.

Kaito stood for a moment. A powerful desire to see what was happening warred with a jolt of fear running down to his stomach.

He could hear screaming now, and a crowd of people coming towards him, some running, others backing away. Another roar of sound rushed through and over them, sweeping down the street, but it was a different sound: not a sudden blast, but a sustained... burn. Like a fusion torch.

Kaito began to run toward the sound, shoving his way past people who were doing the intelligent thing and fleeing. As he ran past *Green Jasmine*, a local cafe, *Elyon* animated a few Embers - fire components that spawned, out of some algorithmical sense of humor, near where hot drinks were brewed. With a hurried left hand swipe, he tried to dismiss the game, but messed up the motion in his rush. Instead, a burning red corona, signifying an active fire spell, surrounded him. He rounded the corner back onto Maple Street, and paused for a moment, jerking to a halt.

Half a dozen UCAF Shells - the same Shells he had just offloaded from the *Nautilus* - had stopped in mid-transit in the middle of the street. Well, four of them were standing in the middle of the street. The one marked *UCAF-X007*, in white paint, he recognized as belonging to Winters. It was pressed up against a building. The Shell's arms and wings were spread, and it was slightly hunched over; not far away, another machine had collapsed in the middle of the pavement. Smoke poured out of the downed Shell, and the four remaining Shells were grouped around it, facing outward, as if to shield it. Above them, a bridge spanned the street. Softly glowing atop the bridge, ridiculously, as people ran screaming in every direction, was the icon of some kind of Air aspected component, and the icon of a player from another Guild.

In the dozen heartbeats it took him to process what was happening, something fell off the bridge toward the Shells below. A loud, deep concussive sound not only hurt his ears but shook his chest and body as another explosion flashed out from within the clump of Shells.

The force of the blast rattled the buildings to either side of Maple Street, and the building on the right seemed to lean forward, casually, onto the Shell below it, as if the massive structure was a drunk making his way home from the bar by leaning on a friend. The Shell's feet ground into the pavement, ripping up chunks of asphalt and concrete as it was pushed out into the street by the weight of the building. As he watched, fusion torches flared out from the Shell's front in a desperate attempt by the pilot to hold the building back.

That's stupid, he thought to himself dully. *There's no way something that small can hold up a building. Why doesn't the pilot just get out of the way?*

That was when he lowered his eyes to the area around the Shell's legs. Any people who had been watching the impromptu parade from the street and sidewalks adjacent to the building had fled. There were still scattered people rushing out of the building's entrance ways on the lower level, and at least a few - he counted four before he stopped - trapped under piles of debris from the damaged structure. As he watched, a young woman in a business suit jumped from a tottering fourth floor balcony to the street below. For an instant, long dark hair streamed above her like a banner, then her legs crumpled when she hit the pavement, and she didn't rise.

That was the precise moment Kaito decided to do something stupid. He saw the woman fall, and knew she needed help, and then his legs were moving, boots pumping against the pavement as he became the only idiot running *toward* a terrorist attack and a collapsing building. It wasn't a moment before he hit the crowd of people coming the other way, and he struggled to shoulder his way through them without hurting anyone, his progress slowed to a near halt.

Kaito saw an opening and tried to dodge left to slip around a young woman carrying a wailing toddler: too late, he saw the hefty businessman clutching a briefcase behind her, and he couldn't get out of the way in time. With a wide-eyed, feral snarl, the businessman shoved past him, and Kaito lost his balance.

He was down then, and after the first foot stomped on his right hand he curled into a fetal position, trying to shield his head, his belly, his genitals. Someone tripped over him, and someone else kicked him in the back. He couldn't breath, and for a moment he wondered if he would die there.

Then all was still. Kaito looked up. The street was empty except for him and the Shells, and the UCAF Military Police, and whoever was dropping bombs from the top of the bridge, where the Military Police were now shooting. If the bomber wasn't already dead, they soon would be.

There were still people in the rubble, and no one seemed to be doing much about it as the building slowly crumbled about the edges, the lone Shell hunching lower and lower. Kaito forced himself to his feet and half ran, half staggered forward, tripping over debris and coughing from the dust of falling masonry. A half-ripe tomato from someone's balcony squished under his boot.

He almost stepped on the first woman. She was thin, white, covered in dust, and her dark hair moved beneath his boot without stirring her; he didn't know if it was the same person he had seen fall, and he supposed it didn't matter. Broken glass and chunks of plaster half covered her, but he couldn't see any obvious injury. He knelt down, put an arm under her shoulders, and gathered her legs up at the knees with his other hand.

She was heavier than he expected. She'd looked as thin and delicate as the bird Mr. Date kept in a cage in the DSI central office, lying there. He'd heard that dead weight was the hardest to lift, and he'd never been the strongest guy around. Lifting her up was bad enough, but then trying to run back away from the collapsing building was like... his mind struggled for a comparison. Like trying to breathe water.

He did it though. More of a staggering shuffle than a run, but he pulled her away, half-tripping over debris the entire time, until they were far enough that the building wouldn't kill them both as it came down. And then, of course, he left her there and ran forward again - because while he was picking her up, he'd noticed a boy no older than ten, leg pinned under an overturned foodcart, a line of blood trickling down his forehead.

Kaito's chest burned. His legs were dead, numb. But he pulled the boy out of the rubble, trying not to look up as the constant hard rain of metal and concrete and glass fell about them both. The boy's legs bounced over the ground as Kaito dragged him down the sidewalk toward where he'd left the bird-woman.

When he told the story later, he'd say that it was pure chance he looked up when he did. But really, it was the damned flashing game icons that pulled his gaze up. The building was crumbling, and it seemed to be happening very slowly, but though he knew it was made of metal and cement and glass those very solid things all seemed to have turned to liquid. The Shell looked like nothing so much as a person standing beneath a waterfall, in some advertisement for a vacation on Mars: 'Visit Elysia Island!' The water foamed around tanned, attractive shoulders and chest, spraying out with violent force, but the person remained unmoved.

It looked like that.

Except that, instead of foaming white water rushing past the Shell, it was a spray of plaster and dust and who knew what else. The pilot he'd spent the past few hours talking to -

Winters - must have decided now was the time to get out, because those fusion torches lit up again, rocketing the Shell up and away from the falling building. With nothing holding it back, the building collapsed, an oceanic wave, a rolling breaker of dust and smoke sweeping up to him in a gray wall and then washing over.

The debris cloud pushed against his body with a physical force that surprised him, and Kaito lost his grip on the kid, bent nearly double coughing, then screwed his eyes closed and curled into a ball as it threw him backward. It actually lifted him off the ground for a second, and dropped him again so that he rolled across the sidewalk. His nose and his throat filled with grit, and he pulled his shirt up over his face, staying on the ground to wait for the dust to settle.

It took longer than he expected. After a count of sixty, he opened his eyes and saw only darkness; the grit stung, so he closed them again and stayed down, still curled in to protect himself. The ring finger of his right hand had begun to ache where it had been stepped on, and the pain was hard to ignore.

Sounds were dull, muffled. Kaito raised a hand to his ear, and felt a thick plug of dust inside. Faintly, he could hear a noise like small stones falling and rattling against a hard surface very far away. He tried to breath through his shirt, but it was like trying to suck a thick milkshake through a straw, and his lungs couldn't get enough air. He imagined drowning here, not from water - that was a thing he'd thought about a million times, the Subtee crushing in and flooding - but from too much dust and grit to breathe. He remembered learning to swim in the Yellow Zone pools when he was a young boy. He, Mizuki and their friends had taken turns to see who could hold their breath underwater the longest, until the pressure had built up so much that you couldn't stop yourself from bursting upward in raw panic, breaking the surface and sucking in air.

Desperate, he lurched to his feet, eyes open now, shirt still held in front of his face. Where the dust had made everything dark before, now it was like... his mind groped for a comparison. Like walking through the hydroponics caverns when the misters were going. He could almost see great hazy shapes around him to either side where the buildings reared up. Kaito tried to suck in a breath again, but the effort doubled him over coughing.

He felt lightheaded, and dizzy, but the dust must have been settling because those fuzzy shapes all around began to take on more definition, and each wracking, painful attempt at a breath got a little bit easier, felt a little more satisfying. He stood there, heaving, struggling not to pass out, as the air gradually cleared.

Everything was white - or maybe a pale gray, it was difficult to tell. The street, the buildings, were all coated in dust, and it looked like a painting in monochrome. Three or four paces away, rolled onto his side by the force of the building's collapse, was the boy. Kaito knelt next to him and tried to find a pulse, but he hadn't taken a first aid course in years and probably had been playing a game on his smart lenses the entire time anyhow. He ripped the boy's shirt down, put his own dust-clogged ear right up against the boy's thin chest, and listened until he was pretty sure there was a heartbeat.

In the distance, muffled, he could hear the approaching sirens of emergency vehicles. He looked toward the bridge; no one was shooting any longer, neither the military police or anyone else, and one of the UCAF Shells had knelt next to the squad's downed vehicle. As Kaito watched, a rope ladder unrolled from a hatch in the kneeling Shell's torso, and a thin man uniformed in black clambered down to the smoking vehicle below. Kaito wondered if the pilot of the stricken Shell was alive or dead.

Time changed, about then. Things had been moving so quickly - or perhaps slowly - since the moment he'd heard the first explosion and began running, that only now did the pace of events seem to return to normal. Kaito wasn't really sure what to do. First, he found the first woman he'd dragged away from the collapsing building and pulled her over by the boy. Then, he just sat there, cross-legged on the ground, watching over the two unconscious people. *It would be nice to have something to wash this dust out of my mouth*, he thought, but his legs were too leaden to get up.

Around the time the ambulances began disgorging medical professionals into the area, his lenses began to light up with a feed of private messages - some from the guild, others from friends or family - anyone who knew that he'd been working today in Green Zone, wanting to know if he was ok.

"Hey," he called out, coughing and waving a hand over his head. "Over here! Two injured!" Then, with his left hand - his right finger was hurting quite a lot now - he tapped out an away message and copied it into all of his messaging apps, even the Guild channel: "I'm fine." He figured that would be enough to shut most people up, pulled up his inventory, and examined the Gold Component while they pulled over stretchers for the woman and the boy.

Somewhere along the line, they insisted on checking him out as well, and that resulted in his finger being wrapped in a splint. After some argument, Kaito was wrangled onto a stretcher face down. They told him there were shards of glass sticking out of his back, but he didn't feel anything, and they also said he was in shock, which was silly, but he was much too tired now to argue with them, and so he let them lay him on the stretcher and then he went to sleep.

They didn't let Kaito go home from the ER of Toshimayr Hospital that night.

Oh, the doctors in the emergency room got the glass out of his back quickly enough, but then they hooked him up to an IV, made him lie in bed on his side instead of on his stitched up back, told him he was being admitted 'for observation' and that they expected to release him tomorrow. It took about an hour to get his smart lenses back, because someone had taken them out while he was unconscious and put them who knew where. No wonder his eyes hurt - he tried not to think about a nurse's fingers on his eyeball.

He was just about to buzz a nurse, there didn't seem to be any painkillers coming through the IV, when his mom and Mizuki came into the room. *There goes any chance of sleeping,* he managed not to say out loud, quickly swiping *Elyon* closed. There wasn't much to do in the hospital room, except chat with the guys, but it was better than nothing at all. Apparently there'd been some monstrously huge raid in progress before the building came down and everyone got distracted by the disaster.

"Hey Mom," he said. Mizuki stayed out of his mother's way, shrugging out of her sharkskin leather jacket and throwing it over one of the chairs hospitals left out for visitors. He'd bought her that jacket, with the ornamental stitching, for her birthday.

"*Akachan*," she fussed, looking about to cry, "My baby! Are you alright? What did they do to you?" Kaito's mother, Hekima, was dressed in one of her work blouses; she must have just come from the office at Date Shipping, where she'd worked since her husband had died. This one was patterned in white and blue.

"No one did anything to me, Mama," he said, trying not to flinch as she hugged him. "It's ok. I just did something stupid and got a little cut up, that's all. Hey, this is why old man Date gives us medical insurance, right?"

From a couple of rooms over, someone started moaning. Mizuki, who had been silent until now, closed the door, then came over to the other side of the bed and leaned in to give him a gentle hug. "Hey, Kaito," she said.

"Hey, Mizuki." It was a little weird to see her here - they'd been on again, off again for years, and he had been pretty sure they were off for good after the fight a couple months ago. The moment she leaned in, the smell of her hair was familiar. He still remembered the kind of shampoo she used, not the name of the brand, but the color of the bottle sitting on a shelf in the shower.

"I brought your old blanket from home," his mother was saying, pulling the timeworn, hand-knitted piece of his childhood out her bag and spreading it out over him. "Hospitals are always cold."

"Thanks, Mom," he said, wrapping his fingers through the gaps in the yarn.

"They won't let us stay long," Mizuki told him, reaching her cool, delicate hand out to ruffle his hair. Despite himself, he still liked how it felt. "I guess visiting hours are done for the night soon." She paused. "You're all over the news."

So that's it. It wasn't a very nice thought, but then, things hadn't ended very nicely with Mizuki. All he said was, "oh?"

"Yeah. They say you saved two people when that building went down. Everyone's saying you're a hero."

All at once, Kaito felt very tired again. Maybe the pain meds were finally kicking in. "I'm not a hero. I just did what I could."

"It's all the UCAF's fault," Mizuki grumbled, and he could tell this was leading into another one of her rants. "If they weren't here..."

"One of their pilots tried to help," he pointed out. *Lieutenant Commander Winters.* "Is that on the news?"

"We've seen the footage," his mother said. "But the UCAF hasn't made a statement."

"I don't even think that pilot was trying to help," Mizuki said with a scowl. "I think they were just trying to stay away from the explosions, and got stuck."

"Hey, it's great to see you guys," Kaito interrupted, suddenly wanting his ex out of the room. *Well, it's good to see mom, at least.* "But I'm really feeling kind of tired now. I think I'm going to try to go to sleep."

"Message me," his mother told him. "When you wake up tomorrow. I'll take time off and come by. Kunari-sama has already told me he doesn't mind."

"Yeah," he agreed, to keep her happy. Company didn't really make being in a hospital any better - only being out would do that. Actually, having people here meant he couldn't play *Elyon* at all, which was definitely worse.

"I've got to work tomorrow," Mizuki told him. "But if

they let you out, come by the bar. You can have some of my mom's soup. Once my shift is over, we're playing."

Kaito thought of what had happened the last time he'd come to see her sing: how he'd found her, drunk, kissing another guy. But even if her parents owned it, it had been his bar nearly as long as it had been hers, and he'd missed it during this self imposed two-month exile.

"Yeah, sure," he relented, and with another few moments of concerned expressions, hugs and kisses, they finally left. Once the door closed behind Mizuki, he shut his eyes and tried to sleep, but then thought he shouldn't sleep with his lenses in and sat up to reach for the case. Then, he finally decided to just do it and called up a search bar. Dreading what he would find, he typed in his name.

"Local Hero Saves Two," read one article. It had pictures, including one each of both bird woman and the boy, whose names he didn't want to read, and one of him from a company holiday party that old man Date must have given them.

Another newsblog featured footage of the building coming down, and a Europa Media Corporation had managed to get a shot of him being loaded into the ambulance from the viewpoint of a well-placed drone. "Shit," he mumbled, clicked for more painkillers through the IV, and fell asleep with his lenses in anyway.

His first stretch of sleep that night lasted maybe two hours before a nurse came and woke him up to check his vitals. After the nurse left, as Kaito lay there in the uncomfortable hospital bed, listening to the nurses talking in the hallway and the beeping of the machines. Time seemed to stretch out, as if the Hospital contained a singularity in its basement which was used to power the whole place, but made all human activities take longer than at all reasonable.

He resisted the urge to toss and turn after the first time, because it hurt his back. A visit to the ER was always stressful, and the visit from his mother and Mizuki had made it worse. Kaito realized his jaw hurt from grinding his teeth, and finally decided there was no way he was going to be able to get back to sleep.

Instead, he reached over to the bedside table on wheels and grabbed his smart lense case. His eyes were dry and scratchy from sleeping with the lenses in. A couple of quick drops of saline later, he was connected and loading up the message boards for *Elyon*. He wanted to see what he'd missed.

He found a thread labeled 'RAID!' in bold type and all capital letters, and began to scroll through it. In another window, he pulled up the Guild Rankings from the event, and began trying to sort out what had happened.

Raids - cooperative assaults on very powerful monsters - came in one of two types in *Elyon*. The first type were planned events, announced well in advance, with pre-published lists of prizes based on individual and guild ranking. The game developers made every effort to make these available to all players, regardless of what city they lived in and what hours they might work: generally, there were entry points located around Europa with predetermined time windows during which the Raid was open.

The other type of Raids were unannounced. They appeared with no warning, for a short period of time, and whoever could get to them did. What had happened in Toshimayr earlier in the day was one of these. When they popped up, word spread very quickly: first among the Guild of the player who found it, and then among the allies of the Guild as they all scrambled for prizes and rewards.

Checking timestamps, Kaito could see that a raid boss had appeared in Yellow Zone about half an hour before the *Nautilus* had docked. By the time the bridge bombing had happened, several hundred players had flooded the public park where the boss had spawned. *Dynasty* had placed alright - in the top 10 of the Guild rankings, even without him. The guild rewards were already sitting in his inbox, he saw.

Starting about ten minutes after the bombing, he could see questions popping up on the forum and the various chat groups he was a member of, checking to see if all the players in Toshimayr city were safe. At first, the players taking part in the raid didn't even seem to know what had happened, and the back and forth messages were confused and garbled.

Kaito closed out the forums and sorted through his rewards, posting a query in *Ōchō's* guild chat as to whether anyone needed anything that he'd received. Then, feeling tired again, finally, he took out his lenses and closed his eyes, trying to relax.

Quite a coincidence, that there'd been a raid right before a bombing, in the same city. It was probably lucky for a few players: odds were that some of them might have been caught near the terrorist attack.

A coincidence. For a moment, something nibbled at the back of his brain, and then sleep took him.

He woke up to a message from his boss, Date Kunari.

Kaito-san, the message blinked as he opened it, his eyes dry and irritated from sleeping with his lenses in for half the night, even after a few drops of saline. *Please take the next three days off to recover from your injuries, and accept my best wishes for a speedy recovery. When you are feeling better, please stop by my office for a cup of tea.*

He closed the message, groaned, and rung for a nurse. "I need to get out of here," he grumbled to himself as he sorted through his game chats and announcements. He shared out some of the rewards from the Raid that he couldn't use, sending items to the players who had responded to him with specific requests, and then put the rest up for sale on the market. By that time, a nurse had come into the room.

"I want to leave," Kaito told her. She was a cute young Europan woman who seemed to have a lot of practice placating irritating assholes like himself.

"Doctor Takeda will be by to see you soon," she told him.

Chiyo, her name tag said. "He'll talk to you about that. Now roll over on your stomach so that I can check your bandages."

Her hands were cold, but gentle. "Ow," he said anyway. "Just give me a prescription for painkillers and get me out of here."

"The Doctor will be by soon," she repeated, and then left him to kill time as best he could.

Soon, of course, didn't mean the same thing to the Doctor as it did to Kaito, and it was afternoon by the time anything much seemed to happen, and another hour after that before the Doctor managed to do whatever arcane paperwork the computer systems demanded of him before the nurses would let Kaito get dressed and leave.

By the time Kaito had been released from the ER, he was seriously considering taking Mizuki up on her offer, and even having a drink or three at the bar. As a rule he didn't do more than sip at a cup of sake every now and then - he didn't really like the taste of alcohol, and never had - and also he knew that after you had lost blood the effects of alcohol upon the body would be exaggerated. As a logical consequence of these two factors, he was fairly sure he could get very drunk very quickly if he just held his nose and threw back most of a bottle. The Doctor who had checked him out this morning and had released him with no more pain medication than a couple of extra strength aspirin would, he was sure, disapprove, but he also would never know.

It wasn't just the trip to the hospital itself which had convinced him this step was necessary. It was the building knowledge, in the form of a malignant, cold, growing tumor of dread in his stomach, much like the tumor that had killed his grandfather here in the same hospital, that reporters were waiting for him to leave. More of it, he could admit to himself, was the fear of people staring at him, talking about him, wanting to talk to him.

Even his guild members, this morning, had very quickly

begun forwarding him links to news blogs and mainstream articles reporting on the attack. They all wanted to talk about his 'act of heroism.'

Leaving the hospital was just as bad as he had feared. His finger was in a splint, and there was a bandage on his back under the clean t-shirt his mother and Mizuki had brought. Half a dozen reporters and bloggers had camped outside the exit, and drone cameras buzzed about to get a good shot. They demanded answers of him, answers that he knew would be blogged and reblogged nearly instantly in Europa's claustrophobic local web.

They skipped right over *What happened*, because of course after all the hours he'd wasted in the ER everyone already knew that pretty well. Instead, they went right for *What made you decide to run in for those people*, and *How badly are you hurt*, and of course the dreaded *How does it feel to be a hero*?

Kaito couldn't remember saying anything coherent. He just kept his head down and walked as quickly as he could, and because he had long legs and walked very fast, he'd outpaced first the reporters themselves, and then once it was clear he wasn't going to do anything interesting and they had all the footage they were going to get, their drones.

He walked quickly out of Green Zone and through Yellow Zone, still with his head down, and then out into Red Zone where he began to relax somewhat. Reporters didn't come out here unless they were writing a story about the unfortunate people caught in the crippling grip of urban decay and poverty, so he figured he was safe for the moment.

In Green Zone and Blue Zone, and even Yellow Zone, the streets were open and airy, the artificial suns above shining down unobstructed until night cycle, when they all gradually dimmed over the course of an hour or so - the hour or so when he left the hospital - before letting Toshimayr fall into darkness. In Red Zone, on the other hand, the orderly blocks of city streets had remained only as the skeleton which supported the neighborhoods, the unseen bones beneath layers of muscle and fat and skin.

Here there were street carts selling hot food and cheap knock off merchandise of all sorts, and stands selling homemade soap and potted young tomato plants. There was a fish market which blocked off one entire wide avenue for what should have been a block, and when he walked past a light squid hanging up beneath one of the awnings he smiled for the first time in hours. There were old men in dirty clothes with long, greasy hair and signs in front of them that said *Homeless Veteran, Please Help*, and everyone walked right past them. There was a young woman playing a guitar with a bowl in front of her to collect cash, and there was a roving pack of street urchins with dirty faces giggling as they shoved their way through these crowded streets.

Kaito knew what the UCAF soldiers thought of Red Zone; it was dangerous here, and this is where the scum of Toshimayr lived, the people who were too poor to live anywhere else. He could understand why they thought that, and those things were even true, in a way. It *was* dangerous for a UCAF soldier to come here: they were liable to get mugged, or worse. They certainly weren't welcome, and they had enough to do keeping Green and Blue zones safe for themselves. There *were* gangs, and this cavern *was* the cheapest rent in the city. But it was a big cavern, and where the occupational forces saw one thing, there were really many different neighborhoods. Most of them were like this one: vibrant, living places where you could go for weeks or months without seeing anyone born offworld, and maybe pretend that the occupation didn't exist.

Kaito slipped down an alley, keeping an eye out for any resources he could nab in *Elyon*, but there were so many people here that the only things around were Common Resources that respawned rapidly. A few twists and turns off the main path, and he stepped up to the door of *Tako To Ama*, identified by the lit neon sign listing the name in *kanji*, and the somewhat pornographic piece of art on the wall.

It looked like a dive bar, but it was *his* dive bar. Tako to Ama was named after a famous print from Old Earth: *The Dream of the Fisherman's Wife*, in which two amorous earth octopuses were depicted pleasuring a pearl diver. Here, the owner had paid a street artist to create a rendition in which two light squid, colors bright and shining against the dark and dirty black of the building's outside walls, raped an off-world woman. While the pearl diver in the original had seemed to be enjoying herself quite nicely, thank you, this pale *Gaijin* was clearly wide eyed and struggling to get away. Off worlders, it said clearly to any who happened to be stupid enough to wander down this alley, not welcome.

He pulled the door open and headed inside.

Annie

Run

June 14th, 2128

Annie's father had taught her that part of being a leader was being seen to do, calmly and confidently, what people expected you to do. That was true of a political leader, like her father, and that was also true of an officer in the military.

She'd unpacked and ironed her dress uniform before going to sleep the night before, even though after what had happened all she'd wanted to do was collapse. This morning, in her new officer's quarters located on the UCAF base in Blue Zone, she'd shined her shoes until she could, as the cliche went, see her own reflection. If there was one thing the military taught you how to do, it was shine shoes; if there was a second, it was to hurry up and wait.

She took a hot shower; it was a luxury the *Scipio* had not afforded her, but here on a volcanically active, oil rich ocean moon, there was no shortage of either energy or water. Then, she pulled back what she could of her hair - buns weren't really possible with her angled cut - and dressed in formal whites and blues for the first time since her promotion to Lieutenant Commander. She wrapped her hand in a roll of duct tape and gave herself a once over for stray hairs, before making sure that the gold pins of her rank insignia were straight. Back in Officer Training School, she'd always had her roomate, Sera, to give her one last check for wrinkles or random bits of fuzz before she walked out of their dorm room; now, she just hoped she hadn't missed anything.

One hour before she was to report to Commander Clavinger's office, she visited Lieutenant Laura Ross at the UCAF base hospital. *Or maybe it's more accurate*, she thought as she opened the door, *to say I'm visiting her room.* She'd checked with Nolan last night after finishing and submitting her report on the insurgent attack at the bridge, and he'd let her know that Laura wasn't awake yet, so she wasn't surprised that the room was quiet save for the beeping of machines. The antiseptic smell of the hospital took her back to the days before her mother's death on Mars: the hush of the hallways and rooms, the quiet chatting of the nurses gathered around their desk, the mechanical noises and occasional moans from the rooms along the hall. She hated it all.

Laura was flat on her back on the tilted hospital bed, plain white sheets tucked up about her chest. An IV tube ran down from several bags of fluids to her left wrist. Her spiky hair was a flat, lifeless mess, her skin was so gray she looked dead, and her eyes were sunken into her skull. It was all Annie could do not to gasp.

Heels clicked on tile.

"Sir!" Lieutenant Traugott saluted, standing to attention. She hadn't noticed him at first: her eyes had gone right to Laura. But it didn't surprise her that he was in the room. Their orders to report for duty this morning had been suspended last evening, so where else would he have gone? She sketched a salute, then stepped toward him.

"At ease, Rafe," she said gently. "How is she?"

"It was the feedback, Lieutenant Commander," the taller soldier told her quietly. "They got lucky with that second IED, messed up her computer systems good. She was still hooked in when an electrical surge tore through everything."

Lucky. It was a one in a million chance, considering the armor on the Shells and the relatively small explosive force of IEDs. Annie considered asking about brain activity, but decided Rafe wasn't the right person to check that with. Anything he told her would be colored by his feelings; she'd find a doctor on the way out, or send a message to Nolan after her appointment with Commander Clavinger. Instead, she put a hand on her subordinate's shoulder and told him, "She's strong, Rafe. She's not going to give up."

Traugott nodded, and for a moment Annie thought he was about to break into tears, but he held it in. "Yes sir," he said instead. "Will she be alright, sir?"

What he wants to know is if his lover is going to come back to him, and laugh with him again, and share secrets with him again, and kiss him like she used to. How the hell am I supposed to know that? I'm not a doctor. "I hope so," was what Annie said, in the end, because she didn't want to lie.

Annie reached the door to UCAF Headquarters, a short walk across Blue Zone from the base hospital, just as another officer was coming out. She had her hand on the door first, so she stepped back as she opened it and stood aside. Her eyes flicked to the other officer's rank insignia, not quite as ostentatious on his duty uniform as on her dress uniform. She noticed his eyes doing the same to her, and figured they both realized at the same time they were of equal rank. She let go of the door, letting it fall shut behind him, and held out a hand.

"Lieutenant Commander Annette Winters," she introduced herself, giving him a professional smile. "I don't think we've met."

The other officer was small and slim, not really any larger than her and quite a bit shorter than Europan average. His black hair seemed just a touch longer than regulation permitted, but it was combed back neatly. There was a couple days growth of coarse black hair on his face as well, giving him a rough look, and dark sunglasses concealed his eyes. His face was motionless, as he shook her hand. "Lieutenant Commander Joel Malik," he said quietly, yet with an intensity that matched his grip. She was glad to get her hand back when he let go.

"It's a pleasure to meet you," she began again. "I just touched down yesterday."

"Yeah, I know," Malik said, reaching up to take off his glasses. His eyes sought hers angrily. "Your flight got shot up by insurgents, so now the Old Man wants my people to stay on until the next transport. We've been here over two years already, been off Mars twice longer, would have taken another eighty-something days to get back. But now I have to tell my people that three years and change ain't enough, we've got to stay longer. They're all going to be real happy to hear that."

"You're the wing we're relieving," Annie guessed.

"That's right. Except we're not going anywhere just yet."

It's not my fault, Annie wanted to tell him but didn't. "I'm sorry," Annie said. "I haven't spoken with the Commander yet, I don't know what's going on."

"Better get in there, then," Malik said, putting his sunglasses back on. "And find out." With that, he strode off toward UCAF base housing, leaving Annie to watch him for a moment, then head inside.

Sitting outside of Commander Clavinger's Office reminded Annie of being called to the Dean's office as a rather naive teenager in her first year of secondary school. The boarding academy her father had sent her to was Exeter Mars, the illustrious descendant of an Old Earth academic institution now reduced to glow in the dark rubble. The chairs outside the office of the Dean of Students had been notoriously uncomfortable, as if designed to make transgressing students shift guiltily while waiting.

Here, rather than the polished wood of Exeter Mars, the hallway floor was the sort of horrible, sickly green tile that seemed to end up wherever UCAF engineers were given free reign to refurbish military facilities. Access was still guarded by the ubiquitous and powerful office ladies who came with any bureaucracy. This particular office lady looked to be somewhere between forty and fifty years old, with dark hair tied back in a bun and actual smart glasses with thick black frames, instead of just lenses, like any normal person would have. The nameplate on the front of her desk read 'Madeline Holt.'

Annie couldn't escape the feeling that she was being judged.

The ugly brown metal door to the Commander's Office

swung open, and voices tumbled out.

"I still can't believe how quickly you picked the game up," said an older man she didn't recognize. She was surprised to see that he was Europan, wearing a rumpled suit with his tie loosened. His english was slightly accented, his beard long and gray. "It takes most people years."

"Well, if you already have a mind trained for strategic thinking," Clavinger said as he moved into her view, following his guest part way out into the reception area, "I expect that's an advantage over a civilian." Annie stood up at attention, but he ignored her for the moment.

"I suppose so," his guest said, crossing the outer office quickly. "Same time next week, Commander?"

"Of course, Date-san," Clavinger said, giving the older man a casual wave.

As the door swung closed, he turned to Annie. "Lieutenant Commander Winters," he acknowledged her, all trace of warmth gone from his voice. He was once again the man she'd seen over the video feed upon arrival: the Commander of all forces at Europa, no trace of warmth in his voice or expression.

She'd read what was publicly available on Michael Clavinger's record; unlike her, he was a pure 'flying' officer, and had worked his way up through the levels of ship command. That was probably bad for her: fleet officers tended to have a low opinion of Shell pilots. While she and her people were fleet officers, the same as the people who crewed ships, there was a big cultural gap between them. In many ways, they were closer to the kinds of Marines who had accompanied ships into battle since the days of combat on the oceans of Old Earth, except that piloting a Shell required just as much technical expertise and training as piloting a battleship. The 'flying' officers, though, tended to see them as ground-pounders who couldn't be trusted with anything other than breaking stuff up close and personal.

Clavinger had been part of Mars Defense Forces twenty

years ago, when everything went to hell on Old Earth. After the Luna and Mars colonies had incorporated both their governments and armed forces, he'd been an XO on one of the ships sent to pacify the asteroid belt mining colonies. He must have done well there, and in the blockade of the Jupiter Colonies that followed, because when the Colony War was over, he'd been appointed Commander Europa, and had been here ever since. Or maybe he hadn't done well enough; he'd never made Captain, and for all his authority here, garrison duty on Europa was a career dead end. He'd never have an opportunity to distinguish himself and move further up the ranks.

"Sir!" Annie snapped her hand up smartly to salute, and the Commander returned the gesture with practiced smoothness.

"Step into my office, Lieutenant Commander." He held the door for her, and she had to step uncomfortably close to him to get by. She tried not to smell his aftershave, and wondered if a male junior officer would have found this as uncomfortable as she did. By the time he'd closed the door and made it back around to his desk, she was back at attention. He hadn't offered her a seat, so when he sank down into his comfortable looking leather desk chair she looked straight ahead at the window and waited. Outside, she could see a view of Blue Zone from two stories up.

"I've read your report on the insurgent attack yesterday," he began slowly. "I'm disappointed, Winters. Not twenty-four hours on world, and you've got one of my people in the ER and one of my machines in the shop."

Annie thought about speaking, but he hadn't actually asked her a question yet.

Clavinger regarded her heavily for a moment, then made a series of tapping motions in the air about a foot in front of his face. "I've read your file," he continued, swiping rapidly through, presumably, just that, in a casual motion. "Top notch schools, top marks in Officer Training. A record like this on anyone else, and I'd know they were smart as hell. On you, all it tells me is that everyone knows who you are, and who your father is."

Annie licked her lips, but stayed silent.

"You can use a different name," the Commander continued, snapping three fingers together to close the file, "Call it for security reasons, and we're obligated to keep it a secret from the media and from your subordinates. But I know as your commanding officer, and I damn well won't forget it. And anyone who says you haven't received special treatment up until now is lying through their goddamn teeth. Christ. Twenty four years old, a year and a half of that in transit, and they've made you a Lieutenant Commander?" He shook his head. "You don't know shit, and you're going to get someone killed, if you haven't already."

"Sir," Annie began, her voice as firm as she could make it, "Permission to speak freely?"

"This oughta be good," Clavinger grumbled. "Permission granted."

"Sir, I gave all appropriate orders when moving my unit, and the system logs confirm that," Annie began, feeling more confident as she went. "My people were on high alert, we had full sensor sweeps going. I regret what happened, but there was nothing I could have done differently."

"You done?"

"Yes, sir."

"Good. Now take that load of shit and stuff it right back up your ass. You went under a bridge, Winters. Opies love bridges. They drop IEDs off them all the fucking time. If you'd ever served an actual tour of duty anywhere to get that butter off your bars, you would have known to order evasive action as your people went under that bridge, and Lieutenant..." He paused, made a motion to check his files, and then finished: "Lieutenant Ross would not be a vegetable right now. So don't give me any of this bull about it not being your fault. Your people get hurt, your people fuck up, it's your fault."

He sighed, looked up to the slowly spinning ceiling fan as if praying, then lowered his voice. "But if I piss in your father's breakfast, I'll get shipped out to some place even more on the ass end of nowhere than this hell hole, like Titan. So here you go, Winters. More special treatment, because I have no desire to see the rings of Saturn up close and personal. I'm noting this in your record, but will take no disciplinary action at this time. Do you know why I'm going to keep extra careful records on you, Winters?"

"No sir," Annie said softly.

"Because I can't just bust you down to Lieutenant and relieve you of command without a reason," Clavinger spat. "So I'm documenting every little thing you do. Another clusterfuck like this? In your file. One of your people reports late for duty? In your file. A goddamn button falls off on your uniform? In your file. And by the time the next transport comes around, you can be goddamn sure I will have covered my ass enough that no one will be able to say shit when I relieve you of command and send you back to daddy. You get that, Winters?" He twisted the surname in his mouth, to show them both he knew it was fake.

"Yes," Annie said softly.

Clavinger stood up, leaned into her face, and nearly shouted. "I said you get that?"

"Sir, yes sir!"

"Good! Now get out of my office. Dismissed." By the time she was at the door, he wasn't even looking in her direction. Madeline Holt stared at her as she made her way to the outer door, and Annie was sure she knew what the old bat was thinking.

And suddenly, she felt that she had to be *out*. Out of Clavinger's office, yes, but also out of the building, out of the cavern in which this city was closed, out from under the miles and miles of water, out from under the ice, somewhere there was open air and sun and she could feel the breeze ruffling the tiny hairs on her arms.

She fled. Annie didn't keep track of where she was going, she just went, at a fast paced walk, trying to find someplace that didn't feel closed in. She almost went to her quarters, where she could have escaped to her simulation of Elysia Beach on Mars, but she hadn't actually been outside in fresh air for over a year now. She felt like she couldn't breath, like the weight of everything around her was crushing in on her, compacting her, and it was all she could do to keep from curling up in a ball and crying. She began to hyperventilate; she knew it was happening, but couldn't stop herself.

The light from the artificial sun at the apex of the cavern didn't feel right, it didn't feel warm, and it made Annie's eyes hurt because it wasn't what sunlight was supposed to be. Instead of being able to close her eyes and feel it warm up her skin with life, she found that it glared through her lids and made her head throb.

Annie didn't realize when she left the Blue Zone for the Green, even when she crossed from one gigantic excavated cavern to another, but when she passed from Yellow Zone into Red, that she noticed. That finally penetrated her raw panic and started to bring her back to a place where she could think, and breath, and notice the sights, sounds, and smells around her.

The buildings crowded tightly about the streets here, and it confused her for a moment: why would this, the great bore into the rock which had become Red Zone, be planned out any differently than the caverns which had become Green, Yellow, or Blue? The artificial sun was the same, fastened up at the zenith of the excavation, and so were the pillar-towers, great columns of stone left in place with tall buildings clustered around them. The streets, though dirty and crowded compared to the other parts of Toshimayr City she'd seen before now, weren't of any different construction than what she had seen in the zones where it was 'safe' for UCAF uniformed personnel to be while they were off duty.

The difference was that here, the buildings hadn't stayed to pre-planned blueprints, orderly and neat. Instead, structures were jammed in everywhere they could fit, including over one side of the divided roads. What had been wide boulevards, with two or three lanes on each side for both vehicle and foot traffic going one way or the other, had lost half their area. Market stalls, food carts, shops with awnings, sidewalk cafes with small tables and chairs jammed together inside a corral of fences, all took up the space that was designed for ground transport vehicles. In between, there were musicians and street artists and beggars all jockeying for cash from pedestrians. Annie couldn't imagine how you could move a troop transport through here, or even a Shell, without killing somebody.

What space was left could only accommodate foot traffic, and the narrow streets and alleys formed by the jumbled on top of each other buildings were jammed with people. All around, the smells of sweat, perfume, coffee and alcohol and tobacco and a thousand other things wafted through the air, and the sounds of dozens of conversations in any direction - a few in English, but most in Japanese - threatened to overwhelm her. Above the shops and cafes and restaurants, the buildings kept going up, with three, four or five floors of apartments crowding the spaces above the street. On the outside of the apartment buildings were fire escapes and balconies, and everywhere on those were potted plants. She saw small, thin trees bearing oranges or lemons or apples; tomato plants with stakes driven into the pots for the vines to curl around, and hanging strings of garlic or other herbs drying in the warm air. There was a lot of greenery up there, and she had no idea what some of the trees or vines were, but she could identify all different kinds of foods.

Compared to this, the secure zones are empty, Annie thought to herself. *Empty and dead. This is the real Toshimayr City - here, where all the people we deny security clearances are exiled. That's why it's so crowded - there's more people living here than it was ever designed to hold.*

She was so lost in the view around her that she must have stopped walking, and with a sudden, violent jolt, someone shoved her from behind. Annie stumbled, caught her balance, and spun to see a tall boy, who couldn't have been older than fourteen, smirking at her.

"*Gomen'nasai,*" he said loudly as a space cleared about them, people in the crowd moving away. "Sorry, *sir*," he continued in English. "You Martians are so short, I must not have seen you."

That wasn't an accident, Annie knew, though she kept herself from saying anything. *That was a push. It was on purpose.* On the edges of the crowd - which was now circled around them, watching - were three or four other teens, both boys and girls, smiling as they trained very steady gazes on her. The whole crew wore a lot of sharkskin - jackets, boots and belts. As her heartbeat spiked, icons began sprouting up in her smart lenses: a reading telling her that her artificial adrenal supply was full and ready to be used, combat programs analyzing the way these kids were standing and predicting that none of them were trained in any formal way to fight. Her UCAF installed wetware and software was gearing up for combat, which was not what she actually wanted. *They're recording this*, she realized. *This is a setup. Get the soldier angry, then post it all over the web. Funny, funny.*

"*Ie,*" she began, putting a professional smile on her face and searching for the right words to respond to an apology politely. Annie was suddenly very aware that she was still in her full dress uniform. *English will have to do.* "There is no need to apologize. This is a crowded street. Have a nice day." She turned, not even sure which way she was going to go, just knowing that she needed to get out of here before she did something that would be judged funny enough to post and share.

"You shouldn't be in this zone, *Kasei-sama,*" one of the teenage girls taunted her, bouncing on her heels and shrugging her jacket straight. "Go back to Blue zone where you won't get hurt!"

"Pardon me," Annie said, trying to leave through the crowd without either pushing someone or needing to run. *"Watashi o yurushitekudasai."*

"Hey, come back *Kasei-sama*," one of the boys called after her. "We're not done playing with you yet!"

Annie ducked down an alley, past a tea shop and a stall that sold clothing, then took turns as quickly as she could to put distance between herself and anyone who might have seen what had happened. After ten minutes, she was both confident she had lost the obnoxious brats, and that she had absolutely no idea how to get back to Yellow Zone.

The buildings here were dirty, she realized as she slowed down, and there was trash along the sides of the street. Annie glanced down once at her shoes, and cringed at the thought of how long it would take to get them back to their perfect shine of an hour ago. She smelled rotting garbage not far away, and stale beer, and something fried. She had moved out of the main drag, or market street, or whatever she'd been on before, and while this alley was quiet, and the lack of a crowd here had given her an escape, now she began to worry not only about whether or not she could find her way out, but also about whether or not she was safe here. With a few hand gestures, she called up her gps map.

At Officers' mess last night, there'd been a lot of talk among the UCAF soldiers stationed here about Red Zone, and about how it really wasn't safe for anyone in a uniform. She knew that standard operating procedure was for any patrol that came here - and that didn't happen often, they didn't have the manpower - to be in groups of four or more soldiers. Now here she was, shined up like she was going to a beauty pageant. She couldn't remember the last time she'd wished so hard that she was wrapped in the armor of her Shell.

Just like I thought. Annie frowned. None of this jumble of back alleys or the buildings around were shown in her mapping software, but she could at least see which direction she needed to go. With a few more swipes, she set herself a marker, bright blue, in the direction of the entrance to Yellow Zone. Right now, it just hovered against the faded wall of a beat up building, but it was enough of a guide for her to start walking again.

Following the marker without a decent street map in her gps was frustrating; she progressed in a series of switchbacks instead of something like a straight line, and she had to turn around twice when she found herself stuck in the dead end of an alley. Once, a cat perched on a dumpster hissed at her, arching its back and baring its teeth. She hurried past it and waved away flies.

A half dozen turns later, she rounded a corner to perhaps the strangest sight she'd yet seen in Red Zone: what had to be a bar or club of some kind, from the neon sign sputtering above the door, casting an angry red glow about the alley. On the cracked and pockmarked wall of the building, she saw a fascinating piece of graffiti.

"Is that an octopus... and a naked woman?"

Unable to resist, Annie stepped closer to the wall for a better look. *Not an octopus,* she realized. *A light squid. Like the one that latched onto my Shell.* She looked to her right, where two of the symbols in the bar's name - she didn't recognize the Kanji - flickered again and then went out. Annie hesitated for a long moment. *Maybe it's a good omen.*

She reached out her hand and pulled the door open, stepping into the bar.

For it was a bar, she realized, once she was inside, not a club, and certainly not the kind of place she was supposed to be in. She'd been briefed on the sanitized and safe bars that catered to the soldiers in Green Zone, with pretty Europan girls tending the bar who would flirt with the UCAF enlisted men, and private rooms upstairs for the officers. Those were the kinds of places to direct your subordinates to, she'd been told. She'd even been given a list of approved establishments. You were *not* supposed to go to Red Zone.

The lighting was dim, but it revealed walls which were hung with a trove of eccentric objects, all of them, as far as she could judge, antiques from Old Earth. Annie walked slowly along one wall toward the bar, hand raised as if to touch, but not actually closing the distance to these precious things: thin books of stapled paper behind glass that she recognized as magazines, with titles such as *Life* or *People*, and faces on the covers that she didn't know. Next, a collection of unit patches and medals that she was pretty sure dated from the wars between the United States of America and the Turkey/Japan alliance in the 2050's, making them nearly seventy-five years old, from just before the Japanese colony ships began leaving Earth for Europa. A framed, large print photograph of a young boy in a desert casting a distorted shadow on a wall. Then, hanging above the bar, a set of curved, sheathed antique swords that she did recognize: a *daisho*, the traditional Japanese set of a *katana* and *wakizashi*.

She lowered her gaze to the bartender and asked, "Are those real?" Annie's shoes stuck to the floor as she walked further into the room, and she tried not to think about what kinds of things might cause that.

The young woman behind the bar was shorter than Annie had come to expect of Europans, but still taller than her by two or three inches. The bartender's black hair was cut in a wild, ragged fall about the lobes of her ears, none of it reaching as far down as her chin, and her eyes were outlined in thick black that only emphasized their different shape. She wore a black tank top that left her pale, delicate arms bare and revealed a small dark tattoo of some kind of octopus or squid in the center of her chest, below her collarbone, with the upper slopes of her breasts rising to either side.

"Real?" She laughed. Her voice was striking: rich, strong. "Who knows? I mean, it's supposed to be, but I don't think anyone's got any proof. Anyway, you lost or something? We don't get many UCAF officers wandering in here."

Annie shrugged. "I saw the graffiti on the wall outside. Thought I'd take a look."

"Uh-huh." The bartender regarded her suspiciously. "You drinking?"

"Um." Annie looked at the bottles behind the bar. "You have scotch?"

"Scotch?" The bartender scowled. "We look like a tourist bar? That shit's expensive. You want hard liquor, try this." She pulled a glass out from behind the counter, set it on the bar, then turned and glanced over the bottles of alcohol for a moment, finally selecting one.

"What is this, some kind of sake?" Annie perched on a barstool that was just a bit too tall for her. "I like sake."

"*Aoi sōrui,*" the bartender told her, pouring something cloudy and dark into the glass.

"Umm, which means?" *Is that blue, or green,* Annie wondered. *I can't tell.*

"It's made locally. Give it a shot."

Annie hesitated, then reached for the glass. She lifted it, swirled it around a bit, and gave it an experimental sniff. "Eww." She wrinkled her nose.

"Go ahead, give it a try." The bartender put her elbows on the bar and leaned forward, watching Annie closely.

Slowly, Annie brought the glass to her lips and tasted the liquor. *Oh my god.* She did her best not to gag, choke, or do anything else which would show her absolute disgust and insult the bartender.

"How is it," the Europan girl asked with a very slight smile curving her lips.

"It's..." Annie coughed. "It's very strong."

The bartender's smile widened. "Yeah. That's stuff's great for getting you absolutely shit-faced in about two minutes flat."

That's exactly what I need, Annie didn't say out loud. "What's it made from? Rice?"

"Algae." The bartender turned around to replace the

bottle. Annie did her best not to be sick, and rather than have to look at the glass full of fermented algae any longer, she turned around on the barstool and looked over the rest of the place.

There was a stage, if you could call it that, in one corner. It looked to be made of cheap wood, painted black and elevated about two feet off the floor. She had a hard time imagining how you could fit more than two or three people on it at a time. Scattered across the floor - also painted black - were tables and chairs, and a couple of big screens hung over the bar and the stage, one showing an EMC news stream and the other a live video feed of what looked to be a concert at Fukami Toshi, one of the other cities sunk into Europa's bedrock.

There were maybe three or four other customers here, all native Europans, all studiously avoiding looking at her. They were grouped around two round tables and a bottle of Sake, and a few of them had bowls of rice or soup half eaten in front of them. She wondered what the Europan equivalent of pub food was.

For a few moments, she watched the news. "Shumokuzame claims credit for bridge bombing," the headline scrolled along the bottom of the screen. *Shumokuzame.* Annie repeated the name to herself. *So that's who hurt Laura.* She knew the name from her security briefings, from all of the files she had read before arriving in system.

The front door opened, and someone she recognized walked in. He was tall and lean, Europan, with a mop of long black hair that he tossed back with one hand as he closed the door with the other. *Katakura Kaito,* she remembered. *The pilot of the Nautilus.* He was wearing a sharkskin jacket over an old ratty sweater, with sharkskin boots, and he seemed to wince a bit as he walked over to the bar, as if he was in pain. Annie smiled as he pulled up a stool to her right, and for a moment found herself confused when he nodded absently back without any sign of recognition.

Of course, Annie realized. *I never turned on the video feed. He only knows my voice.*

"Hey Kaito," the bartender said as she leaned forward onto the bar in front of him. It was the kind of lean - arms in close to push your bust together - that you did when you wanted someone to pay attention to how you looked. When you wanted to get into their personal space. Kaito, however, didn't seem to notice, or maybe he just didn't care.

"Hey, Mizuki," he acknowledged her as he tapped on the empty air in front of him. His eyes were focused on things only he could see.

"You want something to drink," Mizuki offered. "On the house, for the big hero."

Annie narrowed her eyes, confused.

"*Ie,*" Kaito said, shaking his head slightly. "I need food that isn't hospital food. Give me some of your mother's *miso* soup, and *sake.*"

"Sure thing." Mizuki turned and headed back for the kitchen, and Kaito was already lost in his own world again, grabbing, zooming, and swiping invisible icons. Annie bit her lip, considering how to begin a conversation, when a cheer went up from the two tables near the stage.

"Kaito!" One of the men shouted. "Look! Our hero!"

There, on the screen, was an unmistakable shot of Kaito being helped to an ambulance amidst the dust and debris of the insurgent attack yesterday, after the collapse of the office building she'd tried to hold up. There was blood on his back, and the *kanji* scrolling along the bottom of the screen... she racked her memory, and managed to come up with a rough translation: 'Local Hero saves two.'

"Don't even start," Kaito said, leaning forward to rest his forehead on the bar next to her. She realized she'd read the news ticker out loud. "I don't want to hear anything about it," he continued without looking at her.

"I'm sorry," Annie said. "Kaito, right?"

He raised his head, spread the hair which had fallen

down over his face with two fingers from each hand, and regarded her suspiciously. "Do I know you?"

"Not really," she admitted. "But we talked for a while yesterday. Lieutenant Commander Annie Winters." She stuck out her hand for him to shake, and then held it out awkwardly while she waited to see if he would take it.

Kaito's eyes swept up and down her uniform, and he whispered a word under his breath: "*Bijin.*" Then, at a normal volume. "Yeah, wow, nice to meet you in person." He smiled and took her hand, shaking it a couple of times, holding it for a second, and then letting her go. "Sorry. Wow, yeah, I'm still kinda loopy from the painkillers. I should have recognized the voice."

She shrugged, dropping her hand down to hold onto the edge of the barstool. "I never put the video feed on. My fault, not yours. But I didn't know you were there when the building collapsed yesterday! Are you alright? You said you were in the hospital, and on pain meds? What happened?"

He shook his head, looking embarrassed. "I just dragged a couple of people out when the building came down. Got some glass stuck in my back. Anyone would have done it, if they were there. But you, I saw you there - well, I saw your Shell, and I knew whose it was. You held that whole damned building up while people got out. You saved a lot more people than I did."

Annie looked around the bar self consciously. "That's not how the UCAF sees it. They think if I'd given the right orders, that bomb would never have hit one of my people, and then that building would never have come down." She turned back to Kaito, catching his eyes. "And you're wrong. That anyone would have run in and helped, I mean," she said, stumbling over her words. "I was there. Everyone else was running away."

Kaito opened his mouth, then looked over at her glass. Without asking her permission, he picked it up, sniffed it, and made a face. "Oh, tell me you didn't drink this. Who gave this to you?"

"Umm," Annie hesitated, afraid she had done something wrong. "The girl behind the bar."

"Mizuki!" At Kaito's call, the bartender's head and shoulders appeared from the doorway to the kitchen. "Why'd you give her this?" Kaito gesticulated with the glass. "Can we get something decent to drink for Annie, here? And another bowl of Miso soup - it'll help to keep her from getting sick!"

"She told me it was local," Annie began.

"Yeah, it's local alright," Kaito said with a scowl, sliding the empty glass away down the bar. "Local crap. It's the first alcohol they managed to make after landing the colony ships, before the rice crops really got going. Aside from a couple of old guys who claim they like it, it's only good for two things: scaring off tourists and degreasing engines. I'm so sorry. She must have thought you were here to hassle people, or something."

Or she just doesn't want off worlders around, Annie thought, but didn't say out loud. Her suspicions were confirmed when the bartender - Mizuki - brought them a pot of tea and two cups. "Since you shouldn't drink," she told Kaito, but her hard eyes never left Annie until she was back in the kitchen.

Annie took a quick sip of tea so that she didn't have to make eye contact with the other woman. "Oh thank God," she said as she set the cup down, letting the taste of green tea scour away the foulness she'd choked on a few moments before.

"I'm impressed you didn't throw it up," Kaito told her, chuckling softly. "So... how'd you end up here? I mean, this bar isn't exactly on the map, and usually officer-types don't come anywhere near Red Zone."

"It wasn't on purpose," she admitted. "I just had to get off base, and I started walking. Before I knew it I was in Red Zone, and..." She decided to skip her encounter with the obnoxious teenagers, "And I got a bit lost, so I turned on my GPS and found this place on the way back. I saw the picture, and came in. I guess I was curious."

"You saw the pornographic graffiti where an offworld woman gets raped by a sea monster, and you figured this was the place for you?"

She shook her head. "It sounds stupid when you say it like that. But really I was just thinking of the light squid you showed me, so I came in."

Kaito stopped to consider that for a moment, taking another sip of tea from his cup. "Would you let me walk you back to Yellow Zone when you leave? It's not really as dangerous as people seem to think it is, but in that uniform, you might get hassled."

Annie felt her cheeks get warm, and she smiled. "Sure. I mean, thank you. *Arigato.*" She took another sip of tea to hide behind the cup.

Kaito glanced around the bar. "It's not busy this time of day. Do you want to grab a table? I'm starving, and I'm getting more food than they'll be able to fit on the bar."

"Sure." Annie hopped down off the barstool, taking her teacup with her, and Kaito did the same, grabbing the pot as well. They found a table away from the screens, and before too long a couple of bowls of soup were laid out in front of them. Kaito followed that up by ordering sushi and sashimi in great quantities, and before long was telling her how horrible hospital food was.

"Then it sounds like hospital food here is the same as it is on Mars," Annie teased after having a laugh. "I hate hospitals, anyway. I try never to end up in one."

"Says," Kaito joked, "the girl who joined up with the UCAF." He was looking off to one side and scrolling through something or other with his right hand.

"What are you doing," she asked, a little annoyed that he wasn't paying attention to her.

"Just catching up with what's been going on in my guild," he said, then shook himself and made a sign she recognized as closing out an app. "Do you play AR games?"

"AR?" She shook her head, confused. *He's playing a game?*

"Augmented Reality," he explained. "You know, uses the smart lenses to superimpose things over what you actually see? I've played a bunch, usually with the same guild, but there's this new one called *Elyon* that's pretty cool. You go around collecting a bunch of spell components so you can use magic to fight monsters and stuff."

"Oh." *How... lame*, was all she could think. "That sounds... interesting. Magic, huh?"

"Yeah," he said, leaning forward excitedly, then paused. "You don't care at all, do you?"

"Sorry," Annie admitted. "I've never really played a lot of games. I mean, I have a simulation or two that I can play through the shunt," she admitted, touching the implant on the back of her neck, "But that's mostly just places. Like the beach. I recorded a day at the beach just before I left Mars, so that I can go back when I miss it."

Kaito shook his head, a faint smile on his face. "That must be nice. I'd love to afford one of those, but here they're so expensive the only ones who have them are usually getting them on the black market, and using them for, um, things that aren't legal."

Annie finished off her soup. "Yeah, I've heard people use them to record pornography."

"And to record getting high," he added. "And then rich people buy those sims. But mostly the surgery and the hardware are just too expensive."

"Anyway," she said, changing the subject. "That's all I have. I've never had enough time for games, really. Not with school, and then training once I joined the military."

"Tell you what," Kaito told her. "I was a jerk to be checking that stuff when you're sitting right here at the table with me. As an apology, why don't I take you out to dinner? Not here," he waved his hand to take in the rather dumpy bar, "But someplace nice? In Green Zone?"

She thought about that for a moment. Kaito had, on the one hand, been fiddling with a dumb game instead of talking to her. On the other hand, he'd been nice to her on the ride down from the surface, and he'd been nice to her again tonight. She'd already decided to walk with him back to the entrance to Yellow Zone; it would be easier and safer. He leaned back in his chair, waiting for his answer, and absently ran a hand back through his mop of hair, smiling in a slightly roguish way.

"Alright," she said, putting down her spoon. "But no playing games at dinner."

He raised his hands, palms out, as if protesting his innocence. "I promise. I won't pay attention to anything but you."

"Ok, then," she said, satisfied. "So what's this Landing Day I keep hearing about," she asked as Mizuki came over to place a tablet with bill on their table.

"The anniversary of when the first three colony ships sent shuttles down from orbit," Kaito explained, waving his wrist over the tablet to authorize payment from his account with his implanted identification chip. He passed the device over to her. "It's one of the biggest holidays around. Street food, parades, music, fireworks, all that."

Annie swiped her own wrist to cover her portion of the meal. "Sounds like I might need a local guide. You know, so I see the good stuff."

Kaito stood up. "I might know someone who could help you out," he said with a grin. "Come on. I'll show you back to Yellow Zone."

Annie smiled, and followed him out of the bar.

Annie

Shinrai

June 17th, 2128

Like all businesses in Green Zone, the restaurant *Soyokaze* was identified by a sign which gave its name transliterated into the English alphabet, as well as the original *kanji*: "微風." Annie didn't have the slightest idea what that translated as, despite hours pouring through the Japanese language tutorials on board the *Scipio* en route to Europa, and she doubted she'd even be able to pronounce it correctly. With her smart lenses stashed in a hard plastic case inside her purse, she couldn't call up a convenient translation. *Kaito will know*, she told herself as she stepped in through the door. *You can always ask him.*

Hearts and minds, she could hear her instructors hammering into their heads at Officer Training School. This place felt so different from Mars: the smells of the food, the architecture, even the people themselves, the way they talked and looked. *You have to understand the culture you're walking into before you can respect it, and you have to give respect before you will get it.* But languages were just so hard. Other people in her class had sped past her, memorizing lists of nouns and verbs, but she'd only just managed to pass her oral and written exams. The time she'd spent awake on the *Scipio* hadn't helped to do anything but encourage the little she had learned to slide out of her mind like sand through a sieve, despite her studying. In the four days she'd spent in Toshimayr City, she'd hardly been able to do more than recognize a few common words and phrases heard in passing.

She looked around for Kaito, hoping she was in the right place. It felt weird to be without the convenient access to information provided by the tiny interfaces, but she hadn't wanted to dig lenses out of her purse, only to have to take them off again at the restaurant, so she'd found her way here by following street signs and tourist kiosks, because lenses were not the sort of thing you wore on dates. When either party could be recording the other at any given moment for later public or private viewing, leaving the smart lenses at home on a first date was the social equivalent of nuclear disarmament. There were entire websites dedicated to posting embarrassing or pornographic videos taken surreptitiously with smart lenses, and once something was up all the lawyers in the world wouldn't be able to make it go away.

She ran her hands down her hips, smoothing out her black skirt self-consciously. Annie had in some ways looked forward to life in the Unified Colonies Armed Forces Navy because she had, perhaps naively, thought that she wouldn't be judged based on her appearance. That wasn't any more true than it had been when she was a civilian, but at least most of the time she simply had to wear the appropriate uniform. Now that she was going out, off duty and without any other officers, she once again had found herself in a crisis of indecision right up until the moment she had needed to leave her quarters. She'd tried to remind herself that this wasn't a serious thing while she spent an hour putting on and rejecting outfits. *After all, he'll never be able to go to Mars. But he is cute. And he was brave enough to help those people.*

The hard part, of course, was the underwear: in this case, her skinsuit. Most of the time it wasn't visible under her various uniforms, but there wasn't any way to avoid showing off all its awesome sexiness in casual clothing. She snorted at her own sarcasm.

The skinsuit was an old solution - or at least a partial solution - to an even older problem. The human body was designed to exist at a certain amount of gravity - the gravity of Old Earth That Was. If you took a body out of that gravity for very long, muscles and bones, even the heart, began to change because they didn't need to work as hard. Mars, where she'd grown up, had just over a third of the gravitational force of

Earth, and that was the highest gravity that any humans had lived on since Earth had stopped being habitable. As a result, Annie had a bone density and muscle mass that was much more than would be required to deal with Europa's gravity, nevermind the zero-g conditions under which she and her wing had made their transit on the *Scipio*. If their bodies were allowed to atrophy the entire time they were gone, they would *never* be able to go back to Mars - or they'd be wheelchair bound invalids for the rest of their lives.

The gravity decks and exercise machines on the *Scipio* were one part of the solution, and the skin suits were another, designed to precisely target compression on the human body in such a way as to mimic close to 1g. Most of the UCAF forces working offworld for any length of time were issued three skinsuits. Each had to be custom calibrated and tailored to every individual soldier, but Annie had five, a mark of wealth that she didn't feel the need to publicize to her subordinates. They looked something like a white canvas tank top sewn onto a pair of black elastic leggings with stirrups at the bottom.

The skinsuits were not anyone's idea of modest - they tended to point out every little thing you didn't like about your body - and she had confirmed that they did indeed make every civilian outfit she'd brought with her look terrible when they were worn as underwear. Every skirt she had tried bunched up around the hips when she walked or sat down, and her tops all revealed varying degrees of unattractive, sweat-stained fabric. The white and black combination of the skinsuit avoided any eye-bleeding color clashes, but nothing she'd tried on could hide the fact that she was wearing a very expensive, very ugly skin tight garment under her clothing.

So, despite the repeated medical warnings before leaving Mars, she'd taken it off.

How much bone density loss and muscular degradation can I really suffer in a couple hours, anyway? Annie was used to the momentary feeling of euphoric, disorienting lightness at the removal of the skinsuit by now - after all, you couldn't shower in the damn things - but being without it for such a long time when she *wasn't* soaking wet made her feel as if she was naked. As she tugged on a skirt and looked it over in her mirror, she'd realized that it had been nearly two years since anyone had seen her bare legs.

Now, inside the restaurant, she had the impression that literally *everyone* was looking at her. It was a feeling she'd been relieved to leave behind on Mars, and she didn't want it back now. Combined with the sensation of being naked, she had the sudden urge to turn around and run back to her quarters, but she told herself it was silly and made do with avoiding any unnecessary eye contact.

Kaito *was* here already after all, waiting off to one side, and Annie thanked whatever higher powers there might be in the universe for that - she didn't have to stand here alone. He'd dressed up from the ratty sweater she'd seen him wearing over the video feed from *Nautilus*, and she recognized the black shark leather of his shoes, belt and jacket from her brief foray into the tourist shops. His unruly mass of black hair - seriously cute, she had to admit to herself - had been pulled back to reveal where the sides of his head were shaven close to the skull, but what made the biggest impression on her once again was just how tall and lanky he was. Kaito, like everyone else on this moon, had grown up at something like one third of the gravity she'd known on Mars, a little over a tenth of what the human body had been designed for. Like humans who had grown up on Luna or in the asteroid belt, he'd probably never be able to stand up if he went to Mars. Not that the UCAF would ever give him the clearance to make the trip, anyway. Security was tight to prevent terrorists from gaining access to the Martian surface.

"Hi," she said lamely, giving a little wave with her hand and trying not to be too self conscious. How long had it been since she'd been on an actual *date*? She did some mental math: eighty days on the *Scipio*, OTS, AIT... and she'd stopped dating in the year prior to graduating from university. Maybe two years, and the last date hadn't ended well.

Kaito grinned at her; the sudden rush of dread at that particular memory must not have shown on her face. "Hey," he said, shoving his hands into his pockets for a moment and then pulling them out again. "Should have a table in just a moment." He looked her up and down, and that feeling of being naked and exposed came right back. "You look beautiful."

Which was completely not true, but she guessed it was the sort of thing he had to say, and it was nice to hear it anyway. "Thanks," she said. "I like the jacket. Sharkskin?"

He nodded. "Buy local," he said with a short laugh.

"They have them in all the tourist shops," she admitted, "but they're so expensive. And-" she reached out to touch the jacket before she could stop herself "-none of that stuff is this soft."

"It's funny," he said. "They mark this stuff up and sell it to off-worlders as a novelty, but everyone who's born here wants leather from Mars, and it's impossible to get your hands on. Anyway, it takes years to get it this soft," he admitted. "And lots of time with sandpaper, and oil."

"*Konbanwa*," a waiter greeted them, appearing a few feet away with that magic way of arriving from nowhere that wait-staff had on any colony in the solar system. She remembered enough Japanese to translate that as 'good evening," and smiled at the waiter. "This way, please," he said, and then turned to lead them into the restaurant.

The rice-paper screens didn't surprise her: Europa, she knew from her mission briefings, grew a lot of rice in its hydroponic garden caverns, dug down into the rock of the ocean floor. It was an efficient crop in terms of space, and she imagined there was a cultural element to it as well, in a colony settled by ethnic Japanese from Old Earth. The wood, on the other hand, mystified her, and Annie stepped closer to Kaito to quietly ask about it.

"How is there so much wood here?" she almost

whispered, not wanting to offend anyone. "They don't use hydroponics to grow trees, do they? They can't."

"No," Kaito said, shaking his head. The conversation paused for a moment as they reached their table, up two steps and set behind a sliding screen of wooden lattices. It was much lower than she had expected, perhaps only a half a meter high, with no chairs but only cushions on the wooden floor. She must have looked uncertain, because as Kaito walked around her to go to the far side of the table he told her, "Don't worry, there's an opening under the table for your legs. You don't need to kneel if you don't want to."

As she sat down on the cushion, she saw that he was right: the entire alcove must have been built like a small stage, so that you could put your feet in the open box under the table without being obvious about it. Another concession to tourists, she assumed.

"*Domo Arigato*," she told the waiter as he poured her a cup of tea. Hopefully her pronunciation wasn't terrible. Once the waiter had left them a pair of menus and closed the lattice screen, she leaned over the table, took a sip of the tea, and asked, "So do they import the wood from Mars? I can't even imagine how much that would cost. Or is it all brought from Earth when the colony was first settled?"

"Neither," Kaito admitted. "It's all fake. High grade plastic, moulded, painted and finished. We have plenty of oil here, so just about everything is made from some kind of synthetic plastic, unless it's rock, clay, rice or sharkskin. We've gotten pretty good at faking just about everything you can imagine, though."

Annie couldn't help but smile, touching the lacquer of the table. "Fooled me," she admitted. "But even on Mars, we don't really have forests older than thirty, forty years, so I just couldn't see how it was done."

"I can't imagine that," Kaito admitted, holding his cup of tea up and inhaling the steam with obvious pleasure. "How do you deal with having all that open space? Nothing between you and the sky?"

Annie set her cup of tea down and began to scan her menu. "I should ask you how you deal with *never* seeing the sky," she responded, remembering her mad dash through the city, trying to get *out*. "To always know the ocean's above us."

Across the table, Kaito shrugged. "I don't really think about it. Honestly, I think if you asked most people, they'd tell you they don't feel trapped at all: the ocean protects us."

Annie frowned, confused. "Protects you? How? It would kill you if these caverns ever collapsed."

"After all the years since we left Old Earth," Kaito pointed out, "We still haven't figured out a better shield against radiation than water. And that ocean over our heads is one hell of a radiation shield. Anyway, have you ever had Japanese food before? Do they have it on Mars?"

"We've got just about everything," she admitted. "I've liked sushi since my mother introduced me to it as a little girl."

"Huh." Kaito shrugged. "I wonder if they use the same fish..." He raised a hand into the air and a made a couple of waving motions: the sort of thing you used to pull up a search bar with smart lense motion tracking software.

Annie leaned forward. "Are you wearing smart lenses?"

Kaito's eyes focused back on her from whatever he had been looking at. "Yeah, sorry. I won't look up any more random facts, I promise."

What the hell. Annie swallowed to wet a tongue gone suddenly dry. "Take them out."

"What? No." Kaito looked at her like she was crazy. "They're not just tech, I need them to see."

"I don't care. Take them out, or I'm leaving," she insisted, pushing away her cup and sitting back on the cushion to swing her legs out from under the table. Her heart thudded in her chest; she couldn't breathe.

"Why?" Kaito was getting angry now. "You aren't making any sense. I'm not going to sit here half blind for the rest of the night! What, you can't trust me because I'm

Europan, not Martian?"

"What do you mean, you can't see? How do you not get this?" she said, raising her voice without really meaning to. "What, are you clueless? I can't have some video of me popping up online tomorrow. Everyone knows you leave those things at home when you go out with someone."

Kaito looked surprised and angry at the same time now. "You think I'd do that? What kind of asshole do you think I am?"

"I don't know," she admitted, "I don't know you." She stood up, but before she could open the faux-wood screen Kaito was up next to her.

"Wait," he said. "Wait here while I go to the bathroom." And then he was out of the booth, walking away.

Annie shifted nervously from foot to foot for a moment, then picked up her cup of tea. *Maybe a sip will quiet my nerves.* There was a ball of ice in her stomach, and she wanted nothing more than to rush out the door. A few seconds of footage flashed through her mind: a younger version of herself, leaning across a table, the neckline of her dress hanging low enough to reveal the curves of her breasts...

The screen door slid open.

"Here," Kaito said, thrusting a small, hard plastic case at her. She noticed he was squinting. *He really can't see without them,* she realized. *No one has bad eyes on Mars - no one I've ever known. All that bad DNA gets weeded out before you're even born.*

"Go ahead, open it up and check," he told her as he scooted back onto his cushion and arranged his legs under the low table. She unclipped the latch of the case and opened it. Sure enough, she could see the smart lenses inside: two translucent disks of plastic, resting in cups full of saline fluid so that they wouldn't dry out. The lights from the ceiling shone off the plastic. After a long moment, Annie closed the case and sat back down. Keeping the case in one hand, she unzipped her purse.

"I'll give you these back at the end of the night," she

mumbled, looking away from him as she put the case inside her purse and zipped it shut.

"I wouldn't do that," Kaito told her softly. "I mean, I know there's sites out there where people post that stuff, but I wouldn't do that. I don't know anyone who would. What is it, like, more common on Mars or something? More of a problem?"

"I guess so," she finally answered, trying to relax the muscles in her neck and jaw. "It's just a rule that everyone knows: no one wears those things on dates, and if a guy does, he's a creeper and get the hell out." *Or maybe*, she thought to herself, *you only have to worry about it if people know who you are. If you're the sort of person whose name comes up in a quick search.*

"I'm sorry," he said, leaning over the table. "I didn't realize. The last thing I wanted to do tonight was upset you."

"No, I'm sorry too," she said. "I really didn't know you needed them to see." She was grateful when the waiter reappeared; it gave her an excuse to collect herself. When he asked what she would like to drink, she said simply: "Hot sake." With a quick glance at the drink menu, she specified: "The *Kokuryu Europa*." The waiter nodded, and vanished back out through the screen.

"Everyone *says* they would never do something like that," Annie pointed out after a moment, trying to use an even tone of voice. He had given her the lenses, after all. *And he had a good reason to wear them.* "But it happens all the time. At clubs or restaurants, guys take pictures of girls and post them online, and you never know until someone shows it to you. There's not much you can do about that, unless you catch them moving their hands," she sighed. "Video on dates is worse. Usually they just run to the bathroom, set the lenses to record, and come back out. You never even know you're being filmed."

Kaito stewed over things for a moment. "How do you know? I mean, you said everyone on Mars just leaves them home on dates, but how do you know for sure?"

She shrugged. "There's a couple of tricks. I usually had

a girlfriend send the guy a message in the middle of dinner and see if he gets distracted. But I don't know anyone here I could trust to do that."

"What about another soldier," he asked her.

Like Sera. Annie shook her head. "I just got here," she laughed, "as you know. I need to maintain a professional relationship with everyone in my chain of command. I can't ask one of my subordinates to help me out with a date. That kind of thing ruins discipline. And I don't really know any of the Officers who've been stationed here a while, not yet. I haven't even been on a date in years." All technically true, but Sera would have done it, had Annie asked her.

"Years? What, because of the travel time between Mars and Europa?"

"Even before that," she admitted. "Most of my time is spent with other members of the UCAF, but it's against regulations to form personal relationships with anyone above or below you in rank. I can really only date civilians, and I just... haven't really been in a place to meet anyone, until now."

The waiter returned with a white glazed clay bottle of heated sake and two matching cups. They placed their orders for sushi, and then he withdrew behind the screen again. "I still don't get why you were so upset, though," Kaito said, pouring them each a cup a bit more hesitantly than before. *I wonder just how bad his vision is*, she thought and almost giggled. "I mean, you just about screamed at me. One of your friends get burnt by some asshole once?"

"Not a friend," she admitted, throwing back the cup of sake in a single gulp and then pushing it back over to him for a refill. "Me."

Kaito's eyebrows shot up, and he forgot to squint. She could only imagine what kind of images were running through his head. She felt her cheeks get hot, to match the heat of the sake. "Nothing like that," she said sharply. "I was on a date with this guy, this asshole, and the neckline of my dress was loose. I must have leaned over the table at some point, and he got an eyeful, and then the next thing I knew the clip was online."

He poured them both a second cup. "What a sleazeball."

"My father hired a bunch of lawyers to try and get rid of it," she continued, the story tumbling out of her now. A sip this time, not a gulp. "And he sued the guy, but there were too many copies all over the net." She waved a hand, as if to indicate just how large the planetary web on Mars was. "So yeah, it's out there. I don't know if anyone ever bothered to send it to Europa, so maybe it isn't online here, but search my name on Mars and you can get a nice video of my boobs."

Kaito rested an elbow on the table. "Is that one of the reasons you left Mars? Took the assignment here?"

Annie nodded. "Yeah, that was part of it. I mean, part of it is that you go where they send you, but... I knew most of the active duty stations for pilots like me were off-world."

"Must have been pretty rough," he said after a moment, filling their cups again.

"What, when you're wondering if every guy you go out with - every person interviewing you for a job - has seen that video? Yeah, rough is one word for it," she admitted.

"I haven't seen it," he joked.

"Congratulations," she told him, and maybe it was the sake, or maybe it was getting the story out, but she giggled. "There's fourteen million people on Mars, and probably half of them have seen my breasts on the web, but for you I get to be a mystery!"

Kaito grinned. "I'm not sure how I feel about that," he joked. "Like I've been left out or something."

She shook her head. The sake was starting to warm her up, and she couldn't keep a smile off her face. "Tell me about you," she said. "About what's it's like to live on Europa. It's so different from where I grew up..."

Kaito frowned. "My life's pretty boring," he admitted. "My father died in the Colony War," he told her quietly. "So it was just my mom and I."

Annie's smile slipped from her face. "I'm sorry," she whispered.

He shrugged. "It wasn't like you were responsible. I mean, you don't look forty years old," he joked. "I was pretty young. I don't really remember him."

"I was just a kid too," she admitted. She wasn't responsible, sure, but she was a member of the UCAF, and if Kaito's father had died in the war that meant the UCAF had probably killed him. And it meant her father... "I'm surprised they gave you a security clearance with that in your background," she admitted. "That's the kind of thing that they flag when doing background checks."

"He wasn't a resistance fighter or anything like that," Kaito admitted. "Just a shipping pilot, like me. He was in the wrong place at the wrong time. Old Man Date," he said with a shrug, "felt responsible, being Dad's boss and all, so as soon as I was old enough to work he gave me a job. Turns out I'm a pretty good pilot, too. And that's basically it. I work, I play video games when I'm not working and sometimes when I am, I try to take care of my mother, and that's about all."

"Not anymore," she teased him. "You're famous now."

"Don't remind me," Kaito sighed, looking back up at the ceiling.

"You're a hero!" She poured off the last of the sake. "Pulling those people out. You saved their lives."

"I'm an idiot," he said with a laugh. "I got a bunch of glass shards stuck in my back from a collapsing building that I was dumb enough to run toward instead of away from." For a moment, he gave her a strange look, as if he wasn't sure whether or not to say something. He'd been there, and he'd been the transport pilot who brought their equipment down from the docks. He'd already admitted that he had recognized her Shell, and knew how she had tried to help.

But then the waiter came, and the food started piling up on the table, and she ordered another bottle of sake that it turned out they didn't have to pay for because the waiter had recognized Kaito from the news clips, and by the time they finished the second bottle they were both pretty drunk.

"Maybe I should walk you home," Kaito offered after she managed to pick up the bill because he couldn't see clearly enough to realize it was happening until it was too late. "You're kinda drunk."

Not drunk enough to think bringing a local guy back to my quarters is a good idea, she felt guilty for thinking. "This was fun," Annie said as she scrambled up from the table and nearly pushed herself backwards into the wall of the booth.

"Ooops," she said as they both laughed. "Not used to this gravity yet."

Outside, Kaito looked up and down the street, squinting.

"Here." She shoved the lense case into his ribs.

"You trust me, now," he asked her, leaning his head back and putting one lens after the other in with practiced ease.

"I..." *What are you doing here, Annie,* she asked herself. *This is such a bad idea. There are so many reasons you can't be with this guy.* "Yeah, I guess I do," she admitted.

He tossed his mop of hair back and looked at her for the first time in an hour without squinting. "Good."

On Old Earth that Was, they'd had animals that froze when caught in the light of vehicles. Deer. She'd read about them as a kid, and asked her father why they didn't have any on Mars. "They eat leaves, peanut," he'd told her. "We're still trying to grow our trees."

She was a deer. No comforting fabric covering every inch of her, her skirt showing her legs, and he could be recording *right now.*

"I don't want to go back to the base tonight," she said softly.

"What?"

"I don't want to go back to the base tonight," she repeated, louder, maybe too loud. "Take me back to your place."

And, clear eyed, only a little off balance, Kaito took her hand and led her down the street to the corner, where they turned in the opposite direction from the way back to the base, toward Yellow Zone.

For a moment, she thought, *Annie, you're going to regret this tomorrow morning*, but then she pushed it away.

She didn't expect that he would feel so delicate beneath her hands. Birdlike. She'd never really understood that comparison before, but it felt like she could squeeze her fingers and snap his bones.

Afterward, he traced his fingers around the edges of her Neural Shunt where it sat in her neck, while she drowsily pressed her cheek to his warm chest and breathed in their combined scent.

"Does it ever hurt," he whispered, and Annie mumbled a 'no.'

She knew she had to report for duty the next morning, and intended to leave, but before she could summon the energy to get dressed sleep took them both.

Annie stretched her feet through the sand, feeling the fine grains along the sensitive skin in between each toe. The sun baked her skin, but the breeze of the ocean kept her from noticing the heat. The air ruffled the fine, pale hairs along her lower arms in a rhythm that matched the rustling of palm fronds above her.

She shifted her butt on the stretched canvas of a cheap beach chair that she'd bought on her way up; the thin fabric of her bikini was as close as she could get to being naked without actually doing it. The fabric was a little itchy from the salt soaked into it, and still damp. Even with her eyes closed, the sun up above shone through the skin, showing her a vision of dark orange. Sometimes, when her mind was drifting on the edge of sleep here, she thought for a moment she could see things, images or motions, dancing in that orange darkness, but whenever she tried to focus on them they vanished.

She knew that sooner or later she was going to have to check the time, and that when she did that would mean she had to leave. Tomorrow she was shipping out for Europa, and it would be four and a half years before she came back to Mars, but right now she just wanted to feel the warmth on her skin a little longer.

She lifted her hips and rolled on the beach chair, intending to lie on her belly for a while, but there was something in the way, so she only got over onto her right side. It was a warm body, and she snuggled in, pressing her face against skin that smelled faintly of sweat, but not in a bad way. She felt his arm curl around her, hand drifting to her hip, and that was good too.

Wait. This doesn't make sense. Annie felt herself drifting up through the dark of sleep, out of the place where logic fell away and cause and effect weren't necessary. If she was on a beach chair, there shouldn't be anyone next to her. And she hadn't spent her last night on Mars with a man, she'd spent it at her father's house, in her old room.

She opened crusty eyes, and in the dimness could make out for sure that there was, in fact, someone lying next to her in bed. He was still asleep, but yeah, her face was buried in his chest, and his hand was on her hip, and no, she wasn't wearing anything, not even a bikini. It took a moment, but the memories of the night before started to come back: the rice wine, probably too much of it, and asking Kaito to take his smart lenses out, and then what had come after.

This was a mistake. Get out of here quietly, stealthily. Like a cat.

She shifted her hips, trying to let Kaito's hand fall off her on its own, but he must have felt something in his sleep because his muscles tightened just enough to hold her. With the minimum amount of motion possible, she reached down with her left hand and carefully removed it, then slid out of the bed.

She hissed, stifling a cry as she stepped on a shoe - one of her pair of heels from the night before. Nearly hopping on her left foot, she bent down and gathered it up. Her own smart lenses were out, which meant she couldn't see much of anything in the dark, so she got down on her hands and knees and began feeling around.

Pants, definitely not hers. Shark skin boots, also not hers. A bra, impossible to be sure by feel but if it wasn't hers she'd made a bigger mistake than the voice inside was already telling her, so she passed it to the same hand that had the one heel. There - her purse. The stamped leather felt like alligator skin, and she fumbled with the zipper for only a second before getting out the hard plastic lense case. A squirt of saline in each eye, and the lenses were in, the OS loading up and beginning to display all the little icons just on the edge of her vision that she felt so helpless and disconnected without.

One quick hand motion later and her low-light vision was activated. Once she had the world picked out in tones of green and black and blue-gray, she found the other heel, her dress, and the rest of her undergarments - except for one stocking which stubbornly remained hidden. She snuck out of the bedroom, closing the door behind her, and was grateful that Kaito lived alone. It was the work of only a moment to get into her clothes, though she was sure she looked like she'd just been doing exactly what she'd spent the night doing.

She hesitated for just a moment at the door. *Should I really leave without saying anything? Maybe I should leave a note? Or would that make me just more of a bitch for doing this?*

Then, she slipped out into Red Zone's early morning twilight, called up a map of the city, selected the address of her Blue Zone base housing, and followed the direction software as quickly as she could. It had been quite a while since she'd had to make a walk of shame - since college - and if she got in early enough maybe word wouldn't get back to her subordinates. The last thing she needed was Malik, or one of his people, seeing her - she'd get a reputation nothing would get rid of.

One question kept surfacing in her thoughts the entire way back: why had she dreamed of the beach on Mars? Of all nights, why had she dreamed of it last night?

Annie had just gotten out of the shower - she was really starting to get used to having a hot shower again - when there was a knock on the door to her quarters. "One minute," she called, then sat down on her bed to pull on a clean skinsuit. Then, still struggling with the zipper at the neck and with wet, unkempt hair, she got up and opened the door.

"Good morning, Lieutenant Commander," Serafine Moreau, uniform impeccable, greeted her with a cheery smile.

Annie, strangely, wasn't tired. She smiled back at her subordinate. "Come on in while I get dressed," she invited Sera, who closed the door behind her. If she'd had one friend on the trip over, Annie admitted to herself as she stepped to the mirror, picked up her hairbrush, and began to straighten out her tangles, it was been Sera. "So what's going on," she asked as the brush snagged on a particularly recalcitrant knot.

"Nothing *really* important," Sera admitted. "I stopped by last night to tell you that I finished tweaking the movement algorithms in the Shells to compensate for the lower gravity. You were right, the factory settings were lazy: someone just rounded to two decimal places. I tried it out and took a spin around the base, it doesn't feel as sluggish anymore."

"Good," Annie said, using an elastic tie to pull back her hair and then walking over to her closet, where she began to flip through uniforms. "Anything else?"

"Just checking up on you," Sera admitted casually, something Annie would never have taken from Rafe, Laura, or the others. Maybe Nolan, now. "You seem to be in a good mood this morning."

Annie paused with a hand on a hanger, turned her head, and looked at Sera suspiciously. "What do you mean?"

Sera, seated on the bed, shrugged. "You've had a smile on your face since I walked in the room. You've been humming a song when you aren't paying attention. And this bed is still made from yesterday." The junior officer leaned forward, smiling conspiratorially. "Come on, out with it."

Annie bit her lip for a moment, thinking. "You can't talk about this with anyone if I tell you."

"I won't!"

"I met a guy," she admitted, turning back to the closet and pulling out a clean set of black fatigues.

"Last night?" Sera swung her left leg back and forth idly. "Did you go out to a club or something?"

"No," Annie admitted, pulling the uniform on over her skinsuit. "Actually, I met him.. A couple of days ago. We just went to a restaurant last night."

"A date," Sera grinned. "Fancy."

Annie shrugged, then dug out her boots. "It was nice."

"It must have been nice if you didn't come back to base," the other woman joked.

One boot on, Annie straightened up just long enough to elbow Sera, then went back to pulling on her other boot. "I think it was a mistake. I mean, we're only here for a year and a half, and it's not like he could ever live on Mars."

Serafine raised her eyebrows. "Oh. He's... Europan? I just kind of assumed you'd met like, someone here on business, from Luna or Mars, or... somewhere. At least... at least he's a civilian though, right? So there's not technically anything wrong with it."

Annie sat up, then kept right on going, collapsing backward onto the bed. "No, this was really stupid, right? I mean, we're here as an occupying military force. It's a security risk..."

Serafine gently patted her leg. "Well, do you like him?"

"Yes," she admitted.

"That's enough for me," Sera stated, jumping up to her feet and reaching down to help Annie up. "If he was someone shady like a terrorist or something you wouldn't have fallen for him. You have good taste!"

After a moment, Annie took her hand and stood up. "Breakfast?"

"Breakfast," Sera confirmed, and led the way out of Annie's quarters.

In the Officer's mess, Annie and Sera headed straight for the omelette station, where UCAF cooks were cracking eggs over a griddle. "I'm so glad we're back someplace with real food," Sera admitted, grabbing a plate. "Instead of algae slop."

"What'll you have, Lieutenant Commander, Lieutenant," the cook asked.

"Crab and cream cheese," Annie said after looking over the menu board for a moment.

"Right away, sir," the cook told her with a grin. "Go grab yourself some fruit and a drink. How about you, Lieutenant?"

"Add tomatoes to mine," Sera said. "And onions. And peppers."

Annie made a face. "You won't even taste the crab."

"I like onions and peppers," Sera groused, and they picked over the fruit bowls. Back on Mars, Annie remembered, the selection would have been massive. Here, fruit was expensive, but the UCAF didn't want any of its soldiers getting scurvy, so they did the best they could muster: a couple of dozen oranges, melons, apples, pears and bananas, all grown in Toshimayr City's three hydroponics caverns. Annie grabbed an orange, fixed her morning coffee, and piled a heap of grits on her plate before heading back to collect her omelette. By the time she and Sera turned to look for a table to sit at, their trays were loaded with food. Clavinger, Malik, and a group of other Officers were sitting together, and Annie wondered if she was obligated to go to that table.

"There's Rafe," Sera pointed out. Lieutenant Traugott was sitting alone next to a window, stirring his food listlessly.

"We're sitting with him," Annie decided. "I didn't make it over to visit yesterday," she realized with a feeling of guilt. "I need to see how Laura is doing."

The lanky pilot didn't even look up when they sat down, Annie across from him and Sera at his left. "How is she, Rafe," Annie prodded as she unwrapped her utensils.

"Sir!" Rafe looked like he wasn't sure whether to stand up and salute or not.

"At ease," Annie told him, scooping up a spoonful of grits.

"She's... well, they say there's some brain activity," Traugott said miserably. "But she's still in a coma. I think she's dreaming... the Doctors are trying to decide whether to ship her back when the *Scipio* leaves."

"Which won't be on schedule," a man's deep voice came from behind Annie. She looked over her shoulder to see Captain Varga approaching with a tray of his own. "Due to the bombing. May I sit?"

"Of course, sir," Annie said, about to rise herself, but Varga waved her back down.

"Sit, Lieutenant Commander," he insisted, setting his tray down next to hers. "I'm sorry to hear what happened to your officer. It's a shame. But we'll take care of her on the way back, I can promise you that."

"Thank you, sir," Annie said. A message popped up in her peripheral vision. *Kaito*. She hesitated, hand raised, finger hovering over the icon.

"Is it him," Sera asked, leaning across the table and lowering her voice.

Annie glanced over at Varga, who held up two open hands in a gesture of innocence. "Don't let my presence stop you from answering your messages, Winters," he said with a smile. "A gentleman caller, I presume?"

"Something like that," she admitted and opened the message.

Kaito: I really enjoyed last night. Are you OK? Was worried when I saw you gone this morning.

"I shouldn't answer this," she said out loud.

"Why not," Sera asked.

"Because I'm not getting into a relationship when I'm only going to be here a year and a half," Annie protested.

"I did," Varga spoke up, surprising them all.

"What?" Annie was confused.

"I don't stay on base while I'm in system," Varga explained, "Because I stay with a local woman. In fact, I only came to breakfast here to look you up, and invite you to dinner sometime. So I don't see any problem with you beginning a relationship with a Europan."

"A local woman," Sera repeated. "But you're only here like... a couple of weeks every three years."

Varga nodded. "I met Noriko when I began making this run about ten years ago. We get together whenever I'm here. While I'm in port, it's about the closest I've ever gotten to having a wife."

"She's never...." Annie trailed off, not sure how to phrase what she was thinking delicately.

"Found someone else?" Varga shrugged. "We have clear expectations. She doesn't ask what I get up to on Mars, I don't ask what she gets up to when I'm not here. But she could help you learn your way around, Winters," he insisted. "In fact, bring your friend there." He motioned vaguely at her eyes. "We'll make it a double date."

Rafe stood up and lifted his tray, the plates on it still mostly full of food. "Excuse me," he said, and was gone before Annie could stop him.

Varga, it turned out, was a talker. She hadn't spent a lot of time with him while she was awake on the *Scipio*, and in any event he'd had a good deal to occupy himself there. Now that he was in port, however, he seemed to have loosened up, and she'd long since finished her meal, and two cups of coffee, before she could finally get away and respond to Kaito in something resembling privacy.

Annie: I'm sorry I left before you were up. I had to get back to base. I meant to leave last night, but I fell asleep. I guess it's kind of a jerk thing to do.

Kaito: Just glad you found your way back ok.

Annie: I did. Look, I'm on duty at 09:00, but I'm not doing anything tonight.

Kaito: Send me a message when you're free.

Annie hesitated for just a moment. Did she really want to do this? She closed her eyes, remembering Kaito's delicate hand in hers, the taste of his sweat on her tongue, the comforting warmth of his body next to hers last night. *I don't stay on base when I'm in system*, Vargas had said.

Annie: I will.

Annie

Baishunpu

June 19th, 2128

Nolan caught Annie as they were all heading out of the hangar bay. They'd spent the morning ready to give cover to the Military Police, who were raiding Red Zone and arresting known insurgent sympathizers. Clavinger had wanted two Shells on hand in case serious fighting broke out, but the raids had gone smoothly.

"Can I have a moment, sir," Nolan said quietly.

"Of course." Annie tried not to frown. She was due to meet Kaito in an hour and a half, and she still had to get changed and pick something up on the way.

"I've been buying a lot of beer at the officers club," the older soldier began.

"Walk with me while we talk," Annie ordered him, and set off toward her quarters. "I assume you're not turning into alcoholic yet."

"Been that for years," Nolan said with a grin. "But no, I've been buying drinks for other people."

"Alright," she said, still not seeing where this was going.

"Look, it's one thing to get a briefing on the way in," Nolan continued, keeping his voice down. "It's a whole other thing to actually be on the ground."

Annie nodded. "Yeah, I'd say the official reports on Europa are a couple steps to the left of what's actually going on," she agreed.

"So I've made a couple friends who have been here longer than we have. Friends who could be useful."

"What kind of useful," Annie asked.

Nolan dropped his voice. "A guy in intelligence. He says-"

"Am I breaking the law by hearing this," Annie hissed at

him, stopping and spinning on her heel to get up in his face.

"Would you rather know what we're up against, or not," Nolan asked her.

Annie was silent.

"*Shumokuzame.*" Nolan pronounced the word carefully. "That's the terrorist group responsible for the bridge bombing. For putting Laura in the hospital," Nolan explained. "It means some kind of shark."

"I saw that on the news," Annie said.

"Yeah, but here's what you haven't seen on EMC," Nolan continued. "This is not just some small time thing. These people are organized into cells, well trained, and well equipped. We're not talking about a few terrorists here. We're talking about guerillas with a lot of support from the native population."

Nolan swiped at the air in front of his face. "I'm sending you a video file," he told her. "A security drone caught a few frames of the bomber."

Annie saw the incoming file displayed on her smart lenses, grabbed it with two fingers, and pinched it open. Nolan had been right when he described it as 'a few frames:' all the file showed was a person in a sharkskin jacket, leaning out over the bridge. Their face was a pixelated blur. "What's wrong with this," she asked.

"Hackers," Nolan explained. "That's my guess. But look at the jacket."

Annie used her fingers to zoom in. "Ornamental stitching. That's not much of a clue."

"But it's something."

"Thank you, Lieutenant." She closed the video with her left hand, then started back across the base toward her quarters. "And Lieutenant," she called back. "Let me know if you find anything else. I'll buy the beer."

"This is going to be awkward," Kaito reminded Annie

for about the tenth time since they'd set off on their way to the spa.

She rolled her eyes. "I know, and I'm sorry. Look, I tried to talk Captain Varga into dinner or something instead, but it's hard to get a word in with him. He just kind of... keeps talking. And rolls over you."

"Dinner would have been awkward too," Kaito observed. "I mean, I don't know either of these people, and you only kind of know one of them."

"Hasn't one of your exes ever dragged you to a work party before," Annie pleaded. "This is just like that. We stay for an hour or so, and then we leave as soon as we can without being insulting. You help me make a good impression on a superior officer..."

"And his pet Geisha," Kaito finished for her, and the implication stung.

"She's not a prostitute." *How did I end up defending a woman I've never even met,* she wondered. "They have... like a long term relationship. I think."

"In which he gives her money to live, and while he's in port, she sleeps with him." Kaito's voice was getting louder, and fellow passersby in Green Zone were starting to give them sidelong glances. "We have words for women like that. I'm being nice when I say Geisha. That implies she has class. Most people would just call her a *Baishunpu*."

"Do I even want to know what that means?" Annie shook her head. "Look." She stepped around in front of him, bringing Kaito to a halt, and wrapped her arms around his neck. "When's the last time you had an actual, professional massage?"

"I don't know," Kaito groused.

"They feel good. You like hot tubs?"

"Yes," he admitted grudgingly.

"You want to see me in a bikini?" Annie gave him a grin.

"Yes," Kaito relented, cracking a smile now.

"It won't be so bad. Please, just do this for me." A

long moment passed, and then Kaito's arms closed around her, squeezing their bodies together.

"Alright," he agreed. "I won't say anything mean to her. I'll keep my thoughts to myself."

"Thank you. Now," she said, releasing him and slipping out of his grasp, "How much further?"

Kaito made a motion with his fingers in front of his face. "Halfway up the block on the right. *Azuma Tengoku*, it's called."

They found the spa easily enough, and once Kaito had held the door open for her, and the wooden chimes had clanked and rattled notice of their arrival, the young woman at the desk smiled sweetly at them.

"*Konbanwa*," she greeted them. "Welcome to *Azuma Tengoku* spa. Do you have a reservation?"

"Um, yes," Annie said, setting her bag down on the floor in front of the desk. "We're with Captain Varga's party..."

"Oh yes, the Captain!" The receptionist typed on the air in front of her. "He's one of our regulars, and he mentioned he would be bringing guests today. Follow me into the sitting room." She stepped out from behind a desk, pulling two cloth bags down off a series of racks and handing one to each of them. Annie slung hers over one shoulder, along with her own bag, and followed.

The entire Spa had been decorated in the antique Japanese fashion of Old Earth That Was, she saw, just like so many of the Europan establishments that catered to off-worlders, whether tourists or off duty officers. The floors were polished wood; the rooms were separated by *Shoji* screens of rice paper and wood. She wondered how much of it was fake, made of plastics from local oils, and briefly considered asking Kaito, but decided it would be rude.

"Hello, Lieutenant Commander!"

The sitting room turned out to be a couple of comfortable couches in front of a small fireplace, with a rack to store shoes in, a water cooler and paper cups, and a throw rug.

On a coffee table between the couch and the fireplace was a tray containing a pot of tea and two cups. Captain Varga was sitting on the couch, his feet already in spa-provided slippers, one arm around a striking Europan lady's shoulders, the other resting in his lap, fingers curled around a cup of tea. Clumsy in gravity, he set the tea down and stood up. Annie snapped to attention and saluted.

"At ease, Winters," Varga said, reaching out to shake her hand. "No one's in uniform here. This is Noriko Shiroishi; Noriko, this is Ann Winters."

"You can call me Annie," she told Shiroishi as they shook hands. Varga's mistress might have been in her late thirties or early forties; Annie had a hard time telling. In either case, she was in remarkable shape, with the only real marks of age the tiny wrinkles around her eyes that makeup couldn't completely hide.

"*O ai dekite kōeidesu,*" Noriko greeted her with a happy smile.

"And you," Annie replied, hoping she'd translated the greeting correctly in her head. "Captain Varga, Noriko-san, this is Katakura Kaito, a pilot for Date Heavy Industries."

"*Konnichiwa,*" Varga greeted Kaito, reaching over to shake his hand.

"Hi," Kaito said, with a smile that Annie could tell was forced.

"This place is amazing," Varga began, talking at everyone and no one at the same time with the easy assurance of a lifetime of privilege that someone, after all, would be listening. "Noriko took me here on our second date ever - you remember that, honey?" Noriko Shiroishi nodded. "What was that, now - almost fifteen years ago?" Varga shook his head.

"Let's not say how long ago it was," Varga's mistress simpered with a light laugh. Thankfully, right about then, a spa attendant approached.

"Good afternoon," she said, nodding politely to the group. "I know that Captain Varga and Miss Shiroishi have been here before, but I'll give the speech to our newcomers." She smiled to Annie and Kaito. "You have a private hot tub booked for the next hour," she explained, "and then two separate couples massages after that. There are robes and slippers in your bags. Bathing suits are optional inside the hot tub rooms," she continued, as Annie's eyes widened, "And we do ask that you shower in the changing rooms before using the tubs. The ladies changing room is there," she finished, pointing to her left, "And the men's changing room is there." To either side, Annie could see the clearly marked rooms. *What have I gotten myself into*, she wondered. *Bathing suits optional?*

"This way," Noriko told Annie, taking her arm and drawing her toward the door of the changing room. "I'll show you where everything is. Have you ever been to a Spa before?"

"On Mars." Annie risked one glance back at Kaito, who was being herded into the men's changing room by Varga, and then she was through the door. "Did I hear right," she asked. "Bathing suits are optional?"

Noriko nodded, setting her bag down on a bench and fiddling with the shower controls. "Yes. But don't worry, we aren't going to embarrass you at our first meeting!" She laughed, stepping back from the spray. "We'll all wear something to the tubs." With a couple of quick shrugs, the older woman's dress was pooling at her feet, and Annie turned away to fiddle with her own shower. She'd worn her skinsuit under a pair of vintage denim jeans and a cotton t-shirt, with the sharkskin jacket Kaito had found for her over it all. Now, it took her a few moments longer than Noriko to strip, including some rather undignified tugging on her skinsuit before she was finally naked. She reached into her purse, removed a soft plastic plug, and inserted it into her Neural Shunt to keep the water out; finally, she was able to step into the hot spray.

"That skinsuit looks like a new model," Noriko Shiroishi commented, and Annie just about jumped two feet in the air.

"It is," she admitted, not turning away from the wall. She'd gotten used to group showers with other women in boot camp, but that had been a while ago. And she didn't know this woman at all.

"I swear," Noriko continued, "Jeff has had the same three skinsuits just about the entire time I've known him. You should smell them when he dumps them all in the laundry basket at home." She laughed. "Or maybe you shouldn't."

Jeff. Annie blinked for a moment before realizing she meant Captain Varga. "I... can imagine," she said, trying to play it safe. "Do we need to soap up, or..."

"No, just a rinse." The older woman turned off her shower, and by the time Annie had done the same Noriko had pulled on a black, one piece swimsuit that hugged her figure. Annie, dripping and, as always, all too aware of being naked without the familiar presence of the skinsuit, walked over to her bag and pulled out the bikini she'd bought for the occasion. She'd picked it out to look good for Kaito, but now she was having second thoughts. The fabric was bright pink, and the borders and straps black; it wasn't exactly subdued. There was nothing for it but to get it on, pull the robe around her, and step into her slippers.

Noriko led her out through a different door than they'd used to enter, and down a short hallway. There, she paused, and knocked on a door. "Anyone home," she called, and Annie recognized Captain Varga's voice lifted from within.

"We've been waiting for you!"

The older woman held the door open for Annie, and she stepped into a room floored and paneled in wood; the ceiling was tall, with light spilling down through a window from above. Built in steps led up around a giant wooden tub which was tall enough to stand in, and broad enough for half a dozen people to sit comfortably. Inside the tub, Varga and Kaito's heads and torsos remained just above the water.

"Hey," Kaito called out to her, and Annie stashed her bags on the bench by the stairs. "Come on in. The water's nice."

Annie stepped out of her slippers, hung her robe up, and, conscious of the eyes on her skin, scampered up the stairs and slid into the tub next to Kaito. "Oh!" The hot water hit her with a shock. One of the men must have turned on the jets, because bubbles rose all around them and tickled her. She found the bench next to Kaito and snuggled in next to him. A moment later, Noriko Shiroishi slipped into the tub after her. In spite of herself, and the awkwardness of the situation, Annie could feel the heat beginning to relax her muscles.

"So," Varga spoke up, leaning his head back against the rim of the wooden tub, "How did the two of you meet?"

"We actually met twice," Annie explained, assuming that she would need to do most of the talking. "Kaito was the pilot of the Subtee that brought our shells down to Toshimayr. So we talked then," she said, glancing over at Kaito, "But I never turned on the video feed from my cabin, so then when we met in a bar, he didn't recognize me at first."

"Your voice was familiar, though," Kaito teased her. "Maybe if you'd started by just screaming in my ear again, I would have known right away."

Annie playfully slapped his arm. "I did not scream."

"You totally screamed."

"What is this about screaming," Noriko asked with a smile.

"On the way down, all the Shells were riding on the outside of my hull," Kaito explained, leaning forward conspiratorially. "And a light squid attached itself to her Shell, right over one of her cameras. When Annie saw that, she shrieked, I am not kidding you-"

Annie felt behind her neck to be sure her Neural Shunt was still plugged, then slid down in her seat until her head disappeared under the water. She held her breath for a moment, and then surfaced, blinking. "Are you done talking about me," she asked, blinking water out of her eyes and smoothing her wet hair back with one hand.

"Of course," Noriko said.

"It does make a good story, though," Captain Varga insisted. "More interesting than how we met," he admitted, with a glance to Noriko.

"How did you meet," Annie asked, seizing upon the opportunity to turn the conversation away from her and the squid.

"At a gala at the officer's club," Noriko explained. "Someone was getting a promotion or a medal or something- I don't recall-"

"Chuck Lovell," Varga broke in. "He's retired now, back to Mars. And Noriko's father was deputy mayor at the time, so he'd brought her..."

"And this big, ugly man had trapped me against a wall, you know, leaning on his arm so I couldn't get away?" Annie nodded in response to the older woman's unspoken question. She'd had that happen at a party or two, over the years. "So I tasked him to get me a drink, and as soon as he turned around, I just ran right for Jeff."

"So I see this beautiful, scared girl coming my way," Varga continued the story, "And I just did what any guy would do."

"What was that," Kaito asked.

"When the sunnavabitch came back, I told him if he ever talked to Noriko again I'd break every bone in his body."

"So he left you alone," Annie asked.

Varga shrugged. "Well, it helped that I outranked him."

"I'd say that's a decent story," Kaito protested.

"What made you choose-" Annie stopped herself from saying 'Captain Varga.' "What made you choose Jeff? To escape to?"

Noriko studied Varga with an even glance. "He just looked... safe," she said after a moment. "I'm glad I did."

"And we've been together ever since," Varga concluded. "Well, you know. I'm off planet a lot of the time, but whenever I'm here."

"It must get lonely," Annie said softly. *What happens when my deployment is done? Do I just go home to Mars and leave Kaito here?*

"It does," Noriko admitted. "But that's not as bad."

"Not as bad as what?" Kaito rolled his head around, popping the muscles in his neck.

"Noriko's had some trouble here and there over the years," Varga said bitterly. "Being with a UCAF officer. Some people have given her a hard time for it."

Noriko nodded. "One of my landladies kicked me out of my apartment. Do you remember that?"

Varga laughed. "How could I forget? She was throwing our things out into the hallway."

"But most of the time now," Noriko continued, "It isn't a problem. I'm a navigator on one of the cargo runs to Io, so I spend a lot of time in transit, or on Io. And we make enough now that we've bought a place together, and don't have to worry about neighbors or a landlord."

A knock came on the door.

"What's that," Annie asked.

Varga stood and climbed out of the tub. "That's our appointment, Noriko and I, for a massage."

"I thought we had the tub for an hour," Kaito asked with a frown.

"You do," Noriko answered, getting out with a hand from Varga. "We didn't want to impose on the two of you for very long. We thought you might enjoy some privacy."

"They'll knock again when it's your turn," Varga told them, towelling himself off and slipping a robe over his swimming trunks.

"Thank you," Annie said to the older couple, surprised.

"We wanted to do something nice for you," Noriko said, wrapping her hair in a towel. "People like us... people in relationships like ours, we need to be there for each other. Listen, if there's a time when you need to talk to someone," she added, "either of you, please call me. Even if Jeff isn't on planet anymore, or I'm somewhere between here and Io, we'll find a time to get together."

"Anyway," Varga said gruffly, "I've been looking forward

to this massage since we got in system. Let's not keep them waiting."

After the door had closed, Annie turned to Kaito. "That was nice," she said.

Kaito was silent, his eyes unfocused.

"Hey," Annie said, throwing a leg over his body and scooting onto his lap so that they were facing each other. "Are you there?"

Kaito shooks himself. "Sorry," he said. "It just occurred to me that some people are going to think... they're going to talk about me the same way they talk about her."

"Well," Annie pointed out, "I haven't bought you an apartment yet." She leaned in to kiss along his neck.

Kaito laughed, and the movement of his hands stirred the water; they came to rest on the skin of her hips. "How many people," he murmured to her, "Do you think have had sex in this hot tub?"

"Oh, ew!" Annie looked around at the enclosed, private room. "I don't even want to think about that. A lot, you think? Gross."

"Don't worry, I'm sure the water's chlorinated," he teased her.

"I'm not sure I want to sit in here any longer," she admitted.

But in the end, they did stay in the tub - or sitting on the edge to catch their breath, when they overheated - right up until there was a knock on the door of the room. *Just in case we're having sex,* Annie realized when the knock came. *That's why they don't poke their head in. Clothing optional.* The massage that followed, with her and Kaito on side by side tables and soothing music playing in the background, found and loosened knots she hadn't realized she'd been carrying around. There was even tea and dark chocolate at the end, and once their street clothes were on, and they'd checked at the front desk to find that Varga had paid for everything up front, she made a silent promise to do something nice for him before he left the system to head back to Mars.

Rafe looked like he hadn't moved from the hospital chair all night.

Annie knew that he hadn't been in the mess hall for dinner the previous evening, because she'd looked, after getting back from the spa. He'd been spending every moment that he wasn't on duty here, in Laura's hospital room. Annie, on the other hand, hadn't been in days. *Five? Six?* She realized, momentarily washed in guilt, that she didn't remember. When she was with Kaito, she didn't have to think about the fact that she'd lost one of her soldiers during their very first mission. *Not even a mission*, she corrected herself. *We were just moving the Shells from the carrier to the base in Blue Zone. She should have been safe.*

She knew, intellectually, there was really no safe place in war. The Colony War had ended two decades earlier, but Toshimayr City - all of Europa - was still an occupied colony. Annie hadn't expected anything to happen so early in their deployment, and Laura had paid the price for her mistake.

Or rather, Laura was about to finish paying the price. Rafe didn't look up, and Annie didn't say anything. She checked the time, and saw that she was two minutes early. The doctor, she imagined, would probably be late. Bracing herself, Annie stepped over to the hospital bed where Laura lay. There were IV tubes coming out of her left arm, trailing up to a tree-like rack that grew clear plastic sacks of liquid medicine instead of fruits. A breathing tube entered her mouth. Her eyes were closed, her skin pale and leached of color under the fluorescent lights. The spiky black hair was flat and listless, grown out to merely look shaggy and unkempt now, greasy. Annie wondered if the nurses had washed Laura's hair, and thought probably not. *I should have brought some shampoo,* Annie realized. *I could have done that for her. I could have washed her hair.*

The door to the hospital room swung open, and a middle aged man with salt and pepper hair entered, carrying a small tablet. "Lieutenant Commander Winters," he asked, and Annie nodded.

"Yes," she said, making the word come out of her throat on the second try. "Doctor Lagasse?" She accepted his hand, shook it once, and then let him go.

"Yes." The doctor glanced over at Rafe, as if unsure whether to proceed with a third person in the room.

"So," Annie asked, "How is she?"

"There hasn't been any change," Doctor Lagasse explained, in a calm, measured voice. *Then why did you call me down here*, Annie wondered, but the understanding was already blooming cold in her chest. "There hasn't been any sign of recovery of brain function," the Doctor explained. "At this point, we need your approval, as her commanding officer."

"Approval for what," Rafe demanded, his face upturned, now, his voice hoarse and unused. Annie didn't have to ask. On deployments like this, the time and cost to contact a soldier's next of kin was prohibitive.

"Only about ten percent of patients who enter a coma ever recover." The doctor wet his lips with his tongue. "If there hasn't been any sign of brain function after three days," he apologized haltingly, "There isn't likely to be. I know Captain Varga has offered to take her, but the *Scipio* doesn't have the kind of medical personnel trained to transport someone in her condition over a long voyage, and she's unlikely to survive being placed into hibernation..."

"They need me to sign off on pulling the plug, Rafe," Annie said, unable to meet his eyes.

The words dropped into the room like a grenade.

"No." Rafe said. "You're not going to let them, are you?" He sounded like a kid begging his parents. Annie remembered pleading with her father that way, when she'd been a girl and they'd had to have a kitten put down - and then she immediately felt guilty for comparing a human being to a cat.

Instead of responding, she turned to the doctor. "If we take her back to Mars, is there anything they can do that you can't?"

Doctor Lagasse shook his head. "Nothing that I know of. Of course, we're a year and a half behind the breaking medical technology back on Mars or Luna, but I haven't heard of any new experimental medicine or breakthrough in the journals. I can't given you any reasonable assurance that a doctor on Mars would tell you any differently. This is the best military hospital in Jupiter orbit; she isn't going to get any better treatment somewhere else than she is here."

Annie nodded. It had been exactly what she had expected to hear, but that didn't make this any easier. She reached her hand out for the pad, and the doctor passed it over. With a single finger, she signed the form which he had loaded on the screen. Rafe gave a strangled cry, and slumped forward, his head in his hands.

"There's no rush," the doctor said quietly. "I can give you time to say goodby, and come back in a little while."

"Yes," Annie choked out, coughed, and then began again. "Yes, that would be good. Thank you." She turned to look at Laura, and heard the door click shut again as the doctor left. Two steps brought her up alongside the bed, and she looked down at the other woman's face. "I'm sorry, Laura," Annie murmured. "You deserved better than this."

A metal chair leg scraped on linoleum, and Rafe stood on the other side of the hospital bed. Annie watched as he bent over his lover, ran his hands through her hair, stroked her face with his fingers, and whispered in her ear. She swallowed her tears and clenched her jaw until her shoulders and neck were as hard as rocks. *I will not cry in front of a subordinate*, she repeated to herself.

"Do you think she can hear me," Rafe asked her, looking up. His eyes were red and swollen, his cheeks wet.

"I know she can, Rafe," Annie told him, doing her best to soften her voice without letting it break. "It's better this way. She'd want you with her. She wouldn't want to just... linger, hooked up to these machines for years and years."

Rafe nodded, and Annie stepped back to the door, knocking on it once. A moment later, Doctor Lagasse stepped back in. He'd clearly been waiting just outside, and he carried a hypodermic needle in his hand.

"We're ready," Annie told the doctor, and a noise halfway between sob and moan came from Rafe.

"This is an overdose of a sedative," Doctor Lagasse told Rafe as he approached the bed. "She won't feel anything." Annie stepped back, out of the way, and the doctor inserted the needle into one of the IV bags. She watched as his thumb slowly depressed the plunger.

Rafe pressed his face to Laura's, sobbing incoherently. The doctor began turning off the machines that helped Laura's lungs to work, kept her hydrated and full of nutrients. Annie turned away, and watched the electronic screen where the heartbeat was monitored. The spikes slowed in frequency, and then stopped. Eventually, the doctor lifted a stethoscope from around his neck, leaned over the bed, and pressed it to Laura's chest. He turned to Annie and nodded. "I'm sorry for your loss," he said in a subdued voice, and then left the room.

Annie stepped around the bed until she was behind Rafe, and placed a hand on the back of his head. She stayed there with him for a long time.

Kaito

Europa Media Corporation

June 21st, 2128

"When I was ten years old," Kaito told Annie, two days after their trip to the spa, "*Date-san* arranged for me to go to one of the schools in Green Zone. I don't know how he did it; the same way he always gets government contracts to move things for the UCAF, I guess. My mother was so excited - she must have been harping on him for ages about how bad the schools in Red Zone were."

They were in his apartment again, lying on his bed. Annie had met him at the docks after his overnight run to Fukami Toshi. Boxes of takeout rice and sushi were scattered across his bedroom floor. Annie leaned into him, resting her head on his shoulder, and that made it easier to talk - not because she was touching him, though that was nice, but because he didn't have to look at her eyes while he told the story.

"Anyway," he continued after a moment, "She bought me clothes we couldn't afford. Wanted me to look just like all the other kids, to fit in and make friends." He couldn't keep the bitterness out of his voice, and took a deep breath to try and calm down.

"Did you," Annie asked quietly.

Kaito gave a sharp, barking laugh. "It didn't matter how I was dressed. I'm Europan. The only colony founded by ethnic Japanese. I'm not white. As soon as I walked up to the building, we all knew I wasn't supposed to be there. The kids knew it, the teachers knew it, and I knew it. I wanted to turn around and go home, but they wouldn't let me."

She felt for his hand, took it, and held it in hers. "So what happened?"

"They caught me in the bathroom," Kaito said, and he

could still feel the fear, the cold feeling in his stomach from when he was ten years old. "Three of the boys. They... well, they beat me up." That was the easy part to talk about. "Talked a lot about how... you don't want to hear this."

"I do," Annie told him firmly, sitting up so that he had to look at the ceiling to avoid meeting her eyes. "I do," she repeated. "But if you don't want to say it, that's ok."

He concentrated on the feeling of her hand in his. "They asked me if my mother was a prostitute," he remembered. "Talked about how all the soldiers liked Europan whores." *Bet she's fucked the whole barracks,* the largest boy had laughed as he kicked Kaito in the stomach. He'd tried to curl up into a ball, so they couldn't hurt him too badly. *My dad says their slits are sideways,* one of the other boys had giggled.

"Then they said how," he hesitated. "How everyone knew Europan guys had small dicks. How we were practically girls too. They... they worked me over pretty good. Kicking me. That kind of thing." *They kicked me in the balls until I couldn't breathe and then they pissed all over me and my new clothes,* he didn't tell her. "Told me I should've known better than to think I could go to school with them."

He shook his head, and realized with surprise that he was squeezing her hand. "I'm sorry," he said, finally able to look down at her face. "Did I hurt you?"

"No," Annie said, leaning back into his shoulder. "You didn't hurt me. It's OK." Her pocket tablet buzzed from its spot on the floor, and she rolled over and leaned off the bed to pick it up. "Shit," she said. "I have to go."

"What's wrong," Kaito asked.

"Insurgent attack on the MP barracks in Atarashī kibō no machi," she replied. "Probably retaliation for those arrests after the bombing. I have to go."

That afternoon, long after Annie had left, he finally got around to dropping by his mother's place. He'd been avoiding it since the hospital. He took a circuitous route through the neighborhood, designed to let him pick up a good batch of components in *Elyon*, and squeezed in fights against three separate monsters. He'd been playing less, now that he was seeing Annie, and was falling behind his guildmates.

Kaito perched uncomfortable on the edge of his mother's couch, a cup of hot green tea in his hand, as she bustled around cleaning things up and fussing over her apartment. In the background, the Europa Media Corporation nightly news was starting on the 127 centimeter flat screen that he'd gotten her for her birthday and mounted on the wall. The first story was on the upcoming Landing Day celebrations.

"I feel fine," he insisted. "My back's healing up real good." Annie had helped him put ointment and fresh bandages on the cuts this morning.

"You're taking it easy at work, right," Katakura Hekima pestered him, when she finally took a seat at the opposite end of the couch. She reached over to the end table for her own cup of tea and took a sip. "Not lifting anything heavy? *Date-sama* promised me that he would make you take it easy."

Kaito rolled his eyes. "I don't lift anything, anyway. I pilot a Subtee, I don't load it. I sit in a chair and fiddle with switches and dials and read instruments and listen to music."

"I just want you to take care of yourself," his mother insisted. "We were so worried about you when we heard you were in the hospital."

We meaning you and Mizuki, Kaito knew, taking a sip of tea to avoid saying it out loud. *You always liked her. You practically had the wedding planned.*

"Have you been to see Mizuki yet," his mother continued, right on schedule. "It was so nice of her to come with me over to the hospital. She really does care about you."

"I stopped by the bar," Kaito admitted.

"Oh, good. Maybe we should have her over to dinner later this week."

"I don't think that's a good idea, Mom," Kaito demurred. "We broke up, remember?" On the screen, EMC news had come back from commercial. He recognized one of her favorite anchors: a middle aged woman, half Europan-Japanese and half Caucasian. *Prime Minister Executive Order Mandates Reproduction*, the scrolling text along the bottom of the screen read. "Hold on, what's this?"

He tapped at the air, calling up the screen's controls and turning up the volume.

"As we continue to work through the latest news from the inner colonies," the anchor spoke in her polished, educated voice, "broadcast from Mars today, we're now getting to Prime Minister Galtung's executive order on reproductive duty. Let's watch the clip." She painted her face with a placid smile, and the image lingered for a moment before loading the video from Mars.

"Though the Tax incentives for families have resulted in modest population growth," the Prime Minister, a stern, gray-haired man of middle age spoke loudly and clearly to the cameras, "That growth has not been sufficient. We are no longer living at the height of Old Earth's decadence, when the global population passed eleven billion humans. With the loss of our motherworld, we lost ninety percent of our entire species. We need workers for our factories and shipyards, scientists to continue terraforming our colony moons and planets, miners to harvest the valuable metals from our asteroid belt, agricultural workers to grow our food, and teachers to educate our students."

From the audience that the clip scanned over for a moment, Kaito could see and hear applause for the Prime Minister's words. *Fascist son of a bitch,* he thought, but didn't say out loud. The video cut back to the Galtung's face, and his speech continued.

"Therefore, reproduction prior to the age of thirty will now be a mandatory duty for all citizens of the United Colonies who are physically capable of contributing to the population." The applause quieted as the audience listened to the Prime Minister's words. "There will be forbearance for those on active military service, and those pursuing higher education," he qualified his statement. "And we will provide a year's grace time for those currently in violation of this order to bring themselves into compliance. But citizens who neglect their duty to the human race will be subject to fines and possible imprisonment. Additionally, chemical birth control prescriptions will now be subject to a board of review, and the legislature has introduced a bill to criminalize abortion procedures, which I have pledged to sign. We cannot, as a species, afford to throw away a single new life. God bless you all, and thank you."

The clip ended, and the anchor - Kira something or other, Kaito remembered - began to discuss the ramifications of the order. "The new executive order does not apply to citizens over the age of forty," she explained brightly, "But it also brings with it an end to so-called gender reassignment therapy and surgery, which, as the Prime Minister stated, "Removes fertile citizens from the population just when we need them most.' In other news, the first NAAS Lifespa located in the Jupiter sphere is ready to open its doors in Toshimayr City, despite massive protests which continued today..."

In disgust, Kaito swiped away the newsfeed. "What is this, the dark ages," he complained out loud. "It's barbaric. People aren't going to stand for this."

After a long silence, his mother spoke up. "Everyone's been talking about this. I don't know how you missed it, except that you're always playing those games of yours. Don't you think it would be good to get together with Mizuki, dear," she continued, and he could see where this was going. "I know you've had some disagreements, but so does every couple. And you can see," she waved at the dark screen, "You're going to need to pick someone. I always thought you two made such a nice couple."

"No," Kaito said, thrusting his tea cup onto the side table and standing up. All of a sudden, the room felt claustrophobic, like it was closing in around him. "We didn't. And anyway, I think Mizuki cares a lot less about following the law than you think."

"What do you mean by that," his Hekima began, but Kaito interrupted her.

"Anyway," he began, pacing about the room, "What makes you think I don't have someone else, already?" *I shouldn't have said that,* he realized as soon as he saw his mother's face light up.

"Oh, is there someone new, dear? What's her name? Oh, bring her over to dinner the day after tomorrow," his mother insisted.

Kuso. Kaito managed to keep from cursing out loud. "I don't know if that's a good idea."

"Why not?" His mother was positively beaming. "I want to meet her!"

"We haven't really been seeing each other that long," he demurred. "I don't know if she'll be comfortable meeting you yet."

"*Kaikun,*" his mother said softly, standing up and stepping over to give him a quick hug, "If she doesn't want to meet your mother, she isn't worth your time."

Kaito wrinkled his face at the nickname, but after a long moment relaxed and gave his mother a quick squeeze back. "Alright, Mom. I'll ask her." *She's definitely worth it,* he knew. *I'm just not sure how much you're going to like someone who is a member of the same organization that killed my father.*

Annie

Deep Fake

June 22nd, 2128

"I can't even pronounce the name of this city," Rafe ranted over their private comm channel.

"Atarashī kibō no machi," Annie repeated for him, sounding out the syllables slowly. "It means 'City of New Hope.'" Kaito had told her that.

"It's too long," Rafe grumbled. "Why don't we use the English, anyway? I mean, if they're going to be part of the United Colonies, they should at least try to act like it. Maybe if Old Earth had made everyone speak the same language, they'd still be around."

If Annie hadn't been connected to her Shell by Neural Shunt, she would have rolled her eyes. She looked out over the vast algae vats that grew the cheapest food on Europa, over the processing facilities, warehouses and loading docks where the UCAF Military Police were still arresting people. "This colony never chose to be part of the United Colonies," she pointed out to Rafe. "We occupied them, remember?"

"Because they're savages," Rafe continued. "Look at these people. Cooking up drugs illegally and selling them on the black market. If we weren't here to be the law, they'd all just be criminals."

"You hear the same briefing I did, Rafe?" Annie tried to keep the growing frustration out of her voice. She wished that she'd brought Nolan, or Sera, instead of Rafe. She'd known they'd be doing little but standing by to provide cover for the MPs, and she'd thought that it might give her a good opportunity to talk to him about what had happened to Laura, and how he was coping. *This was a mistake*, she realized for about the tenth time. Rafe didn't want to talk about anything but his venom for Europans; it was clear that the way he'd chosen to deal with his emotions was to blame everyone on this colony for what had happened.

"They're not making heroin," she continued, knowing it was probably pointless. "They're making penicillin. Epipens for people who have anaphylactic allergies. Insulin for diabetics. Birth control pills. These aren't narcotics, they're basic medicines that people can't afford." Below, the MPs had started to wheel out the 3d printing machines used to make the epipens. The equipment from the chemistry labs, the drugs themselves, the ingredients - it was all being seized by the UCAF. She wondered how many diabetics were going to die without that insulin. *There must be other underground labs like this one, in the other cities*, she found herself hoping.

"If they need medicine, they should get a job and buy it, like normal people," Rafe argued, condemning them all at a stroke. "And birth control is illegal now. You heard the Prime Minister."

"Importing those drugs is expensive," Annie pointed out. "Even most people with jobs here can't afford them." She didn't know what to say about the birth control; she understood there was a dangerously low population, but...

"I don't get it, Annie," Rafe said, his anger boiling over. "Why are you always defending these people? They're a bunch of criminals and terrorists."

"Not all of them, Rafe," Annie protested. "Most Europans are just trying to live their lives. Only a small number of them are insurgents. Our job here is as much to win the population over as to fight the insurgency."

"We should just bomb the whole damned moon," Rafe continued, as if he hadn't heard her. "Pull up those orbital elevators for good, take our people, and never come back. There's nothing here we need anyway - just oil. And fusion reactors mean we hardly even need that anymore."

"Alright, Lieutenant, that's enough." Annie made her voice hard, like the armor of her Shell. "Keep your eyes on our people down there and stay focused."

After a long moment, Rafe confirmed: "Yes, sir."

He's going to be a problem, Annie thought, and not for the first time. To distract herself, she checked her messages. There was one from Kaito.

Kaito: My mother wants you to come to dinner.

This is going to be so awkward. Annie allowed her sensors to zoom in on the faces of the prisoners being led away by the MPs. They didn't look like criminals: they looked like scientists, lab techs, middle aged professionals. They were wearing safety equipment. None of them were armed.

Annie: I won't be back in Toshimayr until late tonight. Let's do it tomorrow.

Kaito: Sounds good.

Annie: Also, we're buying you a new set of sheets.

Kaito: Why?

Annie: How long have you had those, anyway? Soft cotton. High thread count.

Kaito: A couple of years. Why?

Annie: If I'm going to sleep at your apartment again, we're getting new sheets. No argument.

Does Rafe know I'm dating a Europan, she wondered. How much had he heard at breakfast last week? If he did, he hadn't said anything yet - and she couldn't imagine him keeping quiet once he knew. *This whole thing is such a bad idea*, she told herself, for the thousandth time, and then settled in to continue guarding the MPs.

She had been right about how long the operation would take; by the time they'd unloaded the Shells and walked back to Blue Zone, through now constant street protests at the security checkpoints, it was nearly 24:00. The artificial sun overhead had been powered down, and they moved under the light of street lamps to the hangar bay where their Shells were stored.

Back in her quarters, she had collapsed into bed still half dressed, and slept through breakfast. The early afternoon was spent on paperwork, so that she would have the evening free, and she had met Kaito at the entrance to Red Zone half an hour before they were due at his mother's apartment. Now, she was seated at a kitchen table, trying to make conversation.

Annie blew on a spoonful of *miso* soup before placing it to her lips and tasting it. "You're right, Hekima-*sama*," she agreed. "It does taste differently than what you get in a restaurant." She glanced across the table at Kaito. "The flavor is more delicate. Not as strong - right?"

Katakura Hekima nodded with a satisfied smile. "The *dashi* is homemade, that's why.'

"*Dashi*," Annie mouthed, and thankfully Kaito explained. She didn't want to offend his mother by constantly using her smart lenses for translations.

"It's the stock," he said. "Stinks up the whole apartment when you make it. You boil kelp and fermented tuna..."

Annie waved off the rest. "Don't tell me. It tastes good, I don't want to know what goes into it!"

"It's good for you," Kaito's mother said sternly. "And doesn't use imported foods. The fish, the kelp, all genetically engineered to live in the ocean on Europa. Scallions, tofu, soybeans, all grown here, in Toshimayr." She was in the kitchen nook, not twenty feet away from the small table where Annie and Kaito sat, with a large frying pan spitting hot oil. Into the pan, as Annie watched, went thin fillets of salmon coated in flour. The oil crackled more ferociously, and Katakura Hekima poured in first a portion from a bottle of soy sauce, and then from a bottle of *sake*. She seemed to be measuring by feel rather than with any real accuracy, but from the taste of the soup, Annie didn't doubt what the results would be. Behind them, in the living room, which was really just an extension of the kitchenette and dining room with an old rug on the floor, a flat screen on the wall was playing the EMC news - had been the entire time they'd been in the apartment. Annie's grandmother had done that, too - kept something on all of the time, as if to keep her company.

"So," Hekima began as she let the fish cook, "Kaito tells me you are in the military."

This was the part of the conversation Annie had been dreading. "Yes," she responded, taking a moment to swallow her mouthful of soup before speaking. "I'm here as part of the garrison forces stationed in Toshimayr."

Kaito's mother looked her over. "A nurse," she asked hopefully. "Or a doctor?"

"No." For a moment, Annie wished she could have lied. "I'm a Shell pilot. This is my first tour of duty." If she hadn't been watching for it, she wouldn't have noticed the way Kaito's mother's eyes and mouth tightened at the answer.

"So. You are part of the occupational forces." Hekima busied herself with the frying fish.

"Our mission isn't to hurt anyone," Annie explained. "We're here to build relationships and try to heal the wounds of the Colony War, so that we can all live in peace together."

Kaito was studiously silent, and she felt a flash of anger toward him for not leaping in to defend her, or to change the subject.

"You need that warship, in orbit, to make friends, then," Hekima retorted, her voice still even. "And the machine guns and the missiles. Those are all to make friends with us."

"Most of the weapons we use have crowd control settings," Annie began. "They're designed for riot suppression."

"You wouldn't have riots if you didn't conquer and oppress people," Kaito's mother said, waving her hand at the television, where footage of a political rally back on Mars was playing. "And that Prime Minister," she continued, her voice rising, "Forcing people to have children. It's legal rape."

"Alright, mom," Kaito finally interceded. "Let's not talk politics at dinner, ok? Annie's not like that. She's nice. She really wants to help people."

Annie didn't hear what Hekima said in response to that, because the footage on the screen had drawn her eye. Prime Minister Galtung was on a stage, delivering some of his more popular lines about crushing insurgents, like the ones on Europa, and new security measures that he was enacting on Mars and Luna to prevent terrorists from being able to come from the outer colonies. Galtung looked older than when she'd left Mars a year and a half ago: this recording was from yesterday. While she'd been out of touch for the entire time she was on board the *Scipio*, it only took about half an hour for transmissions from Mars to reach Jupiter and its moons.

But it wasn't what the Prime Minister was talking about that had caught her attention - it was the young woman on stage next to him, clapping along enthusiastically with the applause. She was about Annie's age, and blonde as well, though her hair was much longer - it tumbled down past her shoulders, falling down her back. She wore a dress. The scrolling text beneath the picture identified her as the Prime Minister's daughter.

"Annie?" She looked back at Kaito, realizing she had no idea what anyone else in the room had been talking about.

"I'm sorry," she apologized. "What was that?"

"Nothing," Kaito said, looking concerned. "Are you all right? Did the news bother you?"

Annie shook her head. "No. I was just looking at the fake footage."

"Fake footage?" Kaito turned his body so he could watch the television. "Looks pretty real to me." *I shouldn't have said that*, Annie realized.

"The Prime Minister is," Annie agreed, "And probably the crowd. But she's not."

"Who? Her?" Kaito leaned forward and squinted, a habit she'd noticed he to carried over from the times at night and in the morning when he wasn't wearing his smart lenses. "How can you tell?"

"The face isn't quite right," Annie said. "She doesn't blink often enough, and the image gets a little weird when she turns her head and the camera gets her profile. You can do better if you have a lot of images from a lot of different angles, and shots with closed eyes, to work with when you train the computer programs, but the Prime Minister's daughter was never really a public figure."

"Huh." Kaito watched for a moment, then nodded. "Yeah, I guess it does look a little weird. Actually, she looks a bit like you - different hair, but there's a resemblance."

"That's not the first time someone's told me that," Annie said evenly, but she was suddenly very aware of her heartbeat.

"The fish is ready," Kaito's mother said, bringing two plates over to the table. "I'm sorry to bother you before, dear. I know there are good people in the UCAF just doing their job; I shouldn't take my feelings about the government out on you. You should come to dinner for Landing Day," she suggested. "You can meet the rest of the family..."

Annie nodded, and let the issue drop, turning her attention to the salmon. It was delicious.

After dinner, Kaito walked her to the edge of Yellow Zone.

"Are you sure you don't want to stay the night," he asked, with a shy smile, and she was tempted.

"I'd like to - but I have to be up real early tomorrow." She smiled to take the sting away. "I was nice to meet your mother. I'll message you tomorrow again, ok? It's going to be a long, boring shift." She raised herself up on her tiptoes to brush her lips against his, and then sighed when he put his hands on her hips and kissed back. After a moment, she broke away. "Mmm. Any more of that and I'll change my mind."

"That was the idea," he teased her, and she couldn't help but laugh.

"I'll talk to you tomorrow." With a bounce in her step,

she walked up to the security checkpoint, turned, and waved one more time before going through. In Yellow Zone, she walked in a muddle of thoughts, mostly unaware of what was around her until her eye caught a home goods shop.

"Sheets," she said out loud to herself, and decided to pick some up for Kaito's place. She turned on her heel so abruptly that she almost bumped into a passing office worker, who stumbled. "Sorry," she said apologetically, pausing with her hand on the shop door, and then the crack sound of a gunshot finally arrived.

Her combat programming kicked into gear the moment her lenses registered blood spatter from the office worker - a Europan, she assumed, ethnically japanese, middle aged. Stored adrenochrome was injected into her system automatically, and time slowed to a crawl. Sniper. If they were professional, they were already taking another shot.

She dove into the shop. Cover. No one was shooting at an office worker, they were shooting at her. The glass of the shop door shattered, and she rolled into the shop as far as she could, behind shelves and stacks of packaged linen and cotton and pillows. None of it would stop a bullet, but blocking line of sight was her priority right now.

Annie waited for the third shot.

It didn't come, and time started to return to normal as the chemicals bled out of her system. She used her lenses to contact the MPs, and waited in the shop until they arrived. If I hadn't turned to buy sheets, Annie caught herself thinking, I'd be dead now. Why was I the target? Just because I'm an officer? Her mind shied away from the alternatives, and what they could mean.

She spent the next forty five minutes giving the MPs a report; in the meantime, they set up a perimeter and began searching buildings. Annie trusted them to do their jobs, and it turned out she was right to do so; by the time the MPs sent her on her way back to Blue Zone - with an escort of two men, in an armored car - they were able to tell her they'd detained three suspects.

Whether any of those were actually the sniper remained to be seen, of course.

When she had finally gotten back to Blue Zone, she was wide awake with nervous, manic. There was no way she'd be able to sleep, so Annie went to Sera's quarters instead of her own. She had to knock twice before the other pilot opened the door.

"Sorry," Sera said as she closed the door behind them. "I was messing around with a new AR game. Just about to go for a walk, actually."

"This shouldn't take long," Annie told her. "I want you to look at a file. There's a part of the image that's been corrupted." With a few swipes, she sent the file Nolan had procured from his anonymous sources to Sera, and waited a moment while her friend's eyes focused on something she couldn't see.

"Oh, yeah, I see," Sera said, nodding her head. "But the file isn't corrupted. It's showing you exactly what was recorded."

"How is that possible," Annie asked, as Sera swiped away the footage and focused on her again.

"There's an exploit in the security drones' code," Sera explained. "For when the UCAF doesn't want to risk footage of our people doing something that isn't very PR friendly. Scrambles the faces." She reached over and tapped Annie's arm, right on the wrist.

"Someone hacked the ID chip and set it to black ops mode," she finished.

"So the footage is useless." Annie scowled. "Nolan thought the jacket might be a clue, but I don't see how it helps us. There must be hundreds or thousands of coats with that kind of stitching."

"Let me try an image search." Sera called the file back up and began to cut out frames of the sharkskin jacket, one at a time. "This may take a while, boss," she warned.

Annie threw herself down on Sera's couch. "I'll wait."

Kaito

NAAS

Outside Kaito's apartment, Red Zone was quiet.

At this time of night, most people were either asleep, working third shift jobs for the extra pay, or locked into some hardcore gaming. The bars and clubs had closed over an hour ago, and in another hour the artificial sun suspended from the roof the of the great excavated cavern would slowly begin to glow, gradually bringing the ambient light in Red Zone up to the normal level for a day cycle. Sometimes, Kaito wondered what it would be like to watch an actual sunrise or sunset, on Mars or maybe even from one of Luna's domes. He'd watched videos from old earth using his lenses, but he was convinced that in an indefinable but fundamental way there would be a difference in actually experiencing it.

He couldn't sleep.

A month ago, that would have meant he would load up his current gaming obsession, play until his eyes were sandy with exhaustion, then pass out. He'd tried that already, but for some reason nothing seemed to hold his interest: after cycling between first person shooters and a couple of strategy games without really being able to immerse himself in any, he gave up in disgust.

Kaito threw himself in the bed and pulled the pillow Annie used to his face, trying to find a trace of her scent. Increasingly irritated, he threw off the covers and stood up again, padding over to the bathroom to put his smart lenses back in. Then, he created a kind of nest of pillows, piled up against the drywall, so that he could sit up in bed. He grabbed a couple of DSI invoices, found a pen, and called up the *Elyon* forums. Something had been bothering him since his trip to the hospital.

Scrolling through page after page of posts, he found each event notice and began to make a handwritten list along the left side of the back of an old invoice. He listed each event, wrote the date and time it went live, and what cities the event was running in, or *Global* if it was a game wide event with an access point in every city on Europa. He went back to the beginning of the game - it was only a couple of months since launch - and when he had finished, drew a vertical line, dividing the paper into two columns. Then, he closed out the forums and began to search news sites. Slowly, on the other side of the line, he made a list of every insurgent ambush, suicide bombing, or attack over the last three months.

There was a new one tonight, even; a sniper had killed the manager of a downtown bank in Yellow Zone. There was drone footage of the military rounding up suspects, and stuffing them into an armored vehicle while people protested nearby. Curfews had already been announced.

By the time he had finished and swiped away the news sites, light was coming in the window. Kaito rolled his head from side to side, and his neck cracked. He was exhausted, and he had a headache. But he also had a full sheet of paper in front of him.

He stood up and turned on the overhead lights, looking over the two column list again. *It's not perfect*, he admitted to himself. *And I don't know the other cities well enough to be sure.* But in Toshimayr, at least, the pattern was obvious: before just about every insurgent strike, leading the attack by maybe half an hour, maybe fifteen minutes, an event opened. And looking over the access points for the events, and where the strikes occurred, they were never in the same place. In fact, the events were often at the opposite ends of Toshimayr.

"Someone is using the game to get people out of the way." He had to say it out loud for it to really make sense.

But it still doesn't really make sense. Kaito ran a hand through his hair. "This is stupid. If I can figure this out, so can the UCAF. No terrorist in their right mind would want to give warnings like this, make a pattern like this. This is how you get caught."

And it doesn't even make that much of a difference, he realized as he moved into his kitchenette and started a pot of tea. *So what. A couple dozen people run on over to where the event is. How many of them were even in danger from the attack in the first place? Maybe one? Maybe two? Maybe none at all.*

"If it isn't logical, if it doesn't make sense," he murmured, opening a jar of loose leaf green tea, "Then what does that mean? People do dumb shit all the time. Someone isn't thinking."

As the tea steeped, he called the forums back up and began to go back to the event posts he'd spent the past few hours combing through. *The events are created by coders, but...* There it was. In one thread after another, the same player was on top of every event, putting the call out on the forums to let people know they were live.

Ryūjin, the username read. Guild: 10,000 Oni.

Kaito had an appointment at the hospital, early, to get his stitches out, and then a run over to Atarashī kibō no machi, to deliver a shipment of medicine. He was half asleep the entire way, and let the navigation computer run the *Nautilus* as much as he could while his eyes tried to close. He ate cold, leftover *miso* soup from his mother for dinner, then turned around and took a shipment of crude oil back to Toshimayr. By the time he was back, it was just in time for the artificial sun to turn on, and Kaito went to see the Lifespa.

He was a little surprised that it was in Green Zone instead of Blue, which was much more secure. If it had been located in Blue, he would never have been able to get anywhere near it at all.

On the other hand, he thought to himself as he looked it over, *it's not really for the soldiers, so maybe Blue Zone doesn't make sense.* The building was five stories tall, and fronting the street was a glass atrium turned lobby that seemed to extend up all five of those stories. Inside, he could see a reception area, an elevator- again of glass - and the sort of green, leafy potted plants that no one in Red Zone grew because they didn't bear any kind of edible fruits or nuts. Above the revolving door that led into the lobby was an understated, tasteful logo: NAAS Lifespa. Outside, two UCAF MPs in black fatigues stood guard, semi-automatic rifles slung over their shoulders. On the roof, a UCAF Shell crouched. Not Annie's - he could tell that much. UCAF-X007: he looked for her number every time he saw one. This was X004.

That building must be built like a fortress, he decided, since they seemed perfectly willing to park a fully armed Shell on it around the clock. *Glass or not, everything's got to be reinforced and armored, to support that weight.*

As he watched, a black car with tinted windows pulled up; a woman in dark glasses got out of the back seat, waved off her driver, and walked toward the revolving door. He got a pretty good look at her while the MPs checked her security clearance, and when they made her take off the shades he was surprised to realize that he knew her: that pale, half Japanese, half white skin, the delicate, sculpted features - she was one of the news anchors his mother liked to watch. *Kira Montfort,* he recalled. Unlike the younger people in his generation who had mixed parentage, she was not the typical offspring of a UCAF soldier and a Europan mistress. She was too old for that; he wasn't sure just what age, but at least forty. Her parents must have gotten together before the war, and she had been just lucky enough to take advantage of it.

After a cursory security check, the MPs waved her in. The glass door revolved, and he could vaguely see Montfort make her way over to the desk. Kaito glanced once at the guns the MPs were carrying, took a deep breath, and crossed the street, heading straight for the door as if he had every right to be there. As if he had an appointment. As if he didn't have time to be hassled by MPs, and he was wearing a suit instead of a sharkskin jacket.

The MP to his left held up a single hand to stop him. "Security clearance, please."

Kaito held out his wrist to be scanned, and the MP nodded. "You're cleared for Green Zone. Do you have an appointment?"

"Appointment?" Kaito shook his head. "No appointment. I was hoping they took walk-ins."

"Walk-ins," the UCAF soldier repeated, frowning. "You need an appointment."

"Well, can I go inside and make an appointment at the desk," Kaito asked.

The one MP looked at the other. "Make an appointment," he repeated Kaito's words again.

"Yeah," Kaito said. "For my mother." He leaned in close, looking up and down the street for effect, and raised his hand to shield his words from any passers-by. "It's a surprise. She's been waiting for this place to open for ages, and she doesn't know I'm here. See, I've been working overtime just so I can get her a treatment as a present. She's a really nice lady. Here, let me show you a picture of her..."

The MP took a step back. "Fine. Go inside, try to make an appointment. But if you're messing around with us, they're just going to call security and have you kicked out to the curb anyway."

And with that, Kaito was through the door.

Not in time to catch a word with B-List Celebrity-san Kira, who was already stepping into that glass elevator and heading up to get a full regimen of make you look a decade younger wonder drugs, but that was fine. He stepped up to the desk, where a pretty young Europan secretary smiled at him with perfect teeth.

"Good afternoon, sir," she said, somewhat doubtful, as her eyes roamed up and down his ratty knit sweater. "Can I help you? Do you have an appointment?"

"Actually, I'm looking to make an appointment," Kaito said, leaning over the counter and flipping his hair back to make eye contact with her. He flashed her his best smile. "For my mother. As a surprise. What's one of these treatments cost, anyway? I've been saving up to get her a surprise."

The secretary - she was new, of course she was, the spa hadn't even been open a week - leaned forward, speaking to him in low tones in japanese. "If you have to ask, you can't afford it," she hissed. "Get out of here before you get in trouble."

"Do you have a brochure or something," Kaito asked her in English, raising his own voice. "So I can see the different options? Price ranges, that kind of thing?"

Clearly frustrated that he was giving her a hard time, the secretary hissed at him in frustration, then answered. "A consultation appointment is just over five thousand."

Kaito whistled. "Five thousand? That's like..." he did some quick math in his head. "That's more than I make in a month. Like... a ninth of my yearly salary. Before taxes."

"Five thousand *Martian*," the secretary said with an exasperated shake of her head. "Almost seven thousand local. You can't afford it. And you can't come just once, they don't even do anything except blood and DNA tests and stuff at the consult. The first treatment is even more."

Wow. Kaito stood up straight. "Thanks. I'll see you around." As he turned and headed for the door, he thought, *no one can afford that. No one in Yellow Zone or Red Zone, anyway - no one except Kira-san and the others who've made a killing sucking up to the UCAF. No wonder there were protests - no actual Europans are ever going to get to use this thing. All us regular people are going to get old and die, while the rich stay young and get even richer.*

Annie

The Hakkōda Banks

June 25th, 2128

Below, on the street, the protesters and picket lines had formed for the third straight day.

The computer sorted through the external video feed, running facial recognition software hooked in to the UCAF database maintained by the MPs, as well as the local Europan government records which were mandated to be open to UCAF systems. This time, still on edge from the sniper attack, Annie had come with a purpose beyond what Commander Clavinger had assigned her: to find the bomber in the jacket. She'd distributed the still images Sera had captured from the video footage to all of her pilots, and they were using their assignments to try to identify the terrorist who had killed Laura. Missions like this one were perfect for the job, because she was already doing something very similar for the UCAF.

The cameras and sensors mounted on Annie's Shell shifted and moved in constant, low key activity, like - she smiled at the thought - like the wind rippling through her hair at the beach. Various instruments scanned for high radiation counts, unusual heat sources, faces that had criminal records, and the like. Occasionally, something was matched that she needed to examine manually. Known dissidents were identified, she forwarded their identification to the MPs below, guarding the door of the NAAS spa. If there was no warrant for their arrest, that was where things stopped, though the MPs paid particularly close attention to those people.

If someone had a warrant out, however, both her computer systems and the MPs down below would be notified. Already today, two protesters had been arrested, and at each incident the crowd had riled with anger, threatening to erupt into violence and riot. Each time, so far, a motion from her Shell on the roof of the spa had been enough to quell them. No one below seemed to suffer from the illusion that they had any chance of standing up to her military grade equipment.

They're probably not sure exactly what I'm packing, Annie mused as she watched the crowd. *They must picture me dropping missiles on their heads, or something.* Instead, of course, she was loaded out with riot suppression gear: the plasma cannon she'd gotten such grief from Kaito about, during the trip down through Europa's deep world-ocean, currently calibrated, as she'd promised him, for crowd suppression. Her shoulder mounted machine guns, loaded with rubber bullets, the velocity turned down to the lowest setting. External speakers, ready to shriek out the loudest, highest pitched claxon she'd ever heard. Just the memory of being exposed to one back in boot camp, without ear protection, was enough to make her cringe. *If they do get violent,* she told herself, *I should be able to put a stop to it without seriously hurting anyone. Or without killing anyone, at least.*

She shifted in the seat of her Shell. She didn't have the neural shunt cut in at the moment, though that could change pretty quickly if she needed it. The Shell had been crouched here for three hours now, and it was easier to keep it still by just keeping it powered up, keeping connected to her own body, and letting the computers hold it in one position. Her teachers had emphasized the point that sudden movements on the part of military personnel and vehicles could, without meaning to, provide the spark that turned a police action into a violent confrontation. Unfortunately, feeling her body instead of the Shell meant that she was aware of just how sore her butt was getting from sitting in the same seat for hours at a time, and how tight her lower back was getting. She stretched, and heard something pop in her spine.

No hints on the jacket, and no new arrest warrants, she observed, and then turned back to the text conversation displayed by her smart lenses.

Annie: I don't know how much more fair it can be,

without just giving it to everybody. And it's way too expensive to do that. You think your taxes are high now :)

Her fingers flew on thin air, virtually tapping on the translucent, softly glowing keyboard superimposed over her vision by her lenses. She'd made the mistake of complaining to Kaito about how boring guard duty was, and she'd walked right into a rant about the NAAS facility.

> **Kaito**: So the rich people who already get everything get to have it forever, while the rest of us die.
>
> **Annie**: Or people can work hard, achieve success, and pay for the treatment for themselves.
>
> **Kaito**: Do you even know how much it costs? No one around here can afford that.
>
> **Annie**: I don't remember. I'm sure my father would know.
>
> **Kaito**: As much as I make in two months. Before taxes. And I have a good job, compared to most people around here. And that's just for the consultation, not even a treatment.

Annie frowned. *I didn't think they published prices*, she thought, trying to recall. *One of the efforts to try to keep resentment from building.* Before she had a chance to think about it, she typed back to Kaito.

> **Annie**: How do you know what it costs, anyway? I thought they didn't disclose that information publicly.
>
> **Kaito**: I went in.

Shit. Annie leaned back in her chair, then began to call up records from the UCAF database over the last three days. On her smart lenses, she pulled up a picture of Kaito she'd snapped two days ago with the most ridiculous, cutest bedhead hair she'd ever seen, and fed it into the system. In her peripheral vision, Kaito had kept typing.

> **Kaito**: Yesterday, after I got off my shift. It was so early in the morning the crowds hadn't even got there yet.

Sure enough, there was a match, name and everything. Of course. He'd been in the hospital right after she'd arrived, and he had a Green Zone clearance. Beneath his security clearance picture, matched to a freeze frame from recorded footage of him entering the facility, began to scroll information from the UCAF military police database: age, height, weight, blood type, address, education, employer... She swiped it all aside irritably.

> **Annie**: You shouldn't have done that. They've got you on record as going in now. How did you even get past the guys at the door?

> **Kaito**: I told them I wanted to buy my mother a surprise. Then I leaned in close and started to show them family pictures. They couldn't wait to get rid of me. Anyway, it's not like I was doing anything illegal.

> **Annie**: It doesn't look good to mess around with NAAS. The UC government takes security for these places really seriously. As, you know, from the fact that I'm currently sitting on the roof of the place in a thirty foot tall military vehicle.

> **Kaito**: Yeah, to keep away all us people who aren't supposed to be there. They looked at me like dirt when I went in.

> **Annie**: Well, were you wearing your favorite sweater? The one with all the holes in it and the

raggedy-ass threads hanging off everywhere?

Kaito: And my jacket. But that's not the point. They didn't build that place for anyone who actually lives here. They built it for politicians, for the super rich, and for collaborators who they want to give a cookie to.

Annie: Collaborators? We're not at war.

Kaito: Aren't we? If this place was selling the treatment for a deadly disease that everyone had caught, would it be ok to just let people die if they couldn't pay?

Annie: That's different. If there was a disease, the government would declare it a disaster, and use disaster relief funds to get the medicine to people.

Kaito: How is this any different? Either way, without the medicine, people die.

Annie sighed, closed her eyes, and rubbed at them with her balled up hands. *This is so not what I want to be doing right now*, she grumped internally. *Stuck on guard duty is bad enough without arguing with my boyfriend.*

Suddenly, she froze, then slowly dropped her hands from her eyes. "Boyfriend," she repeated out loud. *Is that really what Kaito is? What happened to... friend? Or just that local guy I was going to sleep with once or twice? What about all the reasons this is still a bad idea?*

Ignoring whatever Kaito was typing at the moment, she mentally rehearsed her list. *One, I'm not going to be here forever*, she began. *About a year and a half. And then I'll be shipped somewhere else. Then, I probably won't ever see him again, because he can't leave Europa.* Well, that wasn't technically true, she admitted to herself. *OK, he could leave. He could take a ship to wherever, and he would be fine in zero-g, he just couldn't come down to the surface.* But even that was only true of some places. *Deimos has even lower gravity than Europa,* she knew. *Maybe he couldn't come down to the surface of Mars, but we could live in system, on a moon. I could still visit home.*

"We," she exclaimed at herself out loud. "Where did this 'we' business come from?" Annie glanced back at the chatlog, where Kaito had kept typing for a while before realizing that she wasn't responding. The last message from him hung, pulsing softly, in her vision:

> **Kaito**: Annie? Are you ok? I'm sorry if I was yelling at you, I didn't mean to. I know this isn't your fault, it just ticks me off. Annie?

Annie thought for a second, then smiled and typed back.

> **Annie**: I'm here. I just realized we had our first fight.

> **Kaito**: I'm sorry.

> **Annie**: It's ok. But let's talk about something else, alright?

As she and Kaito typed back and forth, her smile didn't leave her face, and she hardly even glanced at the data being pulled up by her Shell's sensors. The spell didn't break until two hours later, when she was back at the base in Blue Zone, and the new orders came in.

"So where are you going," Kaito asked Annie quietly, tracing a finger over the smooth curve of her hip and down to her belly. It tickled, and she drew in a breath sharply.

"I can't tell you," she reminded him. "I shouldn't have told you anything at all. I just wanted you to know that if I don't respond over the next day or two, it doesn't mean anything."

"Is it dangerous?" Kaito shifted his weight, and the whole bed shook as he curled himself around her.

"Mmmm," Annie sighed at the feeling of skin touching skin. Intellectually, she knew that when two people touched like this, endorphins like oxytocin were released by the brain, and that was why it felt good. But after so long in transit from Mars to Jupiter's orbit, so long isolated from anyone who wasn't a subordinate with whom she had to maintain distance, physical contact was positively addictive. She craned her head back toward Kaito, breathing in his scent. "I'm a soldier," she murmured, finally. "What I do is dangerous."

Kaito's long arms wrapped around her, and she could tell he was worried. She flopped herself over on the bed so that she faced him, their arms and legs twining together, the sheets twisted and knotted off to on side. "Look," she told him. "I'll just be out of contact for a little bit. I only told you so that you wouldn't worry. Don't get, like, visions of some kind of epic battle in your head here. No one's at war, and no one has been in twenty years. Plus, I'm behind a whole lot of armor, I'm not just some guy with a gun." She leaned her face to his and kissed him lightly. "I'll be fine. I'll send you a message as soon as we're back."

Kaito's brow was still furrowed in concern, but after a moment he sighed. "I'll be out to *Toshi Akiyama* and back, anyway," he admitted. "The trip will take me most of the day tomorrow, by the time we load and unload at both ends."

"That's the nearest city, right? Do you get any time to relax there," she asked, curious. "What's it like there?"

"Yes, it is, and it's a lot like here," he said with a short laugh, and then became more serious. "I guess if I'm going to date a soldier I have to get used to this, and not be lame and get all worried and clingy, huh?"

"Clingy is bad," she agreed, bending so that she could kiss the side of his neck.

Kaito shivered at the touch of her lips. "Are you trying to distract me," he asked her.

With a smile, she left off with her lips for a moment and instead pressed her chest against his. "Is it working?"

Instead of answering right away, Kaito rolled them so that she was on her back, his body held just enough off her that she didn't take the brunt of his weight. No that he weighed much, but it was still considerate. He stared into Annie's eyes for a heartbeat. "Yes," he admitted, "you're definitely distracting me right now."

"Good," she whispered, and then they didn't talk for a while.

Annie had helped her father scrape barnacles off his sailboat when she was a child. They would both start by scrubbing the hull using brushes with stiff, stainless steel bristles, and then her father would get out a plastic putty knife. Sometimes, they had to use an actual knife, but her father warned her that could damage the hull. Once - she might have been six - she asked her father why people had ever brought the small creatures to Mars, anyway.

"Why couldn't we have left them on Old Earth," she complained.

"Do you like to eat mussels," her father asked her.

"Yeah."

"And do you like to look at starfish?"

"I guess."

"Well, they both eat barnacles. If you want mussels and starfish, you need to put up with what they eat, too." He laughed. "It's ironic, though. We spent decades getting them to take hold here, to thrive, and now they're doing so well they've become a nuisance all over again. Just like on Earth."

Feeling again like a barnacle, Annie waited in her Shell, attached to the outside of a UCAF Attack Sub, along with the pilots under her command. Except for Laura, of course. She tried not to think about that, and instead cast her mind back to the briefing.

"Europa," Commander Clavinger had begun, calling up his pre-programmed visuals with a casual hand swipe as he stood in front of both flights of Shell pilots, "Has nearly sixty individual tectonic plates. Where the plates collide, they form underwater mountain ranges with a great deal of volcanic activity, and it's these places - where there are plenty of thermal vents, and less pressure - that most of the native and imported ocean life exists." Next to her, Sera and Semenov were fiddling with some kind of game on their tablets. Annie jabbed her elbow right to get their attention, and glared at them both to pay attention.

A spinning image of Europa painted the plates for them, then zoomed in at Clavinger's command on a particular mountain range not far from Toshimayr City. "These are the Hakkōda Banks, the site of a significant portion of the local commercial fishing industry. Because fishing subs are out there so often, an emergency repair bay was constructed on the banks, dug into the rock. This happened before the Colony War - maybe thirty years ago. There's one of these at every major fishing bank, in case a ship has some kind of problem preventing it from getting home. The crew can take shelter inside, if necessary, and the bya's are stocked with emergency parts, rations, and water."

The visuals routed through Annie's smart lenses continued to move, zooming into a particular promontory within the undersea mountain range and then highlighting a docking bay cut into the rock. As the Commander continued, the blueprints of the emergency repair bay expanded to fill her vision.

"Aside from making sure they're functional, we've never paid a whole lot of attention to these places," Clavinger admitted. "But Intelligence has identified the source of the IEDs used in the bridge attack, and matched them with the bombing of the MP barracks in Atarashī kibō no machi. Yesterday, acting on intelligence gained from the suspects rounded up after the sniper attack in Yellow Zone, our military police raided an apartment complex in Red Zone full of bomb-making supplies and made several arrests. Our suspects have day jobs as fishermen, and coincidentally all of their ships have made stops at this particular facility within the past two months. Intelligence thinks they're using this facility to transfer supplies and parts for the construction of explosive devices."

Clavinger dismissed the visuals, and looked around the room to make eye contact with every pilot. "They've also identified discrepancies in crew lists among the vessels involved - sailors who are unaccounted for. We think this facility may have become a semi-permanent base for insurgents. It's possible that our blueprints are no longer up to date; they may even have bored deeper into the rock, to expand the emergency habitat."

"Shumokuzame?" Annie looked to see who had spoken, and was not surprised that it was Lieutenant Commander Malik.

"Could be," Clavinger admitted. "We don't have confirmation. But either way, terrorist activity always spikes leading up to Landing Day, so we're going to treat this operation as if we're walking into a hostile facility, held and fortified by insurgents. That's why we're sending in the Shell teams," he continued. "You will take and hold the emergency repair bay dock, then proceed into the facility to the maximum possible extent, limited only by the size of the passages. Once you've secured what you can, our un-armored marines will follow with personal weapons. If they run into something they can't handle, you provide a fallback point for them to retreat to."

On a world where you could see the sun rise and set, this would have been a pre-dawn op; on Europa, it hardly mattered, but they'd woken up just after midnight anyway, on the off chance they could catch the insurgents asleep. Now, Annie checked the time. Five minutes to arrival. The attack sub shook in some kind of cross current, and she wondered if the pilot was as good as Kaito.

If the insurgents had someone watching their Sonar on an overnight shift, they'd be seeing the two sub's carrying her wing and Malik's wing by now, if they hadn't already. If so, they'd be sounding alarms, waking up everyone in the facility - and no one even knew how many insurgents that was - to grab whatever weapons they had and get ready for a fight. She almost pitied them; there wasn't a chance in hell that unarmored ground troops would stand up to eleven Shells.

An alarm began ringing in her ears - not out loud, of course, but hooked into the Shell's computers through her Neural Shunt it may as well have been - and she realized that her Shell was detecting a target lock. With a thought, she dismissed the warning and called out to her pilots.

"Everyone off the Sub! Scatter and come in the rest of the way on torches!" Even as she was giving the order, she pushed off from the sub and lit her own fusion torches, instantly boiling the water around her. Shells weren't ideal for underwater operations, but it turned out that fusion-powered thrusters could move you through that medium just as easily as an atmosphere or vacuum, as long as you weren't too picky about maneuvering.

The instant after she was clear of the attack sub, an explosion battered the rear of her Shell, and she suddenly had reason to be glad that Kaito *wasn't* piloting that transport, even if he would have given them a smoother ride.

"Torpedo," Semenov called needlessly over the flight comms. *Well, there's at least one alive*, she thought to herself, then checked her sensors. All of her people had gotten off the Subtee in time, but the torpedo had destroyed their way back to Toshimayr City; it's wreck was drifting downward toward the rough rock of the Banks, broken into two pieces. For a second, she let herself wonder how many people had been part of that crew, but she didn't have time for distractions right now.

"Serafine," she ordered, "Drop your drones. All of them. Everyone else, get to that repair bay ASAP."

Her sensors, muted now, detected multiple incoming torpedoes barrelling through the dark ocean toward them, and she knew that her people had neither the mobility, nor the countermeasures systems that were meant to deal with something like this. She kicked in as much thrust as she could, hoping that her acceleration might cause the torpedoes to overshoot her...

And another set of explosions went off somewhere behind her, throwing her shell forward in a tumbling arc. As she fired off thrusters on different parts of the Shell to bring it out of its roll, she checked her HUD again. Somehow, miraculously, all of her people still showed as active and mostly undamaged.

Dropping the drones worked, she realized, amazed. *We got lucky. The torpedoes locked onto them instead of us. It won't happen again.*

And then they were pressed up against the bay doors, and that made them safe from torpedoes, at least. "Semenov," she ordered, "Check the bay. Serafine, start working with those access codes. Nolan, you and Rafe cover our back sides." A chorus of acknowledgements confirmed her orders, and within moments, Gavriil Semenov's voice greeted her over a private comm.

"Bay is full," he told her, and she breathed a sigh of relief. That made it easier. "Might be we have smart terrorists," Semenov continued. "They rather not risk too much damage when we blow it open."

"Might be," she agreed. "Let's see what Serafine can do before we start wrecking things, though."

She'd asked, of course, what the plan was for actually getting *into* an underwater facility when it's inhabitants didn't want it to be gotten into, back during the briefing. Clavinger's response hadn't been exactly comforting.

"All of these emergency repair facilities are designed to open their bays if they receive a transmission over an open channel," the Commander had explained. "They have to be easy to get into, or there's no point. They're also so vital that no one has tried to take advantage of them before. I guess it was only a matter of time before human nature dragged them into the shitheap. So, first thing is to send a request."

"And when that doesn't work," she'd pressed. *Because of course the insurgents will reprogram the damn thing so they can deny us entry.*

"We think they'll want to minimize any actual damage to the facility," Clavinger had continued. "Lieutenant Commander Malik."

Malik had stood up and laid out the plan. "Winters, your team has people cross-trained in tech, both hardware and software."

She nodded. "Lieutenants Moreau and Semenov."

"So," Joel Malik said, smiling in a way that reminded her of videos of sharks, "Your team goes in first, goes in hot, and tries to crack whatever security they've got on the doors."

Serafine stood up. "That could take a while, sir."

"You've got five minutes," Malik told her. "If you can't do it in five minutes, Winters, you're orders are to blow the bay doors open and enter in your Shells."

Annie shared a glance with Nolan. "If that bay is pumped clear when we blow the doors, the water rushing in will do a lot of damage."

"Can't be helped," Malik said. "If that's the way it goes, you secure the bay and our boys will go in through the airlock in dive gear, cycle the airlocks, drop their tanks, and take the base. Not the best option, since they won't be able to count on us for support, but that's the way it goes. So I recommend your tech people get ready to crack that hangar bay without explosives."

Annie's contribution to that effort had chiefly been as procurer in chief of coffee and snacks: Serafine and Gavriil had pulled an all-nighter, setting up both a transmitter and receiver linked to computers in her kitchen and going back and forth writing code. They'd started with the exact same code they knew the repair facility had been using - provided by the Commander - and then begun brainstorming different ways of modifying it with homebrew security code to refuse access. Nolan kept a whiteboard divided down the middle, with 'Security' written on the left hand side and 'Solution' written on the right.

Unfortunately, even Annie's limited understanding was enough to realize that five minutes was not a lot of time, especially as frustrations mounted around three in the morning.

"We're relying on them to be fucking idiots," Semenov finally exploded. "Because if anyone who knows what they are doing coded this, we are fucked."

Now, in the dark water before the bay doors, Annie said across her wing's secure channel: "Let's hope they're fucking idiots. Start the timer."

"Five minute countdown, confirmed," Nolan answered her.

"Initial Code refused," Semenov spoke up, "As expected."

"Dictionary Attack underway," Serafine said, her voice brittle with excitement. This was the first step. Most people who chose passwords chose real words that they could easily remember, so instead of trying all possible combinations of ten alphanumeric digits, they'd loaded a dictionary into Serafine's cracking program and were checking all possible words in the English and Japanese languages against the password authentication of the receiver. They got their answer almost as soon as Serafine started: there were less than two-hundred thousand words in the English language alone, and even adding in Japanese didn't increase the time required by very long.

"Brute Force it is," Serafine sighed. That meant, Annie knew, that her program was now sending the receiver one code after another in rapid succession, trying every possible combination of letters and numbers in a 10 digit string. There were twenty four letters in the alphabet and ten numbers, for a total of 36 possibilities in each separate digit of the code. That meant the number of potential codes was 36 to the tenth power, or a really long number. She'd forgotten whether it was in the trillions or quadrillions, but that was a lot.

"How many can you try in a second," she asked Serafine again, even though she already knew the answer.

"90 Billion," Serafine reminded her. "If we had four and a half days, we'd be all set."

"Two minutes left," Nolan told them. "Lieutenant Traugot, get ready to blow the bay."

Something niggled at the back of Annie's mind. She thought about her date with Kaito, and how she'd wished she had her Smart Lenses in so that she could see a translation for the name of the restaurant: *Soyokaze*. She'd checked it later, and found that it roughly meant 'gentle breeze.' But in addition to the English alphabet transliteration on the sign, there had also been *kanji*...

"Serafine," Annie nearly shouted, "When you plugged in a Japanese Dictionary, did you just put in the transliterations? The English alphabet? Or did you put in the Kanji as well?"

"I..." Serafine paused. "Oh shit. Alright, hold on. Let me hook in a different dictionary file..."

"Thirty seconds," Nolan said. "Our transports are expecting those doors open!"

Around them, the undersea mount rocked with explosions as Malik's team of Shells continued to bombard any confirmed torpedo launch point, destroying the launching subs.

"Got it," Serafine shouted as the bay doors ponderously began to open, the seawater inside mixing with that outside.

Annie switched comm channels. "Attack subs, hangar doors are open. We are proceeding to secure the hangar; follow us in." She toggled back to her team. "Semenov, Sera, get in there."

As soon as the bay doors had opened wide enough for a Shell to slip through, Gavriil lit off his fusion torches and moved in. Sera followed, while the other three members of the team waited outside. The frequency of explosions caused by

Malik's team seemed to be rapidly decreasing.

"Bay clear," Semenov commed back.

"Alright, let's move in," Annie ordered, heading in herself and trusting Nolan and Rafe to follow. The bay was big: big enough for two Subtee's at a time, she guessed, with room to spare. She found herself a spot above the airlock which lead deeper into the repair facility, then kept an eye on her sensors while the subs transporting marines made their way in.

"All clear," Nolan reported from his position at the hangar doors.

"Sera, close the bay doors and start the pumps up," Annie said. Something fluttered at the pit of her stomach. There hadn't been much time to think about danger when their attack sub was targeted: she'd had to act quickly, give the right orders for her people to survive. And then, in the shelter of the hangar, they'd been safe from torpedoes. But now, she was about to lead her people in a sweep of an enemy held facility, and that meant a lot of opportunities for traps, for things to go wrong, for Shells to get damaged and people to get hurt.

She thought about the number of possible ways she could do this as the pumps activated and began lowering the water level of the hangar. It didn't occupy much of her attention to position her Shell so that she was lowered onto the metal walkway which ran along the inner wall of the bay, not far from the airlock. The trouble was, there was only room for one Shell at a time in that airlock, which meant someone had to go through first, all alone, when the inner door opened. And whoever did that would take everything the waiting defenders could throw at them.

She thought about Laura Ross, lying in a hospital bed, and Rafe Traugott, eyes sunken with exhaustion, waiting for her to wake up. About signing Laura's life away.

"Sera," she sent privately, "Can you open those airlock doors on my mark? Both the inner and the outer doors at once?"

"Yes sir," Serafine Moreau confirmed.

"Good." Marines were beginning to pile out of the transports; there was no need for dive suits with the hangar bay secure, and they were taking up positions centered on the airlock, weapons at the ready. Annie walked her Shell back away from airlock, checking to make sure there was nothing behind her.

She opened her comms to all troops in the bay. "Once that airlock is open and secured, Shells follow immediately, marines behind them." A chorus of acknowledgements from squad leaders came in, and right on the heels of that, a private comm from Nolan.

"Who is going in first, Winters?"

"Three," she said over the open comms, ignoring him as she bent her Shell's legs at the knee into something resembling a runner's crouch. "Two. One. Mark." And then she lit off her fusion torches.

The airlock doors cycled open just before she collided with them, and then she was into a corridor designed for moving cargo. She barely had time to register makeshift barricades of large, spare sections of hulls which must have been replacement parts, and behind them, crouched and firing at her, at least two dozen insurgents. Her shoulder mounted mini guns began to track and fire as fast as she could think, filling the air with bullets as she crashed past the barricades and down the hallway. Insurgents scattered in every direction, utterly unprepared for what was coming their way. Some of them must have thrown grenades, because there were explosions around her as she tried to spin and land at the same time, behind the barricades, the insurgents now unable to use them as cover.

Red warnings popped up in her peripheral vision to inform her that her maneuvering wings had suffered structural damage and could no longer be relied upon to perform within standard operational parameters. Annie swatted the warnings aside, stabilized her crouch, and opened back up with the mini-guns.

Her bullets swept across the groups of insurgents turning to face her, and she watched men and women die in pristine, high definition sensor feeds. Her Shell rocked, more warnings popping up one after the other as heavy weapons were brought to bear on her and there was nowhere to go to avoid incoming fire.

These aren't terrorists, she realized as she watched them react to her. They moved with discipline, following orders from their leaders, even as she cut them down. They all wore gray jumpsuits that weren't quite the same, but looked almost like uniforms. They had military grade weapons: a tripod mounted machine gun was turned to face her by one group of men, and the bullets hit her shell with the sound of rain on a roof. Another insurgent hoisted a rocket propelled grenade launcher to his shoulder, and the explosion rocked her back, but she kept firing.

Nolan came through about the time her fusion reactor was undergoing an emergency shutdown, and with the second Shell in the hallway, they broke. Some of the insurgents dropped their weapons, some didn't. Some had surrendered, she realized as her feeds started to go offline, but a lot more were going to be killed.

"Emergency disconnect initiated," was the last red warning she saw before her neural shunt booted her out of the Shell and back into her own body. She heard screaming, and realized the voice was her own. There was blood - a lot of blood on her, and her cockpit was spraying her with gel. The gel was hardening around the right side of her torso, where she could see shrapnel from the damage her Shell had sustained, a jagged piece of metal, sticking out of her flight suit.

Annie's left hand scrambled around, then slapped a release on the left side of her cockpit. A small compartment opened, and she pulled out a single-use shot in pen form, jabbing it hard into her left thigh. As the painkillers flooded her system, the agony became distant, but it also became hard to think clearly.

Getting out of the seat was a process, but once she was free of the restraints and safety harnesses popping the cockpit was easy. The ground was only maybe two feet below her, because the Shell had tumbled over, so she just let herself drop. She was pretty sure she screamed again when that happened.

The hallway looked secure. Half a dozen insurgents were kneeling, hands crossed behind their heads, along one wall, watched over by two UCAF marines. The battle was sweeping past her, and she could see one of her team's Shells heading down the hall, deeper into the emergency repair facility. She cast about for some kind of intercom or in-base communication system, finally finding one on the wall next to the open airlock through which her comrades were still pouring.

Halfway to it, a marine private rushed over to her. "Need some help, sir," he asked, and she nodded.

"Thanks, private." With one arm over his shoulders, she managed to get to the wall and activate the intercom.

"This is Lieutenant Commander Annette Winters speaking to all insurgents in this base," she began, flinching slightly as her voice boomed out from speakers in the ceiling - and presumably, all throughout the facility. "Surrender yourselves and this facility, and you will be treated as prisoners of war."

The private's eyes just about bugged out of his head, but to his credit he didn't say anything. Military prisoners of war had a hell of a lot more rights than terrorists.

The intercom on the wall crackled. "How do I know the UCAF will keep that promise," a voice asked her.

Annie pressed the button again. "Record what I'm saying so that you have proof. I personally guarantee it. Again, I am Lieutenant Commander Annette Winters of the UCAF 101st Shell Wing, and you have my word of honor that all of your people who surrender will be treated as combatants and prisoners of war."

There was a long pause. "Alright," the voice said quietly, and then the connection was broken.

Annie leaned against the wall, and it took all of her strength not to simply sit down on the floor of the hallway. A few moments later, a sergeant ran over. "Sir," she said as she saluted, "We have reports of insurgents surrendering throughout the facility."

"Good," Annie said, her vision started to gray around the edges. Her own voice sounded very far away. "Lieutenant Nolan is in command until someone gets here to relieve him. I..."

Her legs gave out, and she heard someone's voice calling for a medic, but that was all.

Kaito

Get to Her

June 26th, 2128

Kaito was just about at the security checkpoint when they shut everything down: access to the net, cloud storage, security clearance, everything. He realized what had happened when *Elyon* started spouting errors at him: *Connection Lost. Retry?*

"Shit," he snarled, nearly tripping off the moving walkway as he tried to reload the game. "What the hell?" He'd lingered behind in the dock after the last of the cargo had been offloaded and moved out, taking his time with the shutdown so that he could pick up his new favorite component without anyone else being around. Today, he'd managed to loiter long enough that even Old Man Date wasn't around anymore by the time he'd left, and he'd been getting ready to post an offer on the *Elyon* marketplace for more gold than he was usually able to scrape together in a week.

He closed out the game, pausing in the hallway, and started to reload it, but that didn't work either. *Connection Lost. Retry?* He opened up his chat log to see if Annie was off duty yet, and there it was again: *Connection Lost. Retry?*

He was just about to reboot his smart lenses entirely when the sounds of voices, boots and machinery started to swell from the second docking bay, echoing down the hallways as a whole lot of somethings came in his direction. He turned to see what was coming, and a heavy stone sunk into the bottom of his gut.

Stretchers. UCAF soldiers - medics, probably - jogging down the hall toward him, rolling stretchers, each one with a person loaded onto it. Some of the medics were holding clear plastic bags above their patients, tubes leading from the bags into limp arms. They were talking, too, in that hospital language he didn't understand but remembered from just after the building came down: the tense tones of men and women who were shutting off their emotions while they made decisions about who was going to live, and who was going to die. Some of the people on the stretches were talking too - making noises, anyway, moans or screams - but many of them were silent. That meant they were unconscious or dead.

"Out of the way!" One of the medics snapped at him, and Kaito shrank back against the wall. He knew he should look away, but he couldn't make his eyes move from the wounded soldiers as they rolled past, one after the other. There was blood, soaked into bandages and uniforms, or dried into crusts on faces, arms and torsos. Their skin ranged from pale to burned to so gray they looked not like humans but like some kind of mannequin in an upscale clothing store.

Did Dad look like this, he wondered. *Did someone wheel him away from where he got hurt, and try to save his life?* It was a shock to realize he didn't know, that his mother had never told him.

Only two stretchers left now, coming up on their metal frames with half a dozen medics, and it occurred to him that if he stuck around for the arrival of the UCAF soldiers who *weren't* hurt he was probably going to be in a lot of trouble. There was no way he had the clearance to be here; he must have not been paying attention when the announcement to clear the hall came, and the UCAF must have cut off all access to the net so that no one could take pictures or video. He started to slide back along the wall toward his ship, toward safety, when the last stretcher rolled past him.

"Annie?" Kaito didn't understand it was him who had said her name until the medics looked up at him. "Annie?" He took a step forward, but she didn't move, and her eyes were closed.

"Back up, sir!"

"Who the hell is this guy?" One of the medics stepped away from the stretcher to push him back, and Kaito fought to take a step closer without even thinking about it.

"Is she alright," he asked stupidly. "Where are you taking her?"

A heavy hand fell on his shoulder, and Kaito turned his head to see an officer of some kind - who really knew what those rank pins meant anyway - scowling at him. "Civilians are *not* permitted in this passage right now," the soldier snarled at him. "What are you doing here?"

"I didn't hear the announcement," Kaito said, turning back to Annie, who had been rolled past him and was going down the hall, farther away with each step the medics took. "Is she alright? What hospital are they taking her to?"

"Nowhere you've got the clearance for," the officer spat. "Get down that hallway. Get into bay two, close the damn door, and don't come out until the lockdown is over. You're lucky I don't arrest your stupid ass right now."

She was around the corner, and more soldiers were coming up the hallway now, looking at him. He knew what they were going to start to think: why was this guy here? This Europan? Was he a terrorist? Media?

He cursed, turned, and jogged back to the moving walkway. He had to get out of here. He had to find out where they were taking her. He checked his smart lenses, but there was still no connection. He had no idea how long it was going to take for the corridors to clear and the UCAF to move all their people and equipment out. Kaito turned toward the bay where the *Nautilus* was docked, then back toward the corridor where the soldiers were moving. Then, he turned on his heel and ran to the Subtee.

Inside, he tore through the cabin until he found the standard first aid kit all commercial Subtee's were required to keep stocked. He pulled the whole box out - it was a dull gray, marked with a blocky red cross inside a white circle - and then ran back off the Subtee, down the moving walkway, and into the throng of soldiers returning from their mission. He kept moving, rushing through them.

"Excuse me," he said, trying not to hit anyone but also

trying to look like he was supposed to be there as he dodged in and out of the crowd of moving bodies. He tried not to think about how many assault rifles were in the corridor at the moment.

He made it within sight of the checkpoint before a soldier stopped him. "Hold on," the black uniformed man said with a frown, stepping directly in Kaito's path. "Where are you going? Civilians shouldn't be here right now."

"I know, I know," Kaito told him in a rush of words, holding up the first aid kit. "One of the medics asked me to grab this for him, he said they're out of something... look, I can see the guy right up there, just past the checkpoint!" Reaching over the soldier's shoulder, Kaito pointed at the backs of the last medics in line.

The UCAF soldier hesitated for a moment, and Kaito knew he was screwed.

"Alright, go," the soldier told him. "Hurry up, move!" He raised his voice as Kaito ran by. At the checkpoint, Kaito blew past Van den Berg and Moretti. He thought he heard Moretti say something on the order of 'what the hell?' as he ran past, but he didn't stop or even slow down.

As soon as he could, Kaito turned down a side passage. None of the medics had asked him to bring a damned thing, so if he actually ran up to them he was going to get caught in about two heartbeats. Instead, he needed to get out of the docking facilities and into the city, where he could hook back up to the net.

Kaito had worked here for years; or at least, he'd piloted Subtees in and out of here for years. And while he'd worked here, he'd spent a lot of time finding places where he could hide from Old Man Date for a few moments and chat with guilds, tag in on a raid, or whatever.

He took a back stairway that no one used down to where the maintenance crew kept their equipment, then headed out through the door next to their loading dock. The smell was terrible, as he came out past the dumpsters, but it got him outside and onto a street. He checked the connection on his smart lenses, and yes indeed, he was hooked up to the net again.

"OK," he muttered to himself as he set off down the street. "Does the UCAF base in Blue Zone have its own hospital?" The question had never even occurred to him before, but it would have to, wouldn't it? And he hadn't seen that pilot whose Shell was attacked in the emergency room, or anywhere else while he was in the ER... "Of course it does," he said out loud, heading in the direction of Blue Zone. "But they're not going to let you in, Kaito." A middle aged woman gave him a look, and he decided it was maybe better to stop talking out loud.

Ok, think, he chided himself. *If you were family they'd let you in, but you're not. So how do you get in?* He glanced back the way he'd come, in the direction of the loading dock and the dumpsters. Someone had to take the trash in and out, someone had to clean the toilets. Not soldiers. Locals - Europans, like him, with the right security clearances.

With a couple finger swipes, he pulled up the chatroom his guild kept open to friends from other guilds, former members from games that had died, and the like. Instead of a twenty person chat, it was nearly a hundred, and rarely focused on the game at hand. Instead, you loaded this up if you wanted to see who's kid had a birthday, or who'd finally graduated.

Kaito (Dynasty): Does anyone work at the UCAF hospital in Toshimayr?

He swiped the window off to the side of his vision, where he could still see it, but where it wouldn't hinder his ability to move quickly through crowds. He'd never been into Blue Zone at all; he wasn't cleared for it. He pulled up a map, found the entrance, and set the software to plot him a path. He had to traverse nearly all of Green Zone, he saw, and picked

up the pace of his walk. The UCAF medics would certainly
have had ambulances, or APCs, or whatever it was they put
their wounded in to move them through potentially hostile
territory.

He kept glancing at the chat log as he walked, waiting
to see if anyone had responded yet. He was about a block from
the entrance to Blue Zone when he really started to think about
how he was going to do this without any help, and realized that
every plan he thought of came from dumb action video games
where you just hit a convenient janitor over the head, put on
his overalls (which always fit - the guy was never, say, much
shorter than you) and then you used his security fob to head
on in.

None of that seemed like it had much of a chance of
working now.

A private message popped up. Not in the chatroom, but
it was a name he recognized as a member of one of the top ten
guilds in *Elyon*. It was a name he'd scrawled on the back of a
DSI shipping invoice in the middle of the night not so long ago.
He pulled the message up.

Ryūjin (10,000 Oni): What do you need?

That didn't exactly answer the question he'd asked, but
he paused in front of a coffee shop as if reading the menu
posted in the window and typed a response.

Kaito (Dynasty): I need to get inside and see someone.
One of my friends is hurt, but I don't have the security
clearance to get in.

Ryūjin (10,000 Oni): My cousin works 3rd shift
maintenance. Let me talk to him.

Third shift. Kaito glanced at the time, though he really
didn't have to. That was still more than six hours away. He
looked around the street; it felt like everyone was watching
him. He opened the door to the coffee shop, walked in, and got

in line behind a bunch of off-worlders. When it was his turn to order, he mumbled, "Double Espresso," without even looking at the price. When the Europan barista told him how much his order was, he didn't even bother to point out how ridiculously overpriced the place was. Of course. It catered to off worlders. He just paid, found a seat from which he could see the door, and sipped his coffee while he waited for Ryūjin to get back to him.

About twenty minutes later - just as his coffee was starting to get cold - another message popped up.

Ryūjin (10,000 Oni): There's a men's room at the coffee shop you're in. Go in.

How the hell, Kaito wondered, *does he know where I am?* Had Ryūjin hacked his accounts and gotten access to his gps data? Or was he using some kind of location spell in game? But Kaito didn't have *Elyon* running at the moment...

Ryūjin (10,000 Oni): Now.

Kaito stood up and walked back to the men's room. There was one guy - a janitor, from the look of his clothes - washing his hands, and Kaito walked over to the urinals, trying to look normal. He listened for the water to stop, thinking that when the other guy left he'd send a message asking what to do next.

The water stopped, and then the lock on the door clicked.

"Alright," the other guy - the one who'd been washing his hands - said. "Good. There's a bag in the stall,with a uniform in it."

Kaito looked back and forth between this kid - he looked like he was in high school - and the stall. "Are you-"

"Don't ask me anything, man," the kid said. *Ryūjin*, Kaito mentally labelled him. "Just get in the clothes, put yours in the bag, and meet me out by the door. We're grabbing a

coffee on the way to work. Once you're dressed, follow me."
With that, he unlocked the door and left Kaito in the men's
room, frozen in place.

For a moment, Kaito just stood there, and then he
walked to the stall and pushed the door open. Inside, pushed
against the wall so that it would be just out of view, was a
backpack. *Am I really going to do this,* Kaito asked himself.
Then, he thought of Annie, sleeping naked on the bed next to
him when he'd stirred for a moment in the night, and he saw
her again on the stretcher, covered in blood. *Hai. Yes, I am.*

He threw the janitor's uniform on as quickly as he
could, shoving his own clothing into the backpack and then
slinging it over his shoulder. When he stepped back out into
the coffee shop, he scanned the room for Ryūjin, finding the
younger man sipping a cup of coffee near the door, in the same
uniform as him. Kaito walked over as confidently as he could,
and together they proceeded out the door and into the street.
There, he had to pause for half a step, as he wasn't quite sure
where he was going: just long enough to be able to follow in the
route that Ryūjin led him.

They walked through Green Zone toward Blue - the only
one of the artificial caverns which made up Toshimayr that
he had never once been inside up until now. There, Ryūjin
greeted the UCAF guards with the same familiarity that Kaito
himself was used to in his daily encounters going in and out of
the docking bays. Kaito kept himself silent, and tried not to let
his face show how nervous he was.

"Who's this," one of the uniformed military police
asked.

"Temp guy," Ryūjin said, waving his hand in Kaito's
direction. "Hideo's out sick for the day."

The UCAF guard laughed. "Have fun cleaning the bed
pans, boys," he joked, and waved them in through the full
body scanner. Kaito raised his hands, waited for the scanner
to finish, and hoped there was nothing objectionable in the
pockets of the backpack.

And then they were into Blue Zone.

Kaito tried not to look lost, or like an idiot who had never been there before. Blue Zone had been the most upscale section of Toshimayr twenty years ago, before the Colony War. It had been the cavern which housed municipal buildings like the courthouse, the city hall, and the capitol building. He'd seen images - both still pictures and footage shot from personal devices - of what the UCAF troops had done after the colony government surrendered. They'd knocked down the capitol building and gutted city hall, making room for new structures: barracks, repair bays, housing for officers. A quick search told him they kept the old Blue Zone hospital, but closed off access to anyone without the proper security clearances, forcing a new hospital to be built in Yellow Zone. The restaurants and cafes and other businesses which had always been in Blue Zone stayed, now catering to officers and soldiers. Some of them took a turn for the worse: he knew several of the girls who had graduated secondary school with him now worked as dancers in clubs that catered to enlisted soldiers. At least one, Seijun, who used to sing in the school chorus, had a baby, and it had been the talk of the neighborhood for weeks because no one was really sure *which* soldier was the father.

It was to that old hospital Kaito and Ryujin now made their way. The line of medics and stretchers, and the transports which must have sped their journey, were nowhere to be seen. It must have taken too much time to stop at the coffee shop, to change, and to go through security. Kaito imagined that all of the wounded soldiers were already inside the hospital.

Instead, the Shells were visible, moving into their hangars. There were at least half a dozen, each being hosed down with fresh water to remove the corrosive salt crust from their trip through the ocean. Kaito looked for Annie's Shell - he knew he'd recognize it by the number - and saw it heaped on a flatbed truck. It was blackened and pockmarked from explosions, broken in half a dozen places even to his untrained eye. It looked like nothing so much as a dead body, curled in on itself to try to stop the bleeding. He shook himself, then had to take a couple quick steps to catch up with Ryūjin.

They went into the hospital through a back door, his anonymous companion using a key fob to unlock the way with a quick swipe. Once inside, Kaito followed him to a supply closet where they loaded up a rolling cart with cleaning materials and began to make their rounds. They emptied garbage baskets, swept floors, and worked their way through the hospital as slowly as they could.

"So," Ryūjin said quietly once they were in a hallway with no one around, "Do you know what room your friend is in?"

Kaito had been thinking this over; he'd been in to get the stitches pulled out of his back only two days ago. The scabs still itched. "She won't be in a room yet," he said confidently. "She'll be in either the ER, or in the operating room."

Ryūjin stopped sweeping for a moment. "Your friend wouldn't happen to be one of those shot up soldiers who just got in, would she?"

He thought about denying it, and then decided it didn't matter. "Yeah."

"Nothing can ever be easy." Ryūjin shook his head. "The ER we can check. If she's on the table right now with a couple of surgeons going to work, no way are you going to get in there. Come on, this way."

The ER was arranged with about eight rooms radiating out from a central circular area, where the desk was. There was a hallway out to where patients were brought in, whether by ambulance or by armored transport, and a hallway deeper into the hospital. It was from the second passage that they approached, and that led past the OR, where the windows were covered with shades so that you couldn't see in clearly. Kaito both wanted to find a way to peer in, and also wanted to look away, afraid of what he'd see.

Once they opened the door to the ER, there was a lot

of noise. The nurses were scrambling accompanying doctors from room to room. There was a lot of pained moaning, and every room seemed to be in use. Kaito and Ryūjin slipped behind the nurse's station first, emptying garbages and putting new bags in the cans. "Be careful of anything with a sharps warning or biohazard label on it," he was told, and worried about stabbing himself with a needle bearing some kind of deadly disease for the next few moments.

Then, they made their way around the outside of the room, ostensibly checking to see whether any empty rooms needed their garbage changed. Anyone with half a brain, Kaito knew, would realize this was bullshit and the last thing that needed to be happening with a bunch of wounded soldiers who needed immediate attention, but also it seemed like the two janitors were about the least important people here, and no one was paying them any attention.

At the first three rooms they checked, he shook his head 'no' to Ryūjin quickly. Two of the soldiers in those rooms were men, and he hardly even had to look at them. The third soldier *was* a woman, and he felt his heart trying to tear out of its chest until he realized she had dark hair, not blonde, and so it couldn't be Annie.

It was the fourth room where he found her, though he nearly passed her by. Annie's skin was pale, colorless, and she wasn't moving. The nurses were cutting off her uniform, and there was some kind of - foam? He wasn't sure exactly what - over her side, where all the blood was.

"Penetrating abdominal trauma," the doctor, a middle aged woman announced to the room. "Looks like an IED or shrapnel of some kind. Start her on antibiotics, get her intubated, and prep her for a laparotomy."

The scissors finished snipping the skinsuit under her fatigues, and the nurses had her naked within minutes. For a moment, Kaito remembered her in his apartment, in the dim light, the skin of her chest rising in goosebumps because he kept the temperature so low, and making a quiet joke about warming her up. He remembered the feel of Annie's skin beneath his fingers for the first time. The nurses were putting some kind of tube down her throat.

A hand on his shoulder brought him back to the fact that he was not supposed to be here, and every muscle in his body tensed, ready to either fight or run, before he registered that it was just Ryūjin giving him a shake. The other man jerked his head toward the door, holding up a full garbage bag. The silent message was clear: *we need to leave now.*

Kaito looked back at Annie. He wanted to stay here. But even if he'd been her family, even if he wasn't a Europan without the security clearance to be in Blue Zone just asking to get caught, he realized even then he'd never be allowed into the operating room with her. Drawing a shaky breath, he followed Ryūjin out. He helped empty the other trash baskets around the ER in a haze, watching Annie's room with one eye and nearly tripping or dropping something several times before they wheeled her out of her room, through the doors, and then down the hallway which led deeper into the hospital and to the OR.

A few moments later, when they were wheeling their waste barrels and supplies down a side corridor toward the loading docks and dumpsters, they were alone again.

"That was her," Ryūjin more stated than asked.

"Yeah."

"So you've seen her. Now what?"

Kaito's mind flailed about like a child first learning to swim. "I don't know. They put you in a room after operating, right? Like a more permanent room? So I have to find out where that is. What room number, I mean. And get some kind of clearance to be here."

Ryūjin shook his head. "Ok, we're here for an eight hour shift. She should be out of surgery by then - I mean, unless something goes really, really wrong. And then yeah, we can figure out which room she's in. We can go scout out which rooms are empty in intensive care right now, to cut down on what we need to search through later. And if you've got the money, you can get a security clearance. You live in Red Zone same as the rest of us, right? I'm sure you know a guy. Or at least know where to start asking questions. Then you're going to need some kind of excuse when they ask who's visiting."

Should I just tell them the truth, Kaito wondered. *We're dating? She's met my mother? What does that make me? Her boyfriend? If we were married, I'd have a legal right to be here, but...* "I'll... I'll think of something," he said out loud.

Ryūjin hit the button for their elevator, then turned to look him in the eye as they waited for it to reach their floor. "Are you sure she's going to want to see you? How well do you know her?"

Kaito hesitated. "She will," he said finally. "I mean, we haven't... known each other long, but I know she doesn't really have any family or friends here." *She's lonely,* he thought to himself. "I don't think she'd want to be alone."

"And when her soldier buddies visit," Ryūjin asked as they stepped into the empty elevator, "What's she going to tell them? How's she going to explain you? You sure this isn't going to cause her problems?"

No, he thought, *how could it possibly cause her problems if they find out she's dating a local? What do they call us, Opies? For all they know, I am a terrorist. We all look the same anyway, right?*

"If she says she wants me to leave, I will," was all he could come up with.

The elevator doors opened, and they took their trash out to the dumpsters. "You've got it bad, man," Ryūjin told him. "You know they're probably going to send her back wherever she came from on the next ship out, right?"

He hadn't thought about that, yet, but put it aside for now. "Nothing I can do about that until it happens." All of a sudden, he was sick of talking to Ryūjin. "You said we have an eight hour shift. What's next?"

Annie was only in surgery for about an hour and a half.

By the time their lunch break rolled around, they'd figured out what room Annie was in by making their rounds through the ICU and gathering up the garbage there. Kaito took a broom and swept out all of the rooms, which gave him an excuse to go into hers. Once inside, he made sure the second bed was empty, quietly closed the door, and set his broom against the wall.

For a moment, he couldn't believe he'd actually managed to get into a room alone with her. Since he'd first seen Annie pushed by him on a stretcher hours ago, it was all that he'd thought about, and now, he wasn't quite sure what to do. Kaito brushed his hands off on his pants, then thought about the garbage he'd been handling and went over to the sink to wash with disinfectant. Then, he approached the hospital bed.

They'd tilted it so that she was half lying down, half sitting up, at about a forty-five degree angle, maybe a little less. The sheets were tucked up to her chest, and he could see that they'd put a pale green hospital gown on her. An IV was still taped to her left wrist, and three plastic sacks of fluid hung above her bed, but they'd taken the tube out of her throat. He couldn't see any blood or bandage, and she seemed to be asleep.

Afraid to sit down, in case someone came into the room, Kaito stood there, looking down at Annie for a moment. She still looked pale, drained. Her chest rose and fell quietly, peacefully. He reached out for her hand, hesitated a moment, and then went ahead and placed his hand over hers. Her skin felt cold, clammy.

He waited there a moment, not sure how long he could afford to stay here without getting himself in trouble, then took a deep breath and turned away to leave. As his hand slipped over hers, her fingers curled around his and squeezed.

"Annie?" Kaito spun back toward the bed. Her eyes were half open, fluttering.

"Hey," she said, quietly.

Kaito reached out with his left hand and pulled a chair

over so he could sit next to her. He thought of how obnoxious his mother and Mizuki had been when he was in the hospital, and how after a few moments he'd mostly just wanted them to go away. Well, he mostly wanted Mizuki to go away. "How are you feeling," he asked quietly.

"I'm..." she took a deep breath and closed her eyes, and for a moment he thought she might go back to sleep. Then, abruptly, she was back there with him and her eyes were open. "I feel really weird. It's hard to think."

"You just got out of surgery," he told her. "It's probably the anaesthesia and the pain medication. But you're going to be fine." He felt like a liar for saying that; he had no idea how she'd been hurt, really, or what the Doctors would say to her.

"Mmmm," was all she said, and he wasn't sure if it was an agreement or the sign of someone getting ready to drop back off to sleep. But then she asked, "Is everyone ok?"

Everyone who? I have no idea what she's even talking about. "Your Shell is the only one they brought in wrecked," he recalled after a moment.

"So I did good," she murmured.

"Yeah," was all he could say. "Yeah, I guess you did. Hey, Annie, I've got to leave right now, but I'm going to be back. You just go to sleep and rest up."

"Ok," she said faintly, turning toward him and closing her eyes as she buried the right side of her face in the thin hospital pillow. *I should bring her a real pillow*, he thought. She kept his hand wrapped in hers, and he waited a moment, until he was sure she was asleep, before slipping out of her grasp, collecting his broom, and heading back out to finish sweeping the rest of the ward.

By the time Kaito made it to *Tako To Ama* that evening, the bar was crowded. Deserted during most days, except for a few regulars who lived in the neighborhood getting lunch and a drink, at night it was packed, hot, and loud. Kaito, already hot and sweaty from working an entire shift as a janitor at the hospital in Blue Zone, *right on the heels* of a run up to the ice and back, felt like he was walking on legs made of glass. Each step he took, he waited for them to shatter underneath him.

He paid the cover, got his hand stamped, and managed to get by Hikaru, the bouncer at the door, without getting dragged into a conversation about *manga*. They'd known each other since grade school, and normally he'd have been happy to chat for a while, but tonight he didn't have the time.

Inside, Mizuki was pouring her voice out through the microphone across a crowd of dancers while the band filled the room with bass that moved your bones and made your heart beat in time with the drums. Kaito pushed his way over to the bar and got a cold beer while he waited for her to take a break; he would have preferred ice water, but once *Tako To Ama* got going at night, if you weren't ordering something that cost money, you weren't likely to get very quick service. He didn't recognize either the man or woman working behind the bar, but he'd been avoiding coming at night since his breakup with Mizuki.

She sang for another twenty minutes, and he made sure a cold bottle was waiting for her when she came over. Mizuki, sharkskin jacket long since discarded in the heat of the crowd, smiled when she saw him and rushed over to give him a hug; he couldn't figure out a way to avoid it, and didn't want to start a fight, so he just gave her a squeeze and let her go.

"Sorry," she shouted over the noise of the crowd and the background music that cut in as the band shut the amps off, "I'm all sweaty!" She pulled her tank top away from her skin, trying to get some cool air, but there was none. "I'm so happy you came, Kaito! It's been ages."

"You sounded great," he told her, and it was true: whatever else had come between them, her voice, her music, was still as beautiful as when they'd first met. Mizuki tossed her bottle of beer back, her graceful neck extended as she gulped it down in long swallows. She killed half the bottle in her first drink, then exhaled with a satisfied smile.

"What," she asked with a smile, "are you wearing, anyway?"

Kaito shrugged helplessly. "It's, uh, a janitor's uniform."

"A janitor's uniform." She arched her eyebrows. "Picking up a second job? You short on money or something?"

"Or something," he chose, not wanting to get into details. "Hey, I need your help."

"Yeah?"

He leaned closer and lowered his voice a bit, though he wasn't really worried about anyone overhearing him with all the noise. "I need clearance to get into Blue Zone. You still have a guy for that?"

Mizuki backed off, squinting at him as if he was some strange and previously unknown species of native oceanic life, only now caught under a microscope. "Maybe. I thought you didn't want to get involved in stuff like that?"

Kaito couldn't keep a scowl off his face. "It's not for anything like... like what you're thinking," he told her. "I just need to get in and out of Blue Zone for a couple of days."

"Hey," Mizuki said, her voice softening. "Are you sure about this? If you get caught in there with a fake clearance..."

"I know, I know," Kaito said with a sigh. "I could get arrested. Lose my job, lose my clearance for Green Zone."

"That's if you're lucky." Mizuki studied him for a long moment. "I dunno, man. I'd feel real bad if you got caught."

"I won't," he pleaded. "Look, it's only for a couple of days. I only want to-"

Mizuki held up her hand. "Don't tell me. I don't want to know. Look, I can't get you what you want." Kaito felt as if his chest had plummeted down into the basement, and it must have showed in his eyes. "But I hear if you go hit up the repair shop across the way from the fish market, they're into some shady shit."

"The repair shop," Kaito repeated slowly.

"Yeah. Ummm, I think it's called 'Techs 4U,' like the number and then the letter."

"That's a stupid name," Kaito said with a laugh.

"Yeah, well, maybe you shouldn't got there," Mizuki said, shaking her head. "Like I said, not at all reputable."

"Right." Kaito smiled. "Thanks, Mizuki." With that, he turned and headed out of the bar into Red Zone.

The fish market stunk, and it didn't look like anything special. Everyone knew where it was because of the smell, and most businesses didn't want to be near it. It was a big, factory looking building without any kind of decorations or much in the way of signs, located near the Red Zone docks, which was where fishing subs came and went. The catch was unloaded and sorted there, packed, and then loaded onto ground transports at the loading docks. In one little corner of the building, facing the street, was a long, narrow room with a single counter.

The counter consisted of two registers and a long, glass case where fish and shellfish from the day's catch were put up for sale. Even in Red Zone, most people went to a market where you could get all kinds of food, not just fish, but if you were willing to put up with the smell, with the trip out of your way, and having to go somewhere else entirely to get whatever other ingredients you needed, you could get the cheapest, freshest seafood in Toshimayr. Because they'd often not had quite enough money when he was a child, Kaito had been there plenty of times, first with his mother when he was small, and then after he'd grown old enough by himself, sent with a list of things to pick up.

The repair shop was new, and Mizuki was right: he would never in a million years have stepped inside a place that looked like this if she hadn't told him to. He was pretty sure he remembered this storefront having been an ill-fated attempt at a sushi restaurant for a couple of months around the time he was thirteen; now, with only a glass door listing the hours and dirty stained walls which had acquired graffiti which was not arty and beautiful in an edgy way, but just filled with gang tags and obscenities. Only the flickering blue light of an 'open' sign picked out with neon tubes gave any reassurance that someone would be inside to greet a customer.

Kaito smelled mold as soon as he opened the door; the cheap drop ceiling was stained where the roof or the pipes had leaked, and missing three panels entirely, revealing the pipes and beams hidden above. There was one counter, and a ratty old carpet that seemed permanently stained by the tread of feet coming in the door. Behind the counter was a partition of unpainted drywall, and a door into the back where, presumably, computers were repaired. There was no one at the counter.

He stepped forward, looking for a bell or something to call whoever should be there, but there was nothing. He cooled his heels for a moment, looking around the shop and then loaded up *Elyon* to check the area for components. Then, he re-arranged his inventory for a bit and checked the market to see if anything good was posted at a reasonable rate. Then he closed *Elyon* and checked his chats to see whether anyone was talking about anything interesting.

After he'd been waiting over twenty minutes, Kaito decided he was going to have to either make a fuss or leave. Feeling like he was intruding, he walked around behind the counter toward the door in the drywall. He avoided the stool and garbage can pushed up against the counter, brought his hand up to the door, and rapped against it a couple of times.

He waited a moment, then rapped again, louder this time, and leaned in to raise his voice. "Hello? Is anyone here?" Kaito was just about to leave when the door opened, revealing a young man with most of his dark hair bleached blonde, a scruffy bit of growth on his chin that reminded Kaito of boys he'd known back in his school days, and an annoyed look on his face.

"What?" The kid leaned just far enough out the door to talk, but kept it pulled against his chest so that Kaito had a hard time seeing what was back there. "You need something fixed?"

Kaito shook his head. *How do I say that I want something illegal*, he wondered for a moment. *How do I even know this is the right person to speak to?* "No, not a repair," he began, somewhat aimlessly.

"Then why are you here," the kid asked, and the look in his eye told Kaito quite clearly that he was being regarded as an idiot. "No public bathroom. Go away."

"Mizuki sent me," Kaito said quickly, lowering his voice. "She said you could get me what I needed."

The boy looked at him for a long moment, narrowed his eyes, and then shook his head. "I don't know what you're talking about," he said slowly and carefully. "We do repairs here. Time for you to leave."

"No look," Kaito protested, shoving his arms through the space between door and frame as the kid tried to slam it closed. The impact stung his arm. "Mizuki. She sings at *Tako to Ama*, and I know she hangs around with people in *Shumokuzame*. I need clearance to get into Blue Zone. I can pay."

The kid tried to pull the door closed again, and Kaito wedged his whole body in. "You know her, right? Has a tattoo right here?" He stabbed a finger against his chest, right on the breastbone.

With a curse in Japanese, the kid finally opened the door. Kaito stepped through into a spartan room: besides the same stained carpet and unfinished drywalls, the only things in here were benches, work desks, and chairs, all loaded up with equipment. Behind him, the door shut and locked with a click.

"Blue Zone," the young man said with a scowl. "Fine. And then you get out of here, and never come back."

Kaito followed him over to a laptop on one of the desks. "Good. That's fine, yeah. OK, so how does this work? Do you need my hand?" He held up his right hand, in which the UCAF had long ago implanted an RFID Chip encased in glass.

"No." The kid shook his head, calling up programs on the screen.

"You don't use lenses?"

"Are you an idiot? Yeah, I should store my viruses and cracking software on the cloud," the kid said with a snort. "This isn't connected to anything except the RFID reader/ writer."

Kaito leaned in, curious, to watch programs running on the screen. Though he enjoyed playing AR games, and had since he was about ten years old, he'd always avoided anything more criminal than cheat codes for games.

"Standard UC government encryption," the kid said with a nod. "Not hard to crack. Those don't have enough spare memory for very much code, and they save the good encryption for more important things."

"More important things," Kaito repeated.

"Computer networks, databases, weapons systems, communications," the kid rattled off. "There. Reading." Within just a few seconds, an image of Kaito, along with his security clearances, address, place of employment and other information showed up on the laptop screen. "You already have Green Zone. Why you need Blue?"

Kaito opened his mouth to answer, but was interrupted. "Nevermind. I don't want to know," the kid told him. "There. Blue Zone access. Now," he said, standing up from the chair and closing the laptop, "Twenty thousand yen. And don't ever come back." Kaito counted out the crumpled up bills he'd pulled from his checking account before coming, and the kid accepted them. "Go! Go!" He shooed Kaito toward the door, and a moment later Kaito was walking out of the fish market area, looking down at his hand.

All that was left was to see if it worked. He yawned, swayed on his feet, and used his smart lenses to check the time. He blinked, and for the first time felt just how much his eyes stung. He hadn't slept in nearly twenty-four hours.

For a moment, he debated: should he go home, crash for

a bit, and then try the chip? Or just head back to the hospital now. *I told her I'd be back,* he remembered, and that was enough to make the decision.

Annie

Wake

June 27th, 2128

Annie's back hurt, and her side. She needed to pee, and that kept her from falling back asleep; she was also cold and uncomfortable because the sheets were scratchy and thin. She licked her dry lips and swallowed, and opened her eyes.

She was in a hospital.

There was a beeping machine next to her displaying her vital signs, and a stand from which dangled half a dozen clear plastic bags filled with fluids, all of them feeding into a network of tubes which led down to her left wrist. A curtain cut her bed off from the other half of the room, where the door must be, because she seemed to have gotten the window. The shades were drawn at the moment, but light from the artificial sun came in anyway.

She knew from the moment she woke that she wasn't on Mars, that she was still on Europa, because she felt too light, as if she could bounce off the bed if she rolled the wrong way and just keep falling up until she hit the ceiling.

She also knew because, passed out in the single chair they seemed to have left in her room, long legs stretched out and head leaned back against the wall, was Katakura Kairo. *You just got out of surgery*, she remembered him saying. *You're going to be fine.* And then she remembered holding her hand over her side, to try to slow the blood that was coming out, as she accepted the surrender of the terrorists manning that base. She let her eyes fall closed for a moment, turning her head into the pillow, and realized that it was luxuriously thick, with a soft cotton case. She peeked down at her legs, and saw that a knitted blanket had fallen down away from her chest. *He brought these for me*, Annie realized, and knew it was true because there wasn't anyone else on this entire moon - or even orbiting Jupiter - she could imagine doing that beside him. She fumbled for hospital bed's control wand, using it to tilt the frame down so that it was horizontal instead of at an angle, and managed to get a fistful of the knitted blanket pulled up over her as she gingerly turned onto her side. A stab of pain shot through her side and belly, but she didn't want to look yet. *Just a few more minutes and I'll get up*, she told herself, afraid to try getting to the bathroom.

She'd just closed her eyes when the door opened.

"Annie," a woman's voice murmured. "Are you awake?"

"Who's this guy," was the next thing she heard, and she opened her eyes and turned her head to see Seraphine and Nolan just coming in through the doorway.

"Hey," she said, fumbling for the remote control again. "Yeah, I'm awake. Hold on." Wincing, she used her left hand - the one hooked up to the IV, and that was sore too - to keep the knitted blanket from falling off of her as the bed lifted her back up.

Seraphine threw a glance in Kaito's direction as she stepped up to the side of the bed. "That's the boy," she asked with a smile. "Isn't he?"

Annie nodded, and though compared to everything else that had happened it must have been the least important thing, she felt herself blushing anyway. She hoped the room was dark enough that no one would notice - particularly Nolan.

"How are you feeling," Nolan asked, his expression unreadable to her.

"Sore," Annie admitted, wincing as she tried to sit up.

"Well, shrapnel will do that," Nolan admitted, at last giving her a tight smile.

"How long have I been out? No, wait, don't answer that yet," Annie said. "Seraphine, can you help me over to the bathroom?"

"Of course." Sera tucked her deep brown hair back out of her eyes, behind one ear, and bent down close to the bed so that Annie could hold onto her. Nolan took two quick steps over to where Kaito still slept and shook his shoulder with one hand.

"Hey. Wake up, we're stepping outside in the hall," Nolan said a bit louder than anyone had spoken before, but not unkindly. With a start, Kaito woke, eyes wide as he looked back and forth between the people he didn't know.

"It's OK," Annie told him as she swung her legs out from under the blanket. *How many years have humans been putting people in hospitals,* she thought as she felt cold air on her back, *and we still make them wear robes that open in back?* "I'll introduce everyone in a minute. Just wait outside while Sera helps me up, please?"

Reluctantly, Kaito nodded. "Yeah. Of course." He and Nolan stepped out into the hallway and let the door swing closed, and she wondered for a moment what they would talk about - or whether they would just stand there in awkward silence. The image made her laugh, but then that hurt too.

The steps to the bathroom, supported by Seraphine, seemed to hurt more than being wounded had. Annie couldn't stand up straight, but made her way hunched over, her back curved. It hurt to breathe too deeply, but finally she was in the bathroom, with the door closed, and sitting down. She stayed there for a moment after she was done, catching her breath, and then decided to see how bad it was. She gathered the gown to one side so that she could look down at her belly, where she'd looked and seen the wine-red blood and then felt a light-headed shock of terror.

There were four wounds, ugly and raw. None of them were long slices, but punctures: the shrapnel that had torn into her must have been only small pieces of metal. Each was stitched shut, and covered over with surgical glue. The skin around them had already bruised into horrible shades of yellow and purple. For a moment she thought of what she used to look like, how her skin would never again be the same as before, and she felt guilty and sad in the way of a child who has accidentally broken a toy: *look what I've done.* She swallowed, blinked a few times, and then used the handrail next to the toilet to stand up.

"Sera," she called out through the door, "Is there any underwear out there? Any of my clothes?"

A few moments of noises, of someone rifling through drawers. "I don't see anything," Seraphine answered, her voice close to the bathroom door. "I can bring you some things from your quarters, the next time I come."

"Yeah, that would be nice." Annie pushed the door open, and Seraphine helped her back to the bed. Between the two of them, they'd just finished arranging her, the gown and the bedding so that she was covered, warm, and as close to comfortable as she was going to get when there was a knock on the door.

"Lieutenant Commander Winters," came the voice of a man she didn't recognize.

"Come in."

A UCAF fleet Corpsman stepped through the door, with a tablet under one arm. He gave her a broad smile, and introduced himself as both Nolan and Kaito tried to find space in the room with him. "Hospital Corpsman First Class Novak," he began. "How are you feeling?"

"Sore," she admitted. "It hurts, Doc." All Corpsman were 'Doc,' in a tradition that went as far back as Old Earth.

"It's going to," he confirmed. "Your abdomen was pierced by four pieces of metal, propelled into you when your cockpit was damaged. We call this penetrating abdominal trauma, and it's the sort of thing we often see in injuries that result from IEDs. The danger with this type of injury is what sort of internal damage might have been suffered by your organs. In your case," he continued as she began to feel a bit faint, "A laparotomy confirmed that none of the pieces of shrapnel penetrated any organs. The surgeon removed the shrapnel, stitched you up, and gave you a litre or so of blood. You're going to be on antibiotics and painkillers for a while, and we're going to keep you for a couple of days for observation, but I don't see any reason you can't be out sometime this week."

The air emptied out of Annie's lungs. *I'm not going to die.* "Sometime this week," she repeated. "What else?"

"We're going to take it slow on introducing food to your system," Novak continued. "Clear liquids today, and we'll see how that goes. You've got a clicker for Dilaudid, so if the pain is a problem, use it. Don't worry about taking too much, the computer won't let you. If you start to feel sick or nauseous, call someone immediately."

She nodded. "Alright."

"Other than that, rest up," he told her with a brusque smile. "Any questions?"

"When will I be cleared for active duty," Annie asked.

"That's not something to think about just yet," Novak said with a professional evenness of tone that told her it was a question he heard all the time. "Concentrate on getting well, and then we'll see."

She didn't say anything. *Will they send me home,* she wondered. *More than three years of my life gone, to be here for only a couple of weeks before getting a medical discharge?* She was aware that other people in the room were talking, but couldn't really focus on it until the Corpsman had left. Finally, she shook herself. Kaito had withdrawn to the window, where he was returning Nolan's stare evenly. Seraphine was just closing the door again.

Time for introductions, I suppose. "Kaito, this is Lieutenant Richard Nolan," she began, nodding to her second in command. "And Lieutenant Junior Grade Serafine Moreau. Nolan, Sera, this is Katakura Kaito; he was the pilot that brought us down on the *Nautilus*," she finished lamely.

"It's a pleasure to meet you," Nolan said formally, stepping across the room to extend his hand to Kaito.

"*Konnichiwa*," Kaito responded, uncoiling himself from the wall to shake Nolan's hand. She was surprised to realize that Kaito was actually taller than Nolan, though of course

Nolan was much more solidly built. The two men held the hand grip for a moment, and it occurred to her they might be doing that stupid thing she'd seen men do where they tried to break each other's finger bones as some kind of show of dominance. Luckily, Seraphine interrupted them, sidling up to Nolan and inserting herself between them.

"It's nice to finally meet you," Sera told Kaito with a smile. "But we should be going - we've got to report for a briefing."

"What's going on," Annie asked before she could stop herself, desperate for some kind of idea of what had happened while she'd been unconscious.

"Word is we're going to work our way through every one of those repair facilities," Sera answered before Nolan stopped her with a hard look, a quick jerk of the head, and a hand on her shoulder.

They suspect more are being used as insurgent bases, Annie realized. *And there will be more fighting. My people will be in combat, and I won't be there with them.* "Be careful," she said out loud. "I don't want to get out of here and find out you've trashed all of our Shells."

"Look who's talking," Sera teased her with a smile, leaning down to give her a hug. She lowered her voice. "What you did was really brave," Sera admitted. "We didn't lose anyone in that engagement, and it was because of you. Anyway, I'll be back with a bunch of your things. Maybe this afternoon."

As Sera stepped over to the door, Nolan approached the bed.

"You're in command," Annie asked him.

Nolan nodded. "For the moment. Don't worry, I'll bring everybody home." He hesitated. "Word is the Commander is going to come down and see you sometime today or tomorrow."

Annie remembered standing in Commander Clavinger's office after the bombing at the bridge, and what he had said to her: *...by the time the next transport comes around, you can be goddamn sure I will have covered my ass enough that no one will be able to say shit when I relieve you of command and send you back to daddy.*

"That's very kind of him," she told Nolan with a straight face, suddenly feeling very tired. *That's it, then. This will be all the excuse he needs. At least it won't be for a mistake I've made: he can just give me a medical discharge, and that will be the end of it. There won't be any political mess for him.*

Nolan gave her a long, considering look. "The operation was a success. There weren't any casualties in our team. He'll probably pin a medal on you and send you home."

"That's not why I did it," she protested.

"I figured." Nolan shook his head. "Most officers get visited by the Good Idea Fairy, they get the men under them killed. I'll give you this: you didn't throw away the lives of your men. But Winters, just because you went in the opposite direction doesn't make what you did the right thing. The job of an Officer is to think, to lead the soldiers under them. You can't do that if you die in the first thirty seconds of the fight."

Annie felt heat rising in her cheeks again, for the second time in less than fifteen minutes. "I guess next time I'll have to make sure not to get shot," she tried to joke.

"Yeah," Nolan agreed, although they both knew it was extremely unlikely there would be a 'next time.' He turned to the door. "I'll come by and visit when I can. You'll get sick of seeing my face before too long, I bet."

"I'm already sick of it," she teased him back. "But come by anyway."

And then it was just her and Kaito left alone in the room.

In the silence, Annie closed her eyes for a moment. "Do I remember you being here," she asked Kaito when she opened them again, "Last night? Right after I got here?"

"Yeah," Kaito answered, coming over from the window with his hands in his pockets. After a moment, he reached out and positioned the chair so that he could sit next to her. "Yeah, I was here. You woke up for a couple of minutes, and I had to go. I'm sorry I couldn't stay - I got back as soon as I could."

Annie smiled and reached out for his hand; when she found it, and her skin touched his, she felt like the fusion torches on her Shell had just kicked in at the end of a drop, and her stomach was being pressed up into her chest by gravity. "Thank you," she told him in a small voice, and then continued, "I wasn't sure whether it was a dream, or... I don't know," she admitted. "But I thought you didn't have clearance for Blue Zone? How did you get here? How did you even know I was hurt?"

He smiled sheepishly. "I was killing time on the *Nautilus* after a run up to the surface," he explained, "So that I could have a minute alone to pick up a rare Component that spawns by the docks, with no one paying attention. So by the time I came out, they'd already cleared the hallways to bring the wounded through, but I didn't hear the announcement."

"So basically," Annie chided him gently, "You were so wrapped up in playing your video game you went somewhere you weren't supposed to be."

"Yeah," he admitted. "And then I saw them wheeling soldiers through on stretchers, and I knew you said you'd be out of touch for a while. So I looked for you..."

Annie's smile slipped off her face. "I'm sorry," she whispered. "It looked bad?"

Kaito nodded. "Pretty bad, yeah. But I couldn't follow you, so I knew I had to find a way to get into Blue Zone, to get to the hospital."

This was the part that worried Annie. "What did you do, Kaito?"

"I went to see a guy," he answered, somewhat evasively. "Look, it's probably better if you don't know the details. But as far as the security checkpoints are concerned, I'm cleared to come into Blue Zone."

That's exactly what I'm worried about. Annie squeezed

his hand. "You shouldn't be here," she told him. "I mean, I'm happy that you came, I want you here -" she hadn't realized she was going to say that until it came out - "but I don't want you to get in trouble. You could get arrested."

"I won't," Kaito told her. "Anyway, it's not like I'm coming here to commit a crime or something. I'm sure they've got a lot of more important people to go after than me."

Annie bit her lip. *I should tell him not to come back*, she knew. *It would be safer for him. And they'll be sending me home, soon, anyway.* "Be careful," was all she said, and suddenly she was very tired, and the wound in her stomach was throbbing worse than before. She fumbled for the clicker and hit it a few times, then found the remote and lowered the bed until it was horizontal again. "Come over here," she told Kaito quietly.

He looked doubtfully at the hospital bed, at the tubes leading to her wrist and the medical equipment clustered about. "Are you sure," he asked her.

"Mmm-hmm." She rolled onto her side - not the side where she was hurt - and lifted the hospital sheets and knit blanket to let him in. Just when she thought he wasn't going to do it, she heard Kaito kick off his shoes, and then felt his weight shifting the thin mattress as he got onto the bed and under the covers with her. Once she felt his warmth behind her and his arm around her, she snuggled back into him.

The pain medication must have hit shortly after, because within seconds she was asleep.

It ended up not being that day, but the next, that Commander Clavinger visited Annie in the hospital. Kaito wasn't there - which was a good thing - because she'd told him that she didn't want him to take time off from his job just to hang around the hospital room with her, especially when she was drifting in and out of sleep because of the pain medication. "Just come and visit me when you're done with your shift," she'd told him. "That way you can bring me something besides hospital food to eat."

Clavinger came in the middle of the afternoon, rapping on the door in a quick, sharp knock that was a perfect fit for his brusque personality. The door was swinging inward before she'd even had time to finish saying 'Come in," and Annie was grateful that she was already in bed and covered up with both sheets and blanket.

"At ease," the Commander told her, as if he expected her to leap up out of the hospital bed without his permission to stand down. "How are you holding up," he continued in a gruff sort of way that he must have imagined made him seem down to earth to the enlisted men. It did nothing for Annie.

"Doc says it's looking good, sir," she said, blinking away drowsiness and using the controls to raise her bed up to a sitting position. "No signs of infection. Should be ready for duty again before too long."

The feet of the sole chair provided for visitors scraped across the floor as Clavinger dragged it closer - but not too close - and took a seat. "That's not going to happen, Lieutenant Commander," he told her quietly.

Annie's throat went dry, and she swallowed. "Sir-" she began, but he cut her off.

"This is a good thing," he told her. "Look. You go home with a medal, and an honorable discharge. You and your father get to spin this as a story of heroism. You move on to that political career you were using this to get to. I get a unit commander who's got combat experience, and neither one of us has to ever see the other one again. Hell, we can even part as friends. Have a drink together before you ship out, take some pictures or something for the media."

"That's not what I want," she protested. "I didn't join the UCAF because I wanted to be a politician, I did it because I wanted to do my duty!"

"Your duty," Clavinger repeated.

"Yes! For my entire life, for as long as I can remember, I've thought about Old Earth," Annie said, the words tumbling out of her like water over rock. "That if they'd ever just managed to get their act together under one government, maybe it would still be here, still be a place we could go, instead of a lump of glowing rock. And now we're all that's left, the Colonies, and yeah, I know who my father is, and if I learned anything from watching him it's just how close we still are to *not making it.* The colonies weren't ready for Earth to collapse. Getting enough food and water and air everywhere it needs to go is one constant crisis, and I've watched him try to deal with it my whole life. So yes, I signed up, because these people, these terrorists or whatever they want to call themselves, they'd rather throw everything we have away than just work together!"

"Old Earth," Clavinger said after a long moment. "Only people younger than me use that phrase. For us, it's just Earth, like it always was." He looked up at the ceiling for a moment, then back down at her. "Maybe your heart was in the right place. Maybe I didn't give you enough credit for that," he said with a sigh. "But it doesn't change anything."

Desperate to be heard, Annie leaned forward, even though it hurt her belly. "Sir, if you give me a chance-"

"Listen." Clavinger waved his hand and cut Annie off. "This is the best thing that could happen. You think your father wants you dead? Or a vegetable after being caught too close to an IED? You think that's the best way you can serve the UCAF? The United Colonies?" He stabbed a finger at her as he made his points. "Most people don't have the advantages you have. You want to help us out, here? Then take your medal and your discharge and go home a war hero and run for office and then knock a couple of politicians' heads together. They don't know what's going on at colonies like Europa, and they don't give two shits how many letters I write home telling parents or wives that a soldier is never coming back."

He sat back and sighed. "You think any of the rest of us have a chance in hell of maybe someday being one of the people making the decisions? Never. But you do. I can get any jarhead with good reflexes and a socket in their skull to pilot that Shell.

189

Go do what the rest of us can't do."

Annie subsided. Her anger drained out of her, replaced by a sort of numb feeling. *But that's not what I want*, she could hear herself saying, and it sounded so childish she couldn't say the words out loud. Her stomach was hurting again, and suddenly she wanted very much for the Commander to go away and to let her sleep.

Clavinger stood up. "My official report will say you're a god-damned hero, and I'm going to pin every medal on you I can come up with. When the next transport comes, you're shipping back to Mars, as long as the doctors say you're safe to travel." He reached for the door, opened it, and light from the hall spilled into her room.

"You want some advice? Rest up. When they let you back on your feet and out of here, enjoy the city. Buy some souvenirs or something. Take your soldiers out and treat them to a big dinner and a lot of drinks, and then get your bags packed." He looked her over one last time, and she could only turn away. "Get your strength back. My secretary will let you know when the award ceremony will be. Oh, and I've asked for permission to use your real name," he told her, half out into the hall, "For the ceremony and for any press releases."

"Yes sir," she said quietly, lowering the bed back to a horizontal position and wrapping her fingers through the holes in the crocheted blanket Kaito had brought for her that first day. Once the door was closed, and she was alone again in the dark, she swallowed hard, tried to blink away tears and then had to use her hand to wipe them away instead.

Annie was trying a walk up and down the hall outside her room when the old man came by to visit her.

It was the day after the Commander had visited, and she was feeling a bit more like herself - wearing some clothes that Sera had brought her, underneath the gown they kept insisting she wear, helped with that. The pain didn't seem as bad this afternoon, so she'd held off on using the clicker to get herself really high, and decided that if she was ever going to get out of here and maybe convince Commander Clavinger to change his mind, she was going to have to get herself back into some kind of fighting shape.

The old man was wearing a rumpled suit and a knit hat with a 'DSI' logo on it, and carrying a wooden box of some kind under his arm. It wasn't until he accosted her while she paused to get her breath, one arm on a windowsill and the other clutching the wheeled stand her IV bags hung from, that she recognized him: he was the Europan who had left Commander Clavinger's office right before she'd been chewed out for the bombing at the bridge.

"Lieutenant Commander Winters!" The old man's tone was the sort of obnoxiously upbeat sound she associated with birds which insisted on singing outside your window before dawn. "I am so pleased to see you walking!"

Annie pulled herself up straight, took another two shaky breaths, and tried to smile. "Hello sir," she acknowledged him. "I don't think we've ever been introduced." *And now please go away so I can crawl back to my bed and pass out.*

"We have not," he agreed. "I am Date Kunari, and we have not one, but two mutual friends. Commander Clavinger, who told me you were in the hospital while we were having lunch today, and-"

"Katakura Kaito," she finished for him. *'Old Man Date felt responsible, being Dad's boss and all, so as soon as I was old enough to work he gave me a job,'* she remembered Kaito telling her the night they'd first slept together. Her cheeks felt hot, and she hoped the old man didn't notice. "You're his boss."

"*Hai,*" Date confirmed. "May I help you back to your room?" He offered her an arm, and she was ashamed to feel relieved when she took it. Together, they made their way back to her room, step by slow, agonizing step.

"*Arigatou gozaimasu,*" she thanked him when they had finally gotten her situated back on her bed. "I think I'm not going to be good company in a moment, though," she told him, still hoping he would go away, "once I have some of the pain medication."

"Don't use the clicker just yet," Date requested, pulling up a chair. "You may find that if your mind is occupied by something else, you don't need quite as much medication. And the less you have, the better: for all the things we've discovered out here, we still don't have good painkillers which aren't highly addictive."

Her fingers itched on the controls, but for some reason she held off, even though her belly was burning. "You're here to occupy my mind," she asked with a half smile.

Date Kunari placed his wooden box on the tray that swung over her bed. "*Hai*," he said again, opening up a tray in the side of the box and removing two small cloth bags: he passed one to her, and she saw it was filled with small white stones. "Have you ever played *Go* before?"

"No," Annie admitted.

"It is a game of strategy," Date began to explain as she carefully held a stone in her hand and examined it. It was polished smooth, with a clearly visible grain. "They are made of clamshells," he answered her unspoken question. "Ground and polished by hand."

"I didn't think there were clams on Europa yet," she objected.

"No," the old man agreed. "This set was brought from Earth, by my grandfather. Even then, it was expensive: made by some of the last artisans to make the board and the pieces in the old way. See," He indicated the wood board, with a grid cut into the top. "Cut with the blade of a sword."

Annie abruptly realized how much this set must be worth, how valuable it was. "I'm not sure I should be holding this," she admitted.

Date smiled. "It was made to be used. The people who crafted it wanted it to be appreciated and enjoyed. Don't worry. You will not break it. As I said, it is a game of strategy. Good for a military mind. A game of claiming territory and turning enemy lines."

With seeming carelessness, the old man placed a black piece on the board - somewhere between the edge and the center, and slightly off toward one corner. "Black begins by placing a stone, and then we alternate placing stones."

"Anywhere," she asked, weighing the white stone in her hand.

"Anywhere," he agreed. "But wait. The object is to surround the enemy's stones."

Annie's mind began to work. "So if I had two next to each other," she quickly placed two white stones at adjoining intersections on the grid, "It would take you six stones to surround them, instead of only four. So a larger formation is safer."

"*Hai*," Date said with a nod and a slight smile. "There is much more to understand, but it is best to learn by playing."

"Alright." Annie pulled the two stones she had used as an example back, dropped one into her pouch, and considered. *If I play too close to his stone*, she realized, *He'll already have an advantage in numbers. Better if I make him come to me.* She placed her stone about three spaces out from the edge of the board which faced her, diagonally opposite to the single black stone.

Over the next few turns, Date Kunari's confident, seemingly effortless moves alternated with her own: slow, tentative, and as the game progressed nearly agonized. Somehow, by the time half a dozen stones were on the board it seemed like he controlled two thirds of the territory. When she tried to push on his borders, she found herself surrounded, out-thought and out-fought repeatedly. Eight stones were captured in one formation, calmly deposited off to one side by the old man, and then ten minutes later another half dozen. She was losing, quickly and with accelerating speed, Annie realized, and she had to do *something*.

On her next turn, Annie chose the section of the old man's territory where there seemed to be the most open space, and placed a white stone right in the middle of it.

"Bold," Date commented, the first words either of them had spoken since her last question about the rules some fifteen minutes before. He placed a black stone near the invasion.

"I had to change something," Annie admitted. "I was losing. I couldn't keep doing the same things and expect that to change." She placed another white stone, trying to carve out a large enough space that she could keep her new formation alive.

"It is remarkable," the old man told her as he placed another stone, "How few people ever realize that. In this game, and in life. What is the saying? 'If you do what you've always done, you will get what you've always got.'"

"I feel like you're implying something there," Annie said with a light laugh. "Like next time I should not do the things that landed me in the hospital?"

"Maybe," Date equivocated as they rapidly began to place stones, she trying to keep her invasion alive, he trying to cut off her options. "Maybe I am making a comment on the United Colonies occupation," he proposed, and all of a sudden she felt like they were in deep water. Like the current of this conversation had pulled her somewhere unexpected.

"What do you mean," she asked, her hand hesitating above the board. *Where was I about to place this stone?*

"After twenty years of occupation," Date remarked off-handedly, "There are still regular insurgent strikes on Europa. How long, do you think, will the UCAF continue to do the same things and expect different results?"

Annie put the stone down somewhere, just to do it, but was pretty sure it wasn't placed where she had originally intended. "Once we've won over enough of the population, and captured the insurgent leadership, things will settle down," she told him.

Date placed a black stone, and she realized he was only a move away from capturing her entire formation. "The insurgent leadership is not separate from the rest of the population," he pointed out. "Whoever leads *Shumokuzame* - and the UCAF has captured or killed dozens of their leaders, over the past two decades - those people have fathers and mothers, sisters and brothers, children and friends. Will not some of those people simply step in to take the place of those you have eliminated?"

"Is this what you talk about with the Commander," she asked him, her voice harder than she had expected. Annie placed a white stone desperately, trying to find an escape.

"No," Date admitted. "No, Michael would not appreciate such a conversation. He has been here for too long; he can no longer see clearly what is placed before his eyes. But you - you haven't been here for so very long, yet, and you must be open to other points of view if you have become Kaito's..." he let a beat of silence pass before finishing his sentence, and Annie blushed: "-friend. You must have taken classes in Military History. What was the outcome of the American War in Vietnam? The Russian occupation of Afghanistan? Or the British effort to suppress rebellion in America, for example."

"I've heard this argument before," Annie said with a sigh. "But for every example of a guerilla or insurgent force eventually driving out a foreign occupier that you can cite, I can give an example of the opposite. Should we discuss the effective integration of Roman Provinces into the Empire? Furthermore, there are several drastic differences between any of those situations and the situation here on Europa, or even over at Callisto, Ganymede, or Io. Vietnam, Afghanistan, the American Colonies - they were all capable of supporting themselves independently, of conducting trade with their neighbors. Europa *needs* resources and materials which it can't produce on world. Europa," she continued, "Is also incredibly easy to blockade. You have three Icebreaker Stations where orbital elevators can move goods on or off world, and that's it. Controlling those stations means controlling Europa."

A white stone rested in her palm as she continued, the game forgotten. "And finally, you're ignoring the most important thing. Unlike most of your examples, this isn't some kind of selfish imperialism or colonialism. You know what happened to Old Earth! The colonies can't survive independently - they aren't ready! They're barely able to survive right now, all together."

Date watched her, patiently, calmly. "Are you sure?"

"Yes!" Annie sat back. "Yes, I am. I've had a very good view of just how difficult it's been to make sure all the colonies have what they need: clean water, clean air, enough citrus fruits to prevent scurvy, enough calcium in their diet to combat bone density loss, replacement parts for the computers that run environmental systems, fuel production, keeping enough transport ships running to move everything... I spent my entire childhood watching this turn my father into an old man!"

Across the game board from her, Date nodded. "A difficult task, to be sure. And yet, as the collapse of communist economies at the end of the twentieth century indicated, a healthy and well managed capitalist economy is more efficient than one tightly controlled by a government. Which brings us to the justification Luna and Mars used twenty years ago."

"You say justification as if it's an excuse," Annie argued. "But it's a matter of survival. Old Earth destroyed itself with nuclear weapons because it was made up of hundreds of nation states. We are all that's left. We can't make the same mistake they did; we've passed the point where it's acceptable for different factions of the human race to threaten each other with mutual destruction."

"And so everything is justified for the survival of the species," Date said with a sigh.

"Yes," Annie nearly shouted, slapping her stone down on the board hard enough to rattle all of the other pieces. "If that isn't a good enough reason, I don't know what is. If we don't survive, than there's no point in anything else, is there?"

As if he'd been waiting for her, Date placed a single black stone and captured her entire invading formation. "Perhaps not," he admitted. "But is survival alone enough to justify existence?"

He leaned forward, fixing her eyes with his. "Your subordinate, who was in a room down the hall. The one who did not wake. She was alive, but that was all. You signed the order to remove her from life support, *hai*?"

Annie slumped back onto the hospital bed. "I think you should go now."

With swift movements of his hands, Date Kunari began to gather the stones and sweep them into their two cloth bags, efficiently clearing the board. "Yes. The game is finished. You did well, for someone who had never played before, but the outcome was never really in doubt."

Once he'd packed up the board and stood, Annie used the controls to lower the bed back down. Suddenly, she felt very tired. "Thank you for coming to see me," she told him, more out of politeness than any genuine emotion. She clicked for more painkillers.

"It was good to meet you, Lieutenant Commander," Date told her from the door. "You are, as they say, cut from different cloth than the Commander. Please accept my best wishes for a speedy recovery."

As tired as she was, and even with the painkillers to push her to the edge of unconsciousness, she lingered there for a long while, uncomfortably turning on the bed, but unable to sleep.

Kaito

Complete Control

June 29th, 2128

Kaito woke up with a horrible pain in his back.

He tried to reach for where it hurt with his right hand, even before he opened his eyes, but his hand came up short, caught and held by restraints. Grimacing and working his jaw carefully, he opened his eyes.

He was in light so dim that he couldn't see the room, seated in a hard chair, with his hands fixed behind his back by loops of some kind of plastic.

"He's awake," a man said from the darkness, and a bright light turned on, shining directly into his eyes. Kaito squinted, trying to recoil back from the harsh glare, but all he could do was turn his head to one side.

"Where am I," he asked, pulling with his arms at the bindings.

"Shut up," a second voice said, behind him. "Where did you get your forged security clearances?"

Kuso, Kaito swore silently. *Shit.* As the dim of unconsciousness fled, memory returned. He remembered getting off of his shift at work, stopping by the apartment to change into clean clothes, and then heading over to the security checkpoint for Blue Zone to go and visit Annie. The MP at the checkpoint had frowned, and asked him to hold on a moment, and then... he tried to remember. A sharp burning pain in his back, and that was it.

"I don't know what you're talking about," he said as evenly as he could, and then a fist slammed into his stomach. Kaito sucked in a breath; the way his hands were bound behind him prevented his body from hunching over the way it wanted to.

"Don't bother trying to lie to us, kid," the first voice said evenly. "We're going to get it all anyway."

"I think it's time," the second, harsher voice spoke up from behind him. "Lace him."

Lace? Hands pulled his head back, one on each side of his skull. In front of him, a figure stepped into the light: a man, *gaijin*, his features hard and worn, his right hand raised in a latex glove, holding a kind of needlegun, not unlike what you would see at a tattoo parlour.

"Don't move," the man in front of him said quietly. "You don't want me to slip and put this needle up your eye or something."

And then he understood, every muscle in his body tensing as Kaito strained against the plastic loops binding his hands, against the iron grip clutching his head and holding it in place. *Lace.* He'd heard about it, of course; everyone had, usually some time during their school years when kids were telling horror stories about what the UCAF would do to anyone they caught helping terrorists. Back then, a much younger, if not quite more innocent, Mizuki had delighted in concocting drawn out details about exactly how the neural mesh was inserted into the skull: her favorite theory was that the UCAF used something like a can-opener to slice around the perimeter of the skull and lift the top right off. They'd all known that was garbage, of course, even at ten years old, but they'd also all seen Toru-chan, Mrs. Tanaka's middle-aged son.

"He was a soldier," Mizuki had whispered to Kaito and the other children as they watched Toru-chan playing with his toy trains on the steps of his mother's apartment in Red Zone. "When they caught him, they put the lace in his head. And now he can't think. He's just like a little kid, forever."

Now, in the darkness, the needle hovered in front of him, picked out and gleaming in the bright light. The *gaijin* UCAF man smiled as he watched Kaito's eyes. "You know what this is," the man said. "Good. That will make this easier. I'm going to insert this needle under your left cheek," he explained calmly, "And push it up until it reaches your brain. Once it's in far enough, I will pull the trigger, and that will inject you with the mesh electronics. It will coil about your brain, and after approximately three hours, the neural lace will be ready to begin wirelessly interfacing with our systems. At that point," he continued, "We will be able to directly stimulate your brain."

The needle lowered, and Kaito froze as the very tip touched the skin of his face, just beneath his cheekbone. His arms and hands and legs began to tremble, and he felt a tear leaking slowly down from one eye. "Did you know," the man with the needle explained softly, "The part of your brain that receives pain signals from neurotransmitters is the thalamus? Easy, now." He slipped the needle into Kaito's face.

Kaito screamed.

If his head hadn't been held tightly, he would have probably broken the needle off inside him, trying to get away from its burning, relentless pressure as it moved slowly upward behind his cheek into his head. He wasn't really aware of what he was screaming, or of anything else that might be happening around him, except for that unrelenting *push* deeper and deeper into him. Awareness of the rest of his body - of his wrists pulled so tight against the plastic bonds holding them in place that they bled - was pushed aside by the all-encompassing pain.

It lasted forever; he wished he would die, just to make it stop. When they finally pulled the needle out and released his head, he closed his eyes against the light and slouched forward until all of his weight hung by his shoulders. Heavy, broken sobs wracked his body; his face was wet with sweat, tears, and blood from the puncture in his cheek, and the whole mixture dripped down to his lips where he tasted it. As the pain dulled to a throb, and it occurred to him that he wasn't going to die quite yet, he realized that his pants were warm and wet and recognized the smell of urine.

The light turned off. A door clicked shut.

"Hello," he rasped out of cracked lips and a hoarse throat. How long had he been screaming for anyway? "Is there anyone here?"

The room was silent.

It will coil about your brain, and after approximately three hours, the neural lace will be ready to begin wirelessly interfacing with our systems.

"Three hours," he whispered to himself. *Three hours until they ask me questions again, and this time...* he shuddered, choking back another sob. Would he end up like Tanaka Toru? His mother spending the rest of her life, her old age, caring for the mindless shell that had been her only son?

In a video game, or in an action movie, he would have used the time to escape. He tried, at first; but whatever the plastic loops were around his wrists, they were too tight to slip out of. He had thought that maybe the blood would act as a kind of lubricant, but no; and then he remembered that sometimes the chiseled hero would dislocate a thumb, but he couldn't figure out how to do that, and doubted he'd be strong enough anyway.

Kaito's legs were restrained, as well, loops around his ankles binding them to the legs of the chair. He tried to rock the chair so that he could fall over, and then maybe push himself around the room in search of something sharp, but it didn't move no matter how he threw his weight; it must have been bolted down.

Was it actually three hours they left him there alone, or was it more? There was no way to tell. He'd tried counting, but as the headache built into a pounding, throbbing mass behind his eyes, he lost track of the numbers. He might have slept, at one point; it was hard to say, in the dark. Shapes swam across his eyes, and whether he opened or closed the lids made no difference. He wondered at first if he was seeing something, dim and indistinct in the dark room, that he could use to escape, and then he wondered if they'd left his smart lenses in to malfunction, but finally he decided that he was just hallucinating in the darkness, his mind trying to recognize images that didn't exist.

Hours or days later - he was hungry, and wet, and cold and in pain - the door clicked open again. Light spilled in from outside, for a moment, and then again they turned on that glaring bulb that pointed directly at his face. It blinded him, and by the time he was done blinking away the pain after hours in the darkness, they'd closed the door and there was no chance to look into whatever hallway or antechamber was out there.

"Let's start with something easy," the sharp faced *gaijin* who'd put the needle into Kaito said, enunciating his words carefully. "What is your name? There's no sense lying, we already know who you are."

Kaito thought about that for a moment. They'd had plenty of time to check his fingerprints or retinas or whatever other kind of biometrics they cared to, and his security clearances - both the real and the forged ones - had all been under his real name. "Katakura Kaito," he coughed, then whispered hoarsely. He had to say it twice before it was clear.

"Good." The pain receded, lost in a warm floating numbness that reminded him of when he'd been anesthetized in the hospital. "You see," the second voice told him kindly, "When you answer truthfully, I will dull the pain. I will make your brain release chemicals which will cause you to feel good. Euphoric."

"Now," said the man who had used the needle, "Let's try something a little more difficult. Give us the name of the person who forged those clearances for you."

"I don't know," Kaito said, able to speak more clearly this time. Immediately the pain returned, trebled, multiplied tenfold, and he realized the agonized screaming ringing throughout the dark room was coming from him. The pain crested like a wave, and began to recede.

"And when you do not cooperate," explained the *gaijin* in front of him, "We will instead cause your brain to experience pain. This is much more efficient than the sort of old fashioned, barbaric torture techniques used in the past. No permanent harm will be inflicted on your body; there is no risk of death, or infection, or sickness. We can do this over, and over, and over again, as long as we like, and there is no escape for you whatsoever. Long ago," he continued, "a prisoner could at least wish for death; to slip away on their pain like a receding tide, and escape what was being done to their body. You will find no such release."

Kaito found, to his surprise, that he was crying again.

"Now, give us the name of the person who forged those clearances for you."

"I really don't know the name," he gasped. "It was a kid. Younger than me. He never said his name, and I didn't ask. Blonde. Scruffy face."

There was a heartbeat of silence, and he realized the two men were conferring over his answer. *Of Course. The Lace let's them monitor my brain activity, as well,* he realized. *They'll know if I lie.*

"Tell us where you met this person, then."

"Red Zone," Kaito said. *That isn't giving anything away,* he had time to think before a wave of pain hit. "I'm telling the truth!"

"*Where* in Red Zone," the man in front of him clarified with the tone of an adult speaking to a troublesome child. "Be as specific and clear as you can be."

Kaito hesitated. There were a million places in Red Zone where you could go to get hacked clearances, if you had the money and knew where to look. But if they went to Techs 4U, across from the fish market, and caught that kid and questioned him... would it lead them back to Mizuki? *It might,* he admitted to himself. *I used her name. She's the one who told me about them.*

He thought about the girl he'd known since they were both toddlers on the same street. He tried to summon the anger he'd felt toward her a month ago, before he'd met Annie, right after he'd caught Mizuki kissing that guy. *So we broke up,* he realized after a moment. *That doesn't mean she deserves this.*

To be where I am now. I can't do that to her.

"Somewhere between your nose and my ass," he said, and that was the last clear thought he had for a while, because if the pain had been a wave, cresting and receding, now it was a riptide, dragging him down and bashing him against the rocks on the ocean floor, again and again, not letting up as he struggled for breath. Finally, it dropped him, and he lay in the chair limp and useless.

"We can do this over, and over, and over again," the hard-faced man said. "You may think you've got courage, or that you've got someone to protect, but the real, honest truth is that eventually, everyone breaks. No one can take what we're going to do to you. So, you have a choice. Save yourself a lot of pain, and answer our questions. Or suffer more than you ever imagined possible, and in the end, we'll find out whatever it is you're hiding just the same. You can't actually save anyone; you can only hurt yourself."

"It's ok to be selfish," the man behind Kaito whispered into his ear. "Just this once, think of yourself." The warmth flooded him then, pushing the pain away, and Kaito wanted nothing more than to let himself float away on it. "Tell us where, and you can keep feeling this."

For a long moment, Kaito hesitated. Then, taking a deep breath, he began to speak. "It was across from the fish market," he began. "It looked cheap and dirty..."

Annie

Break

June 29th, 2128

Annie's Shell flew up, propelled by her fusion torches. When the jets had taken her twenty feet or so above the top of the four story office building before her, she cut them, spread her wings, and feathered the directional torches used for maneuvering in zero-g. With a crunch, the feet of her Shell ground down into the roof of the building. She waited to see if the roof would hold her weight, ready to light the jets off again if the building began to collapse beneath her, but when it seemed like everything would hold, instead she moved inward, toward the center of the roof.

Somewhere out in the city, both Sera and Gavril were hunting her. The building would keep her from being seen from street level, because the edges of the roof blocked line of sight, but there were a lot of other ways a Shell was equipped to find someone. Outnumbered, she needed to strike first, from surprise, to have any chance of coming out on top.

With a mental command, she launched two autonomous drones, each loaded with surveillance equipment and programmed to spiral outward and upward from the launch point while sending data to her computer systems. *Mistake number one*, she realized, already angry with herself. *I should have launched those somewhere else, a block away, and then moved before taking my position.* With a few more commands, her sensors were scanning for heat signatures - the telltale mark of a fusion engine. In the meantime, she kept her Shell still, not moving, not using her torches at all, trying to keep her reactor as cool as possible. If she was lucky...

There. I've got you. Was it Serafine, or Gavril? It didn't matter. Two blocks north, a heat signature moving. Annie directed one of her drones in that direction, and mentally selected the AVM-2 ground to ground missile rack she'd loaded onto her Shell's left shoulder - not her usual choice, and certainly not the sort of thing suitable for suppressing riots or providing security, which was still their theoretical function here on Europa. She waited for a second; two seconds...

And then her drone fed her the target data. From the street below it, a minigun opened up, and she knew that drone was done for, but it had done what she needed. She triggered a salvo, and over the next eight seconds a full spread of four guided missiles launched from her shoulder. She had to wait,motionless, the entire time: it seemed like an eternity. Once her Shell was done acting as a stationary weapons platform, she lit off her torches again, spread her wings, and jumped to the roof of the next building, where she didn't stop for even a moment, but kept moving north.

Explosions rocked Toshimayr City as her missiles hit. *Whichever Shell I haven't found*, she told herself as she made a more complicated jump up to a five story building, *Will be heading in that direction. Looking to catch me in the middle of a fight.* She directed her remaining drone north, trying to get a good look at how effective her missiles had been, and opened a view from the drone's high definition digital camera.

Another jump, up to a six story high roof; she was approaching one of the giant structural columns of stone that supported this cavern, and the buildings rose as they clustered around it. Landing, she paused in her forward motion to watch the incoming visual feed. A cloud of dust was clearing. There: a Shell, she couldn't be sure whose, broken and smoking in the crater her missiles had left instead of pavement. The awning of a store hung by one corner, burning shattered glass and debris covered the street. The lobby of a hotel across the way had been blown open completely, the couches, front desk and elevators exposed. *One down,* she thought with satisfaction, and then her Shell's foot shifted underneath her.

"Shit." Before Annie could get her jets opened up to lift her Shell, the roof collapsed beneath her left foot, caving in around her as she fell through. Once the torches were burning again, she was able to get free. The Shell shot up and out from the collapsing building, but as she looked around desperately for a landing place, she knew she'd left herself exposed to whichever enemy was left.

And just as she'd found a decent landing spot - it must have been either a hospital or a news studio, because nothing else ever had helipads on the roof - a runaway train punched her in the shoulder, spinning her around.

It wasn't her actual shoulder, of course; it was the Shell that had taken a hit, but the neural shunt meant that she felt the impact, even though the Shell didn't have the kind of sensors that would translate structural damage into signals that her nervous system would read as pain. *Thankfully.* The Shell spun out of control, crazily, like some kid's ill-conceived paper airplane, and then she felt a second impact as she slammed into something - the ground? A building? - and tumbled along for a few seconds before grinding to a halt.

Dust was everywhere. *I can't see.* Desperately, Annie looked for the feed from her remaining drone, the only clear camera view she had at the moment. The story it told wasn't good: her Shell was crumpled in the remains of a partially roofed ambulance port. There was a paved circle heading out from her to both the right and left; this must be, she realized, where the ambulances pulled up to transfer patients from the vehicle into the hospital. Her armor was scraped up - shattered all along the left shoulder - but seemed to have saved the parts of the Shell she needed to stay functioning. *Somehow.*

She levered herself up from where the Shell had fallen, broken glass and metal girders and other building materials falling off of her. She needed to move, and she needed to find Serafine. *Because this is Sera*, she knew. *Sniping at me from someplace high up. She won't close until I'm crippled.*

I need to get out of sight. Fuck it, I've already ruined the paint job. Crouching down, she shouldered her way further into the building. It wasn't a great fit: her Shell was somewhere between two and three stories tall, but hospitals weren't known for being built to stand up to heavily armored military vehicles. She lit her fusion torches up and crashed through the ER and into some kind of foyer. Her right foot swept through a gift shop, while her left crunched aside a reception desk. *But for the moment, at least, she can't see where I am.* Her left arm - the one that had taken the shoulder shot - got hung up on the pedestrian walkway that spanned the foyer, and she wrestled with the Shell for a moment trying to extricate herself.

This time, she heard the sound of the shot. Not the strange whine of Sera's railgun going off - not from this distance - but the sound of the projectile exploding through the hospital around her. All around her, glass shattered as the hospital shook. The walkway fell across her shoulder, broke in half on the Shell's armor, and then tumbled down. Somewhere nearby, a fire was steadily pouring smoke into the building's interior. *Another shot and this entire building will come down on me,* Annie realized.

The good news was that she could see the main entrance from here, and all of the windows at the front of the building had already shattered, leaving only half a wall between her and open air. She lowered her shoulder and bulled through with the help of her jets, but as soon as she cleared the building another shot from Sera's railgun slammed her sideways. She managed to keep her feet, but warning klaxons began to sounds as various parts of her computer generated displays turned red. *There goes the missile rack,* she realized with a disembodied wince. And there, up above her, perched on the roof of the parking garage, was Sera, Shell undamaged, with a railgun pointed right at her.

An audio feed opened up from Sera's Shell. "Ready to give up, Sir?"

Annie's only response was a wordless snarl as she fired both her fusion jets and the minigun mounted on her right shoulder, throwing herself directly at Sera's Shell in an arc, hoping the suddenness of the assault, combined with the unpredictable movement, would throw off her aim.

The railgun fired, and up close this time she could hear that electric, strange sound it made as it shot a projectile right into her Shell. More klaxons and red as she tumbled forward, guns still going, and she could watch the armor shattering off of Sera's Shell right up until the moment they crashed together and then tumbled off of the roof. And then, everything went dark.

"Shell destroyed," the computer informed her as the simulator ended, giving her mind back to her body. She felt around the back of her neck and pulled out the plug, then unstrapped herself and climbed out of the simulation pod. Gavril was already out, waiting for them as he slowly clapped his hands, and Sera's pod door opened a moment after Annie's did.

"I had you!" Sera shook out her dark hair, clearly frustrated.

"Clearly not," Gavril told her with a chuckle.

"You should have had me," Annie corrected. "And if you'd treated it like real combat, and just shot instead of pointing your gun at me and *asking* for a surrender, you would have won. But you treated it like a game. If you're ever, ever in that position when we're really out there, against insurgents or whoever, you keep shooting until your enemy stays down." *As if I'm still her Commanding Officer in anything but name,* Annie reminded herself bitterly. *As if we'll ever actually be out in the field as a unit again.* She felt healthy; she'd been out of the hospital for two days now, with nothing to do but exercise and drill in the simulator. She'd been spending so much time with Kaito in the hospital that she worried she was turning into the needy, clingy girlfriend. He hadn't returned her messages since her discharge, and she kept telling herself that he must be out on a long run to one of Europa's other cities.

The door to the simulation room opened, and Nolan stepped through. Sera and Gavril sketched quick salutes in his general direction, and he waved back in their general direction. "At ease," he told them, walking over to Annie, and she couldn't help but think how much better, more natural he was at being in command than she was.

"Hey," she said awkwardly. Technically, she still outranked him.

"How are you feeling," Nolan asked her.

"Fine," she answered, then decided that wasn't enough. "Perfect. Ready for duty."

"Good," Nolan said with a nod. "I want you cleared as soon as possible, so that I can get out from under this pile of paperwork they keep throwing at me. Which is actually what I came to ask you about. You mind giving me a hand?"

Annie was confused, and she was sure that it showed on her face. "If... if you want. But you've been in longer than I have, if there's anything there you can't figure out, I won't be any help."

Nolan took a step closer. "Humor me," he said quietly, then nodded his head toward the door.

"Sure. See you later," she told Sera and Gavril, giving them a wave as she and Nolan walked to the door. As soon as it had closed behind them, Nolan spoke softly and evenly, without looking at her.

"MP's have picked up Kaito for forged security clearances," he told her, then grabbed her arm and pulled her along with him as she stopped in her tracks. "Don't stop walking. Keep a straight face. Don't say anything back to me, just listen. Nod if you understand."

Annie nodded. *Kaito.* What did MPs do to suspects, she wondered. *Will they hurt him?*

"My guy in intelligence tells me they think he got the clearance from insurgents," Nolan continued as they turned a corner and stepped into the elevator.

"What does that mean," she asked, unable to keep from turning toward him as the doors closed and they found a moment of privacy.

"It means he's not under arrest yet, officially," Nolan said, "Or charged with a crime. They're going to try to get everything they can out of him about where that clearance came from: names, addresses, anything he knows. And they're not going to be nice about it."

"What does that mean," Annie repeated dumbly, hearing the desperation in her voice but unable to restrain it. She recalled resting her head on Kaito's chest, the bed sheets wrapped about them, and listening to his heartbeat. "They won't hurt him, will they?"

The door to the elevator opened as it came to rest at the second floor. Annie turned to face the exit, taking a deep breath and doing her best to smooth the things she was feeling out of her face. Lieutenant Commander Malik, sunglasses tucked into his pocket, stepped inside to join them.

"Lieutenant Commander," he greeted Annie with a nod, then turned to Nolan. "Your people ready for that operation tomorrow," he asked.

"They're ready, sir," Nolan responded.

"Good." Malik glanced back over to Annie, studying her for a moment. *He knows,* Annie realized. *He can see it in my face, that something's wrong. What am I going to say when he asks me?* But after a long moment, Malik turned back to Nolan. "We'll talk about it more tonight."

"I'll bring the scotch," Nolan said with a smile that betrayed nothing, and then the elevator stopped again and Malik stepped out, leaving them alone. Annie slumped back against the wall as soon as the door was closed, unable to hear what Nolan was saying over her own heartbeat.

"I said they're going to lace him, Annie, if they haven't already," Nolan repeated, and this time she heard it.

"Oh God." *But they only do that to terrorists, to people who deserve it,* she thought in a rush. "But he's not... he's not what they think. I have to go tell them that he's not a terrorist, he was just coming to see me!"

Nolan scowled. "I thought you might say that. And I just want to be clear that I don't think it's a very good idea. But technically, sir, you still outrank me. And so, if you were to happen to order me to tell you where he was being questioned, and I possessed that information, then I would be obligated to tell you."

Annie took a deep breath. "Lieutenant Nolan, I hereby order you to tell me the location of the prisoner Katakura Kaito."

"Yes sir," Nolan replied, stabbing out one hand to stop the elevator. "Before this cavern became Blue Zone, it was the center of the city, with main roads to every other cavern, including the hydroponic caverns."

"Which have been sealed up," she continued for him.

"Yes and no," Nolan told her. "They certainly look sealed up, and officially they are. But there's a hidden passage used for transporting prisoners in and out of our official detainment centers without the bother of paperwork. On the other side of that passage is a fenced off, unmarked building that looks like it probably contains chemicals for use in the hydroponics. If you ask anyone about that building, you will be told that it does not exist. I can't tell you how to get in, because I don't know; I would guess you'll have an easier time going through the hydroponics areas than trying to get through that secret passage from Blue Zone, even though it's the long way around."

"Thank you, Nolan," Annie said softly.

"I'm only following a direct order, sir," Nolan said evenly. "And if this ever comes up in any kind of inquest, that's exactly what I'll say."

Meaning all the responsibility for what happens after this falls on my shoulders, Annie knew, but she was grateful anyway. She licked her dry lips, then reached out to start the elevator up again. "I think I'm going to head out to Green Zone and do some shopping," she said, raising her voice from the quiet tones of her conversation. The elevator stopped on the ground floor, and as the doors opened she could see several soldiers waiting to get in. "I've been wanting one of those sharkskin jackets."

Then, without looking back, she headed out.

Annie couldn't park the black, UCAF Tesla right outside of *Taka to Ama*; it wouldn't fit down the alley. In fact, it had been a pain to get the electric car even within a block of the bar - as blocks were measured in Red Zone - because of the crowded streets. Pedestrians weren't so much the problem; the Europans tended to get out of the way of government vehicles, to avoid trouble. The market stalls, cafe tables and trash bins weren't nearly so obliging.

She hadn't even been able to let the onboard AI navigate once she'd passed through the checkpoint from Yellow Zone; you clearly couldn't rely on the GPS and car sensors in Red Zone, so she'd had to manually override the car and take direct control. Now, she parked just ahead of the alley, against a relatively open piece of sidewalk, her wheels up on the curb so that the car tilted at a crazy angle. When she got out, in her full dress uniform, she remembered the first time she'd come here, and how she'd almost been - what? Jumped? Mugged? Trying to project a confidence she did not exactly feel, she locked the car with a swipe of the finger, the motion recognized by her smart lenses and received by the interface of the onboard computer, and then she strode down the alley.

It was later in the day than the first time she'd come, and business was beginning to pick up. People were just getting out of work, and it seemed like a lot of them were stopping by for a drink or two on the way home. *If,* she thought wryly, *they're planning on going home, instead of just drinking here all night.* She got her fair share of stares upon entering, but she was here for one thing, and she knew exactly what that was. *One person, anyway.*

At the bar, Mizuki looked particularly busy, with a dozen or more customers grouped around the polished wood fixture. As Annie approached, she was pouring out two cups of sake from a large, paper wrapped bottle for two fishermen in the same kind of ratty, knitted sweater that Kaito always wore. The Europan woman, Annie was pretty sure, saw her coming, but avoided eye contact and moved off down the bar to distribute the cups of sake.

I don't have time for this shit. "Mizuki," Annie called out, raising her voice loud enough to be sure everyone at the bar heard. *And I used her first name, with no suffix. That's so rude she's got to react.* With a stare that said 'I'd rather you were dead than in my bar,' Mizuki stalked over, eyes narrowed.

"What is it, *baijo*," Mizuki snapped, leaning over the bar into Annie's personal space.

Annie leaned forward too, right into her, so close she could smell the Europan girl's jasmine perfume. "They picked Kaito up for a forged security clearance," she said quietly but clearly, as close to Mizuki's ear as she could get.

"This is all your fault-"

"Shut up and listen to me, Mizuki," Annie shot back at her, pulling away just enough to make eye contact. "We're going to go get him. Right now. So tell your parents someone else needs to cover the bar, and come with me."

Mizuki's eyes narrowed, her lip twisted in a suspicious snarl. "Why should I help you, *baijo*?"

"Because if you don't," Annie told her, and it was the first time she'd admitted it out loud, "If you don't come with me right now, I don't think either one of us will ever see him again."

"And that's it," Mizuki asked as she pulled the driver's side door shut behind her and settled into the seat. "All you need me to do is drive?"

"Yeah." Annie smoothed her uniform in the back seat. "When I go in, just wait for us to come out. We're going to be counting on you to still be there, ready to go."

"Why don't you just drive yourself," Mizuki asked sharply.

"No one would believe it," Annie said after a moment.

"No one would belief some junior grade lieutenant has

to drive herself?" Mizuki's disdainful expression, eyebrows arched, reflected clearly in the rearview mirror. Annie didn't bother to correct her about the rank.

"No one's going to believe that the daughter of the United Colonies Prime Minister would drive herself anywhere," Annie admitted quietly.

"Wait, what?"

"Just drive, Mizuki," Annie said with a scowl. "I'll tell you where to go."

Mizuki twisted around in the seat to look back at her. "No, wait. What did you just say? What's your name?"

Annie looked away from Mizuki's angry brown eyes. "My name is Karoline Anette Galtung," she said slowly and firmly. "My father is Prime Minister Alexander Hakon Galtung."

"Bullshit." Mizuki slowly shook her head in disbelief. "And the Prime Minister's daughter is just, what, running around Europa, without any kind of bodyguards or anything? Where you could be, like, kidnapped and held hostage against him? We fucking *hate* that guy here."

"The only one who knows who I am," Annie explained, "Is Commander Clavinger. And you, now. I didn't want any special treatment."

"I can't fucking believe this," Mizuki said, turning back around and slumping into the driver seat. "And you're what, just going to walk into wherever they've got Kaito, tell everyone who you are, and order them to hand him over?"

"That's the plan, yeah," Annie confirmed.

"I knew you were bad news."

"Just drive, Mizuki."

"Fine," the Europan girl snarled. "But after this, I want you the fuck out of our lives. Mine, Kaito's, every one. In fact, it's probably best for everyone if you just fly on back to Mars and do whatever it is rich girls do."

Annie looked out the window, silent, and Mizuki started the car. It lurched forward, nearly hitting someone before

Mizuki slammed the breaks on.

"Be careful," Annie hissed.

"Sorry," Mizuki replied. "I've never actually driven before."

For a long moment, Annie couldn't think of anything to say. "I guess it doesn't' matter, as long as you don't hit anything. You know how to get to the hydroponics zones?"

"Of course," Mizuki assured her. "I've lived here my entire life. I know Toshimayr like the back of my hand."

Annie's normal UCAF Officer clearance was enough to get them into and through the first and second hydroponics caverns, and then into the third. This was the first time Annie had seen the caverns where the majority of Toshimayr City's food crops were grown; for an instant, she wished that she'd visited before, because it would have filled her with awe. Now, as the car made its way through the enormous caverns toward where Kaito was being held, and all she could do was wait, she felt sick.

The three Hydroponics caverns were each shaped identically to Red, Yellow, Green and Blue Zones, six outer hexagons grouped around the center hexagon of Blue Zone, in an arrangement borrowed from beehives. Like the habitation zones, the hydroponic zones were carved out of the moon's rocky crust, with the walls arcing up to a vaulted ceiling above, where the artificial suns hung. Scattered through the cavern were half a dozen mammoth, vertical columns of rock which had been left to support the ceiling. In the habitation zones, the lower halves of those columns were disguised by the buildings which clustered about them; here, there was no city skyline to obscure them, and as a result the caverns looked - her mind groped for the right words. Huge? Unnatural? Surreal? She found herself unable to establish the scale of anything in relation to anything else. From a distance, the columns looked as if they were overgrown with moss, or ivy, but as they drove by one, she realized the entire stone surface had been covered in scaffolding, ring upon ring of it, stacked up dozens of stories in the air. Each ring consisted of a catwalk, and then at least six layers of vertically stacked rows of greenery. She couldn't identify what was being grown on the columns from here, but when she looked back and forth between the column they were passing by, and those in the distance, she knew the quantities were immense.

The greenery wasn't limited to the columns, however. The entire floor of each cavern consisted of scalloped, layered terraces green with the crops growing from them. Everywhere she looked, agricultural workers walked the fields, testing the soil, adjusting automated watering systems, and examining crops. With the touch of a button, Annie lowered the tinted window of the car and breathed in the best tasting air she'd felt since coming to Europa.

"It's all the oxygen," Mizuki commented, and Annie saw that her window was down as well. "A couple of our regulars, at the bar, work here. They always told me the air was better, but..." The Europan woman inhaled deeply, a smile spreading across her face.

"Rice," Annie asked.

"Yeah," Mizuki said with a nod. "And then other things on the columns; fruits, vegetables, herbs and spices. Jasmine. The luxury foods, for people who can afford them."

They continued along the roads that wound through the caverns, passing more agricultural workers and the occasional cluster of harvesting or transport vehicles. Once they got into the third cavern, Annie spoke up again. "We need to find the old entrance to Blue Zone. The one they sealed up."

"It should be somewhere to our right, then," Mizuki reasoned. "Since all of the other zones border Blue Zone at the center." They turned down the next right they saw, driving slowly through the artificial rice paddies until they neared the inner wall of the cavern.

"There's a lot of supply buildings," Annie fretted, overwhelmed by the scale. "And the one we're looking for is unmarked, so that it doesn't stand out. I'm not sure how we're going to find it."

"It will be the one no one is going into," Mizuki said confidently. "The one no vehicles are parked outside of. The one with no doors open, or piles of supplies, or..." Her voice trailed off as they drove along the road which parallelled the wall. "That one."

Annie leaned forward to get a look out the windshield. "Are you sure? It looks just like all the others."

"The gate in the fence is closed," Mizuki pointed out. "And see all those warning labels? Hazardous chemicals? That's exactly the kind of shit they put up to keep people from getting too nosey." She pulled the car up to the gate, braked slowly until they came to a stop almost touching the metal wire, and stopped.

As she did, Annie opened an app in her smart lenses which she hadn't used since she left Deimos on the *Scipio* months ago. It wasn't exactly a hack for the ID chip in her hand, at least not legally, because the United Colonies government had made it and installed it for her. It didn't let her make any changes to her ID or security clearances, except for one: the toggle that went back and forth between security clearances for Annie Winters, and clearances for Karoline Anette Galtung. She bit her lip, hesitating for a moment, and then saw the door to the supply building open. A UCAF soldier came out, dressed in standard issue black fatigues, and approached the car. Annie switched her clearances over, then swiped away the app.

The soldier did not open the gate, but talked through it, forcing Mizuki to lean out the window. "This is a restricted area," he called. "Turn the car around and leave."

"My passenger's got clearance," Mizuki told him, pointing her thumb at the back seat. "Open up the gate."

The soldier frowned. "I wasn't told to expect any visitors," he complained. "Turn the vehicle's engine off." He put a finger to his ear and said something that Annie couldn't hear; after a moment, a second soldier came out of the supply building. *Well, they're definitely not storing fertilizer in there,* she joked to herself, trying to keep all trace of nerves from her face. It was a skill she'd had a lot of practice at, first by her father's side as an ornament at state functions, then when paparazzi stalked her through college, and finally as an officer who couldn't afford to let weakness show.

The gate was rolled back just enough to let the soldier step out and over to the driver's side rear window, but not enough that any vehicle larger than a bicycle could fit through. He rapped twice against the tinted window to Annie's left, and she pressed the switch that rolled the window down.

"Identification, please," the MP requested. She knew that his eyes were roaming over her rank insignia, that he was already suspicious, and that seeing the bars of a relatively low ranking, young Lieutenant Commander wasn't going to calm him down. Affecting a bored expression she didn't feel, she held her right hand out to him, as much as she could without stretching or shifting her body. *This is an inconvenience,* she told herself. *And I'm certainly not moving more than I have to for some random grunt who hasn't even got the rank to talk to me in public.*

The MP made a couple of hand motions and swipes as his own app processed her ID and security clearances, sending a radio signal that activated her RFID chip, now in its original mode. She watched, and couldn't help but feel a small bit of satisfaction, even amusement, when his eyes widened. He swallowed once, couldn't quite seem to make up his mind how to address her, and then sketched a salute. "Miss Galtung." He sputtered. I mean, Lieutenant Commander. It's an honor to meet you, miss. We... we weren't warned of your coming. We didn't even know you were in system."

"Of course not," Annie said with an exaggerated eye roll, for the poor guy's benefit. "What is the point of my father sending me on a surprise inspection if we told everyone I was coming? Now open the gate, soldier."

"Yes sir," the flustered MP said, backing away from the car and calling to his partner. "Open the gate!"

Annie rolled up the window, and Mizuki pulled up to the building as soon as the gate had opened enough for the car to fit through. "Remember," Annie told her quietly, "You need to be here when we get out. Try not to talk to anyone, but if they start to ask questions or something, just keep them talking until you see me."

"I get it," Mizuki told her, shutting off the car. She took the collar of her shirt in both hands and pulled it down, then started pushing around her chest with her hands.

"What are you doing," Annie asked her, confused.

"Maximizing cleavage," Mizuki told her. "Go. I'll be here."

"Mizuki," Annie said, pausing with her hand on the door, "Thank you."

"Just go."

Annie opened the door and stepped out of the car, hardly pausing to close it behind her before setting off toward the door. The nervous MP dashed to keep up with her as his partner closed the gate behind them; he barely made it in time to open the door for her and get out of the way.

"If you'll just wait here, sir," the MP told her desperately, "I'll go tell Captain Russo you're here; I'm sure he'll be happy to give you a tour..."

Damned MPs and their old-fashioned army ranks, Annie grumbled to herself, doing a quick bit of mental calculating on whether or not she would outrank Captain Russo. *That should make him the equivalent of a ship's Lieutenant,* she realized. *Just beneath me.* "That won't be necessary," she said out loud looking around the bare room. There was a desk near the door, a couch on one wall, and a hallway to the right leading further into the building, lined with lockers on either side. She set off in that direction. "Show me your interrogation rooms. Do you have any prisoners at the moment?"

The MP scrambled to stay by her side, trying to get out

in front of her and head her off, but she just kept going. "I can't discuss that without authorization, sir," he insisted. "If you would just wait for Captain Russo back in the front room..."

"PFC," Annie addressed him, channeling Nolan's gruff manner as best she could, "It is exactly the effectiveness of Captain Russo and this facility that I have come here to determine." She stepped forward into his personal space, bumping her chest right up against his until he took a step back, her voice rising in volume as her rant continued. "Do you think I'm going to give him time to clean up whatever fuck ups he has let slide around here? No, PFC, I am not. Now show me the interrogation cells, or get the fuck out of my way."

For a moment, she wasn't sure it had worked. But this guy was green, and here was an officer who clearly outranked him getting up in his face. Not just an officer, but the daughter of the Prime Minister. He wilted. "Down the hall and to the left, sir," the PFC admitted in a small voice. "The stairwell leads to the interrogation level, and the cells are beneath that. Captain Russo and Sergeant Brenner are with a prisoner right now, sir."

Kaito. A cold metal lance stabbed through her heart. "That will be all, PFC," was what she said, and then set off without looking to see whether or not Private Limp Wrist, as she'd named him the moment he backed down, followed her. It was all she could do not to run down the stairs, metal steps echoing in a concrete stairwell. The MP guarding the doorway to the interrogation level saluted her and opened the door - after all, if she'd gotten in the gate and this far, she was clearly authorized to be here. He was really more for keeping prisoners from escaping, anyway, she figured.

"Which room is Captain Russo in," she asked him as she went by.

"B3, sir," the MP replied, and closed the door behind her. She could hear the lock clicking into place. *Right. No way out of here unless they let me out,* she realized. *Like what's-his-face. The guy who burned his own ships.*

The door to interrogation room B3, much like the door to this level, was locked only from the inside, so she opened it right up and stepped in, out of the bright light of the hallway and into a dim space. It was really two rooms; a closed door led into the adjacent chamber, and a large glass window - a one way mirror - provided her with a view of what was happening there. It was lucky that both Captain Russo and Sergeant Brenner were on the other side of the window, and that they couldn't see her, because anyone who'd looked at Annie right then would have known exactly what she was up to.

Annie brought her fists up to her mouth to stifle a cry. She sucked in deep breath after deep breath, trying to get enough control over herself to make her face into a mask.

Under a bright light, Kaito was bound in a chair. It must have been bolted to the ground, because as she watched, he jerked and thrashed in pain so violently that he would have toppled both the chair and his own body to the ground otherwise. There was blood on the left side of his face, and he was covered in sweat. Whatever soundproofing was on the room's outer wall and doorway was not present inside, or maybe there was a speaker, because she could hear him screaming. Finally, he stopped, and as he lay there, gulping in air and trembling, one of the two men in the room began to talk. She searched for his rank insignia, focused on that, and was able to put a name to him. *Sergeant Brenner.*

"Now," Brenner said in a slow, even tone, "Why don't you tell us again when your friend - Mizuki, was it? - first got into contact with *Shumokuzame.*"

Annie's eyes widened. *Mizuki? The Mizuki I'm depending on to get us out of here?* She thrust the thought aside. *I can't deal with that now. One thing at a time.* Annie straightened herself, adjusted her uniform, and put her hand on the doorknob. *Is it too late to turn back*, she had time to ask herself. *Yes. Yes, it is.* And then she opened the door and stepped through into the harsh glare.

Brenner and Russo both turned toward the open door.

"I thought I gave orders not to be interrupted," Russo began, but Annie cut him off.

"In my branch of the UCAF," She thrust her words violently at him, "We salute superior officers. But I guess the Military Police are getting lazy."

The sergeant - Brenner - jumped to attention, but Russo moved slowly and deliberately. She could see a low cunning in his dark eyes, already calculating this situation. Why hadn't he been informed someone was coming? Who was she? Had he been caught at one of the innumerable violations of regulations that he was undoubtedly guilty of?

"Sir," Russo began. "Commander Clavinger did not inform us of any visit."

"Then your people must have fucked up the orders at this end," Annie told him, "Because I just came from his office. He wants this prisoner. Immediately. I'm here to collect him."

Kaito was struggling back to some awareness of what was happening around him, and Annie saw him staring at her out of the corner of her eye. *Don't say anything Kaito*, she silently pleaded. *Don't fuck this up.*

"This is highly irregular," Russo protested. Brenner, on the other hand, like a smart NCO, was staying quiet and the fuck out of this. "I'll need to verify those orders with Commander Clavinger's office before I can release any prisoners to you..." He let the pause drag out for a long, deliberate breath as he pointedly examined Annie's rank insignia. "Lieutenant Commander."

"Lieutenant Commander Galtung," Annie answered his unasked question. *If ever there was a time to name drop, it's right now.* "And I do not have time to wait on your fuck ups and excuses. Sergeant, get that man up."

Sergeant Brenner, now put on the spot, looked back and forth between the two superior officers, licking his lips nervously. "Sir," he began, and she knew an equivocation was coming.

Ironically, it was Russo that saved her. "Galtung," he

repeated. As in..."

"As in, not only am I here in this shit-stained basement at Commander Clavinger's orders," Annie cut him off, "But yes, I am here on this world at the Prime Minister's direct command. Now I can either collect this prisoner, bring him back to HQ and get on with my mission, or I can get your superior connected with your comm officers so that *he* can personally ream your ass out for wasting his time."

The room was silent for a moment.

"Or," Annie said, her tone suddenly sweet and reasonable, "I can make sure that when I return to Deimos, my report mentions how orderly and efficient the MP branch on Europa is. What was your name again? Russo? I'll make sure to spell it right in my report, either way."

"I'd like to help you, Lieutenant Commander Galtung," Russo said after a moment.   "But without direct authorization... you understand, regulations are clear."

Annie let her impatience show, and tried to channel her fear into frustration. "Look." She thrust her hand at him, the one with the RFID chip in it. "Would I have this level of clearance if I was going to bullshit you on some stupid prisoner transfer? Stop wasting my time."

Russo tapped at the air, activating the same app the MPs outside had used to verify her identity. "Level one security clearance," he breathed, then made up his mind. "Sergeant, get that man out of that chair."

Annie twisted her face in disgust. Let them think it was disgust at Kaito. "He smells like piss. Sergeant, I don't want to touch him. Get him up the stairs and out to my car."

As they dragged Kaito past her, she thought she heard him mumbling: "A... Ann..." *Shut up, shut up*, she repeated in her head, like some kind of mantra or prayer that could alter reality by the mere process of wishing it. They half dragged, half carried Kaito up the stairs and then out to her car, where Mizuki - the little traitorous bitch - had three MPs clustered around the driver's side window, flirting with her. *At least she's still here,* Annie told herself as they threw Kaito into the backseat and she closed the door.

"Thank you sergeant," she said, accepting Brenner's salute. Russo, in the meantime, had fallen back halfway to the door. *As soon as I'm gone, he'll get in touch with Clavinger,* Annie knew. *We need to move quickly.* Instead of riding in back, like she wanted to, she slid into the passenger seat. "Get us out of here, Mizuki," she hissed, and as the car started one of the MPs Mizuki had twisted around her finger was already rolling back the gate.

"Working on it," Mizuki told her, face frozen in a plastic smile as she waved at the boys. She backed up, turned the wheel, and then drove forward out the gate. With her left hand, she raised the tinted windows. "How is he," she asked, keeping the car at a steady speed away from the interrogation facility, along the inner rock wall of the cavern.

"Not good," Annie admitted, unclipping her safety belt and crawling back between the two front seats into the back.

"Hey," Mizuki complained as Annie's hip knocked her in the ear.

"Sorry," Annie said as she drew her feet after her and sat on the bench next to Kaito. "Once we're out of sight, Mizuki, step on it. They're going to be onto us as soon as they get through to the Commander and he tells them I was full of shit."

Kaito, semiconscious, leaned into her. "Annie," he mumbled, his cheek leaving a smear of blood on her uniform jacket.

"Hey," she murmured to him, wrapping an arm around his shoulder and pulling him close. "It's OK now. I've got you." She buried her face in his hair, breathing in the familiar smell of him through the sweat and the blood and the urine, and realized as he began to shake that he was crying.

Kaito

Shumokuzame

June 29th, 2128

Later, Kaito would realize that he must have drifted in and out of consciousness over the course of that drive. He remembered that Annie stayed with him the entire time they were moving, though he felt a burning shame at the way he had broken down and wept; at the way his pants were stained and stinking of urine; and at the way he had answered all of the questions he had been asked.

How long was it, he wondered as Annie and Mizuki spoke about where to take him, *between when I started answering questions, and when she came to get me? An hour? Two? Or was it less?* Surely he could have taken the pain for such a short amount of time. If he'd known someone was coming, he could have taken just about anything. *But I didn't know. It just seemed like it would go on forever, and ever. Like it was pointless to do anything but what they wanted.*

"I told them about you, Mizuki," Kaito finally said, his voice loud and grating to his own ears as he interrupted the arguing girls.

"What?" Mizuki craned her head around, confused, and momentarily paying no attention whatsoever to driving.

"Watch the road," Annie chastised her.

"They asked who told me where to get a fake security clearance," Kaito explained, unable to look either woman in the eye. Instead, he stared out the tinted window. They were somewhere in Red Zone. "I told them."

"Kuso," Mizuki swore.

Annie gave him a gentle squeeze. "You can't go back to the bar, then, Mizuki," she said. "They'll come for you. Better if your parents don't know where you are."

"I can't just disappear without saying anything to them," the Europan girl argued, and Kaito closed his eyes and let himself drift away from their voices again, into a dim place where he could examine the pain in his cheek and head in great detail. They were dull, now, but he imagined the lace crouched about his brain like some kind of malignant spider, crawling about and poking at him.

After some interminable amount of time the car stopped, and Kaito came back to himself. "Hey," Annie murmured in his ear. "Wake up. It's time to go."

"Where are we," Kaito asked her through dry lips as he stirred.

"The docks," Annie answered softly.

"Why?"

"Because you and I," Mizuki said from the front of the car, "Are getting out of Toshimayr. We've got a ride waiting for us, so we need to hurry up."

"Where are we going," Kaito asked, finding Annie's hand and taking it in his. There was a moment of silence, and he repeated the question: "Where are we going?"

"I don't know," Annie admitted. "It's better this way. If I knew, I'd have to tell someone, sooner or later. If I don't know where you are," she continued, swallowing, "I can't give you away. I hope it's somewhere nice. I'll try to tell your mother you're safe. Or get her a message. You shouldn't, they'll be watching."

And you're not coming with me, Kaito realized. *Of course she's not. I was stupid to even think that she would. It was nice while it lasted, but we both knew it couldn't ever really go anywhere. Now she'll go back to Mars, and I'll go... somewhere.*

While he'd been thinking, Annie had opened the door and scooted out, and now she and Mizuki were pulling him out of the backseat. Touching the two of them at the same time, together, he marvelled for a moment at how Mizuki felt like a bird, delicate and breakable, next to Annie's compact, wiry strength. *Is that how I feel to her,* Kaito wondered. *Fragile? Weak? Someone who needs to be protected?*

Hobbling between the two women, Kaito let himself be

led into the dock facility. Without his smart lenses, he could hardly see: the familiar surroundings were nothing but blurs. "My security clearance isn't going to work," He pointed out, taking a masochistic pleasure in pointing out the flaws in this plan. *Like poking your tongue at a loose tooth,* he thought. *You can't resist, even if it hurts.*

"Mine probably won't either, by now," Annie said with a grimace. "That's fine. Mizuki says that *Shumokuzame* has someone who can get us through."

"Of course they do," Kaito sighed painfully as they levered him onto one of the moving walkways. Here, all three of them could rest for a moment, leaning against the moving rails. *After telling Mizuki over and over that I wanted nothing to do with her terrorist friends, here I am running to them for help.*

"Ready," Annie asked Mizuki, next to him, as they approached the end of the walkway.

"Yeah," Mizuki groaned. "He's heavy."

"After I turn back, you'll have to help him yourself," Annie warned the weaker girl.

"I'll manage," Mizuki promised.

I'm not dead yet, Kaito wanted to say out loud, but as they stepped off the walkway, he fell into the arms of the two women again. A laboured walk and several raised heart rates later, they approached the security checkpoint Kaito had used everyday for years now. Kaito squinted, trying to make his eyes work better. Slouched at the desk, chatting quietly, he recognized Van den Berg and Moretti. And that was it. *No Europan,* he realized with a flash of fear. *No Shumokuzame. We're fucked.*

And yes, there was Moretti, standing up, one hand at the gun on his belt. "What the happy fuck is this," he said in astonishment. If Kaito had felt able to run, he would have run right at the little toad of a man and knocked him over. Instead, they all just kept limping forward.

"Hey guys," he moaned. "I got in a fight at the bar. I need to get something off the ship..."

Moretti was already shaking his head. "Oh no, no do not even try that. Your name is already plastered all over our security alerts. All of you, drop on the ground right where you are and place your hands over your heads." As he spoke, Moretti moved to unclip his service pistol; then, just as his hand closed on the hilt, his body jerked, stiffened, and then fell forward to lay face down on the ground.

Behind him, Van den Berg replaced his taser in its sheath. "Come on," he said. "We need to go quickly."

"Are you fucking kidding me," Kaito exclaimed as Van den Berg came up underneath his arm to take the weight from Mizuki. "But you're UCAF," he protested.

"I'm from Callisto," Van den Berg explained. *Callisto. Not Mars,* Kaito realized.

"I still don't understand," Kaito sighed, then realized what hallway they were going down, more from feel than anything else. "Are we going to the *Nautilus*?"

"Yup," Mizuki confirmed. "Which means you need to wake up enough to pilot."

Kaito shook his head. "I don't want to steal *Date-sama's* ship," he protested. "He always helped my family out..."

"Don't worry about that," Van den Berg told him gruffly as they entered the hangar bay. A strange, detached part of Kaito's mind wondered if his private rare component had respawned yet, and considered collecting it before they left. "We can always drop it off somewhere for the police to find."

The gangplank was still attached from Kaito's last shift, bridging the cold water in the bottom of the hangar bay. Their steps echoed as they lurched across it. Kaito's eyes were drawn by the dark water beneath, and he thought how nice it might feel to sink and let it close over his head, and just keep going down.

"Open the door," Mizuki told him. "Your access code should still work."

And it would, he realized, leaning forward until the pad resolved itself in his vision, then reaching up hesitantly to type in an eight digit string of numbers. *It's not like DSI computers are hooked into UCAF security updates, or something. Someone's going to have to realize I've been arrested, then manually go in and change all of my access codes.* The thought made him feel even more guilty at what he was about to do to the old man. His finger paused over the keypad, then stabbed the last number. The hatch to the Subtee opened, and Van den Berg leaned Kaito against the frame of the ship.

"Say whatever goodbyes you're going to say," Van den Berg said in a low voice, casting a significant look between Kaito and Annie. "But don't take too long. We'll be waiting inside." And with that, he and Mizuki slipped into the Subtee, leaving Kaito alone with Annie.

She was still under his right arm, supporting part of his weight. Now that they were alone, he was suddenly aware of her body heat, of his arm across her back, the press of her hip against him.

"I'm sorry," he apologized to her.

Annie shifted around to face him. She wasn't supporting as much of his weight now; he was mostly leaning against the frame of the hatch. "For what," she asked.

"For all of this. For getting caught, for making you come get me, for whatever trouble you're going to get in."

"Don't be," Annie breathed softly. "I should be the one who's sorry. You got that clearance to come see me. If it wasn't for me, you never would have been... they never would have hurt you." *I never would have been tortured*, he finished the thought in his head that she hadn't been able to say out loud. "I'm just glad that you're alive," she whispered. "I was so worried about you. About what they would do to you."

"I'm OK," he lied, because this might be the last time they ever talked, ever saw each other again. "I'm OK.

"Good," Annie told him. "And don't worry about me. I'll be fine. I mean, I'll get in trouble, but... I've got friends. It won't be too bad."

"You could come with us." He regretted saying it as

soon as the words came out of his mouth because he knew she couldn't, but he wanted her to.

"I can't," Annie said, and it sounded more like she was pleading with him to understand than a statement. "I'll explain why you had the clearance, that you had nothing to do with *Shumokuzame*. I think I can get you cleared of any charges. I'll get in trouble for getting you out of custody, but if you're innocent anyway... I'll probably be sent back to Mars," she admitted. "Look, when I get the charges dropped, I'll send a message to your mother."

You don't sound so confident about that, Kaito thought to himself, but pushed it away: if this was the last time he was going to see Annie, that wasn't what he wanted to spend time thinking about. He moved his tongue around his mouth, hoping not to taste any blood, and leaned his forehead against hers. "I don't want to leave you."

"You have to," Annie whispered, and then her lips were on his, and even after all the hurt he'd been through there was nothing gentle about this kiss. Their arms twined about each other, crushing their bodies together, and he felt as if she was trying to devour a piece of him, and at the same time he was trying to memorize the taste of her tongue, the smell of her body, the softness of her skin as his hand fumbled and then slid under her shirt and jacket, his fingers trailing up her back so that her entire body shuddered. He wanted nothing so much as to rip her clothes off and forget about everything but their bodies, everyone but them.

Somehow, when they broke apart, neither one had given in enough to cry. "I love you," Annie told him for the first time, and then she was gone, dashing over the catwalk and down the hall away from the hangar bay without a look back. For a long, shuddering breath, Kaito watched her go, and then he turned and entered the airlock, slapping the control panel to close the door behind him.

He winced at the pain of moving without aid, leaning against the bulkhead for a moment. *They're going to be coming for you real soon,* a part of him that was beyond and above the pain realized. *And if they get you because you were too slow starting this ship up, everything that woman has done was for nothing.* Somehow, he found the strength to jog through the ship's passageways. He only tripped once.

Mizuki and Van den Berg were waiting for him in what passed for the bridge; the UCAF MP - *Now ex-MP,* he realized - examining controls and looking perilously close to actually being stupid enough to touch something.

"Out of my way," Kaito told him, half-falling into his old, familiar chair. It felt good, and he resisted the urge to let out a sigh, instead rapidly flipping switches and booting up the *Nautilus'* computer. "They took my lenses," he told his two passengers, "So I'm going to have to use the old fashioned control systems. I guess those safety regulations weren't so stupid after all," he admitted as a throbbing hum began to vibrate out from the Subtee's core. "Fusion reactor powering up. Van den Berg, strap in on that bench there. Mizuki, I need you to open up that locker for me."

"Sure," Mizuki said, dashing over to the side compartment and unlatching the cover. "Whatever you need me to do, I'll help. Is this some kind of manual control?"

"It's my spare sweater," Kaito said, holding out a hand for it. Mizuki's face flattened, and she threw the ratty old knit at him. "It gets cold in here. Now you strap in, too." He pulled an actual keyboard out of the panel in front of him, leaned down until his nose was almost touching it, and began to tap in the DSI command codes necessary to retract the catwalk and seal the airlock. "Flooding hangar bay," he informed his passengers. Around the Subtee, the cold, dark waters of Europa's world ocean began to rise, let in through opened gates midway between the catwalks and the ceiling.

Kaito's instruments beeped, and a notification popped up on the screen in front of him. It was so dusty he could hardly read it, even leaning in, and he swiped it once with his sweater, which he hadn't got around to putting on yet. *"Kuso,"* he cursed again.

"What? What is it," Mizuki began to badger him, somehow manning to crawl almost into his ear from the emergency bench where she'd strapped in.

"Back off," he complained, waving the sweater at her face as he tried to exit whatever command menu he'd opened on the touch screen. "I can't drive with you hanging over my shoulder all the time."

Mizuki flopped back on the seat and gave an exasperated sigh. "Now I remember why I cheated on you," she snapped.

"What is it," Van den Berg interrupted.

"Incoming Comm," Kaito told him, putting the message through on the screen and speakers. "Which is bad." Even though the chamber wasn't finished flooding yet, he sent the command to open the hangar bay to the ocean. "Get ready, this is going to be rough."

On the screen in front of them appeared the thin, severe face of a UCAF pilot. Kaito recognized the uniform, and the rank. *The same as Annie's.* "Civilian transport *Nautilus,*" the Lieutenant Commander said after a slight pause, his voice flat and hard as a metal bulkhead. "You will power down your engines immediately and return that dock to its previous condition. When the water has drained to a safe level, you will surrender to the military police unit waiting on the other side of that airlock. Failure to comply will result in the immediate use of lethal force."

Kaito touched the screen, turning off the audio for a moment. "They haven't got control of the hangar bay systems yet. They must not have anyone from Date Shipping here with them, and it will take them a couple of minutes to crack the computers. Until that happens, they can't just shut the door on us."

"And they can't send anyone through the airlock, because this place is nearly flooded," Van den Berg confirmed.

"Right." The entire ship shook, thrown back on a swelling wave as the enormous docking gate began to open.

A vertical curtain of pressurized seawater sprayed into the hangar from just above the water level all the way up to the ceiling; as the opening widened, the curtain turned into a rushing torrent, slamming the *Nautilus* back against the rear wall of the hangar. Metal screamed as twenty feet of catwalk crumpled under the weight of the transport sub, and yellow notices began to pop up on Kaito's screen signalling superficial damage to the Subtee's exterior hull.

Kaito turned the audio link back on. "Lieutenant Commander, do you have units stationed outside this hangar door," he asked.

"My units are fully armed and prepared to fire," the soldier spat back at him.

"Recommend you move them," Kaito said, then swiped away the communication link and engaged the Subtee's engines.

"Is that door - gate - thingy open wide enough," Mizuki asked, leaning forward again, eyes wide. "Can you even see to drive this thing?"

"I said don't lean over my shoulder!" Proximity alarms and warnings screamed throughout the *Nautilus* as she leapt forward through the water, tearing the damaged section of catwalk off as she went. More damage alerts proliferated on Kaito's screen as the hull scraped through the still-opening hangar bay door, and then they were out into the ocean. The fusion engine's hum rose in his bones as the computer began to receive sensor information. "This civilian setup isn't anything like what Annie would have on her Shell," he said, raising his voice to be heard. The sweater was now forgotten, a crumpled heap on his lap, and the cold began to seep in through the bulkheads, bringing the flesh on his arms up in goosebumps. "But we need something for when we're maneuvering around other ships, coming in to port... it should be enough to show... "

The screen lit up in a display of the area around the Subtee. Kaito whistled. "Six Shells incoming," he warned his passengers. *At least Annie's not in one of them.*

"So what now," Mizuki wailed.

"We run," Kaito told them, opening up the engines all the way. "I never get to push her like this," he told them with a sudden, irrational grin. More alarms blared through the cabin, and he angrily swiped them away as the Subtee shot through the water.

"What are those," Mizuki screamed.

"Probably torpedoes," Van den Berg guessed.

The Subtee shook as explosions rocked the water around them, but kept going. "Yes!" Kaito clenched his fist as he watched the Shells drop away being them on the display. "They're not built for this. They can't keep up with us."

After another five minutes, he felt safe enough to pick his sweater up off of his lap and put it on. "Alright," he asked Mizuki and Van den Berg, really anyone. "Now where am I actually going?"

"The Akaishi banks," Mizuki told him. "There's one of those - what are they called - the repair stations, there, right?"

"Emergency repair bay," Kaito said with a nod. "Yeah. But we don't want to go right there, we want to throw off their sensors." His fingers danced across the keyboard and the touch screen, and he pulled back on the engines a bit as they turned to port.

"So what will you do," Van den Berg asked.

"Go someplace they won't be able to follow us," Kaito responded, plotting a course that took advantage of the nearby currents.

"Where," Mizuki asked.

"*Yomi-no-kuni*," Kaito told them with a savage grin.

"I don't like that it's named after the world of the dead," she fretted.

"Canyons," Van den Berg asked, and Kaito nodded.

"Yeah. You must have some like them on Callisto."

"We do. Mostly everyone stays out of them except teenagers showing off."

"Yeah, it's about the same here," Kaito admitted. "Good

thing for you guys I used to win all the races."

The next three hours were by turns boring and nerve wracking. It took nearly forty five minutes to get to the underwater canyons, during which time Kaito's mind wandered back to the dark room and what had been done to him there. He found himself reaching up to gently touch his cheek, where the needle had gone in, and after the third time he did it, Mizuki opened up the first aid kit under his chair and cleaned the injection site with an alcohol soaked fabric swab. He flinched at first, but once she'd stuck on a flesh colored plastic bandage, he was at least able to stop touching it.

The memories were worse.

There was little to do but squint at the sensors and sit back in his chair, and eventually both Van den Berg and Mizuki took his hint and headed back to see what was in the galley. The crew quarters on the *Nautilus* were about the size of his mother's apartment, split between this cabin, a small galley with a miniature refrigerator, microwave, and table to eat at, a bathroom, and a tiny bedroom with hardly enough room for a twin sized bed. *Probably actually smaller than Mom's apartment*, Kaito admitted to himself, *and definitely not meant for three people. Not for very long*. He'd used the bed before - DSI didn't want to pay for a hotel room unless he was going to be docked for a couple of days, and shipping runs often took him out of Toshimay for anywhere between eighteen and seventy-two hours.

Van den Berg doctored up a package of microwave noodles with some of the condiments that lurked in the refrigerator, which was good because while Mizuki was a great bartender, she was a horrible cook. He'd learned that while they were living together.

Kaito finished off his steaming bowl of noodles right around the time they entered the canyons. By then, he'd managed to turn off the proximity warnings, and the next hour and a half solidified the muscles in his neck and back into something with the approximate consistency of concrete.

He hunched forward to see, gritting his teeth, taking the Subtee through canyons that had only ever been mapped by illegal racing. Without his smart lenses, he did it mostly from memory. To distract his passengers, he fed the external cameras into the flatscreen on the wall of the galley and turned on the spotlights. Watching deep sea life scamper back out of the light seemed to keep Mizuki and Van den Berg occupied for most of the trip, which was good, because he didn't want to talk to anyone. Navigating the canyons took all of his attention, which was even better because it meant he didn't have time to let his thoughts wander.

Finally, he took the Subtee up and out of the canyons, following the rising rock and mud up as the Akaishi banks reared around them to every side. When he was finally able to get a sensor read on the Akaishi Emergency Repair Bay, he breathed a sigh of relief, stretched his arms above his head, and began to relax.

"No one's there," he called back into the galley, and his two passengers came forward. "But once I send the emergency code to open it up, it's going to put in an automated notification. We won't be able to stay here long."

"Don't worry about that," Van den Berg told him with a smile. "*Shumokuzame* has all of these things cracked. Let me at the keyboard. I'll send a code that will open it up but keep us dark."

"You guys have been using these as bases," Kaito realized.

"We have," Van den Berg confirmed. "We've lost a couple to UCAF operations recently. One of those your girlfriend was involved in, actually. She's getting quite a reputation."

"Was that where she got hurt," Kaito asked without thinking.

Van den Berg, leaning over him, paused for a moment, then went back to typing. "I think so, yeah. Word is she was the first one through the breach. Killed a lot of good people, got a lot more locked up."

A lot of terrorists, you mean, Kaito had to bite his lip from saying out loud. *Terrorists who almost killed Annie. If it's anyone's fault that all of this happened, that she was in the hospital, that I was arrested, it's Shumokuzame.* Van den Berg leaned back, and the hangar lights came on from the repair facility. Kaito checked his screen, then nodded. "Bay door is opening up. I'll park us inside, set the bay to seal and drain. We'll be off the ship in fifteen, twenty minutes tops."

"Good." Van den Berg clapped Kaito on the shoulder, and he flinched. *Just what are we expecting to find here*, he wondered.

The hangar bay, and the automated docking process itself, was routine - just like any normal shipping run up to an Icebreaker Station, or to one of the other subterranean cities scattered about the ocean floor of Europa. They had no real supplies to unload, and no dockworkers to do that for them if they had, so Kaito set the bay to be pumped down to a safe water level, and then powered down the *Nautilus'* systems after running the safety checks. In twenty minutes, exactly, they stepped out onto the metal catwalk of the Akaishi Emergency Repair Bay.

The only things that looked out of place, Kaito realized as he looked around, were the variety of repair machinery, much of it automated, which had been installed around the bay, making it more functionally similar to a dry dock than to an unloading dock.

The air smelled worse than he was used to, though not as bad as he'd been afraid of. Places like this used air filtration and recycling systems, and there was no spare room to grow any sort of plants. It was chilly, damp, and the air stank of wet, dirty socks, or mildewed towels that had been left in a hamper for too long. Ahead of him, Mizuki shivered, but he couldn't bring himself to feel a great deal of sympathy for her at the moment. Van den Berg led the way, with Mizuki following, and Kaito trudged after them.

While he'd been piloting through the underwater canyons, his pain and exhaustion had been pushed aside by the demands on his attention; now, as he dragged himself through the airlock and down a hall lit by harsh fluorescent lights, he found himself eyeing the cracked floor tiles with the thought that they wouldn't be the worst place he had ever slept.

Their destination, it turned out, was the emergency living quarters set up to keep a stranded crew alive until a rescue ship could come for them. The quarters were larger than those on the *Nautilus*, and better stocked with emergency rations, in a variety designed to actually meet a person's basic nutritional needs. There was a combination kitchen and mess hall, with a long table and benches at one end. There were two dorms, one to each side, which looked like they could sleep half a dozen adults each in metal frame bunk beds. Both dorms had a bathroom with a shower, clothes washer and dryer. Finally, there was a small room with instruments similar to those on the *Nautilus*: sensors, communications software, environmental controls and readouts for the fusion reactor that thrummed in the rock beneath their feet, and a router that provided the whole facility with access to the web, through cables buried beneath the ocean floor.

Kaito dragged himself over to the dorm room on the left and threw himself down on one of the lower bunks without bothering to get any sheets or blankets out of the bathroom closet. He had just closed his eyes when a toilet flushed, and he realized they were not alone. He shot upright so quickly that he slammed his head into the wire springs of the bunk above him, and cried out in pain. *As if my body didn't hurt enough from actual torture,* Kaito grumped to himself, *Now I hit my head on a bunk bed. Wonderful. Could this day possibly get any worse?*

From the bathroom, he could hear footsteps, and then the sound of running water, briefly, before it turned off again. Kaito wanted to shout into the next room to ask whether anyone else was supposed to be here, but whoever was in the bathroom would certainly hear him if he did. Instead, he desperately looked around the dormitory for some kind of weapon that he could use to defend himself.

The metal bed frame. Kaito grasped a length of metal frame with both hands and yanked on it as hard as he could. It didn't budge. He heard shoes scraping on the floor, yanked desperately and unsuccessfully one more time, and then spun to face whoever - or whatever - was coming.

Date Kunari stepped out of the bathroom, still drying his hands with a towel. *"Konnichiwa, Katakura-san,"* he greeted Kaito.

For a moment, Kaito just stared. *"Date-sama?"*

"Hai," his long time employer assured him. "You have forced me to place stones prematurely. I would have waited, if I had the choice."

Kaito frowned. "I don't understand why you're here. Were you on a transport that needed repair-"

"I think you know that is not the reason," Date interrupted him, his voice measured and calm.

"You can't..." Kaito couldn't seem to string the thoughts together in his head, nevermind the words to express them. "You have security clearances. You're a businessman. You play *Go* with the commander of the UCAF forces. You can't be here with me, I'm..."

Date Kunari waved a hand through the air to dismiss Kaito's objections, then began to carefully fold the towel. "Of course I have security clearances. I wouldn't be a very effective leader if I had to hide from the police all of the time."

"Shumokuzame," Kaito was finally able to breath. Even to him, his voice sounded strangled.

"Hai," Kunari agreed. *"Shumokuzame.* For twenty years, I have built this organization." He pointed to the other room, where Van den Berg and Mizuki must still be. "Just planting that one in the UCAF took seven years. And now we will need to find a way to make it look as if the *Nautilus* has been destroyed... you have caused me a lot of trouble, Kaito. But I

think, perhaps, you will be worth it."

Kaito collapsed back on the bed, letting his head drop to his hands. "I don't know what you're talking about," he complained, frustrated.

"I need a pilot," Date continued. "A good pilot. Better than good, if I can get him."

"For what?"

Old Man Date grinned. "To help us liberate Europa from the UCAF, of course. What did you think the point of *Shumokuzame* was? Just a little terrorism every once in a while?"

"You can't," Kaito protested. "I'm not saying that... that I don't want it. But they have guns."

"We have guns, also."

"They have Shells, and ships; they control the elevators," Kaito continued.

"It turns out," Date said with a glint in his eye, "That we have ships also. And with your help, we will take the elevators before they know what is happening. They were right, twenty years ago: whoever controls the elevators, the Icebreaker stations, and the geosynchronous orbital stations, controls Europa. Then, they had all of the advantages: surprise, superior firepower, and a trained army. This time, we will have surprise. We will strike while they have only one ship in system. And most importantly, our people are ready to die for their homes, for their families, for freedom. The UCAF soldiers are simply here to collect their pay."

"But why now," Kaito couldn't help but say out loud, because it was about all that was in his head. *And why me*, his thoughts continued, but he managed to keep that from slipping out just yet. His eyes and his fingers itched, without his smart lenses in. It was just like when Annie had asked him to take them out: like going through withdrawal after being on pain medication for a week, the way his mother had, except this time he didn't have Annie to... distract him.

"Is there ever one, single reason for anything that we

do," old man Date answered in that obnoxious way he had of getting all philosophical about even the simplest questions. "Part of it is my own age. I'm sixty-one years old, Kaito. I've waited twenty years. I can't wait another twenty. Oh, if I had access to the life-extension drugs available to the wealthy on Mars and Luna, it might not be a problem, but I don't. Even that new facility they've opened in Toshimayr - I may have clearances, but I don't have the wealth. Everything I make from DSI is funneled into *Shumokuzame*. Those drugs are harder to smuggle than guns, impossible to get for our people. They want those of us who remember life before the UCAF dead, and the memory of those times dead with us. My body isn't what it used to be, and if I wait another ten years my mind may not be either. My physician says I'm in good health, but I could have a heart attack or a stroke tomorrow, and then that would be it."

Ok, Kaito could understand all that. But it begged the question, "Then how do you actually know that now is the right time? What if you move too soon, because you can't wait, and it all falls apart?"

"It's time," the old man said certainly. "For years, I was pushing a boulder up a hill to get people involved in this, to overcome their fear, their hesitation, and try to get them to move. Now, I'm holding them back. I can't hold them back much longer. A wise man knows when it's time to swim with the tides, not against them. If I don't lead them forward now, they'll go without me, and then I've lost any chance to guide what happens, to steer this in the right direction."

He waved to indicate the room where Mizuki and Van den Berg waited. "Take Mizuki out there. I never ordered her to drop that bomb off the bridge; that was her own idea."

The world froze, and Kaito didn't hear the rest of what Date Kunari said. He was in that rushing cloud of dust and debris again, he could feel the birdlike, brittle frame of the woman he'd pulled to safety, see the unconscious child lying on the pavement. He could see Annie's Shell trying to hold the building up, to give the people inside enough time to get out, to maybe survive.

"Mizuki," he repeated, trying to picture the girl he'd known since they'd both worn diapers on top of that bridge, looking down at the Shells as they marched below, and then reaching over the guardrail to drop her package, measuring the distance to be sure she hit her target.

"I know," Date said with a heavy sigh. "I would never have ordered that kind of strike. Too much risk of casualties to our own people, with no real gain. It's a miracle they didn't shoot her right there. But you see the problem? Her, and people like her - they won't wait much longer. I can't hold them back forever, and if I let them go ahead on their own, they'll lose. We'll all lose, and we won't have another chance for a generation, maybe more. Do you understand, Kaito? These are the people who killed your father. I'm asking you to help me beat them. To throw them off our world, so that we can start over and try to fix things."

"What if I can't do it," Kaito asked quietly. "What if I can't be part of killing people?"

Date was silent for a long moment. "Your whole life," he said finally, "I've tried to protect you. I felt that I owed it to your father. Now, I've put our people at risk to save you. Not just those in the other room, but all of our people, all of our plans. You can't just float through your life anymore, boy. This isn't one of your games. Europans are going to be hurt and die because of what you've set in motion today. Their deaths need to be *for something*."

He turned to face the wall and shook his head. "If you refuse? Then we will take the *Nautilus*, and we will leave you here. You'll have food, and water, enough to survive until the UCAF figure out where you are. And then they will take you back to whatever hole they had you in, and they will learn everything that you know about us before they kill you. You won't get a trial, you won't get justice. You'll get dumped in a ditch in the hydroponics caverns somewhere. They'll use you as fertilizer to grow rice. And I'll have to move quickly enough to stay ahead of them. It will be the end of Date Shipping; they'll arrest and question a lot of our employees, and the ones who are left will be out of a job. They'll seize all the property and assets. And what happens to all of those people, that will be caused by you, also."

"What about Annie," Kaito nearly whispered.

"She seemed a nice enough girl," Date admitted. "With any luck she'll sit this entire thing out in a jail cell. I'm sure she was under arrest before you'd even got the *Nautilus* out of range of those Shells."

Kaito leaned forward, hunched over as he sat on the bed, letting the blood rush to his head as he looked at the floor. "I won't kill anyone," he finally said. "But if you need a pilot... I can do that."

"Then get up," Date Kunari told him. "We have a lot to do, and not very much time to do it. Landing Day is only forty-eight hours away."

Annie

Reap

June 29th, 2128

Annie didn't even make it back to the security checkpoint before the MPs found her.

She raised her hands and said, "I'm not armed," as they pointed their rifles. When they told her to get down on the ground, she did, and then they cuffed her hands behind her back. The man who searched her did so roughly, and she couldn't help but stiffen when his hands explored her thighs and chest. *Son of a bitch. You wouldn't be allowed to touch me with a ten foot pole if...* and there her train of thought slid off the rails. *If what? If I hadn't just broken the law?*

That thought fogged her mind into a sort of stupor, so that for however long they kept her on the ground, and then after, when they walked her out through the docking facilities and then loaded her into a UCAF prisoner transport vehicle, she followed orders but did not really see or hear what was happening around her. Once the vehicle started moving, she shifted her head so that she could see out the small window next to her. *This might be the last time you see anything but a jail cell for a while*, she told herself. *This might be the last you see of Toshimayr City.*

They drove through Yellow Zone, taking the same route where she had marched her wing such a short time ago. She remembered the crowds then, gathered to protest their arrival, but now the relatively anonymous vehicle she was in drew no more attention than any other passing car or truck. She watched people sitting at tables outside a Martian style cafe, drinking coffee, and a young couple stepping out of a sushi restaurant. A mother wheeled her baby past in a carriage. Two businessmen in suits argued as they walked, hands waving expressively in the air around them.

When they approached the bridge, she saw the empty

lot where a building had once stood. It was cordoned off from pedestrians, a bare patch of rock now. A sign hung up next to the lot, advertising that Ishikawa Construction would begin work shortly. *All those people died there*, she thought, remembering that desperate moment when she'd tried to help them. And Kaito had been there too, though she hadn't known it at the time, down on the ground pulling people out of the wreckage and away from the collapse. Despite herself, she smiled. *Maybe we were always meant to find each other*, she tried to comfort herself. *Maybe we were meant to save someone there, some kid who's going to grow up and change the world. It would be nice to think that.*

The prisoner transport vehicle jogged sharply to the right as it passed under the bridge, to avoid potential IEDs dropped from above, and she couldn't help but laugh. The MP sitting across from her stared, but he didn't say anything, and after a good long time she finally stopped, then closed her eyes for the rest of the trip. *I don't need to see Green or Blue Zone. That's not where my memories are.*

Before they put her in the cell, they made her strip in a small changing room. She knew it was coming because the male MPs left the room, and she was left with two female MPs. One of them brought in a plastic box for her to place her uniform in, and the other brought a plastic wrapped light blue prison uniform, which she dropped onto the floor. Neither of them looked away, not when Annie took her jacket off, nor her shirt, nor the shoes and pants. One by one, she folded each piece of her clothing and put it in the box, with her shoes on the bottom, until she stood there shivering in her underwear.

"All of it," the taller MP said, the first words either of these women had spoken to her, and Annie turned away to unhook her bra. She felt their eyes on her as she put her underwear in the box also. "Now," the MP continued, "Your lenses." She held out a plastic lens case, and Annie reached up a finger to one eye, then the other, carefully removing the pieces of technology and setting them safely in the case. That went into the box to, which was then closed and set on the bench.

"Turn to face the wall," the MP demanded sharply. "Place your palms flat above your head and spread your legs." Annie closed her eyes and bit her lip to stay silent while they searched her, the MP's plastic-gloved hands rough and probing. It hurt. Finally, she was permitted to open the bag and put on the light-blue prison uniform inside. It was scratchy, ugly, and shapeless. *But right now*, she admitted to herself, *I'd wear a garbage bag.*

She had a cell to herself. That didn't surprise her; there were only so many UCAF soldiers here in Toshimayr, and most of the time the worst trouble they got up to was getting drunk and in a fight with some locals at a bar.

They took her right past the cells with bunk beds, designed to be occupied by multiple prisoners, and to a single cell at the end of the hall. There was a cot and a toilet, and that was it. When the barred door had closed her inside, and the MPs had walked away, she sat down on the bed. The mattress was hard and thin, and it sagged in the middle from too many years of use. It was covered in plastic, like the kind of mattresses you found in college dorms, and there was a single thin pillow with another plastic wrapped package, this one containing sheets, a pillowcase and a blanket. After a moment, she tore open the plastic and set about making the bed. *There isn't much else to do.* When she was done, she laid down, did her best to fluff the pillow under her head, and looked up at the cracked ceiling.

These sheets are cheap, she could tell with a single touch. *Low thread count.* She ran her finger over them, and thought of how she'd made Kaito buy a new set of sheets for his bed. They were soft, just how she liked, and they'd felt luxurious on her bare skin when they'd both crawled under the covers, after.

The beach. She closed her eyes and accessed the sensory data stored on her internal memory core. When the data loaded, she again felt the sand of the beach at Elysia Island between her toes, the breeze ruffling her hair, the warm sun on her skin. She took in the salt scent of the sea, the taste of it on her tongue, but it wasn't the memory she wanted to lose herself in.

Kaito, she silently sent her thoughts out into the world, *I hope you're in a better place than I am. I miss you.*

No one came to get her or see her for the rest of the day.

After a while, Annie gave up hiding in her safe place and stood. She found that she was able to anchor her feet under the metal bottom of the cell door, so she did sit ups until she couldn't do those anymore, and then she did pushups, stripping down to the ugly prison issued bra when she started to sweat. *I wish they'd given me something that wouldn't bounce so much,* she mourned, *but in the grand scheme of how utterly fucked I am, I guess it's a small thing.*

She did a lot of pushups and sit ups. Eventually, she moved on to stretches and yoga poses she'd picked up in college: Cobra Pose, Upward Wheel, and all the others Sera had insisted would give them both the best butts in the dorm. After that, she did jumping jacks, because well, why not? If she could have found something to serve as a decent bar, she would have done pull-ups, too. Then, lunges and squats. *If there's anything soldiers know how to do*, she thought as she smiled to herself, *besides break expensive equipment, it's how to exercise.*

When they turned the lights off, she went to bed, using her extra sheet to dry off the damp coating of sweat which clung to her skin. She didn't sleep well, and as soon as it was light enough to see the next morning, she was doing sit ups again. By the time an MP came with her tray of breakfast, she was using the cell wall across from the bed to do handstand pushups.

The MP shook his head. "Eat your breakfast and then get dressed. The Commander wants to see you."

All of a sudden, Annie felt as if she was going to pass

out. *Whether from being upside down, or nerves, I can't tell.* Carefully, she extricated herself from the awkward position, then rested on the cool floor for a moment, on her hands and knees, trying to slow her breathing and bring her vision back into focus. *Here it comes. The charges. The Court Martial.*

She picked at the breakfast - some kind of canned hash rations that tasted like they'd made the long trip back and forth from Mars a couple of times over before someone unpacked them. After three bites, she knew she couldn't eat it without throwing up and did her best to clean herself instead. There wasn't much to do; they hadn't given her a hairbrush, and there was no shower. When the same MP returned to collect her breakfast tray, she told him she was ready.

Half an hour later, she was in Commander Clavinger's office once again, this time with her hands cuffed in front of her. The green tile floor wasn't any more comforting for being familiar, now. The secretary avoided looking in her direction, the way that one might look away from a particularly disgusting bug. MPs stood to either side of her chair. Forty-eight standard hours ago, they would have saluted her.

When the door opened, and the Commander's eyes locked onto her own, she stood up. "My apologies for not saluting, sir," she said, the words coming from somewhere that could still find humor in life - a place she hadn't been sure existed until just now. She held her hands up and wiggled the cuffs.

Clavinger's lips twisted into a sneer. "Get in here. You boys," he instructed the MPs, "stay outside." One of them opened his mouth to object, but the Commander cut him off. "She's handcuffed and half my size. Now sit your asses down and follow orders."

"Sir, yes sir," the MP barked, snapping out a salute. Annie stepped forward, and Clavinger held the door so that she could step into the office. There was no chair for her, this time, and he took his time about getting back behind his desk, forcing her to wait. The world seemed to recede away from her, and she hardly heard what he said until after he'd already been speaking a moment.

"...just had to fuck it up. Goddammit, you could have been on a transport back to Mars with a medal, but instead you go and pull this shit. What the happy hell were you thinking?"

Annie licked lips as dry as Martian sand. "I couldn't let an innocent man be tortured, sir."

"Innocent my ass," Clavinger barked. "You were fucking him."

Annie swallowed.

"You don't have to answer that," the Commander continued. "It wasn't a question. I had my people ask around, and Varga finally talked. You found yourself a local piece of ass, which I have no problem with, but you did get snowed by a terrorist, which I do have a fucking problem with."

"Kaito isn't a terrorist," Annie protested, before she could stop herself. "He got that hacked clearance to visit me in the hospital!"

"From insurgent hackers," Clavinger added, each word an accusation. "Who he was introduced to by an *Shumokuzame* sympathizer. A sympathizer who helped you break him out of a military detainment facility, and deliver him to more terrorists. If your piece of ass wasn't *Shumokuzame* before, he sure as hell is with them now. Congratulations, you've saved an innocent man."

Is he right, Annie asked herself. *But they were torturing him. I couldn't just let that happen to him.*

"Yes," Clavinger continued. "You have well and truly fucked the pig on this one, Lieutenant Commander Galtung. The next UCAF supply ship isn't due for another month, which means that's the earliest I can send you back. Until then I've got to keep you locked in a cell, and hope that no one figures out just who the hell you are, or that I've got a royal clusterfuck on my hands. Then you sleep for a year and a half back to Mars, during which time I can forget about you, and arrive with my report, which leads to your Court Martial. A day or two after that, I can expect to be relieved of duty for allowing this steaming pile of shit to happen, which will be approximately two years before my retirement. Your timing is for shit, Galtung."

"I apologize this all couldn't have happened two years later, sir," Annie was amazed to hear herself say.

"What was that? Was that a fucking joke, Lieutenant Commander? Do you realize how much easier my life would be if your spoiled ass happened to get shot full of half a dozen more holes by insurgents? If I ship your body back with a medal pinned to it, I file a hell of a lot less paperwork, and get to enjoy my retirement on time."

"I think," Annie responded hesitantly, "If you were going to do that, sir, you wouldn't be talking to me now."

"No," Clavinger grumbled, "I wouldn't. Because I still give half a steaming pile of shit about something you don't seem to recall the meaning of, Lieutenant Commander. Honor. Loyalty. Duty."

Annie swallowed, but didn't say anything. *I was loyal*, she insisted to herself. *Just not to you. To the man I...*

"Yes, you've shit on my front lawn pretty good, Galtung," Clavinger commanded, leaning back in his chair and opening the drawer of his desk. He pulled out a sheaf of papers; on the top paper was a black and white printed image of Kaito's face, bruised, semi-conscious. "Do you know what this is?"

"No sir," Annie said, then hazarded a guess. "Kaito's file, sir?"

"That's right," Clavinger confirmed. "This hard copy is the only record of Katakura Kaito's arrest and interrogation. I've made sure that all digital records are deleted."

Annie shook her head. "I don't understand."

"You told the officers at a black interrogation facility that you were there on my orders to retrieve a man who had been arrested by mistake," Clavinger said, pulling the paper clip off the sheaf of papers and removing the picture. "I have confirmed to said officers that you were indeed acting on my orders, and that the pertinent details for those orders are classified above their clearance level." Taking the sheaf of papers in his hands, he reached over to the paper shredder on the floor next to his desk and fed them in.

"The security footage at the docks has been classified," Clavinger continued. "The police reports for the stolen Subtee list two members of *Shumokuzame* only. You've revealed a mole in our security forces, which may be the only good thing to come out of this. In one month, you ship back home, as previously discussed, as a God-damned hero. I am not doing this as a favor to you. I am doing this because it is a hell of a lot less paperwork, and does not fuck over my career. Your part of the bargain is to shut the fuck up about all of this, which should not be too difficult as the entire damn thing is now classified top secret, and your soon to be discharged ass will not have the clearance to discuss it with anyone."

Strips of paper curled out of the shredder. "Your alternative," Clavinger explained as he walked over to face her in front of the desk, "Is to be shot for treason. Do we have an understanding, Lieutenant Commander?"

"Yes, sir," Annie managed to choke out.

Clavinger held out his hand. "Do not shit on my lawn again. I do not to see, hear, or even fucking smell you for the next month. Are we clear?"

"Yes, sir," Annie repeated, extending her hand to grip his.

"Good." Clavinger handed her the photo. "I thought you might want this. Now go take a fucking shower. You're confined to quarters until further notice."

It was Sera who came to see her first, of course.

Her timing was good - the knock on the door came just as Annie was pacing the distance between the bedroom and kitchenette, back and forth, eleven steps each way. The shower had been nice after being in a cell for so long, and she'd taken her time, but getting dressed was over real quick, and she still had no access to Europa's local net. No one had given her back her smart lenses, and they'd locked her tablet out of the base network. She had nothing to read, to watch, to listen to, and she had no idea what was going on in the outside world. Her hands twitched, fingers wanting to swipe through her personal messages, re-read the last thing Kaito had sent her, something.

So when the knock came, she was over to the door before she'd even consciously made the decision. "Yes?" She poked her head out, past the MP standing in the hallway. And there was Sera.

"Hey," her old roommate said. "Can I come in?"

The MP looked uncomfortable but said nothing, and so a moment later they were sitting next to each other on the couch that had come with the place. "I heard you went out and made yourself a hero again," Sera said, shaking her head. "What, you caught a spy or something?"

Annie bit her lip, and chose her words very carefully. "Is that what the rumor is?"

"There's all sorts of rumors," Sera told her, ticking down fingers as she listed them. "First when you were missing, people thought maybe you'd been snatched by insurgents; other people thought you went AWOL with your boyfriend." Sera didn't say who those 'other people' were, Annie noticed. *Any of my own pilots? Rafe, maybe?* "Then word came you busted a spy ring or something, and you're under 24 hour protection because *Shumokuzame* put a price on your head."

"It's all classified," Annie told her, truthfully. "And they're shipping me home on the next transport that comes through."

"But what, you're supposed to stay here," Sera waved her hand around the three room apartment, "For a month? Two? That doesn't seem like much of a hero's reward. And that guy outside the door... that's weird. I mean, it's not like anyone's going to get into Blue Zone, and then onto the base, without being stopped."

Kaito did, Annie remembered. "Are they saying anything else," was all she asked.

"One more thing." Sera hesitated.

"What?"

"Word's getting around," Sera admitted. "About... you know."

"No," Annie snapped in frustration, "I don't, I don't know anything. You're the first one I've talked to except for Clavinger." *That asshole.* "What?"

"About your father."

"Shit." Annie leaned back in the couch. "Well if *Shumokuzame* didn't have a price on my head before, they sure as hell will now."

"I haven't said yes or no," Sera promised, "But people know we were roommates in Officer Training School. I don't know how much longer I can put anyone off. I don't think they believe me now, anyway. Lieutenant Commander Malik had his people find a picture of you, from when you graduated from Exeter," she continued. "Your hair was long, but when you put the images side by side, the face..."

"Yeah," Annie sighed. "I guess that secret's out. Shit. There's no point in you lying for me anymore, Sera."

"You still can't tell me what happened, though, can you," Sera prodded.

"Nope. Sorry." Annie stood up and paced over to her kitchenette, where she began boiling water for tea.

"I didn't think so," Sera grumbled. "I don't like this. Something doesn't feel right." She raised her hand, made a few motions, and looked around the apartment. "Hey, did you know you've got an Earth Component that spawns in here?"

Annie rolled her eyes. "You and that game. It was bad enough when it was just Kaito, but now everyone seems to be playing it." She tried not to let the stab of cold ice that pierced her heart when she said his name show.

"It's made its way around base," Sera admitted with a shrug. "It's a decent way to kill time when there's nothing else to do. And it gets you out to some cool places in the city."

Annie wasn't really listening. "How's everyone else," she asked, after a moment. Her electric kettle clicked, and she poured boiling water into two cups, then put a small tea bag into each and carried the hot cups over to the couch, handing one to Sera. The other woman swiped away her game.

"Rafe's still down, but you can't hold that against him," Sera began. "Nolan's buried under paperwork and meetings."

"That's my fault," Annie admitted.

"...and Gavril's about finished the project Nolan gave him," Sea finished.

"What project?" Annie frowned. This was the first she'd heard about it.

"Well, Nolan said there wasn't any point in having two damaged Shells lying around," Sera explained. "So they looked them over, decided yours was in slightly better shape, and Nolan had him start stripping everything that still worked off Laura's Shell, and using the parts to repair yours."

"When did this start," Annie asked sharply. Why hadn't she been told? Sure, Nolan had been acting commander of the unit, but it wasn't like she was dead or off-planet.

"Basically as soon as we got back and they put you in the hospital," Sera admitted.

"Why didn't anyone tell me?"

Sera raised her hands in surrender. "It was supposed to be a surprise."

"A surprise?" Annie didn't get it.

"You know," Sera explained, "For when they let you out of the hospital and back on duty. So we could walk you into the hanger and show you your ride, good as new."

Annie set her tea down on the end table and pushed her palms into her eyes, slumping forward. "I don't deserve that."

"Sure you do," Sera said, slipping a hand around her shoulders. "Hey. You were a good CO. Everyone was broken up when you got hurt. Anyway, Nolan was right. Two busted Shells don't do us any good. Better to have one functional spare, even if they're gonna send you home and leave us without a pilot for it."

Annie dropped her hands down to her lap. "Thanks for coming to see me," she said. "It was a nice thing to do. Tell Nolan... thank you. For everything. He'll know what I mean." She looked out her window wistfully, in the direction of the hangar. "I wish I could climb in one more time."

"You will," Sera assured her, but Annie didn't believe it for a moment.

Sera's tablet, of course, hadn't been disabled, and she was happy to let Annie use it. Kaito's mother's contact information was easily acquired with a quick search on Europa's net, and, as she had promised she would, Annie called Katakuro Hekima.

"Hello?" The tablet's screen opened a video feed, showing Hekima's face. She was in an office; Annie could see calendars posted to a cubicle wall behind her.

"Hello, Hekima-san," Annie said, her mouth suddenly dry.

"Oh, Annie!" Kaito's mother smiled. "How are you?"

"I'm alright," Annie said. "I'm actually calling you about Kaito."

"Kaito?" Hekima frowned.

"Yes," Annie continued. "I wanted to let you know that you might not hear from him for a couple of days, but that he's safe."

"I assumed he was out on a long haul," the older woman said. "Is everything alright?"

"He was... he was arrested," Annie explained. "Over a mix-up with his security clearance."

"Arrested? Where is he?"

"He's safe," Annie assured Hekima. "I got him out, but I'm still working on clearing the charges."

"I still don't understand why Kaito would be arrested. He has a Green Zone clearance through Date Shipping that is completely legitimate."

Annie closed her eyes. "He got a forged Blue Zone Clearance to come visit me while I was in the hospital."

Hekima's eyes narrowed. "So this is your fault."

"You could say that. Yes," Annie admitted.

"Where is my son right now?"

"I don't know." Annie couldn't meet the other woman's eyes through the screen.

"I see. I think I'm going to be contacting a lawyer," Hekima said, her mouth tight. "I should have said something. I knew you were going to be trouble, but I didn't want to upset Kaito."

"I'm sorry," Annie said, and then Katakura Hekima terminated the call.

Kaito

Noriko Shiroishi

June 29th, 2128

Leaving Akaichi Emergency Repair Bay was the most unpleasant journey that Kaito had ever made.

Before they could even leave the emergency repair station, there was work to do; things started badly, and only got worse. Date-san sent him back to the *Nautilus* to pull out anything he wanted to keep - there wasn't much - and then program the computer to take the ship back to the underwater canyons of *Yomi-no-Kume*. After that, there wasn't much need to give the computer explicit instructions, because the plan was to scuttle it anyway. Kaito made sure it would be going plenty fast by the time it got to the canyons, knowing the tricky currents and rock formations would do the rest. He set the computer on a time delay, then hesitated.

I've spent a lot of time on this ship. He looked around at the cabin that had always felt so cramped to him, and now it was the last familiar thing he had left. *Years of my life. And now its going to be gone.* The timer was ticking down; he turned, hurried out of the *Nautilus*, and sealed the hatch behind him, withdrawing the gangplank before getting himself through the hangar airlock and setting the bay to fill with water. Then, he leaned against the airlock door for a moment, listening to the clanking that echoed through the water. Finally, there was only silence, and he knew his ship was gone.

When he got back to the living area, Mizuki was nowhere to be seen; the door to the far dormitory was closed. Date Kunari and Van den Berg were waiting for him, Date-san sipping a cup of tea and Van den Berg pale, sweaty, and unsteady on his feet. There was a bandage wrapped around his right wrist.

"You don't look so good," Kaito told him.

"Have a seat," Date-san replied, standing up and moving

his chair directly in front of the stainless steel sink.

"Why," Kaito asked suspiciously.

"We need to get rid of your RFID capsule," Van den Berg explained, holding up his forearm. The blood which had soaked through the bandage made Kaito's stomach turn. Taking a shaky breath, he stepped over to the sink. On the counter was a bottle of sake, open, and a coffee cup. The coffee cup had been filled to the brim with sake, and the handle of a knife stuck out of the top of the cup.

Kaito shook his head. "I can't do this," he protested.

"You were just tortured," Date-san reminded him in a friendly tone. "This won't be nearly as bad as that. Sit down." The old man took him by the shoulders and maneuvered him into the seat, while Van den Berg pulled the paring knife out of the coffee cup. "You might want to look away while it happens, though."

The two men gripped his arm and roughly held it down in the sink, all three of their bodies crowded together in the cramped space. Kaito tried to look up or down or to his left, but finally just closed his eyes and gritted his teeth. Fingers prodded his wrist.

"There it is," Van den Berg murmured, and Kaito could feel the other man's thumb rubbing against the glass capsule through a thin layer of skin. "Here we go." A lash of fire pulled across the underside of his forearm, and he couldn't help but scream. He felt like he was going to pass out again.

"There it is."

"I see it, I see it..."

"Get it!"

The voices were dim, far away, and they sounded like two boys trying to catch an escaped pet. For a moment, Kaito imagined Date-san running after an escaped gerbil or ferret, the kind of pets rich kids had on Mars or Luna, and the thought was enough to bring a grin to his face. Then, something clinked into the sink. There was a burning splash of sake, poured over the cut, and then they were wrapping his arm tightly.

For a moment, there was silence. "Can I have some of that sake," Kaito gasped, opening his eyes. His arm throbbed, and pain shot through it. He could already see blood blooming beneath the white bandage.

"No," Date-san said with a laugh, snatching the bottle away. "Thins your blood. You need to clot, not bleed." And then he put the bottle to his lips and threw his head back, taking a long drink. Kaito groaned.

"Here," Van den Berg offered, holding out two orange pills. "Take these."

Kaito tossed them back with a glass of water, but didn't feel ready to stand up yet. "What about the lace," he asked.

"What about it," Van den Berg replied with a shrug. "It's not like we can cut it out of your head."

"If they can track it, they'll find us," Date agreed. "Now go lie down, both of you. Our ride will be here in less than an hour, and I need to bleach this sink."

Their ride turned out to be a fishing vessel, presumably owned by members of *Shumokuzame*. Date-san woke them up, dragging a duffle bag large enough to carry a body back into the emergency living quarters. "Time to get dressed," he announced cheerily, unzipping the beg and pulling things out.

Kaito kept one hand on the table just off the kitchen, still not entirely sure he wouldn't fall over. Van den Berg had grabbed a chair, and Mizuki hadn't appeared yet. Date rolled a helmet over to Kaito's feet, and he bent down to pick it up. "Space suits?"

Date nodded, pulling out a large portion of white fabric with gently arcing lines all over it. "You'll need them. The sizes *should* be right - we had measurements on all three of you, though we had to pull yours from DSI records instead of *Shumokuzame* records. They won't notice that unless they have reason to go looking through our access logs, and that takes a warrant." The old man threw one heavy fabric and metal suit to Kaito, who barely caught it. "And for you." He tossed another to Van den Berg. "You can help each other, if you like." Then, he carried the duffle bag, still unzipped, into the other dormitory.

"Hello, my dear," Kaito could hear him say gently. "Time to wake up."

Kaito's face twisted into a scowl, and Date's words came back to him. It was Mizuki's fault that all those people had died when that building collapsed. That he'd had to have shards of glass picked out of his back. And she'd stood there in the hospital room with his mother, all sweet and innocent, as if she was only there to check on him...

Angrily, he hauled the vacuum suit and helmet into 'his' dormitory, where he and Van den Berg helped each other. Kaito had never worn one before, but the man from Callisto had, and he was grateful for the help.

"I thought they'd be bulkier," Kaito admitted, finally standing up. The suit fit his body closely, picking out the shape of his legs and torso.

"You've been watching too many clips from Old Earth," Van den Berg said with a smile, turning around. "Here, do me up. These are pressurized close to the skin, and the lines you see are strips of metal, which maintain the tension and bend with you when you move." After some fumbling, Kaito managed to finish securing the other man's suit. "We still had to wear these on Callisto, when I was a kid."

"There," Kaito said, slapping Van den Berg on the shoulder and bending down to pick up his own helmet. "What are we doing with our old clothes?"

"Garbage chute," Van den Berg informed him, and they gathered the clothing up in a pile to head back into the kitchen where Date and Mizuki were waiting. *Of course*, Kaito realized, *They only had one suit to get on, and two people to do it.* He tried not to look at how the suit revealed the familiar curves of Mizuki's body: the swell of her hips and breasts, the thin, graceful lines of her legs. *I bet Annie looks pretty damned good in one of these, too*, he told himself, and then wondered where she was, and whether she was Okay.

Kaito hesitated to throw the sweater his mother had knitted him down the chute. "This was on the *Nautilus*," he told Date. "There shouldn't be a tracker on it." The old man nodded and took it from him, and then the four of them walked over to the bay where the fishing vessel was docked. "Put your helmets on," Date instructed them, "and seal the suits. Then follow me. No one should be looking out through the external cameras right now, and the Captain's got the entire crew sharing a drink, but I can't guarantee the halls will be empty, and we don't want anyone to see your faces."

But no one was in the halls, and Kaito breathed a sigh of relief as they got into the hold and closed the doors behind them. They walked past the ship's neatly stored supplies, and then Date opened a hatch.

"Oh no," Kaito groaned, but he didn't know how to use the suit to transmit audio out, and he doubted Date would have listened to his objections, anyway. In front of them was the fish hold, an insulated compartment beneath the floor that was filled with hundreds or thousands of dead fish, floating in refrigerated seawater. One of them looked up at him with dead eyes, and chunks of ice bobbed along the surface of the water next to it. With a grin, Date shoved him toward the hatch and said something, but Kaito couldn't hear either. Van den Berg jumped in like he did it everyday, pushing himself down under the water and off to somewhere else in the hold to make room. Mizuki hesitated for a long moment, then knelt down and slipped into the water feet first, and then Kaito couldn't avoid it any longer: it was his turn.

He slid feet first into the cold water of the hold, and when his helmet went beneath the water, a dead fish slapped up against the translucent faceplate, and stared at him with its dead eyes. The pressurized, insulated suit kept him from feeling the ice around him as anything more than vague bumps against a sort of outer shell. He was just about to kick back toward the hatch, to climb out and take his helmet off and tell Date-san that he couldn't do this, when the light went away and he was floating in the dark.

How long are we going to be down here, Kaito wondered. *How much air do I have? They must have figured this out already - we must have enough for... whatever we're doing.* But that thought wasn't very comforting. He knew very well all the different things that could delay a ship in Europa's oceans: tricky currents, traffic at a dock, mechanical problems...

He turned his head, trying to pick out Mizuki or Van den Berg in the dark, but couldn't see a thing. Eventually, he just curled into a ball there, floating in the silent dark, and hugged his knees to his chest.

He must have slept, eventually, because a loud, mechanical clanking sound echoing through his helmet woke him up. The fish and ice sloshed and bumped against him: the hold was moving.

Kaito tried to think through what might be happening. *Most fish are brought right back to one of Europa's colony-cities to be processed and sold,* he knew. *So we could be at one of the other cities. But most of the time, the fishing ships that supply to the domestic market don't have removable holds: they just empty what they have and go right out again.*

He hadn't ever worked on a fishing ship himself, but he knew a lot of guys who did, and had hung out with them around the bar at *Tako To Ama.* The only fishing ships with modular fish holds that he recalled were the ones designed for export. *They remove the sealed holds and ship them right up the orbital elevators,* he recalled. *To be loaded onto cargo vessels and shipped to other colonies in the system.*

Date is smuggling us off-world, he realized. Would he even feel the weightlessness when they left the planet's gravity well? He was already floating in a tank full of water, so probably not. *The cold fish and water mean that we won't show up on any thermal scans, and without the RFID chips... the only thing that could trip us up is the neural lace.* He pictured it crouching there in his head, like a malevolent spider, just waiting for its chance to betray them. With nothing to do, he just waited, drifting in and out of a doze. At some point, he realized that he was hungry, and his bladder became uncomfortably full. Van den Berg had mentioned that the suit had the capability to hook in a catheter, but that they wouldn't be in them long enough for it to be needed... now Kaito shifted uncomfortable, trying not to think about the building pressure.

Finally, just when he was about to scream from the time in the dark and the cold and the hunger, a light filtered down through the chunks of ice and layers of fish. Desperately, he swam up toward the light, shoving aside everything in his path. *There - the hatch!* His helmet broke the surface, and his gloved hands clawed at the edge. Someone grabbed onto his shoulders and helped him out, and then he he was clear, splayed out on the floor like a dead fish himself. He fumbled for the catch on the helmet, not even stopping to think about whether the room was pressurized or not, and yanked it off to take a breath of air.

With a splash, another suited body was deposited next to him, and Kaito pulled himself up to look around. Date directed two men he didn't recognize to help haul out the last of them - from the shape, he guessed it was Van den Berg. A shudder of bone-deep cold ran through him, and Kaito realized that he'd been shivering uncontrollably for some time. Wherever they were, there was some minimal amount of gravity, at least, because he wasn't floating up off the deck.

After Van den Berg had been deposited in his own puddle of cold water, and the hatch closed, Date kneeled down next to Kaito. "Come on, get up," the old man said, prodding Kaito with a hand. "You'll feel better after you get out of that suit and into some warm clothes."

"Where are we," Kaito groaned, pulling himself up into a crouch and fumbling at the clasps.

"You're on the freighter *Mary Ellen*," Date explained. "We brought you up the orbital elevator at Icebreaker Three, passed you through inspection with all the fish, and stowed you aboard on the gravity deck instead of the hold."

Kaito looked around, and realized that he was on top of a giant insulated metal cube - the modular fish hold, now strapped into place on a rotating grav deck. The cube extended about twenty feet in each direction, and the ceiling of the grav deck was only three or four feet above them. "Why the grav deck," He mumbled.

"Less mess," Date confided. "We didn't really want to try to pour you lot out in zero-g, and get ice, fish and seawater everywhere."

"And where are we headed," Van den Berg asked, hauling himself up next to them.

"The flight plans filed before we left," Date answered, "say we're going to Io, to supply provisions to the iron mines there."

"So is that actually where we're going," Kaito repeated, managing to pull his arm out of the suit.

"To begin with," Date said with a smile and a twinkle in his eye. "It's not a long trip; Io orbits Jupiter about every forty-eight standard hours, so if you're willing to wait for it to come around, it's never really very far away. That's long enough to get you all warmed up and filled in on what's happening."

Kaito flopped around for a moment like a fish on a line, then managed to kick out of the legs. He was naked now, and had to clench his jaw to keep his teeth from clicking together as he shivered. Date pulled a thick, soft gray robe over him, and Kaito wrapped himself in it. A moment later, the old man was giving Van den Berg a robe, and Kaito's eyes flicked over to check on Mizuki, who hadn't said anything since being retrieved from the fish hold.

Mizuki had one leg stuck in her suit, and was just able to kick it off as Kaito looked over to check on her. Her skin was pale and speckled with goosebumps, and she was just as nude as he and Van den Berg; Kaito quickly looked away. It wasn't that he hadn't seen her before - they'd dated, even lived together for quite a while - but it felt somehow disloyal to Annie to look at her now.

Once she was wrapped in a robe, Mizuki joined the conversation. "What's at Io," she asked, clutching the robe about her tightly.

"*Narukami*," Date Kunari told them. "The god of war."

The voyage ended up taking them even less time than Date had estimated: the *Mary Ellen's* fusion torches could have taken the freighter from Europa's orbit across the 152,000 miles to Io's orbit in just about two hours, if they were only concerned about going straight in toward Jupiter. Instead, the computers plotted a course that took them in at a gentle angle to meet and match speed with Io as it came around thirteen hours after they left Europan orbit.

It was enough time to eat, sleep, and eat again, and when Kaito - fully dressed now, including his ratty old sweater and a new set of generic smart lenses - met Date, Van den Berg, and Mizuki in the galley, he was feeling much better. When he put in the lenses - which he wasn't allowed to use to access any of his personal accounts, so as not to give their location away - he realized that he hadn't even thought about playing an AR game in days. Annie would be proud, he told himself.

They were all in the sort of nondescript, gray, one piece jumpsuits that were in common use among zero-g crews, complete with lots of pockets to put things in. Kaito didn't have anything to put in the pockets. He didn't have much of anything, period, and the jumpsuit was made for someone both stockier and shorter than he was. It kept riding up in the back. He tied back his hair to keep it from floating in his face.

Date handed them each a couple of plastic pouches with screw off tops. Kaito glanced at the labels: "Strawberry Applesauce," read one, and "Chicken and Rice," read the other. He experimentally squeezed the pouch that theoretically contained chicken. "I don't feel any meat in here," he complained.

Date laughed. "It's all mush. Like baby food. Enjoy."

Mizuki made a face, but Van den Berg just twisted the top off one of his pouches and dug in. "No mess this way," he explained in between long draws of ground up chicken and rice paste. "You can't actually put anything on a plate up here. It would all just float away."

For a moment, Kaito considered just waiting until they'd arrived at Io, but then his stomach grumbled and reminded him how long it had been since his last meal. He twisted the plastic cap off his pouch of chicken-goo and sucked a big glop of it into his mouth. It wasn't the worst thing he'd ever tasted. "So," he began. "Io."

Date Kunari nodded. "Io. Make sure you get a look at the atmosphere as we come in - there's an aurora effect that's absolutely beautiful. Most Europans never get to see it."

"Yeah, I'll get right on that," Kaito said, rolling his eyes. "How about you tell us what we're doing, now? And not just a load of crap about gods from Old Earth."

"Patience," Date cautioned him. "As with all things, the explanation will take time. Did you ever wonder why, even as Mars and Luna were building up their military capabilities, Europa, Ganymede, and the other moons of Jupiter did not?"

Kaito shrugged. "We hadn't been established as long. They had the materials, the manpower, to put into military construction projects while we were still scraping by trying to survive."

"There is an element of truth to that," Date agreed. "But the ability to defend oneself is just as essential to survival as is a supply of food, water and air. Ask the antelope how long it would survive being hunted by the lion without it's great speed."

"I can't," Kaito pointed out. "They're all extinct." Mizuki laughed.

"Just so," Date admitted. "They were utterly and

completely unprepared for nuclear war. I believe there are genetic samples on Luna; perhaps one day we'll recreate them. But the antelope were not intelligent creatures; they lived entirely by instinct, without the ability to consider the future, and make plans for potential threats. We are not antelope."

"Are you saying," Kaito asked, swallowing another lump of chicken, "That the colony government had made plans for the Martian invasion?"

"That is precisely what I am saying," Date Kunari agreed. "Unfortunately, everything moved far too quickly for us. The nuclear war on Earth accelerated existing tensions, bringing things to a crisis point years before we were ready to defend ourselves. By the time Luna and Mars were sending our government messages about unifying the colonies, it was already clear they weren't going to allow us to refuse peacefully, or respect our sovereignty. Within two months, the Unified Colonies government was formed. The invasion fleet was assembled in Martian orbit, and launched, all within a year and a half of Earth going silent."

"When the Jupiter colonies got word," Van den Berg picked up, "they knew they didn't have long before shit hit the fan." Kaito looked at him, surprised to see someone his own age adding to the story. "My father told me some of this," he admitted.

Date smiled. "Callisto, Ganymede, Europa, and the mining facilities at Io," he continued. "They knew that Mars had been arming for some time. They knew that if a response was going to come, it would come before we were ready to defend ourselves." He held up a hand to forestall Kaito's questions. "So. The decision was made to conceal what capabilities we did have. If they were being excessively cautious, and if the invasion had not occurred, no harm would have been done."

Kaito pushed himself over to the garbage chute and stuffed his empty plastic pouch in. "Alright, alright. So what, we had a couple of ships, and stuffed them behind a moon or something?"

"Something like that," Date agreed. "In 2094, the four colonies began construction of a shipyard located in Jupiter's rings, where it's location would be concealed."

Finally, Kaito thought. *Now we're getting to what really matters.* "That's thirteen years before the war on Old Earth. About fifteen before the invasion."

Date nodded. "Just building the shipyard took almost a decade, and getting enough centrifuges operating to begin enriching uranium mined from Io's surface took even longer."

Enriched Uranium. Kaito let himself drift and closed his eyes. "So you have nukes."

"We have a single battlegroup of three frigates, two destroyers, and one dreadnaught," Date confirmed. "All armed with nuclear missiles, capital scale rail guns, and point defense systems."

"It's been twenty years," Van den Berg explained. "The UCAF doesn't even keep a full battle group in Jupiter orbit any longer. A frigate at Callisto, and a destroyer each at Europa and Ganymede."

"Enough to make the threat of orbital bombardment real," Date agreed. "But not enough to fend off our forces. We've spent the last twenty years finishing these ships and arming them. When the UCAF invaded our colonies, they had overwhelming superiority of arms. That is no longer the case."

"But as soon as they find out, they're going to send ships again," Kaito objected.

"They will," Van den Berg admitted. "But think about it. It will take at least a year and a half for any force they get together to make the journey here. That means we have time to be ready for them."

It could work, Kaito realized. *I'm not any kind of military strategist, but...* "What about the Icebreaker stations? The Military Police?"

"We have an operation ready to commence," Date demurred, "which will target not only the Icebreaker stations, but the garrison in Toshimayr, as well. We will launch a simultaneous assault upon the Destroyer in Europan orbit, and take control of the orbital elevators. Once we have control of what comes in and goes out, we are hopeful that any remaining ground forces will be open to terms of surrender."

Annie. Kaito wondered what she would do. Fight, presumably. Was there a way he could get word to her, convince her that the ground forces had to surrender? "What do you need me for," he asked out loud.

"We need pilots," Date said. "All of our ships are operating on skeleton crews. We need to train more people in every position," he acknowledged, nodding to Van den Berg and Mizuki, "But Kaito, you have a talent for driving ships. There's not many people who could have taken a Subtee through those canyons like you did."

"That's underwater," Kaito protested. "Space is going to be completely different."

"You'll be learning from the pilots we already have," Date assured him. "And I have every confidence that you'll adapt quickly."

The ship intercom crackled to life. "Admiral-sama," a male voice pierced the quiet of the galley, "We are entering orbit at Io. The first battle group has already arrived, and indicates they are prepared for transfer of personnel."

"Admiral?" Kaito raised his eyebrows.

"A commision," Date Kunari explained, unbuckling the belt that held him in place and rising from his chair, "That I accepted twenty years ago, in secret, when we still had a government. I have spent the last two decades smuggling supplies to our shipyard, and simpering in that fool of a base commander's ear to distract him from our true aims. Now, Katakura Kaito, will you come with me, and free our people?"

It's not like I really have any choice, Kaito told himself. He remembered being lifted in his father's arms, pressing his face against the rough stubble of his father's cheek. *They killed my father.* He remembered the way he'd been treated by the other students, when his mother sent him to school with off-world children.

"Show me the ship," he said after a moment of silence. "And I'll fly her."

The ship, it turned out, was beautiful.

Narukami, the dreadnought, was the vessel they transferred to, and it was practically invisible until they were on top of it. Kaito didn't so much notice the *Narukami*, as notice an absence: a black hole where stars did not shine. As they maneuvered their shuttle to link up with the warship, it's silhouette passed between the shuttle and Io, and only then could he make out the form clearly.

The ship, much like a Subtee, was built in the rough shape of a cylinder. Kaito understood the engineering behind that on a basic level: the atmosphere inside pressurized vehicles was pressing out on the hull. In the case of a Subtee, there was pressure pushing in on the hull as well, and the danger was that the hull would crumple. In a vacuum, there would be the opposite problem: a breach in the hull would cause atmosphere, and other important things, to explode outward as nature tried to equalize the pressure. As a result, hard edges and corners and protruding forms were nothing more than weak points, begging to be damaged. Designing a ship with them - either submersible, or built for a vacuum - was building in your own Achilles' Heel. The *Narukami* avoided any such weak points; her bow was rounded, giving the whole ship the appearance of a torpedo over 200 meters long, and her aft was a cluster of exhaust nozzles that formed her fusion torch drive. The only things to break her smooth surface were blisters - rounded, again - about her center, which would, Kaito could tell from the schematics on the tablet Date Kunari had handed him, contain her missile launching systems, rail guns, and automated point defense weapons.

With a finger, he swiped through the files, missing his smart lenses. *Narukami* was armed with four railguns designed to fire forward, laid out the long way on her hull. Another eight pierced inward to her core, allowing her to roll past an enemy vessel and fire a broadside from either direction. The two dozen missile launch sites were each loaded with nuclear missiles, half unity warheads that would hit a single target, and half MIRV missiles, which could break apart into a dozen independently targeting and maneuvering warheads while in flight, to engage a mass of smaller enemies in a single volley.

The yield numbers, the military terminology, those didn't mean much to Kaito. He spent more time looking at the kind of acceleration the fusion-torch drive could put out, but he kept coming back to the silhouette of the ship itself. It reminded him, he decided, of nothing so much as a whale.

He'd had a cheap old tablet as a kid, and his mother and Old Man Kunari had loaded it up with educational games and puzzles and stories for him. He was fairly certain they had eventually regretted that, once he'd begun blowing off school work to immerse himself in video games as a teenager, but he still remembered one of the games, in which the premise was that the player was a diver exploring the oceans of Old Earth. He'd loved the animated images of whales, dolphins, jellyfish, and coral reefs, and eventually he'd asked his mother if they could go diving at a reef on Europa, and maybe see some whales or dolphins.

"Kaito-chan," his mother had explained with the soft patience of someone crushing a little boy's dreams, "Those things don't exist on Europa. The ocean here is much too deep and cold. Where would whales go to breath? They can't spend all their time under the water."

"Can we go see them on Earth," he'd asked, with no conception of what that meant. He must have been three, at most, but he still remembered the dropping feeling in his belly when she told him that there were no more whales: everything on Earth had died when the war came.

"They have DNA, on Luna," his mother had tried to

comfort him. "And someday, there will be whales on Mars, when the terraforming is complete."

None of which meant much to a kid told he couldn't get what he wanted, of course - but now, the *Narukami* reminded him of nothing so much as the whales he had dreamt of every night for months as a small boy, swimming through the infinite darkness of space instead of Old Earth's deep blue sea.

Like a whale, the dreadnought didn't swim alone. Against the light of Io, Kaito could see the smaller silhouettes surrounding the *Narukami*, the other vessels making up her battle group. He scrolled down through the file he'd been given, his finger moving easily over the tablet. The destroyers were named *Fūjin* and *Raijin*, he saw, while the frigates were the *Mikaboshi*, the *Kuraokami*, and the *Kagu-tsuchi*. *All named after kami*, he observed, *the mythical gods of Japan. Is it arrogant to call man-made things by their names?* People did it all the time in video games, but ships...Kaito worried that it might be bad luck.

As he had been reading, the shadow of the *Narukami* had grown, and now it filled the viewscreen. He could hear and feel the gentle impact as the shuttle pilot mated their small ship to the black warship, and then the airlocks sealed with a clank. When the atmosphere had pressurized, Van den Berg was the one to open the shuttle's side of the connection, and the first one through. He looked natural, moving in zero-g, and Kaito envied him. He watched as Date motioned Mizuki through next, then brought up the rear himself, trying not to bump his head as he went. The shuttle pilot swung the airlock shut behind them.

The armor of the *Narukami* was over fourteen inches thick, the schematics had explained, and he fought the urge to linger as he entered the airlock, wanting to measure with his hands. The outer layer was a thin shield of aluminum, designed to ward off small meteoroids, which would explode on contact and never damage the anti-weapon armor beneath. A layer of woven ceramics and kevlar insured that any fragments which penetrated the aluminum wouldn't make it any deeper; next, the primary armor layer of boron carbide honeycombed with more ceramics, and then a final layer of kevlar to prevent shrapnel from penetrating the inner hull. All together, it was thicker than the distance down his forearm from his elbow to his closed fist. Shaking himself, Kaito realized that everyone else was leaving him behind, and pushed off to follow.

Just inside the airlocks was a room about the size of the walk in refrigerators used to store fish on Europa, with racks of pressure suits, helmets, and the other equipment necessary for EVA maintenance and repair. They moved through that room quickly and into the kind of cramped passageway Kaito recognized from Subtee construction: it was uncomfortably crowded by the presence of a single woman, dressed in the same sort of spacer coveralls that Kaito and the others had been given on the *Mary Ellen*. In a clumsy, unpracticed fashion, her hand snapped up to her forehead in a salute.

"At ease," Date Kunari told her, in the same tone of voice he had used to order Kaito and his other employees around the docks. The hand fell. "Captain Shiroishi," the old man continued, "My compliments to your crew on the timely arrival of the battlegroup, and the tight formation. Unfortunately, we are going to need to put off the customary tour of the ship for the present time."

Kaito couldn't keep himself from speaking. "Noriko Shiroishi?" He hardly recognized the elegant lady who had accompanied Captain Varga to the spa - the woman he'd thought of as nothing more than a prostitute.

"*Hai*, Kaito-san," Shiroishi said flatly. "You and I will speak later, I think."

"Uh, sure," Kaito stumbled over his words, blushing. This officer before him acted nothing like the pampered mistress he remembered. *Is she a spy*, he wondered. *For which side? Old man Date must know who she's been sleeping with...*

"Your orders, Admiral," Captain Shiroishi asked.

"Calculate a course that will take us to Europa as quickly as possible," Date specified, "And run test diagnostics on the active countermeasures systems. When you have your course, move the battlegroup out."

"Yes sir," Shiroishi confirmed with a tight smile.

"Once we're moving," Date continued, "Stand down as much of the crew as you can. Get your people well rested for our arrival. Forward the same orders to the rest of the battlegroup. Dismissed."

Shiroishi saluted again, then pushed off down the cramped tunnel, her hands tapping exposed pipes, floor grates, and handles to steer her way.

"What about us," Van den Berg asked.

"You," Date Kunari addressed the soldier, "Head aft and find the marines; see about helping out with any boarding parties we need to deploy. Mizuki-san," the old man said, turning his head, "please come with us to the bridge."

"Hai, Date-sama," Mizuki replied, her head still swivelling to take in the sights around her. Of course, Kaito realized, she'd never been in a Subtee until just a few days ago. She'd only ever lived and worked in Toshimayr, which had been designed with large open spaces bored into the rock, where people could live for their entire lives without the crushing fear of claustrophobia. Compared even to the small, cheap apartment she and Kaito had shared while they'd been together, this ship must seem so cramped as to be terrifying, and not at all what she'd envisioned from science fiction VR dramas. For a moment, Kaito felt a twinge of sympathy for her, and then he remembered Date Kunari's revelation that she had been the one to drop the bomb off that bridge and send him to the hospital. With a push that was a bit more forceful than he intended, Kaito followed Date in the same direction the Captain had headed, trusting the old man to know where he was going, like he seemed to know everything else.

The bridge of the *Narukami* would have been called the conn on Subtee's like the *Nautilus*; a holdover from old earth submarines that had not been applied to space ships. Kaito's pilot chair in the old DSI transport had never been meant for a bridge crew, but *Narukami*'s bridge already held half a dozen people when they arrived, including Captain Shiroishi, who had handily beaten them there and was already strapped into her chair.

"Kaito," Date said quietly, taking him by the shoulder, "That is the helm. I'd like you to stay next to the helmsman and watch what he's doing. Don't bother him or interrupt, but learn what you can."

"Sure," Kaito said, wondering if he should have saluted or used the word 'sir' like everyone else., 'Screw it,' he decided and set off along the wall of the compartment, trying to avoid flicking any switches or turning any dials as he moved along. Behind him, he heard Date begin to address Mizuki, and tuned it out. There was no place to sit near the helm that wasn't already occupied, and precious little room to float without being in the way, but he managed to wedge himself in between half-stowed backup instrument panels.

The helmsman, a Europan man about the same age as Kaito, with his hair clipped close to his head and an intense look in his eyes, frowned in Kaito's direction. "Yes," he asked, clearly bothered by the presence of someone unfamiliar while he was trying to work.

"Hey," Kaito said with a nod. "Katakura Kaito. I'm just supposed to stay out of the way and watch. Pretend I'm not even here."

With a grunt, the helmsman went back to his station.

"Do you have a course, Lieutenant Sato," the captain asked someone or other in a firm, clear voice that carried through the compartment.

"Hai, Captain," a young woman to the right of the helmsman replied. "Time to burn: seventeen minutes."

"Time to burn, seventeen minutes," the helmsman confirmed.

"Very good," Captain Shiroishi said with a curt nod,

then touched the air in front of her. When she spoke again, her voice boomed throughout the ship, amplified by the internal speakers and, Kaito presumed, audible in every compartment. "This is Captain Shiroishi. In just over fifteen minutes, we will be burning for Europa. Once the burn is complete, your watch officers will be rotating the entire crew through alternating down-shifts for the next ten hours. I want every member of this crew to get something to eat and some rest when they aren't on duty. Sleep if you can. Once we enter our final approach to Europa, we will prepare to engage the UCAF forces in orbit and reclaim control of the orbital elevators."

The otherwise ever-so-serious helmsman smiled at that, but said nothing.

Shiroishi touched the air again, and the ship's intercom speakers died. "Helm, have you received our course calculations from navigation?"

"Aye sir," the helmsman replied.

"Very good." Kaito risked a glance at the Captain's chair, where she and Date Kunari had leaned their heads together and seemed to be conferencing in whispers, the old man attached to the backrest of the captain's seat by one strong arm.

"So why are you here," the helmsman asked Kaito in a murmur.

Kaito swallowed. He felt very much as if he was intruding someplace he did not belong. "Date-san asked me to watch you, and learn whatever I could," he responded, trying to match the other man's low volume.

The helmsman considered that for a moment. "You ever fly anything before," he asked.

"I've piloted a Subtee for years," Kaito said, but then admitted, "But in space? No, nothing, ever."

"Right." The helmsman sighed. "Look, how long did you train to pilot one of those things?"

"A year before I was licensed," Kaito remembered, "And a while after that before anyone trusted me to do anything solo."

"Sounds about right." The helmsman nodded. "I can show you a couple things while we wait for the burn, but once I'm doing something, you shut up and don't interrupt, right?"

"Hai," Kaito confirmed.

"Alright. My name's Lieutenant Ito. Take a look at this screen." Kaito moved around so that he was looking over Ito's shoulder, and spent the next ten minutes trying to process the massive differences between piloting a Subtee and helming a warship in zero-g.

With the *Nautilus*, there was always a certain amount that he was piloting by feel, by instinct honed over years in the chair. On this ship, Kaito realized, every instinct he had was wrong. The speeds at which the *The Narukami* travelled were so much greater than any Subtee that human reaction times just couldn't deal with them. When taking the *Nautilus* down through Europa's ice, if there was an unexpected bulge or jagged outcropping ahead, Kaito had to be listening for proximity alarms and keeping a close eye on his sensor displays so that he could steer around it. By the time the *Narukami* detected an incoming meteorite, say, or a fragment of debris in orbit, there was no way that any human could react before it hit. Even if the helmsman did, the ship couldn't change course fast enough to make a difference.

"So what," Kaito asked, incredulous, "Every little rock that comes at us, it just hits? We don't even try to move?"

"The little stuff, yeah," Ito explained. "I mean, something big, like a comet or an asteroid or a meteor of some kind of size, we'd see that coming on the sensors pretty far away, and nudge our course to avoid it. But something like this?" The helmsman held up a closed fist. "We just take it on the armor and move on."

"Something like that would sink a Subtee," Kaito admitted, shaking his head.

"We've got a lot more armor than anything down on the surface," Ito pointed out. "And it's designed to take that kind of impact. That's what the outer layer of aluminium is for - little pieces of debris."

"That's completely different from what I'm used to," Kaito realized.

Lieutenant Ito nodded. "Right? That's not the end of it, either. Look, your propulsion is basically always going, right?"

"Yeah." Kaito nodded. "The propellers might speed up, slow down, or even reverse, but I don't turn them off until we're docked again."

"Ok," Ito continued to explain, "So we're going to burn in a certain direction until we've got a certain amount of thrust, as calculated by the Navigator," he said, nodding to the young woman a few feet away. "But then we're going to cut the burn, and until it's time to slow down again, we're not going to use the torches."

"Because," Kaito said with a nod, "There's no resistance in the vacuum like there is in the ocean. An object in motion..."

"...tends to stay in motion," Ito completed the old law.

"So why," Kaito asked, "Do we have a seperate Navigator and Helm? I mean, not to be insulting, but..."

"But it seems like one person could do the job?" Ito nodded. "Yeah, on a merchant vessel, a transport, that's usually how it works. But once we start firing weapons and taking hits," he pointed out, "all of those forces are going to begin acting on this ship, changing our speed, our direction. It's going to be all I can do just to keep the ship under control."

"So you'll deal with the immediate stuff," Kaito reasoned, "And the Navigator handles the big picture?"

"Exactly," Ito said with a smile. "Trust me, it'll get busy enough that even between two of us, we'll hardly be able to keep up." An electronic chiming sound rang out from his screen, and the helmsman reached to silence it, then raised his voice. "One minute to burn, Captain."

"Confirmed," Captain Shiroishi said, emerging from her conference with Date Kunari. "One minute to burn. All hands, either strap yourself in, or find something to hang onto."

"Ten...," Lieutenant Ito called, counting down. Kaito wedged himself as tightly into the bridge machinery as he could, holding on with both hands. "...Two, one. Burning!" Ito's finger touched the air, and the ship went from having zero local gravity to more than Kaito had ever felt before.

His feet hit the ground first, and then, despite his best efforts, his knees buckled and he collapsed to the ground. Thankfully, the ship had been designed so that the compartments were oriented with the floors aft, and the ceilings fore. That meant that on most burns, gravity exerted itself in the direction humans were used to, and they could sit or stand in a way that was consistent with the layout of the equipment. Now, though he could have stood on the floor and continued watching the screens over Ito's shoulder, Kaito was ashamed to find he was too weak to get off the ground.

Annie would be able to stand right now, Kaito realized. *She's used to Mars gravity; her muscles are built for this. Living on Europa means I've never built up the strength I need.*

He wasn't sure how long the burn lasted; a minute, maybe longer. He never asked just how much gravity they'd been under, either - he would have been embarrassed to find it was less than he wanted it to be. Once the burn was over, he cautiously pushed himself back up, surprised to find the return to weightlessness such a relief.

"Burn complete," Ito announced. "We are on course."

"Very good, Lieutenant," the Captain praised him. "You can all expect to be relieved shortly," she informed the crew. "I want every one of you rested and prepared for combat when we enter orbit. When the next shift gets here, get something to eat, and try to get some sleep." The hatch to the compartment opened, and crew members Kaito didn't recognize began to trade places with those who had been manning the various stations.

"Katakura Kaito," Captain Shiroishi called, "With me."

His throat suddenly dry, Kaito swallowed and followed her out.

Kaito squeezed into Captain Shiroishi's quarters, closing the door behind him. The room wasn't more than ten or twelve feet on a side, with a low, thin bunk along one wall, a desk and chair, and hooks to hang clothes on. Panels in the walls with recessed handles indicated more storage, but there was barely enough room for two people to stand in the room.

Kaito leaned back against the closed door and waited for Shiroishi to speak.

"I imagine you have questions," the Captain of the *Narukami* said evenly.

"I-" Kaito took a moment to collect his thoughts. "You were with a UCAF Captain. Old Man Date..."

"Admiral Date," Noriko Shiroishi corrected him.

"Admiral Date. I mean, he knows, right?"

"It was on Admiral Date's orders that I began a relationship with Captain Varga." Kaito searched her face for any change of expression, any clue as to what she was feeling, but he couldn't see anything there.

"That was years ago," he realized. "When we were at the Spa, you said..."

She nodded. "I have given him my body for the past fifteen years. Since I was a young woman. I have given up any chance of a family; I have endured the contempt of my own people. Oh yes," she continued, "I know what they call women like me. Whore. *Baishunpu.* And they aren't wrong."

"But why..."

"Because the Admiral wanted someone close to every man who Captained a UCAF transport on this route," Shiroishi explained. "And so, for my home, for my people, I have been everything but a wife to Captain Varga for fifteen years."

"He doesn't know you're here," Kaito asked.

"No. He knows that I'm a transport pilot on the route to Io; he doesn't know what I do while I'm at Io, or anything about this battle group. If I had my choice, he would never know," she admitted, and for a moment Kaito saw something alive, something vulnerable, flicker in her eyes, before she forced it back down.

"Do you care about him at all," Kaito couldn't stop himself from asking.

"That's none of your business," Noriko Shiroishi hissed. "When we reach Europa Orbit, I will be the one who gives the order to destroy his ship. Nothing that has happened between he and I over the past fifteen years will change that."

Kaito shook his head. The amount of time this woman had dedicated to her cause - what she had given up, the price she had paid - he couldn't imagine doing what she had done.

"But you," Shiroishi interrupted his thoughts. "You're in love with that pilot, aren't you?"

Kaito looked away, unwilling to meet her eyes.

"Could you shoot that girl?" Shiroishi took Kaito by the chin with one hand, turning his head so that she could meet his eyes. "Could you shoot Annie, if the Admiral ordered it?"

He tried to imagine it: a gun in his hand, Annie looking at him.

"No," he whispered. "I couldn't."

Captain Shiroishi released his chin and dropped her hand back to her side. "I didn't think so," she admitted. "The good news is you shouldn't have to. She'll be down in Toshimayr, we'll be fighting in orbit. What happens to her, we aren't going to have anything to do with, one way or the other. But I'm glad you told me the truth, at least."

Miserable, Kaito remained silent.

"Now," the Captain continued, "I'm going to give you a direct order. What we've discussed here - what I've done over the years, and why - you aren't to talk about that with any member of my crew. I can't control what the Admiral asks or doesn't ask you," she admitted, "But I won't have you starting rumors, or undermining my authority."

"You don't think they know," Kaito asked her.

"Some may," she admitted. "Some of it. But most of them? No. And it will stay that way. Understood?"

"Yeah," Kaito agreed.

"Good. If you have any other questions, anything you want to say to me, now is the time," she said, her eyes flashing. "Once we step out of this room, you're nothing more than another member of this crew. You don't look for any special treatment, you don't show up and knock on my door - nothing."

Kaito closed his eyes, trying to clear away the headache that had been building. *It's the lace*, he was certain. *Worming its way deeper into my brain.* He tried to think of what he wanted to ask her, something he needed to know, but realized he didn't care about her background, about the reasons she'd done what she did.

"Do you think we can win," he asked her, finally. "I've heard what Old Man Date has to say. But he's... I mean, he's my boss. And old guy who owns a shipping company. You can call him an admiral, and you can call yourself a captain, but that doesn't make it real. Can we actually do this? Do we have a chance?"

"I believe that we do," Noriko Shiroishi told him without a trace of hesitation. "We're going to lose people along the way. In spite of everything we've planned, in spite of all the preparations we've made, we may still lose. Date-sama, you, I, we may all die. But this is the best chance Europa has had to be free again since the Colony War. And if we don't take it, then it will be no one's fault but our own that we remain a conquered people. No one's fault but our own," she continued, driving the words into him like nails, "That more children grow up without fathers. Oh yes, Date-sama told me about you. More children who are smart will run away from schools where Martian boys and girls made their lives hell. More women like me will whore themselves out to off-worlders, not for a cause, but for money, just to survive. Is this the world you want, Kaito? Or do you want to change it?"

"You know the answer to that," Kaito mumbled.

"Then say it out loud."

"I want to change it."

"Good." Captain Shiroishi nodded. "Because there's something you can do that no one else on this ship can do. Come with me."

The only things that had changed about the hacker kid from the repair shop were that he had shaved - or been forced to shave - and that he was now on the *Narukami* instead of in the backroom of a shady looking repair place across the street from a fish market.

"Hello again," Kaito said as he followed Captain Shiroishi into the undersized closet that passed for the warship's server and tech room. He'd never gotten the kid's name in the first place.

"This guy?" The kid waved a hand at Kaito the way one would wave to indicate a garbage barrel that needed to be emptied. "This guy? He's the one who got me busted!"

"Then we should thank him, Kagawa-san," the Captain said with the hint of a smile. "Or we would not have such a talented man maintaining our computer systems."

The kid sputtered for a moment, and Kaito turned to Shiroishi. "So what am I here for? A login and password for the ship's computers?"

She shook her head. "Well, yes, we'll get you that, but it's not why I brought you here in person. Kagawa, we need you to crack and jailbreak Katakura-san's neural lace. It was installed by UCAF interrogators during his interrogation."

Kagawa's eyes widened. "Oh. Uh, how long has it been... growing?"

"Maybe forty-eight hours," Noriko Shiroishi answered. "He got out just after you did. Had a bit more of an adventure on the way, though," she remarked with a trace of humor. "I understand it involved dead fish and refrigerators."

"Right," Kagawa said with the nod of someone getting down to work. All of a sudden, Kaito didn't feel that Kagawa was looking at him, any longer: the kid was looking at a piece of technology, a system to crack. "That's more than enough time for it to be operational at a base level. Sit down," he ordered Kaito, and pointed to the only chair in the compartment.

"What are we doing," Kaito asked without enthusiasm. "And why are we doing it? Are we taking this thing out?" He looked around the compartment for surgical tools.

"Can't," Kagawa said as he began gathering up tools and instruments. "It'd kill you."

"Right," Captain Shiroishi said sharply. "Kagawa-san, I'm going to leave this in your hands."

"Yes, sir," Kagawa acknowledged in a detached tone of voice that told Kaito he wasn't really even paying attention to the Captain. Shiroishi stepped out into the corridor, then closed the compartment door behind her.

"So..." Kaito flinched as Kagawa waved some kind of scanner around his head.

"I'm checking to make sure it's set up for wireless communication with other devices," Kagawa explained. "They kind of have to be, to be useful for interrogation, but... there. I've got the frequency. Doesn't look like the nanites manufactured any micro-bombs in your skull, either," he remarked, and Kaito flinched. "So that's good."

"Okay, really," Kaito interrupted. "If we can't get this thing out of my head, why aren't we just leaving it alone?"

"Do you know what Neural Lace was originally engineered to do," Kagawa asked Kaito. He set down his tool and began making motions in the air, presumably opening or closing some kind of software that he was using through his smart lenses.

"To fry people's brains if they don't cooperate," Kaito guessed.

"Nope," Kagawa told him with a shake of the head. "That was only after the UCAF got their hands on it. The technology was actually developed on Europa as a therapy for Alzheimer's, Dementia, and other age-based neurological degenerative diseases."

"It was meant to be medicine?"

"Yeah. To grow through the brain, supporting and enhancing the neural pathways. Making them more efficient, backing up memories, speeding up processing speeds, and allowing you to connect wirelessly to medical monitoring equipment," Kagawa explained. "They were even hoping they could eventually use it to control chemical production through the brain. Maybe treat chronic depression, that sort of thing."

"And the UCAF turned it into a way to torture people."

Fitting.

"Yeah. So," Kagawa continued, "once I jailbreak it, we should be able to connect you to the ship's network directly, without smart lenses or anything else."

"So what, I can just think at the computer," Kaito asked.

"Once you develop the right neural pathways," Kagawa confirmed. "I'd kill to get one of these things, but you can't even find them on the black market."

Like Augmented Reality, but better, Kaito realized.

"But that isn't all," Kagawa continued. "*Shumokuzame* has a program that will get the thing to do what it was originally designed to do."

"I don't have Alzheimer's," Kaito protested.

"So it should let you backup your memories," Kagawa told him. "If we can get it to work right. Speed up your processing."

"Like... what?"

"Like calculating pi in your head to twenty decimals," Kagawa said. "Like photographic recall. In theory."

"In theory."

Kagawa nodded. "Okay. We've got the frequency, I've got cracking programs ready to go."

"What do I do," Kaito asked.

"Just sit there."

"Am I going to feel anything," Kaito worried, remembering the kind of pain the lace had caused him while under the control of his torturers.

"Honest answer?"

Kaito nodded.

"I've got no idea," Kagawa admitted. "I've never done this before. I don't think *Shumokuzame* has, either. They've got this program to recalibrate the lace lying around, but I don't think they've ever got a chance to use it before. And they certainly haven't cracked on of these things, because they couldn't tell me anything about the security set up. I'm just going to throw rice at a wall until something sticks."

"Great," Kaito sighed. He leaned back in the stiff, bare chair, closed his eyes, and tried to relax while Kagawa went to war with the monstrous, mechanical thing crouching in his brain.

Kaito spent the next two hours of the burn back to Europa in Kagawa's tech closet, nursing a headache that grew by the minute. Finally, after he'd snapped at the teenage hacker for the umpteenth time, Kagawa suggested that they get something to eat and some sleep. "They don't expect results yesterday," he explained to Kaito as they crammed themselves into a spare corner of table down in the galley.

"Chicken Teriyaki with rice," Kaito read off the label of the heated pouch he'd been given.

"That's a good one," Kagawa mentioned. "I only got Sweet and Sour Pork with Rice."

"That doesn't sound bad," Kaito said, ripping open the top corner of his pouch and letting the steam out.

"The freeze-drying does weird things to the taste," Kagawa explained. "Some things take it better than others. Chicken better than pork. At least, I think so."

Kaito sighed and rubbed his head, giving the meal a moment to cool down.

"Sorry about the headache," Kagawa mumbled around a mouthful of pork and rice. "But we've got it cracked, at least. Now we just need to do the reprogramming."

"I don't even want to think about how my head is going to feel after that," Kaito moaned.

"Cheer up," Kagawa said, swallowing. "The Captain did say she wants us all to sleep before the battle, and once we get to Europa orbit we'll be busy doing other things. If we all die, I won't get around to doing the reprogramming, like, ever. And even if we win, we'll probably have all sorts of repairs and things to keep us busy. I bet its days before we have time to poke around in your head again."

None of that made Kaito feel any better, so he did his best to eat his Chicken Teriyaki without letting mouthfuls of rice float off into the galley. Afterward, Kagawa helped him requisition a sleeping bag, eye mask and earplugs from the ship's quartermaster, and then showed him where the sleeping quarters were. Inside the long room, people had affixed their sleeping bags to all four walls, the floor, and the ceiling, wherever there was open space. The only surfaces where sleeping bags didn't seem to be affixed were the ventilation ducts, of which there were several, working overtime to make sure the multitude of sleeping humans didn't fill the compartment with Carbon Dioxide.

Even with the earplugs, Kaito could hear the snores of other men and women around him in the compartment. He'd never slept in zero-g before, and he tossed in the bag, trying to find a comfortable position in which to rest. *I bet Old Man Date has his own private room,* he grumbled silently to himself. *Captain Shiroishi certainly does. Is this the kind of place Annie slept in, on her way to Europa?*

No, he realized, it couldn't be. Annie had told him that she'd been placed in a medically induced coma for most of her eighteen month voyage from Mars to Europa. An arrangement like this wouldn't have been safe for such a long transit; she must have been sleeping, he thought, in something like a hospital bed. For a moment, he pictured her in his mind, the way she had been in the Intensive Care Unit on Europa: hooked up to medical monitors, IV tubes attached to her arm.

Tired. Drained. That wasn't how he wanted to rembrer her. Instead, he pictured her in the dress she'd worn when they went to dinner that first time. He tried to remember the feel of her skin beneath his hands, the smell of her perfume... and eventually, holding that thought of her in his mind, he drifted off to sleep.

Kaito was on the bridge of the *Narukami* when the ship entered Europa's orbit.

Again, he was wedged awkwardly wherever he could find a space that would be out of the way, biting back a dozen questions at any moment, and feeling entirely out of place. His own anxiety was made worse by the bridge crew themselves: Lieutenant Ito kept gnawing at his nails, for instance, while Lieutenant Sato, at Navigation, kept bouncing her right leg up and down. The only people who didn't show any outward sign of nervousness were Old Man Date and Captain Shiroishi.

"The battle group has maintained formation quite well, during both the burn and deceleration," Date told Shiroishi, his voice loud enough for everyone on the bridge to hear. "Please convey my compliments to the other Captains."

"I will, sir," Noriko Shiroishi assured him.

"Have either of the ships at Ganymede or Callisto broken orbit?" Date looked to Sato.

"The UCAF warship at Callisto is burning for Ganymede."

"Has the *Scipio* altered her orbit," Date asked.

"Affirmative," Lieutenant Sato answered. "She's no longer parked right next to the orbital elevator. She's moved off to a geosynchronous orbit halfway between Icebreakers one and two."

Date frowned. "She's trying to protect both of them? But she can't, at that distance."

"Captain Varga," Shiroishi said, in a tight voice, "Is giving us room. Whatever happens between the ships, he's trying to avoid damage to the elevators, because he knows the people of Europa need them to live."

Date fixed her with a hard gaze, then nodded. "Very well. Then we will oblige him. Once we're in orbit, fire a burn to bring us into the same geosynchronous orbit, and calculate a burn to decelerate when we catch up to the *Scipio*." He lowered his voice. "But he must understand, Noriko, that going toe to toe with us is suicidal. He's outnumbered."

"He understands," Captain Shiroishi said, her face expressionless. "But he will judge the elevators to be more important than his own ship's survival. Once word gets to Mars, the UCAF can always send more ships. Repairing those elevators is a whole other thing entirely."

Date nodded. "Navigation, will *Scipio* have a shot at us as we enter orbit?"

"Missiles only, sir," Sato responded after half a second. "Not with rail guns."

"Order every ship in the battle group to activate point defense systems and prepare to intercept missiles as we enter orbit," Date instructed Shiroishi.

"He won't use nuclear missiles, sir," Shiroishi said.

"What?"

"He won't want to risk what the electromagnetic pulses would do to the colony."

After a long moment, Date repeated: "Give the order anyway. It won't hurt to have our guns and tracking systems on, even if he does hold his fire."

Captain Shiroishi conveyed the order to the rest of the battlegroup, then turned back to the Admiral. "And us, sir? Will we use our nukes?"

"No." Date shook his head. "Not unless we have to. This will be fought with rail guns."

Kaito let out a breath that he hadn't realized he'd been holding. He'd read as much as he could about the *Narukami*'s armor before boarding, and Ito had explained more to him the last time he'd been on the bridge. If he understood correctly, it wasn't meant to stand up to a direct hit from a nuclear missile:

only to protect the ship from the worst of a blast after the point defense guns had shot incoming missiles down. He didn't like the idea of relying on those automated weapons, and it was just fine with him if nuclear warheads were off the table all around.

"Now entering orbit," Ito called out.

Closely on his heels, Lieutenant Sato announced, "No incoming missiles, Captain. We'd have picked them up by now if *Scipio* had fired."

"Captain Shiroishi," Date ordered, "All ships in the battle group have clearance to set their targeting computers to fire as soon as we are in range. Continue to fire through deceleration, and do not cease until ordered otherwise." He frowned. "This is going to be brutal," he said to no one in particular. "Nothing subtle or elegant now."

"Burning to accelerate in ten," Lieutenant Ito called. As he continued calling through the countdown, Kaito got himself down close to the deck. If this burn was anything like the last one, he knew, he wouldn't be able to rise until it was over. He had just enough time to situate himself before the burn began, slamming him down as the *Narukami*'s fusion torches slowed her speed to just over fourteen kilometers per second. While the burn was still in progress he felt the ship shudder and move beneath him, rattling in rapid succession.

"Rail guns fired," Sato announced. "Hits on *Scipio*, *Mikaboshi*, and *Narukami*."

Narukami, Kaito realized. *That's us.* He struggled up to a position where he could see what was happening around him, but it was still just people sitting in front of screens and panels of instruments.

"Damage report," Captain Shiroishi demanded.

"Armor is holding," Sato reported after a tense second. "A glancing bow on our starboard side."

"And the *Scipio*," Old Man Date asked.

"Substantial Damage," Sato said, excitement in her voice. Kaito felt the fusion torch kick in again as Ito adjusted their orbit to compensate for the kinetic energy of both firing, and sustaining fire in return. "At least one of her missile launchers is scrap, and I think one of the rail guns, as well. She's launching drones," the Lieutenant added suddenly.

"Varga won't surrender after a single exchange," Date said, unsurprised.

"I need an open comm," Shiroishi said quietly.

"Very well. Send a signal."

Captain Shiroishi activated her communications equipment, presumably, Kaito realized, on an open channel. "This is Captain Noriko Shiroishi of the Europan Colony Ship *Narukami*. *Scipio*, you are hereby ordered to stand down your weapons and surrender. You are outnumbered and heavily damaged. You've lost this fight. There's no need for anyone else to die today."

For a moment, there was only silence, and then Kaito recognized Captain Varga's voice over the comm. "Noriko? Is that you?"

"Do it," Date Kunari told the Captain in a low voice.

"Voice activation code: *Sazae Oni*," Shiroishi pronounced clearly and firmly.

"*Scipio's* engines are powering down," Sato reported in astonishment.

"Jeffrey," Noriko Shiroishi spoke plainly to her former lover, "I've just activated a virus that I loaded into your personal files before I left. It used your own authentications to install itself in your ship's computer systems, replicate, and shut down your fusion drive. You're dead in the water, damaged, and you're outnumbered six to one. Surrender."

A long, long silence followed, while the Europan ships held their fire.

"This is Captain Jeffrey Varga of the UCAF Ship *Scipio*," came the voice of the man who had treated Kaito and Annie to a day at the spa. "I hereby surrender my ship. I ask that you treat my men with dignity, as prisoners of war."

"This is Admiral Date Kunari of the Europa Colony," Old

Man Date said, leaning forward with a satisfaction decades in the making. "In the name of the independent colony of Europa, I accept your surrender. Your people will be treated honorably. You have my word." He made a cutting motion, and Captain Shiroishi nodded. "Tell the *Kagu-tsuchi* to get a team on board that ship and get her under our control," Date told the Captain. "And then take us to a geosynchronous orbit above Icebreaker one." He toggled up his own ship to ship communication channels. "*Fūjin* and *Mikaboshi*, you will proceed to a geosynchronous orbit above Icebreaker two, where you will interdict the orbital elevator and prevent any ships from leaving Europa orbit. *Raijin* and *Kuraokami*, you will proceed to Icebreaker three, and do the same. *Kagu-tsuchi*, you will stay with the *Scipio*. Once that ship is under the control of our marines, take their officers into custody."

A chorus of acknowledgements came over the communications channel, and then Date cut the feed. "Is that it," Kaito asked, and then shrunk as everyone on the bridge looked at him.

"No," Date said. "This was the clean part. Now we have to chase them out of every military installation they're manning down below. Now it gets messy."

The orbital elevators themselves had no weapons. The first settlers of Europa had needed them to be functional in terms of moving people and cargo, and anything past that was a luxury they couldn't afford. By the time they could have chosen to arm the elevators, if they wanted to, they hadn't.

"For all sorts of reasons," Old Man Date explained to Kaito as the bridge crew waited for their marines to cut through the airlock. "For one thing, the elevators already need to use fusion torches to occasionally correct their orbits. You felt what happened to the *Narukami* when we fired our rail guns; any weapons loaded onto the elevators would push them out of alignment when they were fired. Not a problem for a ship, but when you're tethered to something, that would cause a lot of damage. For another thing, the moment you put weapons on something, people begin shooting at it," he continued, sounding again for a moment like the irritable old boss Kaito had known for his entire life. "We couldn't afford for the UCAF to just shoot them all down when the Colony War started; it would have meant we were completely cut off from trade with the rest of the colonies. By leaving them unarmed, we encouraged the UCAF to occupy them instead."

"The marines are through the airlock, Admiral," Captain Shiroishi informed Date, looking up from her screen. Kaito was able to get a glimpse of her toggling through the camera views from a dozen different marines' smart lenses. *Van den Berg must be with them*, Kaito remembered. *That's where Date sent him. To find the marines.*

The bridge became silent.

"Inform me when they've secured the elevator," Date said quietly. "As soon as we have it under control, I want the commanding officer to have the elevator systems checked for any information about what's happening down below."

"Yes sir," Captain Shiroishi confirmed his order, and the officers settled back to wait. Europa's ice, and the ocean beneath it, was so deep that transmissions often had a difficult time making their way from orbit to the cities below. The most reliable means of communicating between orbit and the subterranean colonies, Kaito knew, was to send a signal to the orbital elevators. Entwined with the carbon nanotube support cables which dropped through Europa's thin atmosphere were fiber optic cables, a hard line connection which carried petabytes of data back and forth every second. Those cables, Kaito realized, and the computer systems they were attached to, would be the best way of finding out what was happening in cities like Toshimayr.

Noriko Shiroishi's posture stiffened. "Incoming signal from First Lieutenant Kobayashi," the Captain announced. A few quick hand motions, and the marine lieutenant's voice spilled out of the bridge speakers.

"...secured, Captain. Repeat, orbital elevator secured."

"Acknowledged, Lieutenant Kobayashi," Captain Shiroishi responded. "Good work. Casualties?"

"Three wounded, one fatality," Lieutenant Kobayashi crackled back a moment later.

Date leaned forward. "This is Admiral Date. Get your wounded back on the *Narukami*," he ordered the Lieutenant. "And secure all UCAF personnel. Any word up the cable?"

"Yes, Admiral," the marine responded. "They received a distress call from Toshimayr Blue Zone five minutes ago. There's fighting around the entrance to the cavern, but it seems like our people haven't taken Blue Zone yet."

There was more, but Kaito wasn't listening to it.

Blue Zone. That was where Annie was.

Annie

Whirlwind

July 1st, 2128

Two deep booms, followed by the heart-rattling honking of the base alarm, woke Annie.

She jerked upright, eyes wide, wrapped at the ankles in the sheets she'd kicked off during the night, her skinsuit sweaty. She missed sleeping without it, but since she wasn't at Kaito's apartment, there just wasn't a good enough reason to justify the health risks of not wearing it for eight hours at a clip; and so, she woke every morning soaked in sweat.

Annie fumbled for the lamp chain at her bedside table, and once the light had clicked on she grabbed her tablet off the charger and thumbed it on. Alerts were already popping up on her screen: "Multiple IDF Impacts," the textbox read in all capitals, and as her eyes flicked over it the base intercom crackled to life and began to repeat the same warnings out loud: "Shelter in place and don IBA where possible."

"Indirect fire?" Annie extracted her feet from the tangle of sheets, tucked her tablet under one arm, and scooted into her bathroom, thrusting aside the shower curtain and climbing into the stall. It was an interior room with no windows; pipes, fixtures, ceramics and tile... it was the most cover she could think of inside her quarters. From somewhere outside in Blue Zone, a third boom set her bones vibrating, and the room shook. Annie called up the EMC news site and glanced over at the sink, where she'd left her smart lenses soaking in saline for the night. As she leaned out of the stall and reached for the plastic case, another impact shook her, and her fumbling hand knocked the lense case to the floor of the bathroom. "Shit," she swore, scrambled to grab it and bring it with her back into the stall. *At least it didn't crack open.*

"Insurgents attack Blue Zone," the headlines read. There wasn't a full article, but there was drone footage of fighting at the security checkpoint between Blue and Green Zones. The blackened, burning wreck of what might once have been a truck had been crashed into the guard station, which seemed to have been blown to pieces. *Suicide bombers*, Annie realized. As she watched, an insurgent shouldered a rocket launcher and fired: a trail of smoke shot past the MPs taking cover near the checkpoint, over their heads, and into Blue Zone. Then, the footage looped around again as the anchor - Kira something, she remembered, the one Kaito's mother liked - began to talk.

"Again, this is drone footage of the insurgent attack on Blue Zone that began just moments ago with a combination of small arms fire and heavy ordnance," the news anchor explained. "We can see bodies, both in the street and at the checkpoint itself; it's not clear how many of those people are wounded, and how many of them are dead, but the fighting is still going on. We've also just received word from the orbital elevators that there is a group of unidentified warships just over nine hours from Europan orbit. These ships seem to be coming from the mining facilities at Io. We have reached out to System Commander Clavinger, but we have not yet received a statement. There are reports coming in of insurgent attacks on UCAF bases not only here in Toshimayr City, but also in both Atarashi City and Fukami City. This seems to be a full fledged rebellion against UCAF rule here on Europa. We strongly advise everyone to stay in their homes and take shelter until the fighting is over. I'm going to repeat this in Japanese: Futatabi, koreha burūzōn de no hangeki..."

Annie swiped the screen away and closed her eyes.

If I stay here, I'm defenseless. She didn't have any kind of body armor to put on - she wasn't infantry, or military police. Her sidearm had been confiscated. She could cower in the bottom of a shower stall, waiting to see whether or not the insurgents made it through the checkpoint, or she could get out of here and do something. Try to arm herself, see if there was a way to help stop this attack. The first step, she decided, was to get herself as ready as she could, take everything that could be useful from the room, and get moving.

She wedged herself into the stall, back against one wall and her feet against the other to steady herself against another blast. Then, she opened one half of her lens case, took a deep breath to steady her hands, and put a smart lens in her left eye. When no explosion immediately interrupted the process, she repeated it for her right eye, closed the case, and waited for her lenses to connect to the base network. As they logged in, she crawled out into her bedroom and pulled on a pair of black fatigues, and her boots. Then, she scooted over to the door - a third explosion rocked the base - reached up to the doorknob, and cracked it open.

Her guard was gone.

Assuming this base was still under UCAF control in a couple hours time, that was going to be bad news for him: he was probably going to get court martialed. In the meantime, it was good news for her. With a couple of hand gestures, she activated the low light and infrared systems in her lenses, and then sent an electrical charge through the carbon nanotubes in her fatigues, heating the outside of her clothing up, relative to the air around her, and creating a wavering, blurred mirage effect in the eyes of anyone who might be watching. Then she set off down the hallway, running low to the ground.

By the time she'd made it downstairs - she didn't even try the elevator - she could feel the scorching heat of the mirage effect even through the insulated lining of her fatigues. She waved the mirage off for a moment and called the EMC site back up to see whether they were playing any new drone footage, but it was just the same rocket strike over and over. She swiped away the news feed and pulled up her map of the base.

At the time Toshimayr City was first built, it had been designed in a honeycomb pattern of hexagons. Blue Zone, at the center of the honeycomb, had been the location of the city's administrative buildings, including a courthouse, and the colony assembly. There had originally been an entrance tunnel to each of the other six caverns, and a road from each entrance leading into a circular drive in the center of the cavern, and within the circular drive, a public park.

Later, when the UCAF had taken over Blue Zone, they had sealed five out of six of the entrances, keeping the southeast entrance to Green Zone as the only secure checkpoint. The buildings had been either knocked down and replaced, or repurposed, to turn the cavern into a military base. The base housing was located in the northwest section of the hexagon, bordered by those now dead end roads to each side; the vehicle bays where the Shells were stored were located in the southwest, immediately adjacent to the security checkpoint. To get there, she either needed to run along the circular drive, cut through the drill field that had once been a park, or try to work her way through the medical sector, where the hospital was located, and then through the various garages and hanger bays that housed all of the vehicles the UCAF forces maintained.

She didn't like the idea of taking any of the roads, and the drill grounds were just as bad. Annie didn't even need to put her ear to the door to hear the sound of gunfire from the cavern outside, and she wasn't armed. Tracing her finger in the air above the door, she plotted her route on her saved base map: she'd head toward the nearest cavern walls, then skirt between the bare rock and the hospital buildings on her way around to the garages. If she was lucky, she'd avoid the fighting.

Annie keyed her fatigues to begin producing the mirage effect again, then cautiously opened the door of the building and headed out. She immediately veered right, moving quickly through the sidewalks, parking lots and alleys that separated the various dormitories and other housing units from each other as she moved away from the fighting. Out in the open air now, the rattling of gunfire was louder, and she could dimly hear the shouting and screaming of men and women in combat from the other end of the cavern.

My people have got to be over there, she realized as she dashed from one corner to another, stopping only to catch her breath and scan her surroundings. *And that means this shouldn't last long.* Small arms, even shoulder mounted rockets wouldn't stand up to Shells - and with what was left of her squad, together with Malik's squad, there should be ten Shells up and running. That was more than enough to put down whatever was happening in Toshimayr. She was into the permanent base housing now, for people like Commander Clavinger who had been here for years: UCAF administrators, bureaucrats, and career soldiers who had lives on Europa, brought their families to live here, or married locals. She easily leapt a fence: even after all of the months aboard the *Scipio*, and her time here, Annie's Martian muscles were more than enough to propel her up six feet or more in Europa's low gravity.

She landed in someone's backyard. There was a slide and a sandbox, both made of brightly colored plastic, and two kids curled up at the base of the fence. One of them had pulled the sandbox cover over them in a haphazard way, and they were trembling, wide eyed. "Get in the house," Annie hissed to them. "Get into the basement."

The boy looked up at her, and flinched at the next report of gunfire.

"No one's shooting nearby," Annie told him and his sister. "That's all at the checkpoint. Come on, move."

The girl stood up, dragging her brother after her by the hand, and Annie ran with them in a crouch, shooing them along until they'd reached the backdoor. "The basement, remember," she reminded them. "Where are your parents?"

"We were at Auntie Mary's house," the girl told her. "And we ran home to find Momma."

"In the basement," Annie repeated, "And don't come out until the gunfire stops." As soon as the kids were safely inside the house, she finished cutting across the lawn and continued on her way.

Those kids weren't the last people she saw, but she managed to avoid further entanglements. There were UCAF soldiers in various states of dress, armed, making their way toward the checkpoint, and there were civilian family members fleeing back away from the fighting. Eventually, after a stop to let her fatigues cool down again behind the dumpster of the hospital, she made it to the southwest corner of Blue Zone, where the garages and hangers were located, and from there into the familiar bay which housed the Shells. Her retinal scan and password sufficed to open the door. She'd been nervous about that right up until it worked, given her time in the brig, but apparently Clavinger really was trying to preserve his fiction about her being a hero. Annie pulled the armored door shut behind her, took a moment to exhale a deep breath, and switched off her fatigue's mirage effect for good. Her pulse was so loud in her ears that, with the door closed, she couldn't even hear the sounds of gunfire or explosions any longer.

After only a few seconds to catch her breath, Annie shook herself and moved deeper into the hanger, the automatic lights flickering to life as she tripped motion sensors. After only a few steps, she paused. *Why are there four Shells here*, she wondered, and made herself count them again. One was Gavril's, she recognized right away. Another two must have been from Joel Malik's squad, because she would have known her people's Shells at a glance. And the fourth... was hers. *But if those three Shells are here*, Annie realized, *there are only seven to fight back Shumokuzame.*

She jogged across the bay until she was standing next to her Shell. Annie didn't realize she'd raised a hand to touch the armored plates of the foot until she'd done it. Scattered around, she could see the salvaged components which were all that was left of Laura's Shell. The decision to sacrifice one machine to repair the other made sense from Nolan's point of view: repair the Shell with the living pilot. He was so logical it almost hurt. Now, she knew, the only question was whether or not someone had wiped the computer or reset the security access. If she had to make a bet - which she'd already done by running halfway across the base to get here - the answer was no.

She stepped around to the rope ladder hanging down from the Shell's torso hatch and scrambled up. At the top of the ladder, she hesitated for half a second, and then forced herself to speak clearly: "Open cockpit."

For the space of two heartbeats, she was certain she'd guessed wrong, and that she'd wasted her time and risked her life getting to the hangar for nothing; that someone had changed the access settings, and she was going to just have to hide in this building until the MPs came to collect her when the fighting was over. And then, whisper smooth, the Chobham armor plates slid apart. Annie couldn't keep from breaking into a grin, and ducked inside the cockpit, the door sealing behind her.

She forced herself not to rush, to go through each step in order, and to be sure she was doing them right. This was a field-repaired machine now, not new off the factory line, and she hadn't been in it since before her stay in the hospital.

"Boots off," she whispered to herself as she untied them one by one, and stashed them in the small storage compartment, before sliding her feet into the restraints and locking them into place. "Five point harness." She continued working her way through the list, making sure that every buckle clicked into place firmly. Next, she pulled the u-bar down over her head, until it touched her chest and locked. "Shunt connection." She felt around the back of her neck, pulling wisps of hair aside, and fumbled the jack into the Neural Shunt. The familiar green icon appeared in her vision, and she secured her hands in their restraints before focusing on it and blinking three times.

In the space of time it took to close her eyes, she fell into the Shell, leaving her body behind. The weakness, the vulnerability she'd felt running between buildings, waiting for a stray bullet or fragment of shrapnel to pierce her frail body, was replaced by strength and confidence. If she could have moved her lips, Annie imagined that she would be smiling. At a thought, the cords which connected her Shell to repair monitors and system diagnostics fell away. She called up a display of her available weapons, and was pleased to see that not only were the lithium batteries of her plasma cannon fully charged, but her shoulder mounted mini-guns were loaded as well. Annie moved the Shell easily to the hangar door, calling up her sensor systems, and painted a map of the cavern which contained Blue Zone.

Besides herself, there should have been seven active Shells registering on her HUD: instead, there were only five, and they were split into two groups. One set of signals was clustered around the security checkpoint between the Blue Zone and Green Zone caverns, while another set was clustered around the sealed tunnel which had once, twenty years ago, connected Blue Zone and Red Zone. Malik's people seemed to be there, which confused her, while Nolan, Rafe and Sera were at the Security Checkpoint. Sera's signal was no longer transmitting as active, but instead giving off the standard distress beacon for an immobile, heavily damaged UCAF vehicle, as was one Shell near Malik.

That decided Annie. Whatever Malik's people were dealing with could wait: she was going to make sure that Sera was alive. That fight was closer to where she was, anyway. She used her Shell's transmitters to key open the hangar bay door, then stepped out into the cavern. She gave herself three steps, to make sure that she wasn't going to melt the hangar behind her, and then lit off her fusion torches and spread her wings. In Europa's low gravity, she and her Shell shot up above the hangars, warehouses, and other buildings which filled the cavern, until only massive stone support pillars reached toward the artificial sun alongside her. Toggling her command channel open, she addressed what was left of her squad: "Incoming fire. Rafe, I'll pin them down: you get Sera out of there."

Her sensors had been populating and tagging enemy targets using telemetry relayed from the other Shells in her wing, facial recognition identifying known insurgents, infrared sensors tracking the blooms of rocket launchers. Now, at the apex of her torch assisted leap, nearly directly above the skirmish, she let her targeting computers work and opened fire with her plasma cannon, at maximum power. Below, the insurgents had seen her, and her sensors tracked incoming rockets, trailing smoke as they arced up towards her; other combatants pointed pistols or rifles, but the bullets they fired were too small for her sensors to track. They were also too small to be any real danger to her, but the rockets... *They shouldn't have anti-vehicle weapons.*

When the Thales-Demios Type II Plasma Cannon had powered up, back in the hangar bay, it had begun superheating its first charge of compressed gas into plasma, the fourth state of matter. Now, at her command, power capacitors inside the weapon activated a ring of magnets which accelerated a toroid of plasma - a donut shaped ring - down toward the insurgent force at over ten billion g's. By the time the plasma impacted the concrete of the street - and the insurgents scattering away from the impact point - it was travelling at over 9,000 kilometers per second, approximately 3% of the speed of light. The explosion that tore outward from the point of impact broke the windows of the surrounding buildings, including nearby hangars, what was left of the guard station, and the nearest repair garages. Next, the wave of force blew in the exterior walls of the guard station and the two nearest buildings; coincidentally, it also picked up the insurgents and carried them along with it. At the same time, the explosion forced the floors of all three of those buildings upward, buckling and breaking them. As the blast wave passed the structures - first the guard station, and then the hangar bay and garage - it began to exert downward pressure on the roof, as well as pressure directed inward on the remaining walls. Within seconds of the wave passing, all three buildings, heavily damaged, collapsed in on themselves.

The insurgents, on the other hand, were not made of concrete, nor were their skeletons metal girders. When the blast wave caught them up, it immediately shattered their ear drums and collapsed their lungs. Every bit of broken concrete, every shard of shattered glass, and every splinter of wood ripped free by the explosion now became shrapnel, accelerated through the bodies of the insurgents by the force of the plasma impact. By the time the her enemies' bodies hit the ground again - or the walls they had been thrown against - most of them were already dead. Those that weren't broke bones on impact; their weapons were torn from their grasps, and they lay bleeding on the ground. None of them moved.

Annie couldn't immediately assess the effect of her strike, however, because one of the shoulder mounted rockets connected. The rocket impacted her Shell on the right side of the torso while she was still descending from her fusion torch powered leap, exploding on impact and spinning her Shell around until it collided with the fractured pavement of the combat site. She didn't feel what the impact did to her body, not with the neural shunt active, and put the thought aside as not useful at the moment. Instead, she mentally keyed the computer to give her a quick diagnostic, then got the massive machine back on its feet.

"Nice of you to finally join the party," Sera's voice cut in across the unit's secure comm channel. She sounded strained - in pain.

"You still in one piece," Annie asked her friend.

"Shell's down, sir," Sera reported. "And I think I have a broken arm. But other than that, yeah, I'm ok."

"Our orders were to deploy light anti-personnel weapons," Nolan's voice interrupted them. "But I suppose you didn't receive those orders."

"That is correct, Lieutenant," Annie confirmed, waiting to see whether Nolan was going to challenge her command.

"Well," he replied after a long pause, "It's good to see the base commander has cleared you to return to duty, Lieutenant Commander. What are your orders?"

"Rafe," Annie began, mentally exhaling, "Evac Sera to the hospital. Nolan, hold this point against any hostile force. I am hereby lifting the restriction against using heavy weapons."

"Using vehicle grade weapons against infantry is against the..."

"You have your orders," Annie interrupted the older pilot. "If someone gives you shit for it, tell them you were firing on their equipment. You were aiming for their belt buckles."

"Yes sir," Nolan responded, and she could envision his satisfied smile in her head.

"Where do you want me after the evac," Rafe asked in a flat voice.

"Here, to reinforce Nolan," Annie decided.

"Yes sir," Rafe said without any great enthusiasm. *What happened to Laura must really be getting to him*, Annie realized. *I need to talk to him, once this is all over.*

"Alright," Annie said. "You have your orders, people. Move out."

"Affirmative," the two other pilots replied in near unison, and Nolan moved his Shell to cover the tunnel. With a thought, she used her connection to the Shell's computer systems to call up the results of her diagnostic scan. If her brain had been connected to her body, Annie would have breathed a sigh of relief. She'd lost a substantial chunk of armor over her Shell's midsection, she saw, and her left wing's control surfaces weren't responding properly, but no truly vital systems had been impaired yet. That could change quickly with another hit, but for now she could move and shoot just fine.

She had a choice, Annie realized. She could move through the repair facilities and garages, and then the warehouses and mess hall, which lay between her and the insurgent strike that Malik's group was fighting. That would take longer, but provide her opportunities for cover. Or, she could take the road from this security checkpoint into the center of Blue Zone and use the ring road to cross to the access road which ran between the base's administrative buildings and the mess hall, kitchens, and supply warehouses, then take that to the breach the insurgents had opened. With a thought, she launched a drone into the upper part of the cavern and called up its camera feed.

Shit. She would have liked to be able to swear out loud, but didn't want her subordinates to hear her over the comm channel. She saw broken Shells, and insurgents swarming up the street toward the administrative buildings, where MPs with rifles were trying to hold them off. *No time for the slow route, then*, she realized. *Let's see if we can make this work a little better than it did last time.*

She aimed her Shell up the street, spread her wings, and leaned forward before firing off her fusion torches. The Shell rocketed along the pavement, and Annie desperately fiddled with the wings' control surfaces as she tried to keep the machine level despite the damaged left wing. It kicked, trying to rise up into the air: she was at the level of the second story buildings, rising up past the rooms. She feathered the jets as she came to the ring road, trying not to crash into any trees as her momentum carried her into the parade grounds. Dust flew up everywhere, and then she had made the turn and was rocketing toward the second force of insurgents.

She didn't bother to slow down, instead letting her targeting computers tag enemies and then opening up with her shoulder mounted rotary cannons. A hail of bullets sprayed out from her Shell, and Annie dimly registered insurgents diving for cover up and down the street. She shot past them before they could get a bead on her, swung the Shell around to face them and put her back to the ragged tunnel leading to Red Zone. Then, she let go with the Plasma Cannon again. As the toroid of plasma erupted from her weapon, small arms fire and rockets began lighting her up, and warnings were displayed in the periphery of her vision: one of her fusion torch exhaust nozzles had been blown to scrap. Her right wing was shot full of holes and only 50% operable. She was losing sensors. A medical alert she didn't even want to look at... she was losing control of the Shell's legs. She kept her shoulder mounted cannons spinning their barrels even as the Shell sank to one knee. The fusion reactor was taking itself offline as a safety precaution, and she had only the power left in her lithium batteries.

"MPs," she broadcast over the UCAF open channel reserved for officers, "Sweep forward and hold that entry point. I want nothing, I repeat, nothing from Red Zone getting in. Someone drive a few cars over from the garage and block that tunnel. Block both tunnels. Seal this whole zone off."

"This is Lieutenant Sterne," a male voice came back to her over the comm. "Orders confirmed, sir. You got here just in time, Lieutenant Commander."

Annie cut to a private channel. "I won't be able to help you anymore," she admitted. "My reactor's down and I'm talking on batteries, here. I'll send our last functional Shell to back you up."

"Roger that, sir."

She switched channels. "Rafe, get over here to the Red Zone tunnel and leave Nolan to hold the Green Zone checkpoint. You two are the only operational Shells left."

"Yes sir," Rafe responded, and Annie checked her drone footage. She didn't see any ongoing firefights... She put in a call to the maintenance crews for a pickup, and sat back to wait. Even with her Shell's reactor shutdown, she was safer in here, behind what was left of the armor, than she was getting out into the open. Once she established that she still had over 90% of her battery power, she called back up the local news site.

That same reporter was still going - a scrolling banner beneath her image gave her full name as Kira Montfort -

was replaying the same couple seconds of blurry, jostled drone footage. "Again," Montfort said firmly, enunciating her words, "We have lost contact with our drones near the battle. As you can see here-" They had a shot of the explosion from Annie's Plasma Cannon - "There has been some kind of high explosive weapon used against the insurgents attacking Blue Zone. Now, if we slow down this footage from right before we lost our drone, you can actually see the projectile."

Keeping one eye on the readings from her own sensor drone, Annie watched as the footage enlarged. Montfort was no longer visible, but her voice was still clear. The footage wound back, and then advanced only a frame at a time. "Here," Montfort said, and the footage stopped. Annie was impressed. Somehow, by luck, they'd caught the bright toroid of plasma in frame. "Now, we've called in an expert from Atarashi City. Streaming live with us is retired UCAF Commander Simon Bauer, a veteran of the Colony War and our longtime military consultant." A picture within a picture opened, showing a gray and stern man in his sixties. "Commander Bauer," the news anchor asked, "Are you able to tell us what weapon was used here?"

Bauer nodded. "That shape is very distinctive. That's a plasma cannon of some kind."

"Now if I understand correctly," Montfort continued, "Plasma Cannons have crowd control settings, for non lethal effect. Is that what we're seeing here?"

"No," Bauer said, shaking his head. "Crowd control wouldn't have fried your drone, and the explosion we're seeing isn't consistent with that. This is a Plasma Cannon set for maximum, or close to maximum, output."

"But Commander," Montfort asked, "Isn't it illegal to use anti-vehicle weapons against infantry combatants?"

Annie closed the newsfeed before hearing the old man's response. She checked her drone feed: the street around her was still clear, and was being fortified by MPs, but she couldn't see into the tunnel, or any of what might be happening in Red

Zone. As she watched, Rafe walked his Shell up next to hers.

"You alright in there, sir," he asked over their comm channel.

"I'll be fine," Annie told him. "Now that you're here and the street is secure, I'll..."

"There's a whole mob of Opie's over there," Rafe interrupted her. "You might want to hang tight, sir."

"I can't see anything," she told Rafe. "Where are they?"

"Packed into that tunnel between Blue and Red Zones," Rafe told her, and she watched as he stalked his Shell past, placing himself between her and the tunnel. "They're doing a lot of yelling. You could probably hear it over your external mikes if you turn them on," he suggested.

Annie considered how much battery power that might drain, then decided it didn't matter. *It's not like I'm going to get this thing moving without a couple hours of repairs, anyway,* she knew. She turned on the external microphones.

It was just like the day they'd walked their shells from the port to Blue Zone - the day Laura had been hit under the bridge. She could hear the yelling, the chanting, of people who didn't want them to be here. *It hasn't gotten any better,* she realized. *If anything, it's gotten worse.* She could make out the phrase 'go home' chanted over and over, in English, and there were phrases in Japanese that she couldn't understand. She turned the volume down.

"Yeah, I hear them now," she confirmed to Rafe. "Just a crowd, or armed insurgents?"

"Hard to say," Rafe grumbled. "The MPs have put up a barricade, but they're all pressed up against it. They could be hiding weapons in there. I've got facial recognition going, but there's a lot of targets..."

"We've got the two entry points secure now," Annie told him, keeping her tone calm and even. She wished that it had been Rafe whose Shell was disabled early, not Sera; she could have trusted Sera's judgement, here. "Just hold tight until Commander Clavinger gives us orders."

"I think they're going to try something," Rafe muttered, and she wasn't at all convinced he was even listening to her. "Don't worry, sir, I won't let anyone get past that barricade."

"Rafe, switch to crowd suppression weapons," Annie commanded him, and that's when she heard the sound of glass breaking over the external microphones. She could just see it on the feed from her functioning sensors: someone had thrown a molotov cocktail at Rafe. The glass bottle broke on his Shell's leg, and the flame from the burning cloth stuffed through the bottle-top caught as the alcohol ran down. A trail of fire streamed out from the Shell's leg.

It presented no threat whatsoever to the Shell's Chobham Armor. A dozen molotov cocktails wouldn't have presented a threat. But as soon as the glass shattered, Rafe opened up with his shoulder mounted machine guns, throwing bullets past the MPs and over the barricade into the crowd. She couldn't see what was happening in the tunnel, but her external microphones picked up the sound of gunfire, and a half second later the screams from the crowd.

"Rafe, stop!"

Annie didn't know whether he had the comm channel off, whether he was ignoring her, or whether his own external microphones were turned up so loud that the sound of his own gunfire and the screams that followed, drowned her out. She wondered if he was thinking of Laura right now, and what had happened at the bridge. It must have been only a few seconds that he maintained fire into the tunnel, but it felt longer, because she couldn't do anything to stop it.

Finally, the sound of Rafe's guns ceased. "Alright, sir," he spoke up over the comm, "I've cleared them out from the tunnel. They won't be any trouble, now."

He says it like he's killing a nest of bees, she realized. *Or checking a mousetrap. Not like they're real people.*

Numb, she powered down her systems and disconnected. The physical sensations of her body came back to her, and as she fumbled at the back of her neck to pull the jack out of her Neural Shunt, she realized that her eyes were wet, and her arm hurt.

Two hours later, Annie sat in the same chair, in the same briefing room where they'd received the orders for the operation which had landed her in the hospital. Then, as now, both Shell squads were present, as well as Commander Clavinger. Before, she'd kept herself from being bored by exchanging text messages with Kaito. Now, there was a tension in the room that kept her back straight, her mind focused. That operation had been a minor strike on an insurgent base. This time, their actions would decide not only whether they lived or died, but whether Europa remained under UCAF control, or fell to *Shumokuzame*.

Nolan was there, and Sera, with a cast on her arm. Rafe sat at the table, as well as Malik. Commander Clavinger, of course, and Lieutenant Sterne, who was in command of the MPs, as well as his immediate subordinates. There was coffee, again, but everyone looked tired anyway. With nothing in the way of preamble, Clavinger began. Annie scratched at the bandage on her left arm.

"Just over two hours ago," the Commander spoke in a raspy voice, "Two trucks, loaded with explosives, were driven at high speeds into both the security checkpoint between Blue and Green Zones, and into the sealed tunnel between Red and Blue Zones. Both of these bombings were followed up by coordinated insurgent strikes aimed at taking control of Blue Zone. Thanks to the actions of our Shell teams and Military Police, those strikes failed."

No one said anything yet. They were all, like she was, waiting for Clavinger to say something new.

"At the same time," the Commander continued, "Similar strikes were launched against our facilities in both Atarashī kibō no machi and Fukami Toshi. Without the benefit of Shell teams in those locations, and with smaller forces of MPs, I can now confirm that we have lost control of those cities. We don't have details regarding casualties, but at least some of our people have been captured."

Annie nodded. That much had been on the news, and no one seemed particularly surprised.

"In all three locations," Clavinger moved forward, "there also seem to have been planned moves against our people who were off-base, just prior to the attacks. Three of our Shell Pilots, who were off base, are not accounted for at this time. A dozen of our MPs, as well as technicians, corpsmen, and a variety of other UCAF soldiers are also missing in action. They all seem to have been tracked somehow. We're not sure how, yet," he added, then took a sip of his coffee.

"Those fucking Opies," Malik cursed. "They've got my men captive somewhere, Commander. Just give the word and we'll go get them out. I don't care how many slant-eyes I have to gun through."

Clavinger waved Malik down with the hand that wasn't holding his coffee. "I'm not finished, Lieutenant Commander Malik." The old man cleared his throat, then continued. "We've also received word that within ten minutes of the strikes launched down here, a force of unidentified warships was detected burning in from Io. Given the timing of the two events, we have to assume they were coordinated by a single guiding command structure. The enemy ships entered orbit and engaged the *Scipio*."

At that, the table of officers erupted. Annie tuned out their voices, working it through herself. *The attacks on our planet-side bases were a distraction*, she realized. *To keep us from reinforcing the orbital elevators.*

"Have we lost all of the elevators, sir," Annie asked Clavinger, and her question cut through the noise. "Or did we keep any of them?"

Clavinger turned to her for the first time since their talk in his office, and his eyes bored into her own for a long moment before he nodded. "I see you haven't forgotten how to think, Winters," he said gruffly. "We've lost all three elevators, *Scipio* as well, according to the last transmission we received. The only installations we currently control are Blue Zone, and the three Icebreakers."

"Lost," Nolan spoke up, "As in she's damaged and boarded, or lost as in *Scipio's* been destroyed?" Everyone waited on the response. The answer meant the difference between a chance to get back home, or an inevitable surrender and imprisonment. Or execution.

"Boarded," Clavinger responded, and Annie, like everyone else, exhaled. "Which means as of right now, I am altering our core objective here on Europa. With a battlegroup of warships, wherever the hell that came from, these insurgents have clear numerical superiority in system. Holding this territory is not practical at this time. Our new objective is to retake control of the *Scipio* and evac as many UCAF personnel as possible from this system back to Mars."

"Are they gonna give you hell for that, sir," Malik asked the Commander quietly.

"I have full operational authority over all UCAF forces in system," Clavinger responded. "And I am making this decision. That's all you need to know, Lieutenant Commander." Which meant, Annie and everyone else in the room understood, that UCAF command was going to crucify him for this, and it would be the end of his career.

"So," Clavinger continued after the space of a breath, "That's our goal, people. We have the resources left to us in Blue Zone. I'd like to get all our people off Europa if we can, but I don't know that it's possible. Never mind the other moons - even if we retake *Scipio* and get her up and running, we can't fight our way past that wargroup to get people off Ganymede or Io. Start throwing ideas at me."

"We put as many pilots in functional Shells as we can," Malik began, with hardly a pause. He'd clearly already been running through scenarios in his head. "We load up our personnel and civilian families into every vehicle we have lying around. We fight our way to the docks, seize Subtees, and then take an orbital elevator by force. We use the plasma torches on the Shells to get them over to the *Scipio*, board, and repair the ship enough to get her moving out of the system. Call in the other two ships in Jupiter's orbit to cover our escape."

"Son," Nolan said, "That's a lot of fighting. You just listed four different points we have to seize along the way, every one of them by force. And if we fail at any one of those objectives, we have no fallback. No retreat. While we're carrying a bunch of civilians with us. It'd be hard enough with a fast, lean group of soldiers - but those civilians are going to slow us down."

"We can't leave our people's families here," Malik protested. "Husbands, wives, children - our soldiers are not going to leave them behind to be killed by terrorists." *We'd have a mutiny*, Annie realized.

"Can we hopscotch this," Nolan asked, burying his head in his hands and rubbing his eyes. "One force to jump ahead and seize a point, while a holding force keeps the civilians at a fallback point? Then we bring them up when it's safe?"

"Seize the Docks, hold Blue Zone," Malik said aloud, running it through as he did so. "Then bring them through the streets to the docks, and send our forward force to seize the Icebreaker." He shook his head. "I don't know that we have the people to be running back and forth doing that. "And it means they're going to be just waiting for that second group to follow along... we're going to telegraph every move we make."

"Our moves are pretty damned obvious already," Nolan insisted. "We don't have a lot of options. Why don't we blow the power on the way out, give them something here at Toshimayr City to keep them occupied, instead of us?"

Malik nodded. "Honestly, the more chaos we cause on our way out, the better. It will not only distract them, it will also deny assets to the enemy. We should blow the entirety of Blue Zone on our way out, and then blow the docks, and so on. The Icebreaker, the elevator."

"People need the docks to live," Annie protested. "To send out fishing subs. To ship goods back and forth with the other two cities. They need the Icebreakers and orbital elevators to get things on and off world. If we blow those things up, people are going to die."

"Fuck em," Rafe said. "They're just Opies. Anyway, they attacked us. They can take the consequences."

"They're not all terrorists," Annie insisted, her voice rising. "There's a lot of people who live here who have nothing to do with what happened to us. Children, old people, people who just work their jobs every day and then go home. It's our job to protect them, not to kill them."

"They don't want us here," Malik pointed out. "They don't want us to protect them."

"Whether they want us or not," Annie argued, "That's our job. That's why we're here."

"Alright, Winters," Malik asked. "What would you do?"

Annie's mind raced. *Thanks for putting me on the spot, asshole.* "How many UCAF personnel do we have on Europa?"

"In all three cities, the Icebreakers, the Orbital Elevators," Clavinger answered, "Counting families, children, and all of that? We have just over ten thousand people."

"And how many can *Scipio* actually take," Annie asked. "Does someone have the numbers?" She looked around for Gavril, but he'd been one of the soldiers off base just before the attack, and hadn't been found. *He would have the numbers when I needed them.* She hoped he was still alive.

"*Scipio* is meant to transport a large number of troops and equipment," Nolan said after a moment of swiping. "She has hibernation chambers for six thousand soldiers."

"That's just over half of our people," Malik said.

"Just Toshimayr," Annie turned to Clavinger. "How many do we have just here?"

"About three thousand," Clavinger said.

"OK," Annie said. "We've already said we don't have the resources to get people out of the other cities. We can fit everyone from Toshimayr, and their families, if we can get them up the elevator."

"Which brings us back around to fighting our way out," Malik said, clearly frustrated.

"Maybe not." Annie looked around the room. No one was going to like this. "What if we just asked them to let us leave?"

"Are you fucking crazy," Malik half-shouted.

"No." Annie shook her head. "Look, what are they going to do with ten thousand prisoners? They don't have anywhere to put that many people. Io can't hold that."

"They'll probably just kill us," Rafe interjected, and Malik nodded.

"I don't think that's the plan," Annie protested. "But even if it was, they know they'll take losses doing that. We'll fight back - we already have. We can destroy a lot on our way out. It's in their interests to just let us leave. That way they get the colony, they get the elevators and the docks and the Icebreaker stations, and they don't lose any more of their people. Can we communicate with those ships up there? Negotiate?" She turned her gaze to Commander Clavinger.

"It doesn't seem like they've physically damaged any of the equipment," Clavinger admitted. "They just aren't responding, and we've lost contact with our people."

"Alright. Something this well organized has to have someone in charge. Let's ask to talk to that person," Annie insisted, looking around the room to make eye contact with her fellow officers.

"We don't negotiate with terrorists," Malik grumped.

"You can not negotiate your way to a whole bunch of dead bodies," Annie snapped back at him, "Or you can give this a try, and maybe get everyone out alive. Almost everyone. Anyway, what do we lose by trying this? We don't give up any material or tactical advantage. You've already said we don't have any other good options."

There was silence for a long moment, broken only by

the scrape of a chair leg on the floor. Clavinger's eyes were focused on the table in front of him, and Annie knew that saying anything more would be counterproductive. He was working through the options in his mind, and whatever came out was going to be the final decision.

"Alright," the Commander said, looking back up after a long moment. "Malik, you get everything prepped to move out and fight our way to the docks. Sterne, detail some of your people to set charges in two groups. I want to be able to blow everything of military value no matter what. I want you prepped for a second set of charges to take as much of this Zone with us when we go as you can manage. Make that second set something you can pull out on my word - ten minutes, twenty minutes tops to disable that second group of charges." His eyes swung to Annie. "Winters, you're with me. This negotiation is your idea, you can be with me when they court martial our asses. If this doesn't work," he said, looking around the room again, "Then we go, go, go, on my order, and we don't stop shooting until we're out of this mess. Understood?"

"Yes sir!" The response was a chorus, and Annie stood up with the rest. As Malik and Sterne headed out the door, she turned to Nolan. "Check on our repairs," she asked him in a low voice. "Make sure we're good to go for a fight. And keep an eye on Rafe," she said, glancing out the side of her eye to where the Lieutenant was heading for the door. "I'm worried about him."

"I could hear some of what happened over the comm channel," Nolan admitted. "He lost it?"

"If we didn't need everyone we have right now," Annie admitted, "I'd bench him and send him for a psych eval. I have a feeling the Commander feels the same way about me," she admitted.

"I'll watch him," Nolan promised. "One way or another, it's good to have you with us again," he said with a smile.

"We've lost enough people," Annie said, thinking of Laura, and now of Gavril, missing in action somewhere out there in a hostile city. "No more."

Nolan nodded, then turned on his heel and headed out. Annie looked back to Clavinger. "My office, upstairs," he said curtly, and walked past her to the door, not even glancing back once to see whether she followed. She did, two steps behind him. He was silent as they walked down the hall, and even during the brief ride up the elevator, when she thought he might say something. It wasn't until they'd moved past his secretary, still manning her station, and into his office, with the door closed, that he spoke.

"This doesn't change anything," Clavinger bit at his words as if he was chewing a too-dry steak. "The only reason you're not back under arrest is that I need everybody I have to pull this off. I did not agree to try this because of anything about you, or your father. We're trying this because it's the best plan proposed."

"Understood, sir," Annie said, keeping her voice neutral.

The old man sat at his desk. "Behind my right shoulder," he ordered. "At attention. Do not interrupt me," he warned her sternly. "But," he admitted after a hesitation, "If you see a chance to do something useful without undermining me, take it."

"Yes, sir." She moved around his desk and placed herself behind him. Clavinger waved his fingers through a dance of menu options, and a small green light above her head drew her eye. There was a ceiling mounted camera pointed at them. If it wasn't transmitting their images yet, it would be momentarily. She assumed there was a microphone somewhere, as well.

"Keying you into the channel," Clavinger muttered, and a blank gray box appeared in her field of vision, courtesy of her smart lenses. If *Shumokuzame* chose to respond with a video feed, she would see it. A smaller box, picture in picture, popped up, showing the image they were transmitting. Annie took a step left to place herself in frame, and the Commander nodded.

With one more hand motion, he began to speak. "Insurgent forces currently in control of Icebreaker Two," the old man barked out, "This is Commander Michael Clavinger, commanding officer of all forces on Europa. I am requesting to speak with your commander," he continued. "To negotiate a cessation of hostilities."

There was silence. Annie started to bite her lip, caught herself, and waited. "Insurgent forces currently in control of Icebreaker Two," Clavinger repeated. "This is-"

"Hold," an unfamiliar voice came across the channel. "Hold on this channel for ten minutes."

Clavinger glanced back over his shoulder at Annie. "We can do that," he said. "Acknowledged."

With a finger swipe, he froze their video feed and turned off their microphones - she could see the status symbols next to the gray box displayed by her lenses - but kept the channel open to receive audio.

"They're going to get someone," Annie surmised.

Clavinger nodded. "Which means there's nothing for us to do, but wait, and see what kind of a person we get on the other end."

Kaito

Kasan-ki

July 1st, 2128

"Again," Kagawa insisted, as both he and Kaito stared at a divided screen. The display was red on the left, and green on the right.

"My head hurts," Kaito complained.

"You've said that like ten times," Kagawa told him, rolling his eyes. "Try it again."

One hand rubbing his temple, Kaito stared at the screen, squinting his eyes. *Green*, he thought to himself. *Green.* He clenched his jaw, trying to think harder at the computer systems of the *Narukami*. Kagawa had cracked the neural lace on their way into the orbital elevator, and the kid had insisted on an hour of practice before Kaito accompanied Old Man Date down the elevator to Icebreaker Two.

"You look like you're constipated," Kagawa laughed.

"Enough of this," Kaito grumbled, rising from the chair to his feet. "My head feels like someone's hitting it with a hammer, and nothing is happening. I've got to be at the airlock in twenty minutes."

A chime sounded, and the red half of the screen lit brighter, while the green half dimmed.

"I can't believe it," Kagawa said, leaning forward. "You actually did it!"

"I didn't do anything," Kaito said, shaking his head. *Ow. Not a good idea*, he realized. He grabbed the door, pulled it open, and then pulled himself out into the corridor.

"Wait," Kagawa called from within his cramped tech closet, but Kaito ignored him and kicked off in the direction of the dormitories. There, he ignored the shift of sleeping crew strapped to the floors, ceiling and walls all around, found his locker, and bundled up what few possessions he had on the ship, stuffing them into his sleeping bag. Then, with it rolled up in his hand, he pushed back out into the corridor and made his way through the *Narukami* until he reached the same airlock he'd used only a few days ago to enter the ship.

Date was waiting there, along with Captain Shiroishi and Van den Berg, who had some kind of assault rifle slung across his shoulder on a strap. "Don't worry, Captain," Date was saying as Kaito floated over, then reached out to touch a wall and bring himself to a halt. "I will be fine," the old man continued. "I have Van den Berg-*san* to protect me, after all. And your people have the elevator firmly under control, now, you have assured me."

"Yes sir," Shiroishi agreed, but didn't look particularly happy.

"Ah, Kaito," Old Man Date said, turning toward him with a smile. "Good. I want you with us - and I'm sure you want to get back down to Toshimayr to see your mother."

With a start, Kaito realized he hadn't even thought of his mother in... he wasn't sure how long. Since the interrogation, probably. "I... yeah," he admitted. "She must be wondering what's happened to me."

Date nodded. "So. Let us move to the orbital elevator. Captain, you will await my further orders."

"Hai," Noriko Shiroishi answered, sketching a salute. Date activated the airlock, and once the chamber had pressurized, he was first through the door. Van den Berg followed, with something of the attitude of a murderous dog restrained by a tight leash, and Kaito followed them. Before he kicked through, he turned back to the Captain. "It was good to see you again," he said. "I hope things go well," he finished lamely.

The older woman smiled. "Goodbye, Kaito," she said. "I'm sure we'll see each other again." She reached out to the airlock controls, sealing the door between them, and Kaito had nowhere to go but forward past a second airlock and into the orbital elevator.

Kaito had never been inside the orbital elevator before -

well, that wasn't quite true. He'd come through just a few days ago, but he'd been packed inside a refrigerated container full of raw fish and ice. He'd never actually seen it from the inside, pushed himself along its corridors as he did now - but he was familiar with its design, from studying it as a child in school, and from the pictures which were widely available on Europa's net.

Properly speaking, what he was walking through wasn't the elevator itself, but the dock attached to it as a counterweight. The counterweight attached to Icebreaker Two was a construction of two parallel space docks, each a long rectangle of girders and solar panels, connected by a habitat through which people and cargo transitioned on their way from docked ships to the elevator, or back from the elevator to ships. Each dock could connect to a single ship at a time, locking it into place. While the ships were docked, they underwent a standard maintenance cycle, performed by local workers using EVA suits and robotic manipulator arms. When it was time for a ship to leave, computers carefully timed it's release from the dock: the force of Europa's rotation was sufficient to fling a ship into space with enough escape velocity to easily clear the weak gravity well, sending it at high speeds along its course back in system toward Mars, or from Europa to another moon, such as Io.

The two docks were attached to the elevator loading facilities themselves, all in zero-g, which made the loading and unloading of cargo easier than if a spinning gravity deck had been inserted into the already complicated contraption. The passageways that Kaito moved through now were the ones that connected the docks to the elevator, and there were miniature moving walkways along all four walls of the corridor, each one with attached cloth handles every two feet. Following Date and Van den Berg's example, Kaito grabbed one of the handles, wrapped it around his hand, and let it drag him forward down the corridor, his legs trailing out behind him as he was pulled through the station.

By the time they reached the terminal, which would normally be filled with soldiers, tourists, and business passengers waiting to ride the elevator down to Europa's surface, there was a small group of *Shumokuzame* marines already waiting.

"Sir," said their commander, who couldn't have been more than twenty, addressing Old Man Date with a salute. "We have a comm signal from Toshimayr Blue Zone, asking to speak with the commander of the Battle Fleet."

Date frowned. "Who is it," he asked.

"Commander Clavinger, sir," the marine answered, face impassive.

"I see." Date nodded. "Where can I take it?"

"The bridge, sir," the marine said, and then led them off down a side passage. The docking facilities weren't designed to hold a very large crew, but like any other kind of operation, there had to be a nerve center, a place for communications to be routed, for supervisors to organize work shifts and direct the docking and launch of the ships moving in and out of orbit. When they got inside, it had the look of a place that did not stand on formality, but was concerned with pragmatism: there was a compact coffee machine that worked on small, sealed pods; a small refrigerator and microwave; and desks with old computer displays and comfortable looking chairs, which were bolted down. Date was directed toward one such chair, and strapped in; Kaito found himself a place to hold onto, and sat back out of view to listen and watch. Within a very short time, Date's computer screen had lit up, and the connection was made.

When Kaito saw who was on the other end, he sucked in a breath. He'd seen Clavinger before on EMC, and the old military man looked the same as ever: bald, gaunt and devoid of any emotion besides impatience. Behind his chair, however, stood Annie. She was in black military fatigues, arms crossed behind her back as she stood at parade rest just behind Clavinger's shoulder, perfectly in screen. Her rank insignia was attached, and her face carefully composed, but a delicate wisp of her blonde hair had escaped whatever she'd used to pull it back, and for a moment he was still in bed with her, and wanted to reach up and brush it back.

He was glad that no one on the other end of the transmission could see him.

"Commander Clavinger," Date Kunari began, speaking clearly and evenly. "This is Admiral Date Kunari of the free colony of Europa."

Clavinger's eyes flickered. This was a man, Kaito knew, who had played *go* one afternoon a week with him. There was a time that the dockworkers used to grumble about how Old Man Date was a suck up to the UCAF administration; Clavinger must now be realizing that he'd been played for a fool all these years, but his stern face didn't show it.

"That's quite a rank you're claiming," was all he said.

Date nodded. "Conferred as one of the last acts of the colony government, as your ships burned in-system twenty years ago."

"I don't doubt it," Clavinger admitted after a moment. "You play a patient game, and you don't bluff."

"So," Date Kunari began, "I assume you wish to come to terms."

"If satisfactory terms can be had," Clavinger demurred. "Any such terms would have to guarantee the safety of my people, and that all captives will be treated as prisoners of war, in accordance with regulations."

"From where I sit," Kunari rejoined, "I don't see that you have much of a choice. You have no way off planet, and no way out of the system in the event that you somehow fought your way to an elevator. You don't have much to bargain with, Commander."

"That's not accurate, Admiral," Annie said, stepping forward, and Kaito's heart pounded so loudly in his chest that he could hardly hear her speak. *What are you doing*, he wanted to scream at her. "It is in your interests for this to resolve with as little damage to the colony as possible, and we could do a lot of damage if we so chose to."

Date remained silent, for a long moment. "Continue," was all that he said.

Annie nodded, and Kaito realized that this was her show. *We're not talking to Clavinger. We're talking to her.* "You don't gain anything by keeping us in system," the woman he loved spoke, beginning to lay out her case. "It will do nothing but cost you resources and space to keep ten thousand prisoners. Ten thousand," she repeated, emphasizing the number. "That's a lot of food, a lot of water, a lot of air - not to mention the danger of escapes, of sabotage, all the things that enemy soldiers can do. I don't even know where you'd get the man-power to guard us all."

"Perhaps," Date's eyes squinted at the screen, "Lieutenant Commander Winters, I am merely planning on throwing the lot of you out the nearest airlock, and saving myself the trouble."

"I don't think you are," Annie shot back, "Because sooner or later word of what has happened here is going to reach the United Colonies government. Sure, they can't get troops here for a couple months, minimum -but at some point, you're either going to have to fight another battle, or negotiate. And when that time comes, it's going to make a lot of difference whether you're perceived as a legitimate government, or an extremist regime that has committed genocide."

Kaito had to give him credit - the old man's face didn't betray any sign at all of what he was thinking. None of this seemed to surprise him; if Kaito had to place a bet, he would wager that Date Kunari had already thought through every step of this, probably years ago, and knew exactly what he was going to do next. His attitude was like nothing so much as a teacher prodding a student to talk their way through a complicated problem.

"Even if what you say is true," Date spoke up evenly,

"You have no way of transporting your people out of Jupiter orbit and back to Mars."

"We have the *Scipio*," Annie said, and Kaito wondered just how much about what was going on in Europa orbit they knew or didn't know.

"You do not," Date corrected her.

"It's still operational, isn't it?" Annie's eyebrows lifted as she asked the question.

"*Hai*," Admiral Date admitted.

"Then if you agree to let us take it and go, we have it."

Date Kunari smiled. "I see. And we would trust you not to use the weapons on that ship? A ship we have damaged, boarded and captured?"

"If you give us back the *Scipio*," Annie promised, "We will load it with our people and burn out of the system as soon we can. If you do that, we will commit to leaving peacefully, without a shot fired."

"You can't fit every UCAF soldier in system on that ship," Kunari pointed out, and Annie nodded.

"We know," she said. "We would have to leave people behind. We would also need a firm commitment from you, and whatever government you claim to represent, that our people would be treated humanely, as prisoners of war."

"So, In reality, Lieutenant Commander Winters," Kunari continued, "We gain nothing, and you gain everything. Your carrier back. A large portion of your people out of captivity, alive and uninjured, to be shipped back to us in a few years, to fight all over again."

"You gain as much as we do, sir," Annie came at him again. "We don't do any damage on the way out. There's no more fighting. All of the orbital elevators, Icebreakers and docks are operational. Less military prisoners to deal with, freeing up personnel and resources on your end. If we take out six thousand, sir, that's more than half of our people in system that you just don't have to deal with at all."

"Let me discuss this with my staff," Kunari said, and cut

off the feed.

Van den Berg looked around the empty room. "Who is your staff, exactly, Date-*sama*?"

Date Kunari snorted. "The two of you, apparently, unless you would like to call in the Marines guarding the door. What do you think?"

"Ask Kaito," Van den Berg said after a moment. "He was sleeping with her."

Kaito felt his face burn. Date Kunari turned to regard him, something like an insect under a microscope. "That's right - and is she also the one who got you out of where they were holding you? I'm surprised she's not in a cell."

"That's Annie, yeah," Kaito mumbled. It seemed that Mizuki hadn't said anything about her true identity. What would Date do if he knew who Annie really was, he wondered. Use her as a bargaining chip? Certainly not let the daughter of the Prime Minister of the United Colonies escape. "You can trust her."

"I'm not sure that I can count on your opinion," Date admitted. "You are... somewhat biased. Lovers - especially new lovers - rarely see each other clearly."

"Look, she..." Kaito took a breath, trying to gather his thoughts. "She's not like most of the other soldiers. She actually came because she wanted to try to bring people closer together. She's not perfect - I still can't believe how sheltered she is, from the world and everything in it. There's a lot she doesn't know, and hanging out with me in Red Zone for a few weeks wasn't going to fix that overnight. But she's not lying to you. Any agreement she makes, you can trust she's being honest, and intends to keep it." He wasn't sure what else to say, so he just looked down at the floor.

"You met this young woman," Date asked Van den Berg.

"I did."

"And," the older man asked.

"She risked her own ass for this sad sack of shit," Van den Berg said, pointing a thumb at Kaito. "That might mean she's stupid, or naive, but it also means she's loyal."

"Naive would be my bet," Date Kunari muttered. "She played a promising game of *Go*, for a complete novice. Better than Clavinger. Kaito-san, stay off screen." He reached forward and turned the transmission back on. "I have an answer for you," he said, and both UCAF officers, who must have been quietly talking, immediately gave him their attention.

"We're listening," Commander Clavinger spoke up.

"I am willing to transfer control of the *Scipio* back to UCAF forces," Date said, and Kaito almost didn't hear what came next over the rush of blood in his ears, "On the condition that UCAF forces pull out of Blue Zone in Toshimayr completely, without any sabotage to the facilities present, and without violence as they move through the city."

Clavinger nodded. "Your own people have done a pretty good job of shooting the place up," he pointed out. "We won't be responsible for that. And we're destroying our computer systems on the way out."

Kunari nodded and waved a hand dismissively. "Yes, I understand. That is perfectly acceptable. The *Scipio* will then immediately proceed out of the system, as soon as she is capable of doing so. We will see that her repairs are given priority. The UCAF personnel that cannot be evacuated on the *Scipio* will be arrested and held in a secure facility pending negotiation for the transfer of military prisoners. Such negotiation will not take place until the UCAF recognizes the independence of not only Europa, but all of the Jupiter Colonies."

"I can't make any..."

"Yes, I know." The Admiral cut Clavinger off. "But tell your superiors that prisoners of war will not be released until armed conflict is off the table. What they do with that report is up to them."

"I can't speak for the forces on Callisto, Ganymede or Io," Clavinger pointed out.

"I understand that also," Date agreed. "And I would like you to understand that, while I will send word down to our people in Toshimayr not to interfere with your withdrawal, I cannot control a mob."

"We can get ourselves to the docks," Clavinger promised. "Are you going to provide transport up to the surface? Our attack subs aren't exactly designed to transport large numbers of people."

"I believe that Date Heavy Industries has several Subtee's which would be more than capable of the task," Date Kunari admitted. "I will make the necessary arrangements. Do we have an agreement, then, Commander Clavinger?"

"We do," Clavinger stated, standing up. "Clavinger out."

Kaito tried to fix the image of Annie in his mind, before the feed cut out, wondering if he would ever see her again.

The hours that followed gnawed at Kaito's guts like bad coffee. It wasn't the waiting, he told himself. He'd had plenty of stretches in the *Nautilus* where long hours passed, alone in the cold beneath Europa's world-ocean. He could handle being alone. He liked being alone, most times.

No, it was the not knowing, not being able to see or hear what was happening except through the news feeds they picked up from Toshimayr. Date Kunari ran the evacuation of the UCAF forces from the orbital elevators command center with little more than a pause for packages of heated rice, or a sip from a water flask. Marines - or what passed for marines, in *Shumokuzame* - kicked themselves in and out of the room on errands, while Date mostly sat strapped into a chair and talked and Van den Berg held an assault rifle threateningly, glaring icepicks at anyone who entered the room until they left.

First, the admiral put in a call to Captain Shiroishi, who was acting commander of the battle group while Date handled other things. If she thought agreeing to hand the *Scipio* - the ship she'd just defeated in battle only a few hours earlier - back over to the UCAF was foolish, she didn't say it out loud, and

Kaito couldn't read it in her face. As tight as she and Old Man Date seemed to be, it wouldn't have surprised Kaito if this had been the plan all along, and the reason they didn't destroy the ship outright. In any event, it took less than an hour from the time of their communication with Annie and Clavinger for the *Scipio* to be docked up next to the orbital elevator, automated repair systems hooked up and busily performing surgery on her hull.

In the meantime, Date had been in communication with a whole lot of people that Kaito did not recognize. A UCAF officer down in the Icebreaker below them, to which the orbital elevator was tethered. That officer confirmed that he had orders from Clavinger to move the evacuating UCAF troops through his station and up the elevator to be transferred onto the *Scipio*; he insisted that his crew be the last up the elevator, and that only after all the other troops were out would he turn control of the Icebreaker station over to the crew Date was sending to relieve them.

Next, to Europa Media Corporation, where Date calmly informed the producer that he wanted airtime for an announcement to the free Colony of Europa. That got their attention, and about twenty minutes after that, Kira Montfort was breaking into the audio/video feeds of every device and screen across Europa using the UCAF codes for special announcements from the colonial government. Kaito tried to judge whether or not she looked younger, and wondered how long it would take the lifespa treatments to do their job.

"We interrupt your feeds now for a special announcement," Montfort pronounced calmly and clearly, her eyes seeming to look through the camera straight to the viewer. *She looks just the same as she always looked making announcements for the UCAF,* he realized. *Does it even matter to her who is in charge?*

The feed he was watching - he'd split the screen between this and repair assessments on the *Scipio*, which he at least sort of understood - replaced the news anchor's placid face with an image of Date Kunari, not ten feet away from Kaito. There was an ever so slight lag between the feed and Date himself, but Kaito had already muted the sound so as not to interfere with the transmission.

"*Konbanwa*," Kunari began in Japanese. "Twenty years ago, one of the last acts of the democratically elected colonial government of Europa was to create a special task force, code named *Shumokuzame*. As part of the creation of that military unit, I, Date Kunari, was commissioned Admiral and given command of all colony forces that were ordered not to engage the UCAF invasion force. Our mission was simple: to liberate our home, by any means necessary. Since that day, construction continued in secret, at our facilities near Io, on the battle group of ships currently in orbit above Icebreaker Two. Today, a joint operation between this battle group, and irregular military forces operating in all three of Europa's major cities, has liberated our home from UCAF occupational forces."

The old man paused, as if anticipating the reactions this would bring among the viewers, and that they might need a moment to subside before anything he said would be heard. "Exactly one hour from this announcement, UCAF personnel will evacuate Blue Zone and make their way to the Toshimayr docks. We are permitting them safe passage out of this system." He leaned forward, as if to address his audience in confidence. "I know many of us have suffered these twenty years. Some of you are too young to remember a time when we were truly free - free to elect our own leaders, free to make our own laws, and free to live where we wished. This is going to be a time of great change, and times of change are never easy. They require us all to act in accordance with our best natures: with honor, compassion, and dedication to the common good. Until such time as we can organize elections, the Europan Military will govern the Colony. Now," he continued, "I have a request to make of you. Clear the streets between Blue Zone and the docks. Do not interfere with the evacuation of

UCAF troops. Enough of our people have already died, enough damage has already been done to the colony we worked so hard to build. As much as you may desire vengeance, as much anger as you may feel, put it aside, and let these people leave unmolested. Thank you. *Sayōnara.*"

With Date's curt nod, the feed cut back to Kira Montfort in her news studio, and Kaito tapped once at the mute symbol on his screen so that they could hear what she said.

"...again," Montfort was saying, "That was Admiral Date Kunari of the Europan Armed Forces. Admiral Kunari has provided us with authenticated records from the colony government dated over twenty years ago which verify the legitimacy of his claims to rank, and that the insurgent force popularly known as *Shumokuzame* was in fact acting under orders from the democratically elected colony government." A drone video-feed of the security checkpoint at the entrance to Blue Zone replaced Montfort's smooth features, and Kaito swore softly.

"Do you see that," he asked Old Man Date. It looked like the security checkpoint, and the entrance into the Blue Zone cavern, had been hit by a bomb.

Date nodded. "Yes. That was the plan, of course. A vehicle loaded with explosives. It seems that we did not, however, allocate sufficient forces to Toshimayr Blue Zone. The UCAF garrison held. There is footage, I believe - but I need to speak to our people holding the UCAF prisoners in Atarashī kibō no machi and Fukami Toshi."

"Yeah, sure." That meant, Kaito understood, be quiet and stay out of the way. Which was pretty much what he had been doing ever since he was unpacked from a cooler of ice water and fish. Date had asked for his help; since then, he'd really been nothing but awkwardly shaped cargo to be inconveniently carted around in the old man's wake. *Maybe*, Kaito thought as he searched for footage of the fight at Blue Zone, *that means he doesn't need me after all. Maybe that means that after today, I can just go home.*

There. Drone footage of the fighting at Blue Zone. Kaito started the video stream, and muted the commentator, in favor of captions. Most of the shots were blurred, shaking, unable to really capture what was going on. There was an in depth analysis of a few frames of some kind of weapon blast, which he didn't pay attention to until he heard the words 'plasma cannon.' Annie's voice drifted back to him, from the day they'd first met: "It's not a rocket launcher. It's a Thales-Demios Type II Plasma Cannon...Standard issue for UCAF occupation forces. It can be calibrated for crowd control." *Please*, he begged whatever un-named forces might still exist in this universe and pass for gods, *Don't let her have been involved. She was supposed to be locked up in a jail cell for all of this.* And yet, he knew, she'd been standing next to Clavinger, negotiating on the behalf of the UCAF. That hadn't looked much like Annie was in trouble at all.

The next clip was titled 'Blue Zone massacre.' He almost didn't play it.

The footage was clearly from someone's smart lenses, from the point of view and the nauseating motion. The view was from inside a crowd of people, native Europans, swaying and jostling and surging toward... where were they? It took Kaito a moment to recognize the location, because it had been a dead end all his life: someone had blown open the tunnel from Red Zone to Blue Zone. He could see fires, and people in the crowd throwing things - explosives? There were guns, and he knew if the feed had included sound, he would have heard the crack of shooting.

The person filming things ran into the tunnel and lifted a rifle of some kind. The footage jolted, presumably from recoil as the gun fired, and then jostled around as the insurgent ran forward. Kaito could see a wrecked Shell smoking off to one side, and UCAF soldiers using it as cover. As he watched, one fell, and the crowd surged forward into Blue Zone. And then, too quick to follow, the view snapped violently around, and for a few still frames he could see only the ground. The footage replayed, slowed down to go frame by frame. As the viewpoint jerked suddenly, there were just a few frames of another Shell, wings spread. It must have been moving at great speed, because it was blurred - and in one of the maybe three frames that had caught it, whoever had edited this together and uploaded it had circled the puffs of smoke, faint but visible, from the rotating gun barrels of the shoulder cannons.

He recognized the Shell. He'd watched it, in the moments before the building came down and the dust swept over him, trying to hold everything back from collapsing: UCAF-X007.

It was Annie.

Forty-five minutes later, Date Kunari seemed to have completed all his pressing business, and Kaito, at his request, pulled EMC"s drone footage of the UCAF exodus from Blue Zone up on their largest screen. He kept the volume low, but didn't mute the feed.

"They didn't listen," Date complained.

"Did you really think they would," Van den Berg asked.

"No," the old man sighed. "But I had to try."

All three of them watched the footage in silence for a long moment. The streets, Kaito could see, just as clearly as the other two men, were not empty. Instead, they were lined with crowds of people carrying signs: 'UCAF Go Home,' read one, and another, 'Babykillers.' There were Europans obviously carrying guns - not pistols, but military style semi-automatic rifles. Kaito hoped they were *Shumokuzame*, and that they would follow orders.

"This could be really bad," he said out loud. No one else said anything. They didn't have to.

A Shell led the procession out of Blue Zone. Not just any Shell, Kaito realized, as soon as he saw it. Her Shell, the serial number clearly visible. It was damaged - he could tell that, even without any military or technical training. There were parts of the armor that were blackened and scored by explosions, fire, something. And then, right up next to those, divided only by the seams between the plates, was armor that looked brand new. *They must have just torn off the old stuff and strapped on whatever they had lying around to replace it*, Kaito thought. That doesn't look like a finished job, at all.

Behind Annie's Shell, ground vehicles followed: armored personnel carriers, trucks meant for moving supplies, even cars that didn't look at all like regulation military equipment, but instead like someone's personal, private vehicles. Alongside and behind the vehicles marched UCAF soldiers, rifles in hand, wearing their black fatigues and body armor.

"Why aren't they riding in the vehicles," Kaito asked out loud. "Were there really that many soldiers in there?"

"Noncombatants," Van den Berg explained. "They've got the vehicles loaded with noncombatants. Families, doctors and nurses, mechanics, secretaries... everyone who lived and worked for the UCAF in Blue Zone, but who wasn't actually a soldier. They're trying to protect those people, in case something happens."

Kaito shook his head and watched as the long parade of soldiers and vehicles snaked out of Blue Zone into Green Zone, and down the streets, moving toward the docks at no faster than a walking pace. "This is going to turn into a riot."

"Get me that news anchor again," Date snapped to Van den Berg. "I'll make another announcement."

"Too late," Kaito said. On their screen, a drone's camera zoomed in, catching a sake bottle as it shattered against one of the armored personnel carriers. Instantly, the alcohol running down the side of the vehicle erupted into flames. UCAF soldiers swung their guns around to point at the crowd, which fell back in a panic. Clavinger must have given an order, because the convoy picked up speed, the soldiers jogging next to the vehicles.

The mob had held back, waiting only for the first act of violence, and now was released from restraint. The air filled with detritus of all sorts, thrown by Europans: chunks of concrete, garbage, and more molotov cocktails. There was one line the mob wasn't ready to cross, yet, however: though they surged and roiled like waves around rocks, they did not charge the UCAF convoy. Fear of the guns kept them back. And somehow, the soldiers didn't fire back.

"If nothing else, their soldiers are disciplined," Date admitted with a grudging note of admiration.

"But if the crowd sees they aren't going to use the guns, that's just as bad," Van den Berg pointed out.

And yet, for long moments, the worst did not come. Kaito became aware that his jaw was clenched, his shoulders hunched, as they watched the progress of the long line of people and machines through Toshimayr. The front of the line had reached the docks, where the lead Shell - Annie - stepped aside to protect the ongoing parade as they passed into the complex and out of the reach of the mob. He began to think that, somehow, this might just work.

The newsfeed wasn't showing the right part of the convoy for them to see when it happened, but the drones had cameras on everything, and a second later someone had spotted the breaking point and switched feeds. The screen zoomed in on a downed UCAF soldier, their face bloody. Another soldier ran over to help him up, and for a moment, Kaito focused on the brick on the street nearby. A third soldier stepped forward to cover them, pointing his gun at the crowd, which surged forward at the sight of blood, and the crack of a shot rang out. Kaito wondered, for the space of a heartbeat, whether it had been anger or terror that tightened that anonymous finger on the trigger. It didn't matter. The drone camera swept to the crowd, where a body was down, and then, with an inarticulate cry of rage, the mob charged. More gunshots rang out as the soldiers tried to hold them back, and then one of the Shells stepped forward.

"They've got riot weapons, right," Kito asked. It wasn't Annie's Shell, she was already at the docks. Date and Van den

Berg were silent, and he realized that no one knew.

The machine guns on the shoulders of the Shell began spitting bullets into the crowd.

Annie

Ascending

July 1st, 2128

"And remember," Annie emphasized, looking at the Shell pilots clustered around her, "Riot settings only. No machine guns or railguns or anything like that." The two wings of Shell pilots had been combined into one for this operation; they'd lost too many people and machines to be fussy about it. From her people, Nolan, Rafe and Sera remained, with Sera riding Gavril's Shell, which had been hastily transferred to her. Thankfully, the cast around her broken arm wouldn't slow her down as a pilot: the Neural Shunt didn't even need her to *have* an arm to function. Annie had been lucky; the wrench-monkeys had managed to replace most of her armor and get her Shell up and running.

The final two pilots with her were Malik and the only other pilot from his squad who was still fit for duty, Lieutenant Annabella Bianchi, a sleepy eyed young woman who always looked like she was thinking about something else during briefings. Annie didn't trust either of them to follow her orders: Bella because it was anyone's guess whether or not she'd heard the orders, and Malik because he'd just about thrown a fit when Clavinger had put her in charge over him.

"Excuse me, sir," Malik had said, his jaw clenched so tight he might as well have screamed 'what the fuck are you thinking' at the top of his lungs.

"You hear me, Lieutenant Commander," Clavinger had said, his voice full of iron. "Winters' wing has four pilots left, yours has two. I'm merging the smaller wing into the larger to preserve the operational integrity of the unit. Is that clear?"

"Yes sir," Malik responded, and his eyes had flicked to Annie with a clear message: I'm going to get you for this.

Now, she searched his face, and Bella's face, for any sign they were going to give her crap. Both pilots expressions were guarded, carefully blank. "Alright," she said, even though it clearly wasn't, "Get your Shells heated up, people. We move out in ten minutes." She watched as Malik and Bella clambered up the dangling rope ladders into their Shells; Rafe was right on their heels, but Nolan and Sera lingered next to her for a moment.

"Trouble," Sera asked in a hushed tone.

"You bet your ass," Nolan answered.

"Watch them both," Annie ordered. "I don't trust them not to fuck this up. I don't trust them to obey orders. And watch what you say over the comms." Sera opened her mouth, but Annie cut her off. "Now get in your rides, before their external mikes come on." The three split up, each heading for their own Shell. Annie couldn't help a grimace at her mismatched plates of armor, hastily swapped in from Shells that had been deemed too damaged to repair in the time available. "We'll get you looking pretty again once we're back on Mars," Annie promised the machine.

She felt a stab in her heart: she'd pushed away thoughts of Kaito over the hours since she was woken by an explosion, as she ran from one thing to another, but now, saying that out loud, she remembered that going to Mars meant she was never going to see him again. Annie swallowed, grabbed the rope ladder, and pulled herself up. If all went well, this would be the last time she rode a Shell into combat until they got back to Mars. And after that... well, who knew. There was a year and a half of transit in a medically induced coma ahead of her. As she slid her feet into the boot restraints, connected her harness, and ran through her mental checklist, she imagined the cushions and padding were still warm from the battle just hours ago. Everything done, her body secure from the impacts that came with battle, she reached back to the nape of her neck and plugged in.

The world lit up as her mind merged with the computers and sensors of her machine. Around her, the rest of her jumbled together wing were powering up weapons systems and walking out of the hangar. The battle scars of the *Shumokuzame* attack on Blue Zone had been left as they were a few hours ago, and the wing walked their machines over scorched and broken pavement to take positions around the convoy that was forming up in the central parade grounds. As she watched, her field of vision, fed by the external cameras of the Shell, zoomed in on wounded soldiers being loaded into the base hospital ambulances. A young mother was shepherding her two children into an armored personnel carrier; neither looked older than ten.

"I'll take point," Annie transmitted to the rest of the Shells. "Nolan, you've got rear guard. Sera and Malik, you're behind me, then Rafe and Bella. Space yourselves out so that we cover the whole convoy - I want everyone within line of fire of at least one other Shell at all times."

"Roger that," Nolan confirmed quickly, and the rest of the pilots sounded off in a chorus. Annie placed herself at the blasted out security checkpoint, where she waited for the order to move out. While the convoy continued to load, she readied a drone for launch and booted up the same visual identification program she'd used the first day she'd arrived on Europa.

With little warning, her audio-visual feed displayed Commander Clavinger's face: from what she could tell, he was in one of the APCs, and her computer told her he was broadcasting to all UCAF personnel, not just her Shell. "Listen up, people," the Commander barked. "This is our chance to move non-combatants out of here safely. There are going to be crowds; there is going to be a lot of noise, and probably a lot of things thrown at you. Do not respond. Keep moving. The last thing we need is someone shooting into the crowd and turning this into a riot. If we need crowd suppression, Lieutenant Commander Winters' Shell team will use riot suppression tactics. MPs, protect the vehicles. We will do this, and we will get our people home. Move out." The feed cut, and Annie moved out.

She could have sent Nolan, or Malik, out first, but she didn't trust anyone else to keep their finger off the trigger. If Annie could have guarded the entire convoy herself, been in half a dozen places at once, she would have done that. She set her Plasma Cannon for crowd control, and the moment she stepped into Green Zone she launched a drone to begin scanning the crowd.

If she'd thought the people lining the streets when she and her pilots had arrived in Toshimayr was overwhelming, it was nothing compared to this. All of Red Zone and Yellow Zone must have crowded into these streets, with the security checkpoints abandoned. Men, women and children, old and young; there were signs everywhere, and news drones hovering above the buildings, recording everything and sending the feed to the people in Atarashī kibō no machi and Fukami Toshi. Sending it up to the Icebreaker Stations, she was sure, and the orbital elevators, and the ships in orbit. Was Kaito watching, right now?

Annie turned her external microphones down, so that the sound of the mob was only a dull roar, and then she led the convoy forward. She kept her weapons pointed straight ahead, down the street, being careful never to swing them out over the crowd. *If even the slightest thing goes wrong*, she realized, *this is going to turn into a bloodbath.*

"Keep your weapons pointed up the road," she ordered over her wing's private channel. "Don't point them at the crowd. And get your drones in the air. If you see any trouble, you tell me immediately."

"Confirmed," Nolan and Sera responded, and the rest followed suit.

The entrance to the dock complex was in sight, and Annie was just beginning to think that they might somehow get through this without a complete disaster, when something happened back on the line. "We've got fire on an APC," came Sera's voice over the audio feed.

"Keep them moving," Annie told her. "Hold your fire,

you understand?"

"I've got it, sir," Sera assured her, and then Clavinger's voice cut in on the open channel to all personnel.

"Do not, repeat, do not fire on that crowd," the Commander said sternly. "Pick up your pace, people. I want everyone on foot jogging; drivers, pick it up to five miles an hour. Go, go!"

"Sera, is that small arms fire," Annie asked as soon as the Commander was offline.

"It's fire, sir," Sera answered. "Flames. Molotov cocktail."

"Alright," Annie said, and she would have exhaled in relief if her neural shunt hadn't been cutting her physical responses off from her body. "That's not going to hurt an APC anyway. Just keep them moving. Hurry it up. I'm waiting for you at the entrance to the docks."

Annie stepped her Shell aside, staying out of the way of the vehicles and people moving past her into the dock complex, and turned around to face back up the road. She kept her weapons parallel to the road, not facing into the crowd, and launched a second drone to head back down the line of march and give her an eye in the sky over the rear. She set up split video feeds so that she could watch the entire convoy, and then had nothing to do but wait.

More and more people passed beneath her into the docks; more and more UCAF soldiers out of danger for every second that ticked by. Sera's Shell was coming up on the docks now, and Annie opened a private audio channel to her. "Sera, once you're up here, I want you to stand watch on the opposite side of the column from me. Remember, keep your guns pointed along the road, not at the crowd."

"Roger that, sir," Sera confirmed. "Are we rotating as the rest of the Shells get here?"

"Negative," Annie told her. "I want Malik and his people into the docking facilities and away from this powderkeg ASAP. Sorry, Sera, you're going to have to wait a little longer with me. I'll send you in when Nolan gets here."

"I understand," Sera began. "I don't-"

"Man down!" Rafe's voice cut across the wing's channel. "Man down! Shots fired, I repeat, shots fired!"

With a thought, Annie magnified her drone feed from above Rafe. One of the UCAF soldiers was down, the crowd surging toward him, and another soldier standing guard was firing into the mob. "Riot control, Rafe," Annie shouted. "Back that crowd off, but do not, repeat, do not use lethal force!"

"I see anti-vehicle weapons," Rafe practically shouted back. "I'm not letting any more of our people die today." On her drone feed, Rafe's shoulder cannons spun up and began to spit bullets into the crowd.

"No!" Annie's Shell was a step forward before she had even thought about what she was doing. "Sera, guard this point! Get these people inside!" She couldn't fire off her fusion torches; there were non-combatants all around her. "Cease fire, Lieutenant, I repeat, cease fire," she transmitted to Rafe, but there was no response.

All up and down the line of march, the mob was surging forward, spurred on by twenty years of occupation and the sound of Rafe's guns. Annie brought her external speakers to life to address them: "Back away from the road," she broadcast sternly, aware that the news drones would be picking up her voice. Then, she swung her plasma cannon out to cover the crowd. She might as well have been screaming at the waves on Elysia Island. She checked to make sure that the weapon was set for crowd control, and then fired.

At the lowest setting, the touroid of plasma that pulsed from her cannon into the crowd detonated as a flash of light and sound. Around it, people fell back, hands over their eyes, temporarily stunned. "Repeat," Annie broadcast over her speakers. "Move away from the road and disperse. My next shot will be calibrated to blind." With a thought, she turned the setting of the plasma cannon up to the next level: a flare bright enough to induce temporary blindness, but no permanent damage to the eyes.

Behind her, Sera was handling the other side of the route, and at least near the two of them the crowd was beginning to pull back. Annie could see people going down, trampled under the weight of others in the mob, and she wondered how many would die. *Less than if I was using my shoulder cannons.* With a moment to think, she looked back to the video feed from her drones, hoping that Rafe had listened to her command.

Along the line of march, dead bodies, twisted and thrown by the anti-vehicle machine guns, were heaped like trash in an alley. The pavement was red and slick with blood. The vehicles of the convoy were moving forward as fast as they could, no longer waiting for the soldiers on foot, who brought up the rear. Rafe's shell had stopped firing, for the moment, it's shoulder-mounted cannons smoking as they cooled in the open air. Much of the crowd was gone - either fled away from the killing, or already dead, she assumed.

A block back from the road, however, her drones spotted a mass of people. With a thought, she zoomed in. *This is trouble.* While the mass of ordinary citizens had run from the guns, here was a knot of well armed *Shumokuzame* forming up for an attack. Her camera spotted both long rifles and carbines, as well as anti-vehicle arms like rocket launchers and shoulder fired missile launchers. Annie didn't even bother wondering where they had gotten this stuff anymore - that had stopped worrying her around the time the battle group of warships had hit Europa orbit. "Rafe, get a move on," she transmitted privately, and then opened a channel to the entire convoy.

"I have eyes on an organized, well armed group of hostiles forming up about a block out," she announced. "Recommend everyone who isn't in a Shell make best speed to the docks before this turns into a full on clusterfuck." Switching over to her wing channel, she continued: "Nolan, you're last man out. Don't leave anyone behind. Everyone else, back him up and protect the line of march. Crowd control settings only. Rafe, or anyone else, if I see those machine guns light up, or railguns, or fucking anything, I will shoot you down myself, and leave your insubordinate ass here to be thrown in whatever hellhole passes for a prison."

Her progress back down the line of march was slow: she had to be careful of hurting people, who were now fleeing in all directions, or of slowing down the evacuation. As a result, she could only watch the video feed from her drones when the insurgents formed up into small groups and advanced on the road the convoy was using, piggybacking forward from one piece of cover to the next until they had a line of fire on Rafe and Bella's Shells.

However sleepy-eyed Bella was, Annie had to give her this: she followed orders. She began by launching three tear gas canisters, arcing them up and over the insurgents' heads. Then, she cranked her external speakers up to maximum and bombarded the insurgents with an ear-splitting, high pitched siren. Annie cut her own external audio feed, but *Shumokuzame* and the fleeing crowd could do nothing but crouch with their hands over their ears. Those exposed to the tear gas began coughing, crying and vomiting all at the same time. Rafe opened up with a pulse from his plasma cannon, stunning the insurgents with another flash-bang, and for a moment Annie thought it was going to be enough.

There were more and more armed people - all *Shumokuzame*, if she had to guess, rather than just civilians - coming up the cross-roads toward the line of march, and she just didn't have enough Shells to protect the strung out groups of vehicles and soldiers. She saw a rocket strike Bella's shell, fired from a low rooftop, and explode against the upper left leg, sending her crashing to the ground. Annie could do nothing but watch as insurgents swarmed over the downed Shell, planting charges and then dashing away.

"Fuck this," she heard Rafe mutter over the open squad channel, and then he opened up with his machine guns again, cutting down the hostiles who were trying to get away from Bella's Shell. He wasn't quick enough to stop them, however, as a string of small explosions popped, one after the other, around her armor.

Annie switched to a private channel, direct to Bella's Shell. "Lieutenant Bianchi, what's your status," she called out desperately. "Bella! Are you ok?"

There was no response.

"Dammit," she cursed to no one, and then re-opened the wing channel. "Nolan, as soon as you're in sight of Rafe support him."

"What about Bianchi," Malik's tight voice cut in.

"No response," Annie admitted.

"Goddammit take these handcuffs off us," Malik demanded. "This isn't a riot. This is a fucking assault!"

Annie wanted to close her eyes and be somewhere else. "Authorization is given for the use of lethal force in defense of the convoy," she said, simply. "Don't lose any more of our people."

Following her own orders, Annie changed the settings on her plasma cannon and spun up her shoulder guns. Now that she'd made the decision, there was nothing to do but to follow through with it. She was close enough to see Rafe, now, and her drones had a good view of the insurgents coming up behind him. *I need a better angle*, she realized, and cut down the next side street, away from where the UCAF soldiers were evacuating. Once she was reasonably sure that she didn't have any people clustered around her Shell's legs, she lit up her fusion torches for a short burn, propelling herself up above a nearby apartment building. She cut the burn, and as soon as her Shell's feet hit the roof, it started to crumble beneath her. Not knowing how long the building would support her weight, she targeted the enemies coming up Rafe's six and let loose a shot from her plasma cannon on full power.

A toroid of shining plasma flashed out from her Shell faster than the human eye could track, exploding in the middle of the side street where *Shumokuzame* was advancing. Her drones, programmed to automatically go high when she was powering up her plasma cannon, to avoid being shorted out themselves, took a moment to come back down and focus on where the explosion had been: a quick look told her there was nothing left but scattered body parts and debris from collapsed walls.

In the meantime, however, Rafe was being swarmed by rockets, small arms fire, and molotov cocktails. She could see Nolan bringing up the rear of the column, almost in range to support them. "Rafe, I can't get a clear shot without hitting you," she sent over the squad channel. "And you're right in the middle of our troops. I need you to get clear."

The roof beneath her Shell shifted, and she decided that was as good a time as any to get off of it. She lit off her fusion torches again, aiming for a rooftop garden on top of a luxury high rise. When she landed, the carefully manicured shrubberies blackened and burnt beneath her jets, and the raked sand melted into glass. She changed the setting on her plasma cannon, back to flash bang mode, and aimed right for the street at Rafe's feet. Her drones flew high again as they communicated with her computer systems, and she fired.

The flash bang stunned the insurgents and UCAF troops alike around Rafe, throwing many of them back with their hands to their eyes. Inside the Shell, however, Rafe was unaffected, and he took advantage of the opportunity to advance up the side street, extricating himself from the convoy. As Annie watched, the people who had been stunned by the low intensity explosion of plasma began to help each other away: the UCAF troops retreating toward the docks, *Shumokuzame* fighters away down the side streets. Many of them ran right toward Rafe, still only half able to see and not aware that he'd moved. His machine guns cut them down with a short, staccato burst.

"They seem to be breaking off," Nolan transmitted over the wing's channel.

Annie checked her drones. He was right - with all six Shells in action, the insurgents were breaking, fleeing from superior firepower. "Alright. Stay sharp, let's get our people out of here. I'll put in a call to have our medics crack open Bianchi's shell and get her out." With the passing of the crowds, and the retreat of the more organized insurgents, she was able to see more plainly the bodies left crumpled on the streets. Many of them were wearing civilian clothes - but others were wearing UCAF uniforms.

She switched to the channel reserved for calling in medical support. "I need those bodies checked. Evac anyone who still has a heartbeat."

"What about the dead, sir?" The voice sounded tired.

"Leave them," Annie said. "We won't have room on the *Scipio* anyway." She cut the channel, waited another moment for Nolan's Shell to draw even with her, and helped him guard the end of the convoy during the last stretch into the docks. Rafe had gone ahead of them, and she wasn't surprised when a private signal from Nolan broke into her thoughts.

"You've got to pull him," the older officer said.

"I know."

"He's not following orders. We can't rely on him."

"He's also one of only five Shell pilots left," Annie reminded Nolan. "And with what just happened, there's no guarantee that this cease-fire is still on. We may have to fight our way off world. Look, I'll tear him a new asshole after this is all over, if he's still alive. We can court martial him when we get back to Mars, but I can't throw away a gun until our people are safe."

"I get it," Nolan said. "But I don't like it. I can't shake the feeling he's going to do something stupid and fuck this up worse than it already is."

"Him and Malik both," Annie agreed. "He was already ready to go at it with me, and now we've lost the last member of his team."

"Malik will follow orders," Nolan reassured her.

349

They'd reached the entrance to the docks, and Annie brought her Shell to a halt before heading in. Nolan stayed with her as she turned to face the blood-soaked road. Her drones were still flying, and they showed clear side streets - for the moment. "Everyone who's got half a brain is hiding somewhere," she commented. "But I'm not taking any chances. You and I stay here until we get confirmation everyone else is loaded."

"Roger that," Nolan confirmed, taking up a position to guard the docks with her.

Annie switched to the wing channel. "Sera, Rafe, Malik, get yourselves attached to a Subtee and get out of here," she ordered, then switched to a private channel with Commander Clavinger. "Nolan and I have rear guard, sir," she told the Commander. "We'll hold until the last Subtee is ready."

"Roger that Winters," Clavinger said. "Should be ten, fifteen minutes, tops. I saw one of the Shells go down. Who did we lose?"

"Bianchi, sir," Annie answered.

"That leaves five of you if we need to go in hot at Icebreaker Two," Clavinger pointed out. "Are your people ready?"

"Yes, sir, we are," Annie confirmed, and then sat back to wait. *Don't do anything stupid*, she begged silently, but she wasn't sure if she was saying it to *Shumokuzame*, or to her own pilots.

Annie stayed keyed up until she was latched onto the hull of a DSI Subtee, the compartment flooded, hangar door opened, and they were out into open water. Even then, with her drones collected, she fretted about not knowing what might be waiting for them out in the world-ocean of Europa. If *Shumokuzame* had managed to construct warships secretly, maybe they'd armed submersibles? If so, there could be an attack at any moment, with only a couple of attack subs and a handful of Shells to act in defense of the helpless transports. She tried to imagine what it would be like fighting attached to the hull of a transport, with a mile of open water in every direction, instead of being just off a bank, like when they'd raided *Shumokuzame* held repair facilities. It could well end in her Shell sinking into an undersea canyon, far enough away from anything that she would never be found.

After fifteen minutes of trying to keep herself alert for threats, she realized there was little point. The journey back up to the ice caps was going to take at least another hour, and her sonar systems would warn her long before any enemies arrived - it wasn't like there was any cover to hide a ship behind. Instead, with a sense of deja vu, she loaded up her sensory recording from Elysia Island.

It was the first time the sun had kissed her skin in... well, since the last time she'd loaded up this recording. Annie looked up at the clouds for a moment, then closed her eyes and focused on the sound of the breaking waves, on the rustle of the palm leaves overhead. She tried to relax, but something kept bothering her. First, it was some sand that had gotten into her swimsuit. Then, it was the way the wind tickled her hair. Finally, it was the cry of a gull overhead, shrill and insistent. Irritated, Annie banished the simulation with a thought and called up the visual feed from her Shell's external cameras. She looked out into the blackness and wondered if she would see a light squid.

Annie hesitated, then called up a different recording from her internal memory core. This one had been taken only a few weeks ago, and she had felt a bit ashamed for doing it at the time, and especially for doing it without asking. She'd never called it up before, not even when she was in a cell. The simulation came to life around her, fed directly into her brain, and she was on her side on a bed in the dark. She was naked, under a soft sheet, and pressed up against a warm body. She could feel Kaito's arm draped across her middle, his chest against her back, and his breath on her neck. She could smell him. She didn't turn around, didn't move, didn't do anything to spoil the illusion. Instead, she set her Shell to pull her out if there were any sonar contacts, or when they were five minutes out from the ice. Then, safe in the simulation, she closed her eyes, wound her fingers through his, and dozed.

It ended up being the sonar that pulled her out of the simulation.

She had to force herself away from the comfortable warmth of the bed, but when she summoned a heads up display of the sonar readouts, she could see three contacts that read as UCAF attack subs coming at them.

Clavinger's voice came over her audio channel, and she observed that she was linked in with Nolan and the captain of each ship in their makeshift flotilla, including both their two attack subs and the DSI subtees. "Listen up, people," he began. "We do not, repeat, do not have contact with those attack subs. They are not responding to our signals. Now, you all know that the UCAF bases in both Atarashī kibō no machi and Fukami Toshi were captured by insurgents; they may well have seized the attack subs docked in those cities, as well. We have to assume those sonar contacts are hostile until they respond to our signals. I want our attack subs to take rearguard, while the DSI subtees head up through the ice. Lieutenant Commander Winters, how many of your remaining Shells are outfitted with torpedos?"

Annie quickly called up current schematics of the remaining four Shells under her command, even though she already knew the answer. "I asked the techies to load us up with whatever underwater gear they could before we headed out," she told Clavinger and the assorted captains. "Every Shell has two depth charges strapped to their legs, ready to be released. Lieutenant Moreau's railgun was designed to fire underwater, if necessary, before we ever came to Europa. I asked about torpedoes, but the techies said there was no time to retrofit the Shells for them."

"Alright," Clavinger said after a moment. "Deploy your

remaining Shells as best you can to cover our ascent through the ice. Once your people have dropped their charges, however, I want them to get up to that Icebreaker station. We may need Shells to secure it, if things go badly. Does everyone understand their orders?"

A chorus of answers greeted the Commander, with the DSI Subtee pilots markedly less enthusiastic than the UCAF officers. The channel went silent, and Annie opened up audio to the rest of her pilots.

"Those incoming contacts you see are assumed hostile," Annie told them. "Sera, detach and get out in front of us. Unless you hear otherwise from me, you fire that railgun as soon as they come in range. Everyone else, look for a chance to get above them and use your depth charges, but do not, I repeat, do not detach from your ride. I want you to have an open channel to whoever is driving your sub; you're going to have to work with them. Once you've dropped your charges, you don't wait around, you just go. Understood?"

The next five minutes were the kind of tense waiting that she hated. It was easy to act in the moment, when the threats were obvious, and a soldier only needed the mental clarity to see what had to be done, and the courage to do it. It was the waiting that frayed her nerves.

As the sonar display showed the attack subs closing on Sera's maximum range, Annie opened a private channel to Clavinger. "Unless they say something in the next thirty seconds, we're firing."

"Proceed, Lieutenant Commander," the old man said, and she could hear the exhaustion in his voice. Her display began tracking smaller contacts accelerating away from the attack subs, toward her and her team: torpedoes.

"Sir?" Sera had opened her own private channel to Annie.

"Fire," Annie ordered.

The charged capacitors in Sera's railgun pulsed energy through magnetic coils, propelling a shaped projectile through the ocean at well over eight thousand feet per second. The ocean water was over a thousand times more dense than air. As a result, the projectile began to disintegrate almost as soon as it was fired. Not so much as a splinter or a fragment ever reached the attack subs - but that hadn't been the point. The shot created a massive shockwave that moved through the water, throwing Sera's Shell backwards toward the rest of the flotilla, but also catching up the incoming torpedoes and throwing them about like a child scooping up a handful of toys. Some of the torpedoes hit each other - Annie couldn't be sure how many - and the resulting explosion triggered the rest. By the time anyone had any idea what was happening, the forward subs had begun escaping up into the chasm that led through Europa's ice cap.

"How are you, Sera," Annie asked over the wing's channel.

"Shaken up but alive, sir-"

A flashing red warning icon and high pitched audio tone drew Annie's attention. "More torpedoes," she warned her pilots. "Sera, get back here!"

Ahead of and beneath them, Sera lit up the fusion torches in her Shell's legs and began to move. While her team had been modified to be able to maneuver in water, Shells were designed for surface fighting. They could hang off the side of a ship in orbit and light off a few rounds, sure, but what they excelled at was crowd control, or dealing with unarmored infantry attacks. Not outpacing torpedoes in the water.

As her other pilots rode the ships at the rear of the flotilla up into the chemically melted water between the ice, Annie dropped off of her ride, waiting for Sera. She could tell, even without the computer's calculations, that her friend wasn't going to make it. Below, the attack subs were coming up at an angle, following their torpedoes. Sera must have realized she wasn't going to get to the ice, because her Shell abruptly changed course, angling not away from the torpedoes, but to get over the attack subs.

Annie opened up a private channel, furious. "Sera, what are you doing? Get up here!"

"Bye, Karoline," her friend's voice came back. Annie's visual feed showed the depth charges released from the legs of Sera's Shell; they must have fallen past the torpedoes, because just a few seconds after the Shell exploded in a flash and a cloud of bubbles, there was an explosion on the hull of one of the attack subs. Across the private audio channel, there was an inarticulate wailing, and Annie released she was the one making the noise.

The attack subs were still coming. Annie lit off her fusion torches and moved up into the crevice.

"All Shells," she sent to the three pilots left under her command, "release depth charges."

"Won't we hit you sir," Rafe protested.

"Follow your damned orders, Lieutenant," Nolan snapped.

In the meantime, Annie had found herself a fissure in the ice to wedge into. She watched the charges fall past her, all six of them, and continue down toward the incoming attack subs. There was another explosion.

"Malik," Annie transmitted, "You're in command. Get everyone up in one piece. I'll deal with these subs."

Feathering her torches carefully, she moved out into the crevice. Below her, one of the attack subs had broken apart into two pieces and was drifting down, trailing its oxygen in bubbles, but the other was moving up into the crevice.

There you are, Annie thought to herself, with no one left to talk to. It was too close to fire a torpedo at her without damaging itself, and before anyone in the sub had an idea what was happening, she'd affixed her magnetic clamps to it and begun to move across it's hull.

Beneath her, the attack submarine shuddered as it launched torpedoes up between the walls of ice that surrounded them, toward the retreating UCAF forces. She couldn't do anything about that except to hope that her people were dropping chaff, or getting lucky. Instead, she kept working her way around the hull until she reached the doors that led into the attack sub's weapons compartments.

Unlike a Subtee, UCAF attack subs weren't designed to haul large cargo. They didn't have large bay doors, and the food, medical supplies, and other things needed by the crews were carried in by hand. But they did need to be able to load one thing, and that was torpedoes. With the Shell's articulated hands, she held onto one magnetic clamp while slamming an artificial fist into the loading doors until they began to crumple. Then, with the Shell's fingers, she pried the doors apart and opened the interior of the sub to water. Just to make sure, she jammed the barrel of her plasma cannon into the breached compartment and fired off one shot at maximum effect. Beneath her, the hull buckled and cracked; shards of armor flew into her Shell, and a warning icon appeared in her display: something was wrong with her comm system.

Beneath her, the attack sub's turbines stopped, then reversed. *That's fine*, Annie thought satisfied, *Get out alive if you can. As long as you aren't shooting any longer.* She released her clamps, kicked at the ice shelves around her with her feet, dropping chunks of ice onto the retreating sub, then lit her torches again and began to move up through the canyon.

"I'm on my way back up," Annie sent over the unit channel. "Hold an elevator for me."

There was no response.

Annie focused on the red warning icon, and it expanded into a small window that spelled out exactly what was wrong, in exhausting detail. She only needed to read the first line: "Transmitter inoperative." Even muted by the Neural Shunt, there was a sudden stab of fear.

Alright, fine, she told herself. *I just need to make it up myself, and establish visual contact.* She lit her torches. The flotilla was far ahead of her, and moving faster than she could through the ocean, but it would take time to load the elevators. On her sensor displays, the Subtees moved further and further ahead of her as the minutes went by. The last time she'd made the trip through Europa's ice cap, it had only taken half an hour, and Kaito had been doing the driving. She hadn't even known who he was, then, she realized as she continued to use her torches to maneuver around jutting crags of ice, but something about his confidence had convinced her that there was no danger in the trip.

She'd been wrong. There was plenty of danger: she could never have made this journey at the speeds he had, and certainly not in a transport as large as the *Nautilus*. She didn't know the ice like he did, hadn't made this trip a thousand times like he had, and now she understood just how good of a pilot he was. In spite of her fear, dulled by the separation from her body's bio-feedback mechanisms because of the neural shunt, she felt a flash of pride in him. If she'd been able to control her body, she would have smiled.

By the time she was a quarter of the way up, the entire flotilla had docked at the Icebreaker. She could still hear Clavinger giving orders over the command staff channel - he hadn't bothered to kick her off the channel, maybe, or was just assuming she was gone. Or he'd made the decision already to leave her behind.

"First elevator away," someone - the MP commander, perhaps? - transmitted over the command channel. Annie was trying not to bounce off a sheet of blue ice that scraped into the channel at a sharp angle. She pushed her Shell upward as fast as she could - she needed to make it before the last elevator went. For over two hours, she worked her way toward Europa's surface at what felt like breakneck speed. She was only a hundred meters from the Icebreaker Station when she heard Clavinger's voice over an open channel.

"Alright," he barked, "That's the last elevator. If there are any UCAF personnel within reach of this signal who have not boarded, respond now."

Annie lit her jets and tried to transmit again. "I'm here!" Beneath her, the water of Europa's ocean bubbled. The ice to either side of her fell away: she was in the bowl of melted sea-water that surrounded Icebreaker Two. Freed from the danger of collision, she burned at maximum force.

The Shell shot out of the water as if from a cannon. She cut the torches, and for a moment she hung in the air as her visual feed showed her the last Orbital Elevator ascending toward where the *Scipio* was docked. Out of habit more than anything else, she feathered her jets and found a place to land on solid ice, away from the station. It would be in *Shumokuzame* hands now, and she was the last UCAF soldier on Europa who wasn't already captured.

Ice crunched beneath the feet of her Shell as she landed, and Annie tried not to think about the radiation her body was soaking up every moment she was out on Europa's open ice fields. *I can't stay here*, she realized. *And there's nothing for me below except prison.*

Karoline Anna Galtung looked up at the stars, and knew that directly overhead the *Scipio* hung - her only way home. She'd come all this way, but there was nothing she could do to cross the last distance between her and safety. She wasn't going to go home; she wasn't going to see her father again - she was going to spend years here in a prison. Shells had limited atmospheric mobility - they could use their jets to jump up onto a rooftop, or a cliff but that would never take her into orbit... something in Annie paused.

The gravity on Europa is only a third as strong as the gravity on Mars. The mass of the Shell is unchanged, but...That means it only takes a third as much energy as it would on Mars to lift this Shell out of Europa's gravity well.

Karoline flashed through a branching menu of system settings with a thought, overriding the recalibration Sera had made on all the Shell's to adjust their fusion torch output to Europa's lower gravity. She looked up at the stars again, then triggered her torches. She kept the burn going, as long and as hard as she could. Somewhere that Karoline wasn't aware of, her body was pressed back into the cushions that cradled it, and she could only hope she remained conscious. Beneath her, the long, low plain of ice dropped, and the horizon turned from a line into a gentle curve. She angled toward the Orbital Elevator, and saw that she was catching up to it. Closer, she took the Shell, and closer, until her external cameras could pick out the window in the passenger compartment. It hadn't been so long ago that she was pressed up against that glass, staring down at Europa.

She drew even with the elevator, and her display began to zoom in on faces. There was Nolan and Rafe, Malik and Clavinger, and others she didn't recognize, eyes wide, mouths open as they watched her race them. Karoline wanted to smile, and suddenly the hand of gravity fell away from her, and she had to start burning her torches to slow herself down instead of speed up. She'd never flown in zero-g before, and the Shell wasn't really designed for it, but she managed to work her way over to where the *Scipio* was and match its orbital speed. Her comm opened up.

"UCAF Shell, this is *Scipio*," Varga's voice came to her clearly. "Is that you, Annie?"

"It is," Karoline said, but knew he couldn't hear her, so she just held up one of the Shell's half-broken hands and waved.

"Lieutenant Commander Winters," Varga said after a moment, "We have visual. Wave again if you are unable to transmit."

Karoline waved again.

"Understood. As soon as we have everyone from the Orbital Elevator loaded, we're going to bring you in through one of the cargo bay doors. Until then, just hang tight."

She had long moments to look down at the moon, or out at Jupiter. Her systems were waiting to identify each star in view by name and number, but she dismissed that function to just look at the view. In a few hours, Karoline knew, she would be going to sleep in a hibernation chamber. The trip back to Mars would pass in the space of a dream. Maybe she would even dream about Kaito.

Not far distant, her sensors picked out the dark shapes of the Europan warships. She didn't look at those. She was going home; what happened next was out of her hands.

"Alright, Annie, we've got the Commander and everyone aboard," Varga's voice came. "Move around to our port side and look for the hangar door. We'll open it up and let you in. Move quick, because we're going to begin burning for Ganymede ASAP, and things are liable to get hairy."

Ganymede? Karoline began moving to the *Scipio's* port side, going around the scaffolding that held it to the orbital dock. There was the hangar door, opening now. *But we're supposed to be going back to Mars.* As she approached, the arms that held the *Scipio* to the orbital dock began to release, and the ship's fusion torches - the exhaust ports a thousand times larger than hers - lit. Slowly, the *Scipio* began to move away from the dock as Annie slipped along it's hull and into the hangar bay.

"*Scipio*," a man's voice came over the open Comm channel, "Your heading is not toward Mars." Date, she realized. The man she'd negotiated with. Her Shell's feet hit the deck of the hangar bay.

"That is correct," Clavinger's voice answered. "Optimal launch window to Mars won't come back around for two years. We are proceeding to Ganymede, where we will affect further repairs with UCAF forces there until a better launch window to Mars opens."

"That was not our agreement," Date protested.

"I agreed we would go to Mars," Clavinger said, "But I never agreed we wouldn't stop at Ganymede first."

"I cannot allow you to reinforce Ganymede," Date said coldly. "Change your heading."

There was silence from Clavinger. *Oh no*, Karoline thought, *he's killed us all.*

The hangar door began to close, sliding a dark curtain across her view of the stars and of Europa below. She could see the Europan warships lighting their engines. *You idiot*, she screamed at Clavinger, though he couldn't hear her. *Varga's already lost this battle once.*

Her sensors detected missiles incoming from the Europan warships. The hangar door was nearly closed - could she survive a hit, here?

Dammit. Karoline lit her fusion torches one last time and rocketed out through the gap between the closing bay door and the hull. She charged up her plasma cannon and locked on to the leading warship.

"Winters, what are you doing," Varga shouted in her ear.

Karoline fired, and fired again as the ship to ship missiles lanced past her. She hardly even slowed as the leading warship grew in her visual feed, but only fired off shot after shot as fast as her plasma cannon could charge, trying to blast a hole through its armored hull. Just before she hit, she ducked the Shell's shoulder, plowing into the hull where her shots had damaged it, like a bull charging.

She didn't feel the impact.

Kaito

Epilogue

July 4th, 2128

The *Narukami* didn't have a brig equipped to hold more than one or two people at a time, so most of the UCAF prisoners had been transferred down to Europa, where they'd been put in one of the repair facilities that *Shumokuzame* used to use as hideouts. The prisoner that Kaito was going to see, however, had been under intensive care in their medical bay until just this morning.

The salute snapped to Kaito by the guard was a bit slow and off kilter, but he wasn't used to receiving them, anyway - or to the uniform. It felt tight and uncomfortable as he put a hand to the wall to stop his movement. As tight and uncomfortable as his new haircut - short for zero-g.

"I'd like to see the prisoner," he said, and winced inside because it hadn't really come out as an order, but as a request.

"Ensign," the guard began. Kaito technically outranked him, hence the salute, but everyone knew that Kaito was only a recent addition to the ship's crew.

"Captain Shiroishi has already approved," he interrupted the enlisted man, putting as much force into it as he could. "You can call her, if you like. She's pretty busy, though."

A moment later, he was past the guard room into the brig proper. There were only two cells, separated by a walkway. The one on his left was unoccupied. He turned to the one on the right, and grabbed a bar to steady himself. It was smooth: the cell had probably never been used, until now.

Annie was floating in zero-g in the center of the cell, curled into a ball. She was still in a medical gown, but they'd given her a blanket for warmth, and she was wrapped up in it. Her eyes were closed, and there was still a bandage on her head. He could see where they'd shaved some of the hair off to repair the skull fracture.

"Annie," he said, and his voice seemed to echo.

"Kaito." She breathed his name out in a whisper, and then he was looking into her open eyes.

"You scared me," Kaito said, leaning forward until his face was only inches from the bars.

"I didn't think I would live through that," she admitted. She swallowed, visibly, as if she hadn't used her voice in a long time. "What happened? After..."

After you rammed your Shell into a warship, he didn't say out loud. "We broke off pursuit of the *Scipio* to save everyone we could on the *Kuraokami*," he answered her.

"So the *Scipio* got away," Annie said, a faint smile curving her lips.

"Annie, you killed over a dozen people," Kaito said. She was silent. "Yeah, they got to Ganymede. Congratulations. And they've pulled in the *Cincinnatus* from Callisto. So now they've got three ships grouped together. It's going to be a pain in the ass to dig them out, the Old Man says."

"But that won't stop *Shumokuzame* from trying. You look good in the uniform," Annie told him, still curled up in a ball, floating tantalizingly far away from him. He wanted her to come closer. He wanted her to tell him she loved him.

"They've got me learning to fly this thing," he said, motioning vaguely at the bulkheads around them. "We're heading out soon."

"To Ganymede," Annie guessed. "But I won't be going with you. No reason to bring a prisoner of war to the front lines."

"No," Kaito admitted. "You're going to Io."

"That's where you're putting the prisoners," Annie concluded. "It makes sense. No one's getting off that hell-hole without a ship. You haven't told them who I am, have you?"

Kaito shook his head.

"Thank you." Annie uncurled herself, and drew the blanket up like a cloak. Her long legs were bare, and she kicked off from the floor with her toes to come toward him. Holding the blanket closed with one hand, she folded the other over his fingers, gripping the same bar. Their faces were only inches apart.

"I came to say goodbye," he whispered. "It might be a few months before I can get back..."

"Clavinger has three ships and knows you're coming, this time. It won't be quick or easy." She took a breath. "Don't come to Io," Annie told him. In a thin blanket and a backless hospital gown, she gave orders better than he could in a new uniform. "I don't want you to see me there."

"Annie, I-"

"Kaito," she said. "I want you to kiss me. I'm going to record it, and I want you to kiss me so that I can take it with me." *And in case you don't make it back.*

He nodded, and then they were pressed against the bars awkwardly, mouths meeting while the cold metal touched the flesh of their faces. He was able to reach through just enough to place his hand on her hip, and she wrapped her arm about his shoulder to trace her fingers through the hair on the back of his head. For a long moment, the cell was silent.

"Good bye," Annie whispered, her eyes closed.

———————————

END NOTES

Kaito and Annie did not end up where I thought that they would when I began writing this novel, which seems to be a pretty good indication that they've taken on lives of their own. I have ideas - and even a few chapters - for where they go next, and if this gets to 100 reviews on Amazon I will press forward with a sequel.

Large parts of this novel were written while I was on a long weekend at Fairleigh Dickinson, being inspired by a variety of workshops and the other authors around me.